The
SCOURGE
NOSTRUM

The
SCOURGE

NOSTRUM

Roberto Calas

47NORTH

Published by 47North, Seattle

www.apub.com

Amazon, the Amazon logo, and 47North are trademarks of Amazon.com, Inc., or its affiliates.

ISBN-13: 9781477808887
ISBN-10: 1477808884

Cover design by Salamander Hill Design Inc.

Library of Congress Control Number: 2013940105

Printed in the United States of America

For Rina and Nick, who once had nothing,
and so give me everything.

Episode 1

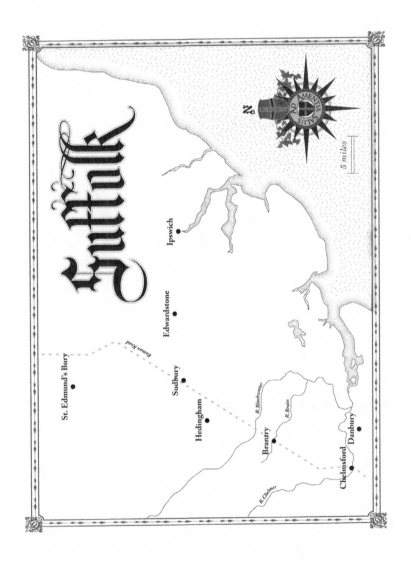

Chapter 1

WHEN I WAS A CHILD, I watched a man burn at the stake for mixing tinctures to cure the Black Plague. I remember him smiling just before the flames seared his flesh. A haunting smile that has bewildered me to this day. The monks who burned him told the lingering crowd that prayer is the only true and righteous weapon against illness. That alchemy is a sin.

Some weeks later those same monks dunked a saint's body into a vat of wine in the hopes of creating a cure for the same plague.

I am a simple knight. It is difficult for me to see the difference between a tincture and a corpse's bath water. But after two days of prayer I understand that neither God nor the saints will heal the woman I love. I must look to alchemy, even if it means burning in the very fires of hell. And I, too, will smile as the flames lick my flesh. For I will have saved the woman I adore and earned eternal salvation in her eyes.

"You are stealing from the church!" Brother Phillip is the last remaining monk in the monastery of St. Edmund's Bury, my current sanctuary. He is not happy today. "You imperil your very soul, Sir Edward!"

"I am not stealing from the church," I say. "I am stealing from *you*." I stare at him until he takes a step back. One of his eyebrows twitches.

In my experience, monks are quick to threaten God's Fury. They wave His wrath like a whip whenever you stray from the path they have chosen for you. But I believe every man must find his own road to salvation. Job, from the Old Testament, followed the road of perseverance. Saint Edmund, the martyred king who gives this town its name, put faith in his principles. And me?

My own personal path to salvation depends on chickens.

I roll a wheelbarrow full of the feathered creatures through the churchyard of St. Edmund's Monastery, toward the prior's house. The massive monastery buildings rise around me like mountains of cut stone and stained glass. Brother Phillip walks beside me, holding my great helm and prattling on about the loss of essential food.

Essential food. There are only four people left alive in this abbey, and yet there are enough animals and provisions to feed a small village for a year. But I am tired of explaining this fact to Brother Phillip. I have spent two days listening to his ceaseless whining on every conceivable topic. Perhaps he is God's punishment for my sins. I have murdered, stolen and lied, but surely not even those sins warrant an affliction by this man. I understand now why the other monks left him behind when they fled the monastery.

I look at Brother Phillip and feel a momentary pang of pity for him. I, too, must leave him, for I have found new purpose.

"Chickens are clever," Brother Phillip says, desisting from his complaints to offer this golden insight. I suppose, when compared to him, chickens might be clever. "Thomas Cockerel told me that chickens can dream. Just like you or me."

If chickens dream like I do, then I would see the tears in their tiny eyes each morning. I would see scars on their knuckles from the stone walls of the abbey. If chickens have dreams like mine, then I pity the creatures.

"Why must you take them, Sir Edward?" Phillip asks. "How can chickens help Elizabeth?"

The birds coo, sounding like tiny monkeys, and they peck at the canvas stretched over their heads. I stare at Phillip for a long moment, the black mist settling into my stomach as I think of my wife. "She's getting worse, Phillip. I have to do something."

Phillip fusses nervously with the wooden cross at his neck and his eyebrow twitches again.

"You'll take care of Elizabeth, like you promised?" I ask. An icicle stabs my soul when I utter her name. "You and Sister Mildred?"

There is a nun here in the abbey. A kind woman who cooks for us every day and tries to restore some shred of order to the world. She has nursed Elizabeth while I have prayed.

"Mildred will care for her," Brother Phillip says. "But it is an imposition. Sister Mildred has to tend the livestock and the gardens as well."

I glance sidelong at Phillip. "It wouldn't kill you to help her with her chores."

"I do help her," he says. "I pray every day for her health and for our continued safety."

I reach the prior's house and set down the wheelbarrow so I can open the door. My armor feels heavy after two
days of wearing a tunic. A sack containing more of Phillip's
essential food—dried meats and bread—hangs from my
shoulder. "Prayer is good, Brother Phillip," I say. "But God
helps those who help themselves."

He crosses his arms. "If that is true, Sir Edward, then
why do you need the chickens?"

Has Brother Phillip found wit?

I open the door and roll the wheelbarrow to a sparse
room at the back of the house. "I need these birds because
they are loud. And because they can only fly for short
stretches." I reach down and take hold of an iron ring set
into the floor, pull upon it until the trapdoor swings open.
The stench of rotting flesh nearly knocks me over.

It is cloudy outside, but enough light streams down into
the pit to reveal the swaying, groaning, clawing mass of pale
bodies at the foot of the ladder.

"But most importantly," I say, "I need chickens because
they are fast."

I untie the front of the canvas and tilt the wheelbarrow
forward toward the pit. If chickens have dreams, then this
is their nightmare.

"Brother, if you would?"

Brother Phillip shakes his head but sets down my great
helm and stretches the canvas forward, so that the chickens
can't escape their fate.

"This is madness," Phillip says. "Absolute madness."

In these times of madness, only madness will save us.

A knight who is now my enemy once spoke those words,
and I think I should have them chiseled onto my tombstone.

Madness defines my life these days. I spent more than a week with two of my knights traveling from my home in Sussex to this monastery in East Anglia. I would have traveled into hell itself to save my angel from the plague that has ravaged England. But the plague ravaged my angel, too.

I thought perhaps God was punishing me. I have sinned more than I care to think about and, perhaps, as punishment the Lord took the one thing in this world I could not be without.

I have tried prayer. I tried a relic from Saint Luke, the healer. I even flogged my own back until it bled. I would be there still, in the cathedral with my Elizabeth, flogging and praying, if I had not noticed the black marks on her wrist.

The plague forced me to bind my angel to a torch bracket so she could not afflict others. But she hated the bonds. She struggled against the silk cords, yanked her arms, and hissed. And the cords left their mark. Black rings of dead flesh.

Her body will not heal. Every bump. Every scrape. Every cut. Every wound she suffers will be hers for eternity. Her body will fall apart in time. And though I would love her no matter what physical state she is in, I wonder if her mind is falling to pieces as well.

I padded the silk cords with feathers and hay and tried to put such thoughts from my mind, but they would not go. For two days I gave myself to God and prayed that He would heal her. But He did not listen. And I understood that Elizabeth's only hope lay with an alchemist who might not exist, on an island that might never be found.

So I stood with tears in my eyes and kissed Elizabeth's fingers, said good-bye as she hissed, as she tried to bite through the padded silk gag around her mouth. Before I left, I drew a silk glove and a phial of lavender oil from a pouch at her belt. I sprinkled her scent onto the silk and tucked the glove into a pouch at my belt. "God helps those who help themselves, my angel," I said to her. I'm not sure where I first heard that phrase. Brother Phillip assures me that it is not in the Bible and that, in fact, God wants us to rely on Him and not on ourselves. But if that were true, the Jews would still be slaves, and Goliath's army would have crushed the Israelites.

I have no sling and I have no staff, but I am fairly certain that I can part the sea of plaguers beneath the prior's house.

The chickens squawk and cluck as they tumble into the pit. I hear wings fluttering and pray that some of the birds make it past the plaguers.

Most of Phillip's chickens die swift and horrible deaths. A few make it to the wet tunnel leading out of the monastery. The mob of lurching plaguers pursues the screeching birds down the passage. The creatures were human once and are perhaps human still. But they do not look human. They look like demons. Bloody, snarling creatures with terrible wounds on their bodies and eyes as black as the Abyss. I hope Phillip's clever chickens can wade the river at the end of the tunnel, or my Red Sea will crash upon me before I am through.

I wait for a time, calculating the speed of chickens chased by demons. When I imagine the animals would have cleared the tunnel, I take a deep breath. I don my great helm, light a thick altar candle, and say good-bye to Brother Phillip. He is a bastard and a coward and it is because of him and his brothers that my Elizabeth needs this alchemist in the first place, but I cannot stay angry at him. There is not enough spine in Phillip for the anger to take hold.

"Godspeed, Sir Edward," he says.

I descend the rungs quickly and draw my sword when I reach the bottom. It is the sword of Saint Giles, and Saint Giles is my saint. Not because he is the patron saint of the insane, but because he is the saint of Bodiam, the village where Elizabeth grew up. She loves Saint Giles and so I adopted him. I only hope the adoption is mutual.

"If any of the chickens survived," Brother Phillip calls, "can you bring them back before you go?"

I would like to believe this is more of his newfound wit.

I walk through the long tunnel holding my candle as far forward as I can. The thick flame flickers and glistens back at me from a hundred moist stones. Halfway through the passage, the candlelight gleams off something metallic. I nearly fall to my knees at the sight.

It is Tristan's blood-soaked helmet.

Chapter 2

THERE IS NO OTHER TRACE of Tristan. Just the great helm, half-submerged in water and spattered with blood. I can think of no reason to take a helmet off in a tunnel filled with demons. Demons whose bites inflict plague. I scoop up the helmet and pin it between my candle arm and my chest.

If Tristan has come to harm, it is my fault. I should have left with him. We should be searching for this alchemist together. He stayed by my side throughout our journey to St. Edmund's Bury, and I should have been at his side when he left.

Dozens of bodies litter the tunnel floor. I pause at each one to make certain that Tristan is not among them. He is not. I am not certain if these are the plaguers that we killed on the way in or fresh ones cut down by Tristan on his way out. The bodies of the afflicted are dead and decaying from the moment they succumb to the plague, which makes it impossible to tell when they were finally destroyed. A faint breeze in the tunnel makes the candle flame dance.

I hear footsteps in the distance. The uneven gait of the dead. I hold Saint Giles's sword as far forward as I can and walk quietly onward. The candlelight makes the blade glow like molten steel.

Snarls echo in the passageway. I pad forward, readying myself to fly back toward the rungs. My sword trembles. Something darker than the tunnel's darkness moves in the distance. My heart pounds. Not because I might die, but because I might die before healing Elizabeth.

Candlelight washes over the living dead. One of the chickens was not clever enough. Or fast enough. Two plaguers fight over the carcass like wild dogs. One of them sees a bigger prize in me and abandons the chicken. It is a female. A slim girl of no more than fourteen wearing a tattered chemise and walking with bare feet. She steps drunkenly toward me. The bright flame of my candle glints from her soulless eyes.

If there is a cure for this plague, then I pray God will forgive me for the scores I have murdered. And for the murders I must yet commit. I let Tristan's helmet drop and whip my blade across the girl's throat. She gurgles and claws at her neck, and I am reminded of Allison Moore, whom I slew upon the banks of the River Medway when I mistook her for a plaguer. But this girl does not die like Allison Moore. She advances again, blood seeping onto the collar of her chemise, spreading and blooming like a liquid rose.

I strike again, and this time she falls. Her companion, a man wearing a soiled silk doublet and cap, finishes with the chicken and approaches me. The bird's blood is smeared across his face. It takes seven hacks of my sword to keep him from rising again. The massive candle gutters dangerously with each blow. I wipe my blade on his doublet and retrieve Tristan's helmet before moving onward.

Light streams into the tunnel from the entrance 150 yards further along. The birds must have cleared the river, because I see the last of the plaguers shuffle out of the passageway and into the water. Clever chickens.

And there, at the mouth of the tunnel, I find a message from Tristan.

My hand cannon leans against the wall just inside the open gate, where we left it when we arrived two days ago. A blood-soaked shred of fabric has been draped over the barrel of the cannon. There are words scrawled across it; Tristan must have painted the message before leaving the monastery.

> *Good of you to come*
> *Heading toward Brantry to find a lustful horse. (Don't tell Morgan.)*
> *Chelmsford after that*

A skin and pouch lie next to the cannon on the muddy floor. The skin contains powder for the gun; the pouch holds five iron shots, wadding, and two powder-coated firing cords. I put away my sword and lean the cannon against my shoulder.

The clouds drift away from the sun. The light shines warm against my face. Tristan is alive.

Or at least he was when he left this tunnel. I stare down the River Lark toward St. Edmund's Monastery, where my Elizabeth waits, tied with padded silk to a torch bracket.

I pray to God and Saint Giles that I find this alchemist, but I know they will not help me. Alchemy is a sin.

The clouds blot out the sun once more.

The cobbled streets of St. Edmund's Bury are empty. Deserted stone buildings sit shoulder to shoulder, monuments to a dead civilization. I doubt even the rats remain in them. A chicken wobbles past me and disappears into an alley between a butcher's shop and a candlemaker's home. One of Brother Phillip's, I'm sure. Clever chicken.

My ankle burns with each step. It is a wound from a week ago, the result of a disagreement with a brown bear in Rayleigh. Sister Mildred applied Saint-John's-wort and bound the ankle tightly with linen strips. It is a remedy that worked well enough in the confines of the monastery, but not even Saint John can ease the pain I feel after the first mile.

I leave the town and make my way into the countryside, drawing out the glove I borrowed from Elizabeth and breathing in her scent. She gave me this glove once before. At the Earl's Tournament, in Nottingham; the only tournament I ever won. When I returned the glove to her after the contest, she cherished it more than the golden rod I was awarded, or the four horses I won from other knights. She kept it in a pouch at her side from that moment on.

I stop to rest every hundred paces or so, making it slow going. During one such break I decide to load my cannon. I have never loaded a cannon, but I have watched Tristan do it. It is a nervous business. These weapons explode when packed improperly. I have seen it. It is unpleasant.

The barrel is wet, so I wrap a stick in strips of cloth and run it through the iron cylinder before carefully packing the powder. I roll a strip of wool wadding around one of the iron projectiles and jam the slug deep into the barrel with the stick.

I continue my journey, stopping at every stable I see, but I have little hope of finding a horse. The afflicted have an uncanny ability to find life and to take it. The horses I do come across are little more than ribs and hooves. Sometimes the plaguers leave a skull.

The land here in East Anglia is supposed to be flat. So flat, they say, that a man can watch a horse run away for two days. But here, near St. Edmund's Bury, this is not true. My ankle feels every hill and valley. I will have to find a horse soon or my journey will end in Suffolk.

My wrist itches. I slide the steel gauntlets off and stare. The world spins. I look away, take several deep breaths, then look back again. It is the same. I am cut. A small gash across the top of my wrist. Hardly noticeable.

But I do not know how I got it.

I search my memory of the encounter with the two plaguers in the tunnel. Did either of them get close enough to bite me? Could the man in the doublet have caught me with his teeth while I hacked him to bits? Sweat dampens my entire body. I study the wound. It is probably from the metal of my gauntlet. Or perhaps I scraped it on the crude rungs of the ladder when I first entered the tunnel. Maybe the gauntlet slid forward and I ran my wrist against the stone walls without noticing. I look away, then back again. Nothing has changed.

I am cut.

I continue southward and cross a field that is littered with cattle bones.

Perhaps I scratched myself with my nails and broke the skin.

Another farmhouse lies ahead, and a stable. It will be the fourth stable that I search. When I am twenty yards from the structure, I see a man dressed in a tattered robe on his hands and knees in the grass, his arse in the air. A tuft-eared red squirrel stands on two legs a few paces from him, nibbling at something in its paws.

Maybe I brushed my wrist against the edge of the wheelbarrow.

My foot snaps a twig and the squirrel's keen ears catch the sound. The animal drops the morsel and scurries off. The man rises to his feet and runs after the squirrel, but it is a hopeless chase. The animal disappears in a quicksilver dash up an elm trunk. The man throws his arms skyward and shakes his hands.

"What you ask is impossible!" he screams toward the heavens. "Send the demons! Take me now, for I cannot do it, oh Lord, I cannot do it!"

He hears my footsteps when I am only a few paces away and he whirls to face me. His head is more beard than face, and his eyes grow wide when he sees me. He runs in the same direction as the squirrel, throwing his hands up and shouting, "I am sorry! I will do it! I will do it! *Mea maxima culpa!*"

He trips on the dangling fabric of his robe and falls to the ground. "I am sorry! Oh, Lord, I am sorry!" He sobs and makes no attempt to rise.

I remove my helm and kneel at his side. "I didn't mean to frighten you," I say.

The man rolls on his back, his eyes shut tightly. "Do it. Finish me. Bring an end to my pitiful life. I can strive no longer. *Mea maxima culpa.*"

I recognize his Latin from mass: "my most grievous fault." He is riddled with guilt, as every good Christian should be.

"You want me to kill you?" I relegate the wound to the cellar of my mind and give the man my full attention.

"Plunge your fangs into my throat. Rend me with your claws. Burn me with your fiery breath. I am ready."

"I have a sword," I say. "Will that do?"

He opens one eye.

I shrug. "I could light you on fire, but it will take some time."

"Are you a demon?" he asks.

"That depends on whom you ask," I say.

He sits up. His robe is soiled by grass and Lord knows what else. "You are not here to take my life?"

"I've killed enough today, I think. Maybe I'll keep you around until tomorrow."

His eyes grow wide again and I smile, then feel a storm of guilt for smiling when Elizabeth is locked in a cathedral. *Mea maxima culpa.*

"I'm not here to kill you." I rise to my feet and help him stand. "I'm sorry I spooked your meal."

He stares at me and cocks his head.

"The squirrel. I scared it off." I set Tristan's great helm down and reach past the hand cannon into the sack that hangs from my shoulder. "I'll break bread with you to make amends."

He looks horrified. "I was not going to eat the squirrel! I would never have eaten it! Not ever!"

"Weren't you trying to catch it?"

"Yes," he says. "Our Heavenly Father instructed me to catch it."

"God wants you to catch a squirrel?"

"Two squirrels," he says. "And two deer. And two badgers. And two magpies. And two hedgehogs. Two of every animal. A male and a female."

"I see." I clear my throat. This man is not a clever chicken. "Have you built your ark yet?"

He wrinkles his nose and looks at me with mild disgust. "What a ridiculous thing to say."

His name is Peter and he was a clerk in St. Edmund's Bury. He tells me that he has lived in the stable for the last two months.

"The Lord led me here," he says. "And Osbert found me a few days after I arrived."

"Osbert?"

"Osbert is God's messenger," he says. "God speaks to him. And Osbert tells me what Our Heavenly Father wishes of us."

God speaks to many people these days. If He had spoken to us earlier, perhaps there would not have been a need for this scourge that has afflicted us.

"So the barn is full of your animals?" I ask.

Peter licks at his lips, and his brows twist with anxiety. "Animals…they are difficult to catch. We have captured two rabbits."

"Two rabbits?" I say. "That seems like a slow start, Peter."

He shakes his head vigorously. "That is not all! We have also found a lark."

"You caught a lark?" I ask.

"We found it. It fluttered on the grass. Something was wrong with its wing. But God did not say the animals had to be in perfect health."

"No, I imagine he didn't," I say.

"We have a hedgehog."

"Healthy?"

Peter looks as if he might cry. "I do not know what is wrong with it. Osbert says it may be plagued." He wrings his hands, then holds up his forefinger and brightens. "But we caught a healthy chicken once."

"A chicken?" I ask. "Does it dream?"

"Dream?"

"Yes," I say. "Chickens are clever, Peter. They dream."

I wonder if chickens can sense that something has gone catastrophically wrong with the world. I hope their cleverness does not extend that far. I pray the chickens live in blissful ignorance and that their dreams are full of grain and sunshine.

Peter is talking. His words soak through the veil of my thoughts.

"…will never stop, no matter how difficult the challenge becomes. God wishes to purge the world once more. Osbert and I will be the caretakers when the slate is washed clean."

"Is this the new Flood, then?" I ask. "Does God want a fresh start?"

He raises his hands and closes his eyes. "Thus says the Lord of Hosts: 'Now go and strike Amalek and devote to destruction all that they have. Do not spare them, but kill both man and woman, child and infant, ox and sheep, camel and donkey.'"

I have never heard of Amalek, but I wonder what they did to deserve such a fate. Even the donkeys must suffer. This would upset Tristan.

I glance at my wrist. Just a line of red among the hair, filthy with muck from the tunnel. Is this wound God's Fury as well? Am I to be purged?

"And what does Amalek have to do with the plague, Peter?"

"Amalek shows us the strength of the Lord's intolerance for iniquity. Those who do not yield to our Almighty Father will suffer, as those of Amalek did. For this is the End of Days! The seas will turn to blood! The earth will shake! The stars will fade from the sky!"

I scratch at my neck. "Do you or Osbert know of any horses in the area?"

Peter thinks about this for a time. "There is a horse near the Lutons' Manor house."

"A living horse?"

"Yes. We have seen it through the window of the stables. Osbert says I must get the animal. But there are demons." He covers his mouth with a filthy hand and shakes his head. "So many demons."

I have heard of Lutons Place. It has changed hands many times over the last twenty years. One of the owners was a friend of that Chaucer poet Elizabeth is so fond of. I think the manor is owned by Thomas Clopton now. I met Sir Thomas in London once, but I have never been to Lutons Place and I do not know its precise location.

"Can you show me where the Lutons' Manor is?"

"No!" He shakes his head and backs away. "No, the demons are there!"

"I don't want you to take me there," I say. "Just tell me the way."

"No!" He crosses himself. "You will lead them here! You will bring them down upon Osbert and me! Our work is too important!"

I study him for a time. People talk about this new sickness, this scourge that turns people into mindless demons. They call it the second plague. But no one talks about the third plague, this affliction of madness that has swept England.

I decide to try a different approach. "I didn't want to explain all of this. It would have been better had you never known. But God is upset with your progress, so He sent me to help you. My first duty is to find two horses."

He looks at me without expression for a long time. "God is upset?"

I nod slowly. "Not terribly. Annoyed, really. A bit irritated."

"Osbert never said that."

"I'm sure Osbert didn't want to worry you," I say.

Peter paces back and forth with such speed that I think he might wear the grass away. He halts and stands perfectly still after a few heartbeats. His gaze rises, one brow arched. "How do I know God sent you?"

"Faith."

He thinks on this, then walks toward the stable. "I must ask Osbert."

Perhaps Osbert has more sense than this poor creature. I follow Peter into the stable, staring at my wrist as I walk. The stalls reek of urine and feces and rotting flesh. It is the kind of smell that only shit and decay and dampness can create when exposed to day after day of warmth.

I understand now why the plaguers have not found Peter and Osbert.

A massive silver crucifix, tarnished and soiled, leans against the rear wall of the first stall. Next to it is a small etching of the Virgin Mary. The etching stops me.

Mother Mary was a constant companion throughout our journey from Bodiam to St. Edmund's Bury. Silent and ever present. And, it seems to me, not always kind to us. Wherever our travels took us, we found her churches. Whenever anything went horribly wrong, I felt her touch. Perhaps she is trying to tell me something. I'll be buggered if I know what it is.

Peter walks down the center aisle and I follow. We have to squeeze past a carved wooden pew with velvet seat cushions powdered by straw dust.

"Do not look into the stalls," he says.

I nod to him and look into the stalls as we pass. Each one contains a melting candle and a cage made out of woven branches. All of the cages are empty except one, which holds a half-starved hedgehog.

"Where are the animals?" I ask.

Peter spins toward me and puts his hands to his face. "You should not have looked! I told you not to look!"

"I thought you said you had a lark and rabbits," I say. "And a chicken. What happened to the chicken?"

He groans and pulls at his hair, then screams loud enough to make me back away. "*I have to eat, do I not? How can I do God's work if I do not eat? Why does no one understand that?*"

I hold my hands toward him, palms up. The cut on my wrist catches my eye again. "God understands, Peter. It is a difficult thing He asks of you. That is why He sent me to help. But He truly needs to know where the Lutons' Manor is." I hope Peter is far gone enough that he doesn't ask why God would need directions.

He is. The former church clerk stomps to the back of the stable, where a blanket mostly covers a cage that sits on a chair. No, not a chair. It is a hinged wooden seat set into a great panel of burnished wood that leans against the back wall. Carved wooden faces provide the platform to support the seat when it is in the down position, as it is now.

We have seats like this at the back of our Church of St. Giles, in Bodiam. The carved wooden platforms are called misericords. The name comes from the French word *miséricorde*, which means mercy. Apparently priests or parishioners can gain a modicum of mercy by leaning against these platforms when they are required to stand for long periods during mass. Father Aubrey was proud of the misericords at St. Giles. He told me they were among the finest he had seen and spent ages explaining who each of the carved faces belonged to. I wonder where Peter took the panel from. Father Aubrey would seethe if he saw this fine example of Christian craftsmanship in a stable like this.

Three candles burn on a shelf built into the panel above the cage. Dozens of prayer beads have been hung from a nail above the candles. Peter kneels and whispers into the blanket, glancing at me suspiciously as he does. I cannot hear what he says. After a moment he stands.

"Osbert says that he is not certain that God sent you. He wants proof."

"What is in that cage?" I ask.

"Osbert demands proof!" he shouts.

"Peter, what is in that cage?"

"Give us proof! You say are you from God; Osbert says you are a demon! *We need proof!*"

I shake my head and brush past him.

"No!" Peter throws himself at me and we fall against the back wall. I elbow him in the chest and reach for the blanket.

"Get away from him! Get away from him!" He wraps his dirty hands around my forehead and pulls my head back. His hands smell of shit. I pry his fingers off me and rip the blanket away.

"No!" Peter shouts.

The gnawed remains of a rodent lie in the cage.

"Osbert is a rat?" I ask.

Peter slumps away from me and sobs, covering his face with his hands.

"Honestly, Peter, did you eat Osbert?"

Peter wrings his hands. "Osbert...Osbert said it was acceptable. He said I could just have little nibbles."

I wipe at my forehead and sniff my fingers. "I don't care. God doesn't care. Just tell me where the Lutons' Manor is."

"I cannot," Peter says. "Osbert requires...Osbert requires proof."

This is a stubborn sort of insanity. If God was this frustrated with that Amalek city, I can understand his judgment now.

I take the candle off the shelf, then draw my cannon from the shoulder sack.

"Here is your proof." I aim at Osbert and light the cannon. Peter dives shrieking to the floor at the sound of the explosion. The smoke from the gun dissipates, making patterns in the shafts of light that enter through the stable windows. Much of the cage is gone. There is no sign of the rat.

"You...You killed Osbert."

"*Mea maxima culpa*," I say.

Peter tells me where the Lutons' Manor is.

The manor is near the village of Sudbury, about three miles from where I am and not far from Hedingham. I take a deep breath when I think of Hedingham. I planned to stop there on my way down. Sir Morgan of Hastings is imprisoned in a nunnery there. He was infected by the plague because of me—because I insisted on bringing two of my knights on my journey to St. Edmund's Bury. And in so doing, I risked both their lives and have likely orphaned Morgan's daughter.

I tap a pouch on my hip and feel the edge of a thighbone inside. Morgan is not the only one I need to see at the nunnery. I made a promise to a nun there.

The wound on my wrist has not changed. I wonder if wounds inflicted by plaguers look different. Will the wound blacken or run with pus? Will it change over time until I am certain it carries the plague? I rub at it and manage only to push grime deeper into the wound.

An hour before sunset, I spot a tall Norman church tower in the distance. The Lutons' Manor house crops into view two hundred paces later. It is a handsome home of Suffolk flint, rising several stories. And it is entirely surrounded by plaguers. There must be survivors inside.

May God protect them.

A scattering of outbuildings sit neatly upon the grounds. I focus on the only other building that has attracted the attention of plaguers. Many plaguers. Twenty-five or thirty of them surround the stable. That is twenty-five or thirty too many. I need to draw them away somehow. Burning mint attracts the afflicted, but I have no mint and do not want to waste my hour of sunlight searching for it. I should start carrying chickens with me.

I unsheathe my sword and stare at the molar that has been lacquered into the hilt. It is said to be a tooth taken from the body of Saint Giles. I pray to him for guidance, then I have another thought. I stare up into the cloud-strewn sky.

Mother Mary, I am sorry for any wrongs I have committed against you. I will do what you want of me. Show me the way. Blessed Virgin, just show me the way.

Nothing happens. Why should anything happen? God has forgotten us, so why should the Virgin remember? If this plague was wrought by God, why should the saints help me thwart it? We are on our own now, here on earth. We—

A shout from the manor house disperses my thoughts. A man has fallen off the tiled roof and landed among the afflicted. Men and women look down at him from the manor windows, some of them screaming or sobbing. The plaguers climb over one another to get to the fallen man. They swarm over him like ants on an apple slice. The poor fool. He must have been trying to reach another wing of the manor. Perhaps there are plaguers inside the home.

I rise out of my crouch and take a step toward him, then check myself. What can I do for him? A woman screams over and over again. The scent of blood must be in the air, because the plaguers from the stables pull away and lurch toward the manor house.

I might reach the man. Maybe make his end a little quicker. But he will die regardless, and my Elizabeth still lives. I clench my hands and try not to speak angry words at God. Is this Mary's work? Is this man's sacrifice her guidance?

All of the plaguers leave the stables. It is an appalling trade—a man for a horse—but Mary has shown me the way.

I lope across the manor grounds, past magnificent cedars, over a delicate arched bridge and finally to the stables. Invisible nails seem to bite at my ankle but it does not matter. The Virgin Mary is on my side again. She has found me a horse. I feel guilt for doubting her, shame for questioning her intent.

Mea maxima culpa.

I rip open the stable door and once again my thoughts are dispersed.

Apparently the Virgin Mary has a sense of humor. A thousand pounds of Suffolk dairy peers over the stall at me and moos.

Chapter 3

I'M DISAPPOINTED WITH PETER AND Osbert. Rats must not have good vision. Dead rats even worse, I imagine.

The heifer is dun colored, with white around her nose and over her eyes. The sunken flesh of her flanks reveals the curve of her ribs. She looks like she has not eaten in days. She is alone. She is scared. And she is my only hope.

"There's a girl," I say softly. She shuffles away from me and bawls. "Shush. There's a horde out there looking for you. And I don't think they want milk." A rope around her neck has been tied to a hook in the wall. I unfasten the rope and lead her out of the stall so that she faces toward the stable door. I set a milking stool beside her. "I don't think either of us is going to enjoy this," I say. "But we don't have much choice, do we?"

I stroke her neck and her tail swishes. "What's your name, girl?" She stares at me blankly, her wet nose glistening in the dying light. I step onto the stool beside her. "You look like an Abigail to me. How does Abigail sound?" I rest one hand on her side and she shuffles back a step and tosses her head to one side. "We're going to take this easy at first. Slow movements. No panicking. We're just going to get used to each other, isn't that right, Abigail?" I put both hands on her, catch my breath, then hop forward, plopping my breastplate onto her broad back. I pivot and drop my legs to either side of her as she shuffles forward.

"Just nice and slow and gentle, you understand?"

She doesn't.

Abigail bolts from the stable. I have never ridden a cow before. Apparently it is a learned skill. I topple from her rump and fall with a clatter to the stable floor. Cured meats and loaves of bread tumble from my shoulder sack. Tristan's helmet, which I have tied to my belt, flops against my side. I pick up the food and hobble after her, terrified that she will run off into the countryside. But it is not Abigail that I have to worry about—she comes to a stop a few paces outside the stables and tears at the grass with her teeth.

No, my biggest concern is the army of plaguers staggering toward us from the manor house.

The fastest of the plaguers are no more than fifty paces from us. Growling demon-faced creatures with eyes that promise oblivion.

I run back into the stable and return with the milking stool. I set it beside the cow and glance back toward the manor house. The plaguers are thirty paces away.

"Abigail, I don't want to sound dramatic, but we are going to die here if we can't work this out." I hear the edge of panic in my voice. Her ear flutters. I think she hears it too. "I'm going to get on, and I need you to be a good girl. Can you do that for me? Can you be a good girl?"

The cow turns her head and I stare into one of her gentle eyes. I look back again. The mob of plaguers is fifteen paces away. The nearest is a man whose neck and lower jaw are riddled with weeping sores.

Mother Mary, I don't care if you don't save me, just save Elizabeth.

I hop onto the cow as far forward as I can and straddle her, throwing my arms around her neck. It must be a lot of weight for her, but Abigail doesn't flinch. She takes a few steps forward, then stops.

"Let's go!" I glance back at the plaguers. They are close enough for me to see teeth. To see blood in their fingernails. "Move! Move! Move!"

Abigail lowers her head and picks at the lush grass.

"Oh, for God's sake!" I smack her rump and am rewarded with a tail twitch.

I draw my knife.

"Sorry, girl, but this will hurt you a lot less than those demons will." The first of the afflicted reaches her flank. It is the man with the sores. Tall and haggard, with a bloody piece of glass jutting from one of his eyes.

Abigail becomes aware of the plaguers. She lurches to one side and lashes out with one of her back legs, sending the man crashing backward. I lose my balance and drop my knife, and Abigail finds the strength to gallop. She hurtles forward, so I have to throw my arms around her neck and clutch the rope at her throat. The lurching of her broad back knocks me off again. My feet hit the ground but I do not let go of her neck. She staggers and tilts sideways, dragged downward by my weight, but she keeps moving toward an abandoned field of rotting rye. My legs drag along the clay and plaguers dive for them.

One of the afflicted, a woman, gets a hand on my boot and is dragged along as well. She is dark haired and the skin around her black eyes is peeling away in bloody strips. She opens her bloodstained mouth and hisses. Abigail struggles to move the two of us and more plaguers throw themselves upon me.

My gauntleted hands are locked together so that Abigail cannot shed me. We will live or die together. The cow's head tilts closer to the ground. Her back legs dig for purchase among the dewy clay. A man missing part of his scalp throws himself at me, his clawed fingers hooking onto the back edge of my breastplate. I roll to one side, but the afflicted man won't let go. And the weight becomes too much for Abigail. She crashes sideways to the ground in a shower of flesh, plaguers, and armor.

I seize the opportunity to drive the steel cowter on my elbow into the face of the man holding my backplate. His nose splatters like a mouse beneath a millstone and he lets go. The other plaguers struggle to their feet, but Abigail and I are faster. I clasp my arms around her neck and throw one leg onto her back as she rises. The rest of the afflicted are upon us. Their hands clutch at Abigail. She pounds away from the horde, fear at last giving her strength and speed.

I dangle from her neck with one leg over the top of her. The plaguers are falling away. But if I cannot get back on Abigail, she and I will fall to the clay once more. And there will be no second escape from the afflicted. The steel greave on my leg slips against the cow's smooth hide. Each stride sends me one inch closer to the ground. I gather every ounce of my strength and pull myself upward, reclaiming one inch at a time. Abigail slows and kicks at me.

"Not…nice…Abigail…" I groan. She tries kicking again, but it is too late. I shift onto her back. She puts her shoulders into her strides and pulls away from plaguers.

I am riding a cow.

But I am not riding quickly. Abigail slows to a trot after a few strides, then stops altogether. She dips her head and tears at the grass.

"They're still back there!" I slap her rump and she swishes her tail again. This is not going to work. I kick at her flanks and she glances back at me, her jaws working the grass. Her ears twitch forward.

I can hear the erratic thudding of the plaguers' footsteps. They are once more within striking range. I point to them.

"Look! Look, you stupid cow!"

Abigail peers at the plaguers and then lurches sideways and shakes her head as if she had never seen them before.

"You're no chicken!" I shout at her. She bellows and lurches forward again. "You're no chicken!"

Her hooves kick up dirt as she gets started, but it is too late. The fastest of the plaguers have arrived. Abigail loses her bovine calm and begins spinning and kicking. It is all I can do to stay on. I wrap my arms around her neck and wind one hand in the ropes. Five of the fastest plaguers have reached us and try to get close, but Abigail's kicks and wild spins keep knocking them down.

When I am sure of my balance, I let go of her neck with one hand and hack at the plaguers with my sword. They will reach Abigail's flesh soon. She will go down, and I cannot outrun this tide of plaguers. The brunt of these wretched creatures is almost upon us. I bring the sword down harder than I have to and hurl curses at the afflicted as I send them to purgatory. And then something peculiar happens.

Six or seven of the approaching plaguers fall to the ground. They simply topple backward. A few scream as they fall. I jab my blade through a man's throat and look back again. Another few plaguers lurch and fall backward. The marching hordes behind these stumble over their fallen comrades but continue their relentless approach. Another five or six fall, to the ground.

There are three of them around Abigail now. The others cannot get close enough to us. They simply fall to the ground whenever they get near. As if God were striking them dead. Perhaps Mary is making amends for the cow.

I kick an old woman and hear something in her chest crack. She howls and claws at her breasts and I cleave her head from crown to mouth.

Abigail is whirling dangerously. Riding a cow is not like riding a horse. A cow's back is broad, so that your legs cannot rest comfortably around the animal's flanks. And its skin is looser than a horse's: it slips forward and backward and pulls you along. I think it is only the terror of falling and pure strength of will that keep me on her while she spins and kicks. She sends a plaguer twirling to the lush grass with a kick and sees an opening. She bolts forward again.

The old woman comes with us for a few paces, until I can free my sword from her skull. And when I look back at the rest of the plaguers, I see what is bringing them to the ground. And I consider leaping off of Abigail and letting the afflicted take me.

Chapter 4

ARROWS. THE PLAGUERS ARE RIDDLED with arrows.

I look ahead and spot the archers behind a low hedge. They are arranged in a row a hundred yards from the stable, not far from the stone church I noticed earlier. I count ten of them.

They angle their longbows upward, draw back the strings, and let loose the arrows. I can just see the shafts in the darkening sky, impossibly thin geese flying in a chaotic formation. But these geese have teeth. Some of the arrows bite only dirt, sinking almost to the feathers in the soft grass. But most bite deep into afflicted flesh. The plaguers shriek and fall to their knees or topple backward. Most rise again and continue their clumsy pursuit.

I think of Sir Gerald, the enemy I made on my journey to St. Edmund's Bury. His men used crossbows, not longbows, but perhaps he has broadened his arsenal. Who else could it be? I have no doubts.

I yank the rope around Abigail's neck hard to the right, but a rope is not a halter. She shakes her head and continues toward the archers.

The plaguers behind are undeterred by the ceaseless rain of arrows. They plod on fearlessly. Some have three or four arrows jutting from their bodies. And still they come.

The archers fire volley after volley. If they are Sir Gerald's men, then I should let the plaguers have me; it would be a much more pleasant death.

I think about leaping to the ground and running away from both the archers and the plaguers, but I know I cannot. My ankle would not allow me to escape either of them. Abigail trots toward the longbowmen. I breathe a quick prayer and put my life in the hands of Mary, Giles, and God.

One of the three responds. Abigail becomes aware of the archers, and she does not like them any more than I do. She wheels and pounds away from them toward the field of rotting rye. A thickset man among the archers points toward me. He shouts something. I think they intend to pursue. But I see no horses. Abigail may not be a racer, but a cow can outrun a man when she makes up her mind to.

But she cannot outrun arrows. Several of the archers turn their bows on us and the arrows plunge silently into the earth around us.

"Run, girl! Run!"

But Abigail needs no encouragement. It may have taken her time to realize her danger, but now that she knows, there is no stopping her. We plunge into the withered rye, where the archers cannot see us. I smell fertile earth and rotting crops. An arrow clanks against the spaulder upon my shoulder, striking sparks and deflecting into the field. I duck low against the cow's neck and concentrate on staying upon her. She stumbles on the ploughed ridges but forges onward. Arrows hiss into the dry stalks until we clear the field and move beyond the archers' range.

And then we are free.

I rub Abigail's ears and smile. "There's a girl," I say. "I'm sorry I spoke ill of you."

She slows to a walk and peers behind us, then lowers her head and eats. I dismount and let her feast for a time. She has earned it. Abigail and my holy triumvirate have kept me alive. I say a brief prayer of thanks and allow myself another smile.

My coat of arms is a cross, engrailed, crested with a unicorn upon a helmet. The cross symbolizes that we Dallingridges are a God-fearing people of England under Saint George. The helmet, because we have always been warriors and knights. And the unicorn, because I like unicorns. Many people ask me about the unicorn. Must there be meaning to everything?

Perhaps I should add Mary and Giles to my coat of arms. Elizabeth would be pleased if I added Saint Giles. I can see her smile in my mind. The small hop she makes when she is truly happy. I can feel her sweet lips against mine. Her fingers curling around the hair that falls at my neck. The memory changes. Her fingers are in my hair, but we are at the monastery two days ago. She tears at my locks and howls, and I have to push at her face to keep those beautiful teeth away from my flesh.

I open my eyes and sigh. Abigail cranes her neck back and stares at me as she chews. Saint Giles would go well on my crest. He watches over the insane, so perhaps I could change our family motto from *Amor, honor, regnum*—"love, honor, kingdom"—to *In tempore insania, insania salvábit nos*: "In these times of madness, only madness will save us."

I feel a sharp burning pain in my wrist. The wound and all it might imply had slipped from my mind. I snatch the gauntlet off. The wound throbs. It is red and swollen and angry. I close my eyes and take a breath, then look again. It looks terrible.

Maybe the gauntlet sleeve scraped the cut in that wild escape.

I slip the gauntlet back on and think of Elizabeth. I think of our coat of arms and the castle we are building at Bodiam. I think of anything except the throbbing gash that could end my journey. I have killed so many of these plaguers. Am I to become one? Will Tristan find me staggering toward him? I force myself to breathe normally. I don't feel sick. I do not think I have the fever. It is simply a scratch.

I recall the black marks on Elizabeth's wrists and shake my head. Time is her enemy. Nothing must stop me. I am not plagued. I am *not*.

I have no bridle, so we plod aimlessly toward the south until the darkness becomes a danger to Abigail and I am forced to dismount. We find a cluster of abandoned cottages near the River Stour: wattle and daub structures with rotting thatch on top and rotting bodies inside. We pick one with passable thatch and no bodies. I take off my armor and throw myself onto a straw mattress against the back wall.

Abigail stares at me.

"Well, we can't both sleep on the mattress, silly cow." She doesn't stop staring, so I turn my back to her and toss for a while. I find a murky half slumber, a limbo between wake and sleep. My dreams are of eating flesh and being hunted. I drift out of my slumber for a time and, before falling asleep again, wonder if morning will bring the plague to my body.

Chapter 5

I WAKE THINKING OF ELIZABETH. IT is a good sign. I am not certain I would think at all if I were plagued. The wound doesn't look any better, but if it were plague, I would have turned by now. Would I not? I think of the villagers of Danbury, who we inadvertently afflicted. They drank from tainted phials. Those who drank more turned faster. Could my wound have been so slight that it will take days for me to plague? I have killed scores of plaguers and yet I do not know enough about this affliction to be sure. I feel pain in my head, but I am not sweating, nor sick to my stomach.

I strap on my armor again and fashion a crude halter for Abigail. The cow stamps and backs away from me, but I am able to fit her with a crude bit whittled from a branch. It allows me to aim Abigail in the general direction I wish to go. And that direction is southwest, toward Hedingham and Chelmsford. I will visit with Morgan, then try to find Tristan. If I do not run across Tristan, I will begin my search for the alchemist and his island fortress on my own.

I pass near the town of Sudbury. It is a wool town, prosperous and—before the plague—full of the Flemish. I understand that the Flemish were put in Sudbury by King Richard's grandfather, Edward III. He settled them here to help revive England's dismal cloth trade. Richard told me once that Edward "would not even wipe his arse with English cloth." Fortunately, the Fleming transplant took root. Sudbury flourished in the cloth trade, and Edward could safely wipe his arse with English cloth.

I suppose it may still be full of the Flemish, but they likely have lost most of their Flemishness. All plaguers speak the same language, and it is not French.

I become aware of the riders shortly after passing Sudbury. Two of them. They are a half mile from me, but they ride swiftly. I consider veering off into the countryside, but I am certain they have seen me already. If a man can watch a horse run away for two days in the flat East Anglian plains, how long can he watch a cow?

"Maybe they're friends," I say to Abigail. She farts.

I nod and place one arm over the cannon so it is partially hidden.

The men reach me and slow their horses. One wears a rusted chain-mail tunic, the other a leather jerkin. Both are armed. They fall in step with Abigail, one on each side, and laugh. Abigail twitches her ears. I shift uneasily on her back and try to gather as much dignity as I can. I could not find a long enough rope to make Abigail's halter, but I stumbled upon an old maypole with a long pink ribbon dangling from it. That ribbon is Abigail's reins. I am certain it is not helping my knightly bearing.

I nod to each of them. "It is good to see other healthy men in East Anglia." I hope I am still healthy.

"Oi, Stephan." The man in the chain mail ignores me and calls to his companion on my left. "What would you call a knight that rides a cow?"

Stephan gives me a long look. "An udder failure," he says.

The two men laugh again. I keep my eyes on the road ahead. I have enough strife with the afflicted. Must I have it from the unafflicted as well?

"Unless he comes from Jerusalem, Henric," Stephan says. "In which case I would call him a Mooooor."

Henric bends over in the saddle as he laughs. "A Mooooor!" he says, catching his breath. "A Mooooor!"

I remove two flints from a pouch at my belt and hold them in one hand as I rummage through my shoulder sack. Stephan smirks at me.

"Moors are from Spain and Africa," I say.

Henric finally addresses me. "Stephan's got a gift with words," he says.

I nod my head but do not meet the man's gaze.

"My father was a punster," Stephan says. "I wasn't any good at 'em till he died. Just as we dropped him into his grave, his way with words passed on to me." I can see him smiling up at me from the corner of my eye. "You could say it was a gift from the Lowered."

Henric bursts into a fit of laughter again. "Gift...gift from the Lowered! Ain't 'e just the funniest man you ever 'eard?" He doubles over with laughter again and punches Abigail in the side. "Gift from the Lowered!"

I turn my head toward him and draw a firing cord out from the shoulder sack. "If you strike my cow again," I say, "I will grind you into grain and feed you to her."

Henric seems to think this is as funny as Stephan's puns. He hoots with laughter, then mimics me. "If you strike my cow again...hooooooo!"

I place the firing cord in my lap. "I'm glad I could provide some entertainment," I say. "Godspeed to both of you." I kick my heels into Abigail's side and she accelerates to a slightly faster walk. It is not what I was hoping for.

Henric wipes at his eyes, then grows sober. He takes hold of Abigail's pink reins and halts his horse. "I'm afraid you need to get off the heifer now, Sir."

I begin striking the two flints together, creating a shower of sparks in my lap.

"You deaf, cow-knight?" Henric says. He draws a short sword. "I said get off."

"What's that he's doing?" Stephan asks. "You lighting yourself on fire?"

"No," I say.

Henric lets go of Abigail's reins and draws his horse away from me. "What are you doing?"

"I'm lighting a firing cord," I say. The cord catches and begins to smolder. I put the flints away.

"What's a firing cord?" he asks.

"It is a length of hemp that has been soaked and rolled in flammable powders." I draw my gun from the shoulder sack and aim it at Henric. "It is used to light cannons like this one." Henric stares at the weapon. "I appreciate the friendly banter," I say. "Really I do. But it is time you fellows continued toward wherever it was you were heading."

Abigail chooses this moment to explore the high grasses on the roadside and I have to rotate my torso to keep the gun facing Henric.

"You...you got one shot," Henric says. "You won't 'ave time to reload."

Abigail walks further off the road, toward a line of coppiced trees, and I pivot until I am almost facing backward. I am unhappy with Abigail's priorities. I lift one foot so that it rests on her back and prop the cannon upon my knee. The movement shows off the hilt of Saint Giles's sword. "Why would I want to reload?"

Stephan creeps his horse toward me, so I turn the cannon to face him. He stops, holds up a hand, and smiles. I wave the end of the cannon southward.

"Move on. Both of you."

Henric smiles. I do not like the way he does it. There is a confidence to that smile. "It's a fine sword you 'ave, cowknight. A shame that swords can't kill people from far away."

"If people are far away, you don't need a sword," I reply. "So shut your mouth and get far away."

"Stephan, what would you call a weapon that was part cannon and part sword?"

Stephan has the confident smile now too. I look from one to another. They know something that I do not. If I do not find out what it is soon, I might well be dead. I study them. Their hands are on the reins. Their horses are calm.

"I would call it a cannord," Stephan says.

"Cannord sounds a bit French, don't it?"

Stephan nods. "Perhaps a swannon?"

Henric makes a sour face. "A bit flimsy. Like a girly bird."

Stephan makes a great show of thinking, tapping his chin with a finger, then his eyes widen. "Why, Henric, there's already a name for such a thing."

"Is there?"

"Yes," Stephan says. "I believe they call it a *longbow.*"

Neither of these men has a bow. I shoot glances toward the coppiced trees, but there is no one waiting in ambush. Then I catch motion to the north on the Roman road. Horsemen. Several of them. Everything falls into place. The archers from last night. Sir Gerald's men.

I need a horse. There is no time for thought. I raise the cannon and touch the firing cord to the powder hole. Henric holds up his hand and backpedals his horse, but he has no time to escape. His confident smile is gone and I have a heartbeat to savor it. The cannon fires, cloaking all three of us in thick smoke and the bitter smell of spent salt-peter. Abigail tenses and leaps to one side. I have to jump clear of her to avoid falling clumsily to the road. Pain jolts from my ankle all the way up my leg. I hear Henric's horse shriek and see its silhouette as it rears. Stephan's horse bolts southward. I can hear the drum of the other horsemen's hooves on the road.

I reach blindly for the reins of Henric's horse. The smoke clears enough for me to get a good look, and I am stunned by what I see.

Henric is unharmed. There is not a mark on him.

"You...you missed!" he says.

I do not know how I could have missed from four feet away. I'm glad Tristan wasn't here to see it. Damn these blundering cannons.

Stephan trots back to us. The confident smiles are back. The horsemen are almost upon us. "We are not cowed by your fancy cannon."

Henric laughs. "Cowed!" He leans over and smacks his saddle. "'E's got a gift! Cowed!"

I throw the cannon down in disgust as the horsemen surround me. There are eight of them. All broad-chested men wearing leather jerkins, with unstrung bows in leather cases upon their backs.

A horrible death awaits me.

Chapter 6

THE HORSEMEN ARE THE ARCHERS I saw back at Lutons Place. I ask if they will take me to Sir Gerald, but they do not know who he is. Hope smolders in my heart.

Perhaps they are from a lord's militia. Deserters or survivors. I ask who they fought for as they strip me of my sword and my shoulder sack. None of them reply. They cut Tristan's helmet from my belt and bind my hands.

One of the archers flexes his bow, bending the stiff yew until he can string it. Without a word of warning he nocks an arrow, draws the string back with a grunt, and shoots Abigail in the flank. She kicks with her legs and tries to flee, but two of the archers hold the rope around her neck. The men laugh.

"No!" My scream echoes across the countryside. I run at the archer and send him crashing to the ground. The man struggles to rise, but I shatter his cheekbone with one of my boots. I draw my leg back for another kick, but two men drag me away. Another knocks me senseless with a blow to my jaw. Archers have brutal strength, and this one puts everything into the blow.

I regain my senses as three more archers string their bows and aim at Abigail. "No!" I scream. "*Why?*"

The two men guarding me hold knives in my direction and peer over their shoulders at Abigail. She is lowing and tossing her head. She raises one hind leg halfway to the arrow, then puts the leg down again.

The archers fire. Four arrows strike Abigail. I have never heard a cow shriek, but that is what she does. A long, high-pitched grunt. She bucks and yanks against the ropes, then falls to one side and lows. I break away from the men guarding me and kneel beside her as the archers continue to fire. I touch my head to hers and stare into her eye as the men fire arrows around me into her flesh. They laugh and try to land arrows as close to me as they can. I whisper soothingly to her. Her long tongue slips in and out of her mouth.

I am sorry, Abigail. Mea maxima culpa. Mea maxima culpa.

I add another name to the list of snuffed lives that I am responsible for.

I turn on the men. The rage is upon me. It is difficult to see anything. Only shapes, which I run toward. But there are too many. They knock me to the muddy grass and hold me down. I mutter curses, promise them that every one of them will die. I scream and make threats, until one of them hammers me in the temple with a fist.

The archers brought two spare horses with them. Henric takes one and Stephan the other. When I regain my senses they sit me on a horse in front of Henric. Three men cut at Abigail's body while the rest of the group rides leisurely along a worn track that heads eastward. I look back at Abigail's corpse and swear to Saint Giles and the Virgin Mary that I will avenge her. Perhaps I am losing my mind.

"She was all dried up," Henric says. "No milk. We can't use a dry cow. She'd have slowed us down and brought the demons on us. But now we'll have meat."

"What do you want with me?" I ask. "Why am I bound?"

"A knight like you?" Henric says. "Must be a ransom for your return."

"Release me," I say. "I promise, on my honor, that I will return with my ransom. I have money in Sussex."

"Money?" he says. "What do we need money for? We need horses. I imagine we can get ten horses for a knight."

Is coin finally worthless? Are we to barter horses and goats now like the savages that wandered Britain a thousand years ago? I think of Brother Phillip and his wealth of live-stock back in St. Edmund's Bury. The monk could be a king in this new land.

I spot a cloud of crows in the distance. It is another two miles before I see the first of the wheels.

One end of a thick log has been driven into the fertile earth. The log rises to about the height of a man. A carriage wheel has been affixed to the top of the log, facing toward the sky, so that the entire assembly reminds me of a mon-strously big mushroom. The wheel is not perfectly parallel to the ground, so it rotates a few inches to one side, squeal-ing in the wind, then slowly back again.

A man lies bound upon the top of this wheel with his arms and legs spread wide. I am not certain I can call the poor creature a man anymore. Someone has shattered his limbs countless times with hammer blows, so that his arms and legs seem to ooze bonelessly through the spokes of the wheel. Pus, buzzing flies, and clotted blood cover the man's body.

I jump in the saddle when his eyes open as we pass. He is still alive. Dear God, he is still alive. The eyes are blue within white, not black within black. He hisses a word. It takes me a moment to realize he is speaking French.

"Miséricorde."

The man wants death. If my hands were not bound, I would oblige him. Not even the French deserve such torture.

There are nine more carriage wheels along the old track. They must have run out of carriages, because the last wheel looks like a simple iron hoop with boards lying across it. Each wheel supports a man whose arms and legs have been beaten into jelly. Some have smashed faces. Some have had their stomachs opened so the flies and ants can feast on their entrails. Most of the men are still alive. A few still have the strength to moan. The wind or the men's spasms make the wheels spin slowly and creak gently in the East Anglian afternoon.

The afflicted are not the worst thing about this new England. Plaguers are hungry and desperate. I understand those motives. What, then, are the motives of the survivors? Power? Avarice? Cruelty? Of the two groups, the unafflicted survivors are the greater threat. I am uncomfortable with what this implies about my kind.

I stare at the wheels and wonder who is responsible for such barbarism.

"They're French soldiers," Henric says. "Our troop captured them in Essex. Mad. Every one of them."

"Mad?" I ask.

Stephan nods. "They were gibbering when we found 'em. Said they fought a battle against Lucifer, near Hadleigh." He laughs. "One of them said that demons chased them all the way to Halstead."

The men are not mad. Those were not Lucifer's demons they fought near Hadleigh, they were mine. I led an army of the afflicted against Frenchmen who had landed at Lighe a week ago. The enemy had never seen plaguers, and they were terrified of them. These men were fleeing me. Poor bastards. Apparently I share the blame for this barbarism.

"Were you two responsible for the wheels?" I ask.

Henric shakes his head. "I don't have the stomach for it. It were Alexander who did it. If you're lucky, you won't meet him."

"If you were decent men," I say, "you would end their suffering."

"I would, truly I would, but then Alexander would 'ave me up on one of them wheels," Henric says. "Besides, they're French."

One of the men stares at me as I pass, and a single tear rolls down his cheek.

Most of my life has been devoted to hating and killing the French. But here, on this lonely road in Suffolk, I find myself pitying them. What strange days these are.

In these times of madness, even the French deserve sympathy.

"If they 'adn't been French, they would be dead already," Henric says. "Alexander likes to use the Spanish donkey. 'Orrible to watch but kills them in a lot less time."

The Spanish donkey. One of the vilest forms of torture in existence. The simplest version is a log placed horizontally on tall supports. The log is trimmed with axes and filed so that the portion facing upward becomes a long, sharp edge. The victim, whose hands are bound to a rope that is slung over a tree branch or bracket above the log, is lowered gradually onto the sharp edge with his legs on either side. Heavy weights tied to his feet force him downward and the wedge of wood splits the man. The heavier the weights, the faster he is split. Sometimes the man holding the rope will pull the victim upward a bit to prolong his life. If the torturer feels pity, he can release the tension on the rope and the man is split in seconds. But torturers rarely pity. I have heard that sometimes a man can survive for hours when he is split from crotch to sternum.

"Alexander sounds charming," I say.

"'E's tough," Henric says. "Had nine women raped and split last week. Left them alive for most of the day. They were pagans. All of them. The donkey was just a taste of the 'ell they 'ave waiting for them."

We leave the wheels of anguish behind, and I promise myself that I will come back to give the soldiers *miséricorde.* And if I meet this Alexander, I will end his misery too. And I won't end it quickly.

Henric, Stephan, and the archers lead me another mile to a tiny village. A wooden sign as we enter proclaims it to be "Edwardstone." I don't think much of the coincidence until they walk me toward a stone church at the village center. It is another church devoted to Saint Mary, the Virgin. It makes me think of Sir Morgan, who was convinced that Saint Giles was guiding him. I wonder if Mary is doing the same for me, although every fourth church in England seems devoted to Mary, so maybe I am overthinking things.

Five grimy military tents are squeezed in among the tombstones of the churchyard, the canvas snapping in the wind. Eight equally grimy men mill around a fire pit. They watch us as we approach. One of them raises a hand and Henric waves back.

They duck me into one of the tents. The canvas keeps out sunlight, so candles sit on two tall candlesticks at one end. A shaggy soldier sitting in a chair by the candles looks as if he has just woken. He nods to Henric.

A man and a woman sit back to back in the darkness at the center of the tent, their hands bound around the thick pole that supports the entire tent. Someone has placed a burlap sack over the man's head. It is hard to see in the faint light, but it looks as if the woman wears a nun's habit.

"Another one?" the guard in the chair asks.

"Yeah," Henric says. "He was riding a cow with pink reins." The two men laugh. "Had an unhealthy affection for that cow, he did." They chuckle again and sit me against the tentpole between the man and the woman. They run a rope around my tied wrists and bind me to the pole.

"I am a knight of Sussex," I say. "I hold the favor of the earl of Arundel and King Richard himself."

The two men laugh again.

"You can tell that to Alexander." Henric bids farewell to the guard and slips out of the tent.

I seethe in silence for a span, imagining the things I will do to Henric and Stephan. And Alexander. And the archers who killed Abigail. And this woolly guard in the chair. And those men by the campfire. All of them. Every one. I will bring Amalek upon this encampment when I am free. Not even the donkeys will be spared.

"It is no use talking to them," the nun says. "They have gone outlaw."

"There must be laws for outlaws to exist," I say. "Men like these have been reduced to savagery in this new world. And we may be their prisoners for a long time. God has blessed us with a trial, Sister."

The man in the hood cocks his head toward me. "Hallelujah."

I stare at him for a long time. My heart pounds with the truth but my mind cannot accept it. "Tristan?"

The man nods his head. "Hello, Edward."

A thousand questions spring to mind, but only one makes it out of my mouth. "Why do you have a sack over your head?"

"The question you should be asking," he says, "is, why aren't *you* wearing a sack over *your* head? It is the height of fashion on the Continent these days. A bit restrictive when it comes to range of view, but really, what is sight in the face of fashion?"

I feel a smile creep over my face. "Tristan!"

"I hope you didn't bugger that cow, Edward," he adds. "I understand God frowns on that sort of thing."

I laugh. It is the first time I have laughed in days. I have found my brother-in-arms. My most loyal knight. My worst influence. And my best friend.

I have found Tristan of Rye.

Episode 2

Chapter 7

"TELL ME ABOUT THIS COW," Tristan says. "Supple skin? Firm udders? Was she worth it, Edward? And, out of curiosity, where is she now?"

The nun beside me hisses a breath. "Must everything you say be so vulgar?" she asks. "In these vulgar times, Sister," Tristan says, "only vulgarity will save us. Enjoy some humor while you can. Death's sweet release may soon be upon us."

"If this is what passes for humor," the nun says, "then death will indeed be a sweet release. Vulgarity is not wit."

"Vulgarity is the height of wit, Sister," Tristan says. "God loves a good impudence here and there."

"If vulgarity is wit, then you are a saint."

It takes a moment for all the possible meanings to sink in. Tristan barks a laugh and then a peculiar thing happens. He cannot find a retort. He stammers, then falls silent. I look skyward, expecting the Angel Gabriel to blow his horn.

When I am certain the seas are not turning to blood and that the earth is not shaking, I speak. "It is good to see you, Tristan. I thought you would be in Chelmsford." I am careful to keep the emotion from my voice. It is a mistake to show the enemy what you value.

"I was heading to Chelmsford," he says. "But I heard about this fine establishment. Pastoral. Romantic lighting. Clever women. The staff could use a good scrubbing, but at these prices, how can I complain?"

"I hope you didn't pay in advance," I say. "We won't be here long."

"I told you to keep your mouth shut, didn't I?" The guard stands and pulls the burlap hood from Tristan.

"No," Tristan says. "You told me to hold my tongue. Which I am incapable of doing when my hands are bound. A rather peculiar thing to ask, really."

The guard draws a swath of linen from a pouch and tears a long strip from it, then ties a knot in the center.

"What's your name?" Tristan asks. "I'm going to speak to the owner about your rudeness. And where's my wine? I asked for it more than two hours ago."

The soldier gestures to Tristan and turns to me with a pleading look in his eyes. "Does he ever stop talking?"

"He sleeps sometimes," I say.

The guard puts the knot between Tristan's teeth. It is good Flemish cloth. I hope King Edward didn't wipe his arse with it.

"Pull it tightly, please," the nun says.

A man wearing a rich, knee-length tunic enters the tent. The guard pulls the linen away from Tristan's mouth and hides it behind his back. "Afternoon, Gilbert," he says.

Gilbert has long mustaches and closely cropped hair. He studies me with his head tilted upward slightly, a gesture that no man I admire has ever used.

"Another knight?" he says.

"Not a chance," Tristan says. "I'm leaving today. The staff is awful. And this room is not at all adequate—I specifically requested a view of the river."

The man studies Tristan, then clears his throat. He lifts a small rack that holds a dozen ceramic phials. "We found these among your things. Would you care to tell me what they are?"

"They contain a cure for the plague," Tristan says. "Please don't drink them."

The nun gasps. "A cure?"

"He jests," I say. "They are full of poison."

Gilbert studies Tristan, then me. He runs his finger along the hilt of an oversized knife at his hip. "If they are poison, then perhaps the two of you should drink them."

"I've had some," Tristan says. "But you can't ever be too safe. Bring it here."

"Tristan, stop it." I say. "He's not being serious. The liquid in those phials causes plague."

Gilbert sighs monumentally. "Shall we not play at games? I have been a scholar my entire life. I studied at Cambridge, gentlemen. I can see through your lies. I can see into your hearts."

"Then you have poor vision," I say. "If you drink those, you will contract the plague."

"What is your name?" Gilbert asks.

"I am Edward of Bodiam. And I am a knight of Sussex. Who are you that would hold me here against my will?"

"Sir Edward," Gilbert says. "Do you know that lying is not a natural instinct? When someone asks us a question, our first instinct is to tell the truth. Your friend answered my question very quickly. Too quickly to have lied. After he spoke, you realized that he had blundered. You took more time and came up with your response." He points a finger at me. "A lie."

I sigh, and Gilbert mistakes it for confirmation. He smiles and paces with his hands clasped before him. "You then further weakened your credibility by changing your lie. First you said the phials contain poison, then you said their contents cause plague. Do you see how you have defeated yourself?"

"You are an idiot," I say. "Believe what you wish."

"I don't have to believe. I know the wonders of *reason*."

Reason. I have heard many men speak of it. It is a fashionable topic these days. Lords fill their manors with men from the Continent, from Italy, and from the Arab lands so that they may learn about reason.

I have not had a great deal of teaching on this Greek philosophy. I know that the old monk Bede—a scholar whose writings have survived for nearly a thousand years—was versed in the teachings of the Greeks. He used their *reason* to conjecture that the world we live and walk upon is not flat but spherical. I would not believe such nonsense, but the Church denied it with such fervor that I know it must be true.

Reason, when used to delve into universal truths, is an indispensable tool. A torch to light the shadowy corners of the world. But these days, when men speak of reason, it is as a molten forge to twist and shape the world for their pleasure. And so I do not place a great deal of faith in *reason*.

"Here is a sample of reasoning, Edward," Gilbert says. "Phials contain medicine. You are carrying phials. Therefore, you are carrying medicine. Do you see the simplicity of it?"

"That *is* simple," Tristan says.

"Here's another," Gilbert says. "Humans avoid danger. The plague is dangerous. Therefore you would not carry the plague near you. Breathtaking, isn't it?"

"Breathtaking," I say. "Precisely the word I would have used."

"Why would your friend carry phials of plague with him? It is not *reasonable*. It makes no *sense*."

"Tristan never makes sense," I say.

"I don't," Tristan agrees. "But it adds to my charm."

"You must possess charm to add to it," the nun says.

Gilbert waves one hand to silence them. "Reason is an arrow," he says. "And it always strikes right where it means to. In the middle part of the target, Sir Edward. In the center of the target wreath, where only the best archers strike. And the center of that wreath, where the arrow strikes, that is what we like to call the truth."

"Such eloquence," Tristan says. "I never stood a chance against you, did I?"

"I have studied the works of all the masters," Gilbert says.

"Please, Gilbert," Tristan says. "Use the cure for good. That is all I ask."

Gilbert nods reassuringly. "Now, tell me, Sir Tristan, how do the phials work?"

"One drop will cure the afflicted. And one drop will protect the unafflicted for two weeks." Tristan shakes his head. "Damn you and your reason, Gilbert."

Gilbert stares at the phials and smiles broadly. "Alexander will be pleased when I show him what these phials do. Perhaps he will give me my own horse."

"He may give you more than that," I say.

Gilbert shrugs. "I will satisfy myself with a horse."

"I wouldn't." Tristan shakes his head. "God frowns on that sort of thing."

Chapter 8

WE HEAR THE FIRST SCREAM well after sunset.

There is a certain scream that only plaguers can elicit. A cry of unholy terror. After twenty years of war I thought I had heard every type of scream a man can make. But there is something biblical about a man's cry when he is surprised by a plaguer. Something that taps into the fear of eternal torment. When a man shouts in battle, it is from the lungs and from the throat. But when a man sees a plaguer, the scream comes from his very soul.

The guard wakes and peers out of the tent.

"What in Christ's name..." He squints, then dashes outside.

"Well, that's sorted then," Tristan says.

"What, exactly, is sorted?" I ask.

Tristan gestures vaguely with his chin. "That. Out there. Sorted."

"Tristan, nothing is sorted."

Tristan cocks an eyebrow, takes on Gilbert's tone. "You obviously have not studied *reason*, Sir Edward. All of our enemies will either be dead or plagued. If you had been to

Cambridge, you would realize that we can now escape from our bonds and leave at our leisure. Here, let me put it in the simple terms of reason: only bandits can hold us captive. Plaguers are not bandits. Therefore we are not captives anymore. Breathtaking, isn't it?"

"No, I did not study at Cambridge, Tristan. But let me make an attempt at reason: plaguers eat those who are not afflicted. We are not afflicted. Therefore—"

"The goal then is to not be here when the plaguers arrive," Tristan says. "See the simplicity?"

I sigh. "Can we try to get these ropes untied?"

Another scream rings out somewhere in the churchyard.

"Please tell me that you fools did not infect this entire camp," the nun says.

Tristan listens to the cries and winces. "Humans can run very quickly. We are human. Therefore..." He shrugs.

"Tristan." I feel the heat of frustration rising in me. Elizabeth tells me I need to breathe deeply when this happens, so I do. I breathe deeply three times and smile. "Humans cannot run when they are *tied to tentpoles*." I grit my teeth through the rest. "We are tied to thick tentpoles. Therefore..." I trail off, as Tristan did.

A man shrieks just outside, right next to us. Something falls against the tent behind Tristan. The tent shudders. More screams, including one from the nun. The light from the candles is just bright enough for me to see a dark stain spreading across the canvas.

"Knights are fools!" the nun says, and there is a touch of hysteria to her voice. "The two of you are knights!" She doesn't finish. She drops her chin to her chest and sobs. "We're going to die here because of your stupidity!"

"Edward and I may hold your life in our hands," Tristan says. "You might consider being a little nicer to us."

I dig my feet into the earth and shove with my legs. The tentpole shifts slightly, but not as much as I had hoped. They must have buried the oak shaft deep into the earth.

"Tristan, push against the pole with your back. Hard."

The pole shifts a little toward me. I shove back. The pole tilts toward him, and he shoves again. We slip into a rhythm. Forward and back, forward and back. The entire tent rocks with us. Just a few inches at a time. Back and forth.

Tristan spouts poetry to the rhythm of our rocking.

"Here's a riddle to leave you appalled..."

The cries echo all across the churchyard. A wild-eyed man with blood smeared across his cheek looks into the tent, then disappears again.

"I'm hairy beneath..." Tristan continues.

The pole shudders.

"...above I am bald..."

The canopy rattles over our heads as guy lines snap.

"I'm purple and red..."

A man enters the tent, almost falling as he does. It is Gilbert. Or was Gilbert. There is no *reason* left in the man that stares at us now. He stares at us with a vacant look of surprise.

"...and stand up in the bed. What am I called?" Tristan sees Gilbert and smiles. "Shall I repeat the riddle for you, Gilbert? A Cambridge man should have no trouble..." He trails off. "Oh."

A line of bloody spittle dribbles from Gilbert's mouth. He staggers toward us, moaning. The nun shrieks and thrashes against the pole. Gilbert reaches a hand out toward her. She shrieks again.

"Keep rocking, Tristan!" I lean toward the nun and pound Gilbert in the face with my foot. He howls and falls back, then turns back to me with a snarl. My boot has gashed the skin of his forehead. The pole tilts toward me, shoving me forward so that I have to curl in on myself. I shove back with all my strength. Gilbert lunges toward me and I use both feet to keep him at bay. He bites at the toe of one of my boots, so I use the other to knock teeth from his mouth. The pole tilts back toward me. The nun will not stop shrieking. I set one foot down and shove back against the pole. The tent tilts in Tristan's direction. Gilbert grabs at my leg. I lean to one side, gather all my strength, and swing my free leg in an arching kick that catches Gilbert in the temple and sends him tumbling to the ground.

Tristan groans and shoves at the pole. More guy lines creak and snap outside. The canvas loses its tautness. Folds of the tent sag toward us. The thick oaken pole pushes against my back, bending me almost double. Gilbert staggers to his feet. Tristan groans again and something at the base of the pole cracks. The full weight of the tent shaft falls upon me. I rotate my shoulders so that the pole is free to fall onto the ground. The candles flutter madly in the far corner.

Candles.

The broken tentpole creaks and falls slowly. The canvas drifts downward, fluttering the candles on the other side of the room. I have time for one more calculation of reason before the darkness descends.

Canvas burns. Tents are made of canvas...

Chapter 9

GILBERT GROWLS IN THE DARKNESS with what might be frustration. I empathize with him. The thick folds of canvas lie upon us and I can see nothing. I lie on my side, my hands still bound to the fallen tentpole. The nun has stopped screaming, but I can hear her weeping quietly and muttering prayers beside me. Tristan is silent, but I can feel his hands pulling against his ropes. My wrists are bound below his and just above the nun's. I feel her hands moving too.

"Sister," I say. "Can you slide your hands off the edge of the pole?"

"I am trying," she shouts. "They are tied tightly."

"Try harder," Tristan says.

"My wrists are at the bottom of this pole," she says, her fear momentarily forgotten. "You should be a little nicer to the woman who holds your life in her hands."

The canvas ripples toward me. Gilbert.

"Fair maiden," I say, trying to keep the panic from my voice. "Wouldst thou be a dear and please slide your fucking wrists off the miserable fucking post that we are attached to before Gilbert the demon uses his pox-addled *reason* to find me and *eat my bloody brains!*" I might have failed to keep the panic from my voice. I take three deep breaths and smile. "If you would, my lady."

"I cannot!" the nun shouts. "The ropes are too tight!"

"Rock back and forth," I say. "Use your weight to loosen the ropes."

The nun rocks back and forth. Tristan and I rock too. The canvas rises and falls as we rock. I hear a wooshing sound at the far end of the tent and notice a faint glow through the tent cloth…

…therefore this tent will burn.

We rock harder and the glow brightens.

"Is it…is it getting warmer?" Tristan asks.

I smell smoke.

"I am free!" the nun shouts. She stands, and the fabric rises in a peak around her. The far side of the tent is blazing.

"Run!" Tristan says. "Flee!"

The nun flees.

I watch her tunnel through the canvas, stooping and prodding it upward with her hands until she is gone.

"Tristan, can you slide your hands free?"

"There's a nail beneath my ropes," he calls. "I'm caught."

A hand slips toward me from beneath the canvas. It lifts the fabric, and Gilbert's ebony eyes stare into mine. I scream. It is a girlish scream, I will admit it. But Gilbert's sudden appearance startled me beyond words. I pivot on my hip to kick him again and the pole moves with me. Gilbert's nose shatters. I have an idea.

The smoke makes me cough. I know we do not have much time in here.

"Lean to the right hard as you can, Tristan!" We both struggle as Gilbert crawls back to me, his fingers squeaking against my breastplate. I put everything I have into sitting up but something is pinning us to the floor. Sweat trickles through my hair. It is miserably hot in here.

Gilbert's hands find my face. I open my mouth to bite his fingers, then think better of it. One of his nails gouges my cheek. I crane my neck away from him. His teeth crunch against the mail at my hip.

"Are you pulling, Tristan?" I shout. "Lean, you miserable bastard, lean!"

"I am leaning!" He coughs. "What is the purpose of this?"

"To sit up!"

He falls silent and the realization comes to me. "To your left! My right, your left!"

Tristan and I groan. I can hear him coughing too. The ropes bite at my wrists but slowly the tent post rises until it is vertical again. The tent is still attached to the pole, so the canvas spreads, although it sags downward without the support of the guy lines. I can see the hellish blaze that engulfs the far side of the tent. The guard's empty chair is on its side and on fire. Bits of smoldering cloth fall from the canopy. We can see the church through great flaming rents in the fabric on the other side of the tent. Figures lurch across the graveyard. The dead walk. And we burn.

The heat makes the skin of my face tighten. I can hear little over the roar of the fire. Gilbert bites the cuisse on my thigh as I kick at him. But he has room now. He stands, pushing the sagging canopy upward with his head. He snarls and approaches from the side, where my legs cannot get to him. I kick meekly and brace myself for his final leap. I feel shame that my death will come at the hands of this idiot. Crushing sorrow for failing Elizabeth.

But Gilbert does not leap. He jerks and grows rigid, sways on his feet. Then jerks again and falls lifeless onto me. The Virgin Mary? Saint Giles? A seizure of the heart? I don't question it.

"Stand...up..." I can't stop coughing. I feel dizzy with the smoke. "Stand up, Tristan!"

We struggle to our feet, lifting the tentpole with all our strength.

"Never...never seen...a two-man caber toss," Tristan says.

And that is exactly what it is like. The Scottish barbarians have a sport where they hold twenty-foot poles by one end and flip them into the air. The pole Tristan and I hold is only half that length, and there is no possibility of us flipping it, but I feel, for the moment, like a savage Scot.

The pole tilts to my left, so that the burning wall of canvas rushes toward us. I lean to the right. The pain in my ankle is too great. I stand on one foot and the pole pitches to one side. Tristan stumbles and the two of us groan as we right the pole again. The canopy above is melting into flame.

"Edward?" Tristan says.

"Yes?"

He looks over his shoulder at me. "It's good to see you."

I smile in spite of everything. It is good to see him too.

"Edward?" he says.

"Yes?"

"Our situation has not improved." Tristan coughs. The sweat on his grimy face glistens in the orange light of the flames.

No, it has not. My ankle throbs with pain. I do not think I can bear the weight of this tent much longer. The pole feels heavy as a ship's mast. All of the canvas rests upon the shaft, and the shaft rests upon our wrists. The heat is unbearable. My chin touches the bevor above my breastplate and the metal is hot enough to cause pain.

"Lean..." I cannot talk. I am coughing too much. "Lean...right..." I cough, then shake my head. "No...your left..." We lean to my right, and the weight of the pole and burning canvas topples us. We tumble sideways to the ground and the burning canopy falls upon us.

I hear Tristan's screams. The fires of hell have found us. I will not smile as the flames sear my flesh, because no one will heal Elizabeth.

Chapter 10

THE HEAT FADES AS I die.

Purgatory is dark and smells of burnt flesh and canvas. An angel stands before me. Perhaps I have been reunited with Elizabeth in the afterlife. But Elizabeth holds a smoking shovel, which seems odd to me. And Elizabeth has dark hair. I look more closely. It is the nun.

Her habit dangles mostly off her head. Soot and dirt smudge her face. But seen in the moonlight, she is a handsome woman.

Thick lengths of black hair have come free of her habit and fall across her face and onto her shoulders. Sculpted cheekbones and clear skin speak of a well-bred woman, but it is the lips that truly define her. Healthy, soft lips, emolliated by lanolin and rosewater. They are the lips of a woman who *demands*, and whose demands are always met. She was never meant for a nunnery. She was broken with the nun's habit as a wild horse is broken with saddle. I wonder which of this woman's demands got her banished to the convent. And I thank all the saints that my Elizabeth is not like her.

Most of the tent cloth has been pulled away from us, so that we can see the night sky. We lie on one wall of the tent and the rest of the fabric lies to the side in flames. Gilbert's body lies a few feet away. His legs are on fire and the smoke of it fills the air with the gagging scent of burning flesh. It won't be long before the flames reach the fabric beneath us. Tristan coughs beside me. I remember his screams when the canvas fell.

"Gilbert's knife," I croak.

The nun pokes at the knife hilt with the shovel head until it falls from the sheath. She rips a strip from the hem of her robe and uses it to pick up the hot metal, then saws at my bonds.

"You injured, Tristan?" I ask.

"I think my neck...has melted," he says, still coughing. "Nothing a fashionable sack over my head won't fix."

A dark shape lurches toward us from behind a gravestone. The nun is intent on cutting my bonds. She doesn't see him coming. My wrists are almost free. "A little faster, love," I say. I don't want to panic her.

"It is never enough, is it?" she says. "I saved your lives, and all you can do is goad me to move faster. Where I was raised a humble 'thank you' was the proper show of politeness from a grateful knight." She scowls and saws with both hands. The ropes fall away from my wrists. I stand, scooping up the shovel and pushing the nun aside with one hand. The sharp spade flashes upward, splitting the plaguer's skull with a clang and sending him to the ground in a lifeless heap.

"Thank you." I lean the sword on my shoulder and extend a hand to the nun. "Sir Edward of Bodiam."

She takes my hand and I help her to her feet.

"Sister Belisencia," she whispers and shivers at the sight of the dead plaguer. I recognize the man. It is Stephan. The nun's pampered lips tremble.

"It's all right," I say. "He's with the Lowered now."

Tristan and Belisencia look at me. I shrug. "He had a gift."

I take the knife from her hand and slice Tristan's bonds with one slash.

He dabs at the back of his neck and winces, then studies the long, slender shape of the nun's body. "You were in a convent?" He shakes his head. "Bit like feeding roasted sturgeon to a pig, isn't it?"

"You would be grateful for roasted sturgeon, would you?" she asks.

"I've eaten all types of fish, my lady," he says. "And I find the nobler fish to be the bitterest and most unsavory." He takes her hand and kisses it. "Sir Tristan of Rye."

"Where did you get the shovel?" I ask her.

"Next to a gravestone," she says, shuddering.

"How did you know it was Gilbert you were hitting with it?" Tristan asks.

"I didn't," she says. "I was rather hoping it was you, Sir Tristan."

More figures lumber through the graveyard. I cannot tell if they are plagued or wounded. Screams echo from the church. Giant shadows play across the stained glass windows as torches inside capture the struggles. God has looked away and hell has found His church.

I walk toward the battlemented stone walls, feeling the familiar ache in my ankle. Tristan follows.

"Where are you going?" Belisencia asks.

I look back. Her hands are splayed out to the sides, her shoulders shrugged.

"To hell," I say. "You coming?"

It is a massive arched door—traced and studded with iron— that leads into the Church of St. Mary the Virgin. And it is ajar. I hold Gilbert's knife in one hand and draw the door open. The church is like most other Norman churches. It is a thing of feathered arches and table tombs, of effigies and stained glass. And tonight it is also a thing of dark corners and lurking horror.

Wooden chandeliers dangle from the ceiling and cast enormous shadows of themselves on the walls. Bracketed torches bathe the church in quavering orange and create even thicker shadows behind the arches that lead to the aisles.

We walk down the narrow nave. I lead. Tristan walks behind me, and Belisencia clutches at his arm. Hisses echo. Shapes move at the edges of our vision. A man howls somewhere in the gallery above and all three of us jump. Belisencia shrieks, then covers her mouth when Tristan and I look at her.

The gallery is a masterpiece of burnished wood, with faces of bishops and cardinals at intervals and a tapestry showing Christ feeding the masses with five loaves of bread. Once it was a place from which a choir flooded the church with celestial song. But the only sounds I hear tonight are the dying man's broken screams and the loud slurping of plaguers as they feed. Belisencia buries her head in Tristan's shoulder.

Two faces peer down from the gallery at us, and they do not belong to priests or bishops. I can just make out the dark stains around their mouths.

"Check the nave and chancel first," I say.

Tristan nods.

"Why...why are we in here?" Belisencia asks. She is holding Tristan so tightly that he stumbles on her robes.

"They have our swords and cannons," I say. "And a dead man's leg."

"A dead man's leg?" she says.

"The nuns will be pleased that you remembered," Tristan says.

The waxing moon sends a faint shaft of silvery light through the stained glass windows. Flickering torches give life to the carved angel corbels, turn them into demons that leer and scowl. I think of my angel back in St. Edmund's Bury and the state I have left her in.

A hulking figure drags itself across the moonlit floor over sunken tombs and toward the back of the church. It is a great bull of a man wearing mail and a tabard. The links of his armor scrape against the limestone as he slithers forward. A carved wood panel spans the rear wall of the chancel, similar to the panel the madman, Peter, had moved into his stable.

The man reaches the panel and pulls himself upright onto one leg. His other leg hangs limp and at an odd angle. He becomes unbalanced and crashes downward with a wail, his elbow striking one of the hinged seats and pushing it open. He moans softly and looks up to the web of beams on the ceiling, then notices us. His face is seamed with pain. He holds a hand out. "Thanks be to God. Help...help me."

A plaguer wearing leather armor and carrying an unstrung bow on his back lurches toward the man. I discover my shoulder sack hanging upon the edge of a pew a few paces from the altar. Two other sacks lie on the floor. I assume they are Tristan's. The two cannons are on the bench, as are our swords, helmets, and knives.

I draw my sword from its sheath and approach the plaguer. It hisses at me and I take its head off with two swings. The body collapses in a spurt of blood that pools around the altar. The nun takes a sharp breath and covers her eyes. Tristan gathers our items while I walk toward the kneeling man.

"Who are you?" I ask.

The kneeling man gurgles, spits. "My name is Alexander."

Something explodes behind us, sending thunderous echoes through the church.

I whirl but it is not an explosion at all. A plaguer has leaped from the gallery and fallen to the stone floor of the nave, striking the chandelier on his way down. Shadows lurch dizzyingly across the church as the candles swing.

The plaguer tries to rise but his leg is broken and his cheek shattered. He struggles to one knee, then is flattened by another plaguer falling on him from the gallery. Tristan picks up his sword and draws it from the scabbard. "Finish your chat," he says. "I'll entertain our guests."

I turn back to the wounded man. "So you're Alexander the Cruel?"

He stares at me wordlessly. The crest on his tabard is the gold engrailed cross of William, earl of Suffolk. A steel arrow brooch on his shoulder marks him as a ventenar, a man who leads twenty archers. Alexander the Cruel is nothing but an up-jumped longbowman.

It is not just the man's leg that is broken. One of his arms hangs limp. Perhaps he fell from the gallery too. His fingernails are cracked and broken from the limestone floor.

"Just a name," he says. "Just…just to…scare people."

"You scared those Frenchmen on the road," I say. "They must have been terrified when you strapped them to those carriage wheels."

"Invaders," he says.

"People," I say. Two figures lurch from the shadows of the north chapel. I jam my cannon into the shoulder sack, then strap my sword belt around my waist.

"Kill them," Alexander says. "Please, dear God, kill them."

I look into my shoulder sack to make sure the thighbone of Saint Luke is still there. It is. But something else is missing. I search the pews, fighting down panic, then drop to my knees. The pouch containing Elizabeth's glove lies beneath a pew. I open the small leather bag and breathe in her scent before running my belt through the loop at the back of the pouch.

Tristan returns from his grim task and tugs his helmet onto his head. "Thanks for finding this," he says.

"They'll eat me while I live," Alexander hisses. The first plaguer stumbles on a fallen candelabra. The metal clanks loudly and scrapes along the floor, chains jangling and echoing in the nave.

I look back at Alexander. I think of nine women raped and split slowly in half. "Do you see that carved shelf beneath the seat that you are leaning on?"

His eyes glance away from the approaching plaguers to the platform, then back to me. "They're almost here! For the love of God! I have money. I have horses. Whatever you want."

"It's called a misericord," I say. "It's a French word. Do you know what it means?"

"Mary and Joseph, they're going to kill me!"

Tristan shakes his head. "No, I think that would be, *Marie et Joseph, ils vont me tuer.*"

I give Tristan a look that makes him back away, then address Alexander again. "Do you know what it means?"

The plaguers have found a way around the candelabra.

Alexander tries to drag himself away from them, but with one arm he can only creep. The pain makes him cry out. "Why are you talking about French words? I don't know what it means! I don't have any idea!"

"No." I say. "I imagine you don't." I don my great helm and motion Tristan and Belisencia toward the door.

"You're killing me!" Alexander shouts. "You are killing me!"

There are no words to his next scream. Only unholy terror. Alexander screams from the soul.

Chapter 11

BELISENCIA TURNS ON ME AS we step outside. "You left that man to be torn apart!" She glances into the church one last time and crosses herself. "He's still alive! Oh, Mother Mary, he's still alive!"

"*Mea maxima culpa*," I say.

There is an old stable behind the church, a three-sided structure of weathered oak with short partitions separating it into ten stalls. Eight horses are tethered in the stalls, but a pair of plaguers ravage one of them. The horse lies on its side and nickers softly. One leg kicks out occasionally as if in a spasm. The acrid smell of blood mingles with that of horse-shit. A plaguer has thrust most of his face into the animal's ravaged stomach. Another tears strips from its flanks. Tristan and I draw our knives and bring *miséricorde* to all three.

We unhook saddles and harnesses from the partitions and ready the horses. I turn to Belisencia and offer my hand to help her onto a pale gelding. She steps into the stirrup and pivots, so that both her legs are on one side of the saddle.

Tristan snorts. "Are you going for a tour of the orchards? Or perhaps sauntering to the fishpond for a bit of air?"

I hold out a hand to silence Tristan. "We may have to ride swiftly, my lady," I say. "Neither of us will be able to guide your horse."

She glances at the gelding, then back at me. "But I am not dressed to ride astride."

"The dead rise to feed on the living and entire villages cram into churches seeking safety," I say. "I think modesty is a luxury of the past."

"Modesty is what separates us from animals," she replies. But she pivots and lowers her legs to either side of the horse. The robe slips upward to her thighs. Tristan grins and his gaze sweeps along the curve of her leg.

Belisencia tugs at the robes but they will not fall any lower. She glares at Tristan. "Anyone who looks at a woman's body with lust has committed adultery with her."

"Truly?" Tristan's grin is devilish. "Did you enjoy it?"

She clears her throat and tugs at the robes again. "I think I mixed up the verse."

I toss her a saddle blanket. "Everyone who looks at a woman with lust has already committed adultery with her in his heart," I say. Father Aubrey loves that verse. Perhaps because he spends so much time committing adultery, in his heart, with all the girls of the village. "What sort of a nun are you?"

She unfolds the blanket and drapes it so that it covers her legs. "The kind that saved your lives. Shall we head out?"

"We are bound for Hedingham," I say. "And you?"

"Somewhere safe," she says, kicking her horse forward. "Without demons."

Tristan holds his hands up and sighs with exasperation. "You gave her a blanket? Now we have nothing to look at on the long journey."

"Modesty, Tristan," I say. "It's what separates us from animals."

The moon is bright but we ride slowly. I have a new respect for horses. They are the gold coins of this new country and I will not risk them needlessly. We ride west until I spot the carriage wheels. I stand in my saddle and check each of the Frenchmen. Most are dead. One wheezes and opens his eyes, giving me a start. I hold up my knife and speak to him.

"*Miséricorde.*"

His face crumples, but there are no tears left in him. He nods his head over and over again and I slit his throat.

"I'm sorry," I say as his life dribbles out. "*Mea maxima culpa.*"

I look at the wound on my wrist and wonder if someone will have to give me the same mercy soon.

We turn southwest, toward Hedingham and the nunnery where we left Morgan of Hastings. Belisencia will be safe there, and I have recovered Saint Luke's thigh from Alexander's church, so the nuns will be happy.

Tristan turns to me when we are a safe distance from Edwardstone.

"So, riding a cow?" he asks.

"Leave it," I say.

"Tell me about the pink reins. Were they a pale pink or more of a foxglove pink?"

"At the monastery in St. Edmund's Bury," I say, "how did you get out of the tunnel?"

"Raw meat," he says. "Threw a dead goat down the pit, then ran."

"How'd you get the goat past Brother Phillip?"

Tristan laughs. "I had to pry the monk off my leg. He told me I was eternally damned for starving a monk."

We laugh. It feels good to laugh. But the wound on my wrist and the thought of Elizabeth quell the laughter swiftly.

Tristan rubs at his lower lip and becomes pensive. "I overestimated the plaguers' interest in the dead goat, though. You remember that dead deer on the road to Hadleigh?"

I nod. We tied the dead deer to a rope and lured an army of plaguers to a battlefield five miles away. The same battlefield those Frenchmen on the wheel fled. But I was nearly torn apart when the plaguers spotted me as I attached the rope.

"Similar sort of thing," he says. "Except there was no horse waiting to whisk me to safety." His gaze grows distant and he does not say anything more.

It must have been bad.

"And you?" he asks me finally. "It's a surprise to see you out of the monastery."

I think about my response for a time.

"Elizabeth...I was washing her arms. Found marks on them. Black bands near the wrists from the ribbons."

We ride in silence until I can speak again.

"She slammed back against the wall once and it...it left a thick black mark on her shoulder."

Tristan nods. "Is she safer now?"

"We padded the ribbons. And Sister Mildred helped me fix a mattress to the wall. But..." I shrug.

"We need to hurry," Tristan says. "We'll find the alchemist and he'll have the cure. We should look for the simpleton that Isabella spoke of. The people of Chelmsford will know. I'm sure they'll know of him."

"Alchemy is a sin," Belisencia says. "The Lord says, 'Do not turn to alchemists; do not seek them out and so make yourselves unclean by them.'"

"Morgan said that to me once," Tristan says. "Except it wasn't alchemists; it was sorcerers and mediums."

She dismisses him with a wave. "It applies to alchemy as well. Prayer is the only true cure for this plague."

"I've seen a lot of prayer these days," Tristan says. "And not one plaguer brought back because of it. If prayer is the cure, then we're all doomed."

"Perhaps that is as God wishes it," Belisencia says. "Perhaps he is finally calling us all back to the Kingdom of Heaven. Although I don't think I will see you there, Sir Tristan."

"No," he says. "I'll spend eternity with the merry folk."

"Merry? You mean the ones who defy God?"

"No," he replies. "I mean the interesting ones. You zealots spend your entire lives simply waiting for the next. You pinch your noses and sit quietly, never looking to the sides, hoping you won't make a mistake before God calls you back to the Kingdom of Heaven. What kind of existence is that?"

"A pious one," she says. "A glorious one. You sinners spend your life chasing every pleasure. Lasciviousness, perpetual drink, lies, violence, vulgarity. You blunder from one mistake to the next, hurting all those around you, risking eternal damnation, never knowing discipline or faith. What kind of existence is that?"

"Sister," Tristan says. "That sounds like heaven to me."

"How odd," she says, "that someone like you, who has no faith, wears a cross."

Tristan touches the wooden cross at his chest. It is the one Morgan gave him before we left Hedingham. A peddler sold it to us, claiming it to be an artifact made from the wood of the True Cross upon which Jesus Christ was crucified. At first I scoffed at this claim, but I witnessed Morgan performing what I can only describe as miracles with it. Parting mobs of plaguers. Shattering a charge by mounted knights.

"It is also odd," Tristan says, "that you who have faith wear none."

Belisencia tries to retort but when her mouth opens she bursts into tears and covers her face. I own neither sword nor shield that can protect me from a woman's tears. Tristan and I look to each other awkwardly and ride to either side of her.

"I...I am sorry," I say, not certain what it is I am sorry about.

She buries her face in the blanket and cries for a time. I look at Tristan and he shrugs nervously. He pats her back with his gauntleted hand, then glances at me and shrugs again, motions to Belisencia.

I am more comfortable dealing with an army of plaguers than a sobbing woman.

"I am sorry," I say again. Women like apologies. "I am so sorry."

Tristan rolls his eyes at me. And I throw my hands up, then point to the nun. He started this. He can resolve it.

Tristan sighs and pats her on the back again. He clears his throat. "I'm...I'm sorry," he says finally. I shake my head.

After a few more paces, she wipes her nose with the blanket and stares forward, the tears looking like dew on her eyes. "The nunnery was overrun," she says. "Sister Agatha escaped with me. But she...she..." Belisencia bursts into tears again.

"I'm sorry." Tristan and I say it at the same time and glare at one another.

"She changed into...into one of those...those..." She wipes at her nose. "She was the most devout of any woman I know. Why...why would God do such a thing to someone like her?"

"They are in a better place now," Tristan says. "They are with God and all the pious, glorious people."

Belisencia stares at Tristan quietly for a moment, then bursts into even greater sobs. "No," she mumbles through the blanket. "No, many of the sisters escaped. But so many of them were bitten. What if they are possessed by demons? They will walk the lands, possessed for eternity! They can't be saved! They will live in eternal torment!" She wails uncontrollably. I strike Tristan in the shoulder as hard as I can.

"Why?" she shrieks. "Why does God punish them?"

Neither Tristan nor I have an answer. Not even an apology seems right. Belisencia's sobs quiet after a time and she rubs at her eyes with the heel of her hand. "I lost my rosary." She sniffs. "I can't even pray properly. What sort of nun has no rosary?"

"We will find you a rosary," I say. A quest. Quests are good. I am good at quests. I will find this nun a rosary on our journey to the alchemist.

Tristan slips the wooden cross from his neck and places it over Belisencia's head. "It's not a rosary," he says. "But they say it was made from the True Cross."

Belisencia takes it in two fingers and studies it. She nods her head. I see the trembling in her lips before she bursts into tears again.

I think about apologizing again but restrain myself. Apologies will not help Belisencia. I speak the words to the Hail Mary instead.

"*Ave Maria, gratia plena. Dominus tecum. Benedicta tu in mulieribus, et benedictus fructus ventris tui, Iesus.* Amen."

"Amen," Belisencia says. She stops crying.

"Hallelujah," Tristan says.

We sleep that night inside an old windmill. Tristan and I are forced to use all the saddles and saddle blankets to make a bed suitable for Belisencia to sleep on. She does nothing but complain about the makeshift mattress while Tristan and I remove our armor, yet she is asleep before we are done.

I check my wound in the morning. There is more pus. Worse, I feel a pain in my throat and my body feels warm. I will have to tell Tristan soon. He needs to be prepared.

We set off again at dawn, toward Hedingham. The sun is hidden by the forests to the east, and that is the excuse I make when we reach the River Box; the river should be on our right but it is directly in front of us. I believe we have traveled more south than southwest.

We follow the Box westward until we come to a large stone mill with a squat bridge beside it.

"Where are we?" Belisencia asks.

"I don't know," I reply.

"We could ask him." Belisencia points to a man standing in the break of a long, high set of hedges. He wears mail and a filthy white tabard with the red cross of Saint George upon it.

"We should ride away from here right now," Tristan says.

I cannot agree with him more, but Belisencia trots toward the bridge.

"Good morning to you," she shouts. Her horse clomps across the flat wooden bridge. "We are lost."

The man turns his head and speaks to someone behind the hedges.

"Belisencia, come back at once!" I canter over the bridge, my horse's hooves drumming on the wooden planks. Tristan follows.

"Might you tell us how we can reach Hedingham?" she calls.

The man walks toward us holding a short spear. "Are you plagued?" he calls.

I reach Belisencia and grab the reins of her horse. "Have you learned nothing about what this plague has wrought? You must assume everyone is an enemy."

"That is not an England I wish to live in," she says.

The soldier stops a few feet from us and stares warily. "Are you plagued?"

"No," she says, smiling. "We are all three healthy."

I hope that is true.

"You're not here to see Hugh the Baptist?"

Tristan chuckles and goads his horse forward. "Hugh the Baptist?"

"He is our shepherd," the soldier says softly. "He is the Light and the Word."

"We just need to know how to get to Hedingham," I say.

"You can cut through the Holy Lands," The soldier says. "Hugh won't mind."

"Jerusalem seems a bit out of our way," Tristan says.

"No, the new Holy Lands." The soldier gestures beyond the endless stretches of hedges. "These are the very lands where the Lord showed himself unto Hugh."

"I knew a man who used to stand behind hedges and show himself to girls," Tristan says.

"All of these lands are sacred now," the soldier says.

"We used to call him Cocky Tom," Tristan says. "And not because he was confident, if you understand my intent."

"Is there no end to the filth that pours from your mouth?" Belisencia asks.

"Filth pours from all of my other orifices, Sister. Why should my mouth be any different?"

We dismount and the soldier leads us through the break in the hedges. My ankle irritates me, but the pain is lessening. I give thanks to Saint John and his wort. But all thought of saints and ankles vanishes when I see what is in the fields of the Holy Land. I draw my sword before I can think. Tristan does the same.

"What in God's name are those?" I shout.

But I know what they are.

Plaguers. Scores of them dressed in white and wearing crudely carved wooden masks.

Chapter 12

THE PLAGUERS ARE SEPARATED INTO groups. All of them seem to wear the strange masks: rounded pieces of wood with large eyeholes and either vertical slots or small round cutouts for breathing.

The ones nearest us seem to be ploughing a field. Ten or fifteen of them have been rigged to a plough with ropes and leader poles, with a healthy farmer walking behind them to square the plough. Two hulking mastie dogs, also hooked to the plough but with longer ropes, walk ahead of the plaguers. The hair on the dogs' backs is matted with what looks like blood.

A woman without plague dressed in white stands at the edge of the field. As I watch, the dogs reach her and she feeds each of them something, drips blood onto their backs from a dead chicken, then motions to the opposite edge of the field.

Poor chicken. Not clever enough.

The woman backs well away from the edge of the field as the dogs loop around in the manner of a horse on a familiar track. They stay out of reach of the plaguers on their arc, then walk in a straight line toward the other end of the field. The plaguers follow behind, dragging the plough and snarling at the dogs. A man on the far end of the furlong, also dressed in white, waits for the dogs to arrive, presumably with another nugget of food for them and another not-clever chicken. Three more fields within the border of hedges are ploughed in the same manner.

"I don't know if this is genius or madness," I say.

"I find the best ideas often have a bit of both," Tristan replies.

Belisencia crosses herself.

The soldier smiles. "They've been saved," he says. "Every one of 'em. Doing the Lord's work now, on the Lord's Holy Lands."

"Saved?" I ask.

"Aye," he says. "I'll be just like them one day too. But Hugh needs protection, so it'll be some time yet."

"What do you mean?" I ask. "Are you saying you will be plagued? Like these people?"

His smile is wistful. "Aye. And so will you. Except you three are fortunate. You get to be saved today."

"Like bloody hell we will," Tristan says.

"We'll take the long way to Hedingham," I say.

But when we turn back to the opening in the hedge, there are eight men in mail blocking the way out.

I think of Belisencia's comment about my lack of trust and sneer at her. "You may not *have* to live in this England much longer. I told you to stay away, didn't I? I told you."

"Why are you so angry?" the soldier says. "You are about to receive the everlasting glory of God. You will earn eternal salvation today."

Tristan shakes his head. "Hallelujah."

Episode 3

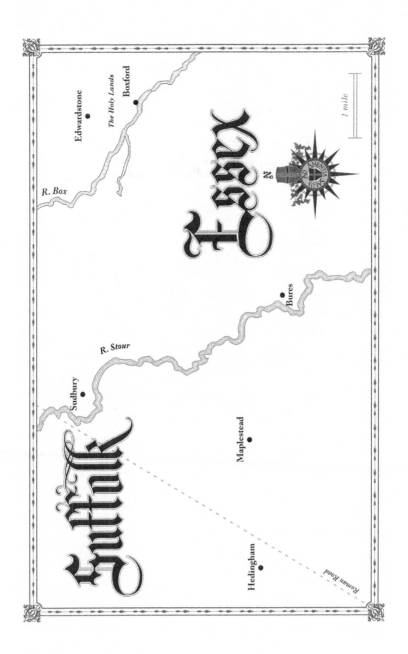

Chapter 13

WE ARE PRODDED ON SPEARPOINT across fertile fields belonging to Hugh the Baptist. I do not know who this man is, but I am wary of anyone who would presume to take such a name. Perhaps I should accustom myself to such things: in these dark times, England is awash with new kings and self-anointed saints.

On either side of us, plaguers wearing wooden masks pull ploughs across what one of these soldiers calls the Holy Lands. I study these new sorts of oxen as we pass. The masks are all slightly different. Some have simple rectangles for the eyes. Some have large stars or half moons or crosses. I notice something else I missed when I first saw these plaguers: they have no hands.

"Must you lose your hands to be saved?" I ask.

"Not at all," the soldier says. "But it helps."

I spot an old ox mill operated by the afflicted. The plaguers lurch in circles after a bloody goat, their bodies harnessed to a shaft that rotates with them and transfers their energy to the millstone.

The soldiers lead our horses behind us as we climb a shallow slope. On the other side of the hill lies a small village—ten or twelve thatched homes arranged in a straight line. Opposite them, a few hundred paces away behind stone walls, sits a manor house with a tiled roof. The gates are open, and I see a fishpond at one side of the home. The manor is modest in size, but the owner is expanding.

A new wing, half-built, rises on the east end. Plaguers wearing the bizarre wooden masks and leather harnesses are tied together into groups of three and four. They strain and lurch, reaching for men who walk backward. The men hold clay pots in their hands and stir something inside with wooden spoons. As the plaguers stagger toward the men, they drag large blocks of sandstone roped to their harnesses.

"Hugh the Baptist has an army of slaves," Tristan says.

"You say such things because you are ignorant of the truth," the soldier replies.

"I'm sure you're right," Tristan says. "Those harnessed plaguers probably enjoy doing the work of draft animals."

"You will be enlightened by Hugh the Baptist. He will free you from your darkness."

"I'm sorry, but I find it difficult to be enlightened by someone named Hugh the Baptist," Tristan says. "What sort of name is that? It's not even biblical. He might as well be called Ralf the Baptist. Can you imagine if Jesus had been named Ralf? Ralf of Nazareth. Doesn't really invoke the same sort of awe, does it? I don't think Christianity would have had quite the—"

"Silence!" the soldier shouts.

"Do not make things worse with your blasphemy, Tristan," Belisencia says.

"Worse?" Tristan scoffs. "They are going to plague me, cut off my hands, and harness me to a plough until my body falls apart. I'm interested in your definition of worse."

"In hell," Belisencia says, "your body will not fall apart. You will continue to plough for eternity. But the plough will be ten times as heavy. And the harness you wear will be made of fire."

"I'm not sure you completely understand how harnesses and fire work, Sister."

"I understand how the fire in that tent worked," she says. "And you would have had an intimate understanding of it if I hadn't scraped the burning canvas off you."

"Did I ever thank you for that?" Tristan asks.

"Not once," Belisencia replies.

"Good."

We approach the gates and the first soldier points to an outbuilding of stone that lies to one side of the manor house. Flowers have been wreathed around the door and an intricate crucifix made from bits of curved wood hangs from the eaves. "That's the sacred temple of Hugh the Baptist."

"That name again," Tristan says, laughing. "Hugh. Hugh the Baptist. I knew a man named Gruelthorpe. Now there's a name. Not a biblical name either, but I can respect a man named Gruelthorpe. Gruelthorpe the Baptist is a man who will dunk you whether you want to be dunked or not. He'd have converted thousands."

The soldier nods to the others and I know what is coming; I have seen Tristan elicit that nod more times than I can count.

"Tristan..." I shout, but it is too late. One of the soldiers swings his spear shaft and cracks Tristan in the back of the head. I turn and drive my shoulder into the soldier and he falls backward. Two of the other men grab my arms. Tristan is on his knees, one hand on the ground, the other on his head. I struggle against the two soldiers and free an arm. But a third and fourth man join in. They each take hold of a limb and drive me into the ground. They hold me motionless while another soldier draws back his spear to slam the end of the shaft into my face. I close my eyes and turn my head away.

"Leave him!"

I wait two heartbeats before opening one eye and glancing toward the gate. A man with long ringlets of black hair steps toward us. He wears a monk's robe and a smile that holds so much goodwill that I am instantly suspicious. His hands are covered in blood. "He struggles because he does not yet know the Truth. Cease your struggles, Knight. I am Matheus, king of the Holy Lands. Cease your struggles and listen to the words of the Lord."

Another king.

King Matheus raises his bloodstained hands in a gesture that I assume is meant to convey holiness. But the blood and his overreaching smile make him look malevolent. He walks back through the gate and stops halfway to the manor house at a marble font that looks like it was taken from a church. Two priests near the font fix us with solemn stares. A young man in a white robe holds a platter of strawberries.

The soldiers shove us forward until we are a few paces from Matheus and the marble basin. Many more soldiers stand guard around the manor house, including two scarred men with hard eyes and the olive skin of foreign mercenaries.

These two towering predators stand by the door to the manor house, ten paces from Matheus and the priests.

Six or seven people in white robes form a line that leads to the font. A girl who cannot be older than nine is among them.

"How are there pilgrims already?" Tristan asks. "People will follow any cause if they believe there is a breath of religion in it. I should set up my own font. Change my name to Gruelthorpe."

"Knights will follow any cause if there is a breath of violence in it," Belisencia says. "I should set up my own throne. Change my name to Richard."

"You don't look much like a Richard," Tristan says. He studies her. "You're more of a Ralf."

I look at the pilgrims, and I understand them. These are people starved of hope. When you are starving, you will eat whatever is given to you in the hope that it is food. I, too, am starving, but the Church has not fed me. Nor has it nourished my wife.

My breath catches when I think of Elizabeth. The machinery of sorrow rattles in my head, but I shut down the mill before it can grind out tears. I will feast on alchemy. I will leave this hellish place, find the cure, and devour the love of my woman.

At the front of the pilgrims stands a freckled woman with hair so blonde it is nearly white. Blood runs in rivers down her face and soaks the collar and back of her robe. The dark red looks black against her pale tresses. She wipes blood from her eyes and smiles rapturously.

There is an instant where I see Elizabeth in this women. My beloved has few freckles upon her face, but her legs are

spattered with them. I have spent many drowsy hours trac-
ing figure eights between these marks with my forefinger.
I wonder if those freckles will still speckle her legs when
I bring her the cure. Or if her flesh will be blackened and
stained, her mind lost in the madness of this plague. Every
heartbeat I spend here brings my angel one heartbeat closer
to destruction. The machinery in my head clanks again, but
this time it is rage I feel, not sorrow.

I shrug the soldiers away and bellow at Matheus. "I am
Edward of Bodiam, a knight of Sussex and friend to King
Richard and the earl of Arundel! You cannot hold us here!"

"I will not hold you here, Sir Edward," Matheus says.
"I only wish to save you." The serving boy plucks a strawberry from the platter and feeds it to Matheus.

"Forcing us to contract the plague is not salvation,"
Tristan says.

The cut on my wrist throbs, but I think perhaps it is simply a festering of the wound. It could not be the plague. Not
after two days. I wipe sweat from my brow with the leather
palm of my gauntlet and take a deep breath. Matheus gives
me a bemused smile. "You have misheard," he says. "No one
will force you to contract the plague."

Belisencia covers her face with her hands. "Thank Mary
and Joseph," she says. "Thank the saints and the angels."

Matheus steps forward and strokes Belisencia's hair
with bloody fingers; it leaves streaks of gore in her hair.
"My poor sister. Did you really think I would force you to
do such a thing?" He shakes his head and the boy feeds him
another strawberry. "The three of you will listen to Hugh
the Baptist," he says, chewing the strawberry. "And then you
will afflict yourselves."

Chapter 14

MATHEUS WHISPERS TO ONE OF the priests, a bald man with a pocked face, then walks a dozen paces to a stout oaken table beside the fishpond. He stands beside one of the benches and waves us toward him. The guards reinforce his request. When we are seated at the opposite bench, Matheus sits and smiles at us. The young man brings the platter of strawberries and sets it on the table.

I think of my Elizabeth again, bound and dying in St. Edmund's Bury, and I fight the rage that builds within me once again. We are wasting time. We are wasting Elizabeth's time. "There is nothing you or your baptist can say to make us afflict ourselves."

"And yet," Matheus says, "you will." The boy feeds him another strawberry and Matheus speaks as he chews. "Hugh the Baptist will bring peace to your soul. He will free you from the darkness."

I hear the bald priest speaking to the next white-robed person in line. "You were baptized in the name of the Father, the Son, and the Holy Spirit," he says. "And today you will be baptized in the Blood of Christ." I glance over. The priest lifts the silver ladle from the font and tips it over the head of a young man with dark hair. The man stiffens as the blood slips past the collar of his robe and down his back.

"Whose blood it that?" Tristan asks. "Is that from the afflicted?"

Hugh shakes his head. "It is lamb's blood. But during the sacred ritual, the blood becomes that of Christ."

"How do you know that it becomes Christ's blood?" Tristan asks.

"Because God told Hugh the Baptist that it does," Matheus replies.

"Have you ever considered that perhaps a mule kicked Hugh the Baptist in the head?"

The second priest leads the blonde woman toward the small stone outbuilding the guards first pointed out. The temple of Hugh the Baptist is little more than a storage hut.

I turn back to Matheus. "I have an urgent matter to attend to." I try to keep the edge from my voice. "You have no authority to hold us here."

"I am king of the Holy Lands," Matheus says. "I have been given the authority by God and Hugh the Baptist."

Tristan taps my shoulder. "If Hugh the Baptist gave him the authority, we really can't argue."

"Quiet, Tristan," I say.

Matheus chuckles. Despite my contempt for this man, I see the eloquence of speech and demeanor that makes people follow him. He has a warm gaze and a quick smile, and though his geniality seemed affected at first, I am not certain of this now. When cruelty surrounds you for long enough, you learn to fear kindness.

I do not know if Matheus is sincere or not. Perhaps he truly believes what he says. But I despise him either way, because he keeps me from my Elizabeth. The door to the stone outbuilding opens with a creak. I glance back. The blood-spattered woman takes several deep breaths, nods as if to herself, then steps inside. The priest follows her and shuts the door.

The bald priest at the font continues to shout: "All of us who were baptized into Christ Jesus were baptized into his death. We were buried therefore with him, by baptism, into death. Just as Christ was raised from the dead, we too will walk in newness of life."

I look back at Matheus and he smiles again. A peaceful smile. "You do not know Hugh," he says. "He is the shepherd in the storm. He gathers the lambs and sends them home. He will bring peace to your soul. He will free you from your darkness. You will understand soon."

A woman's scream from the outbuilding shreds the reverential silence of the manor grounds.

"I think that woman understands now," Tristan says.

Belisencia puts a hand to her chest; her gaze darts from the outbuilding to Matheus. "Why did she scream?"

"It is Rapture," Matheus says.

"Rapture sounds a lot like agony," Tristan replies.

The door to the outbuilding opens and the priest steps out. A moment later, the woman stumbles forward, one hand on the doorframe, head low. There is more blood on her now. Something has savaged her shoulder just above the collarbone. It is a wound that only teeth can create.

She has been afflicted.

My stomach roils. It is likely that this lovely woman was someone's Elizabeth. And Matheus has murdered her.

"Is she…? Did she…?" Belisencia covers her mouth.

"She has received eternal salvation," Matheus says. "God has freed her from her darkness."

"If I believed in hell," Tristan says, "there would be a place for you in Lucifer's fiery garderobe."

"Sir Tristan, is it?" Matheus asks. "Do you not believe in hell?"

"I do," Tristan replies. "I rode a unicorn through it once."

Matheus smiles. "What if I were to show you hell?"

"You don't need to show me hell," Tristan says. "The longer I am forced to talk to you, the more I believe in it."

Matheus turns away from Tristan and the veneer of sincerity slips for an instant. In that moment, I catch sight of the real Matheus, the puppet master behind the curtain. He glances my way, sees me staring, and smiles.

"I will show you hell, Sir Tristan. It is a short distance from here. I will show you hell and I will tell you what God said to Hugh the Baptist. And when I am done, the three of you will, of your own volition, do precisely what that virtuous young woman just did."

I stand and lean toward Matheus, my arms trembling with rage. I see soldiers move toward the table at the corners of my vision. "And if we don't do what she did? What then, king of the Holy Lands?"

Matheus shrugs, his eyes on the afflicted woman. "Then you will have rejected God." He glances at the two hulking mercenaries by the font. "And you will burn as heathens."

The dark-haired young man in pilgrim's robes is escorted toward Hugh the Baptist's temple next. I look at the woman who afflicted herself. She sits on the grass by the manor house carving and whittling at a rounded block of wood. A stocky man sits beside her and helps her with the work. It takes me a moment to realize that she is making a mask. The mask she will wear when she turns.

"Do you know why God brought this plague upon us?" Matheus asks.

"Horse buggery," Tristan says.

"No," Matheus replies.

"Because we have sinned," Belisencia says. "We have sinned, and this is our punishment."

Tristan glances at me, closes his eyes for a moment, then opens them again. I respond in the same way. It is an old signal from our days in France. It means action. The guards have lost interest in us. They watch the baptisms. I glance at the outbuilding, only a few dozen paces away, and nod.

We leap to our feet and sprint toward Hugh the Baptist's temple. Despite our armor, we do it so quickly that no one has time to react until we are halfway there.

The two mercenaries are the first to respond. They run to intercept us. Tristan draws open the door to the outbuilding. I know he wants a hostage, and Hugh is the perfect choice. I stop outside the temple, but I have no time to pivot toward the oncoming soldiers. One of the mercenaries explodes into me and we crash to the clovered grass. The second mercenary pulls at Tristan before he can get inside the temple. Tristan locks his fingers against the doorjamb.

I try rolling to my feet but another soldier throws himself onto me. More soldiers help pull Tristan from the door. All of them tumble to the ground beside me when Tristan's fingers lose their grip. Armor flashes. Men grunt. Fists swing. Someone's blood splatters against my cheek. A booted foot knocks a man away from the scrum. I swing with all my fury at an olive-skinned face near me. My blow is hard enough for the jolt to travel all the way up to my elbow.

And then it is over. Spearheads glint before my eyes. Swords are drawn. A dark-haired mercenary holds a hand to his cheek and stares at me with murder in his eyes. The door to Hugh's temple is open still. I peer inside. A man sitting in a chair leans toward me, just a silhouette in the tiny building. The sun catches a corner of the man's misshapen, scarred mouth. The skin is wrinkled and brown and split around the lips. He whispers something as a soldier shuts the door.

Matheus looks down at Tristan and me, shakes his head.

"Hugh the Baptist will bring peace to your souls," he says. "He will free you from your darkness."

Chapter 15

TWO SOLDIERS REMOVE MY GAUNTLETS and bind my hands behind me with thick linen cords. I wince as the cords bite into the wound on my wrist. The soldiers do not take any notice of the festering gash, but the pain from the cords is so great that tears come to my eyes. They bind Tristan's hands as well but leave Belisencia unfettered.

I cannot seem to catch my breath. Perhaps I am too old to be wandering the countryside in armor.

Matheus barks an order to one of his soldiers: "Fetch the tapestry."

The soldier nods and runs into the manor house, holding his scabbarded sword with one hand so that it does not flap. He returns with a rolled tapestry.

Matheus leads us toward a small church on the manor grounds. Eight soldiers, including the two foreign mercenaries, join us on our walk. The mercenary I struck in the scuffle watches me the entire way, snarling anytime I look toward him. He has close-cropped black hair and an old scar at the corner of one eye. His cheek is swollen and blue and bears a lobstered imprint from a finger of my gauntlet. I wonder at his nationality. Spanish or Italian maybe. Both breeds are fiery. This one seems an inferno.

"Where are we going?" Belisencia asks.

"Sir Tristan wanted to see hell," Matheus says.

"I've seen hell," Tristan says. "It's full of crying women."

The church is similar to the one in Edwardstone, only smaller. Long and stony, with a square Norman tower at one end. The double doors open with a clank of iron latches and the creak of old oak. The smell of stone dust and lamp oil wafts from inside. The cool air of the church feels good against my skin, and I realize that I have been sweating. I wonder if I am developing a fever.

Matheus leads us up the spiral stairs of the tower. The steps curl anticlockwise, as stairs do in most fortifications. Elizabeth wanted the stairs in our castle at Bodiam to curl clockwise. She said she wanted our stairwells to be different. It is one of the few times that I overruled her without trying to see her point. Stairs must be anticlockwise so that defenders are able to swing their swords freely from above. Attackers climbing the stairs have the wall at their right side, so they can only thrust. Tristan once joked that the French should train their soldiers to fight left-handed. But the Church would, of course, be outraged by such a thing. The left hand is the devil's hand, and all who favor that hand are evil. Elizabeth is left-handed, so this is another of the many subjects upon which the Church and I disagree.

We reach the crenellated summit and stare out at the Suffolk landscape. Lush, green fields and forests spread before us. Matheus's plaguers drag ploughs across his furlongs and grind wheat with their endless circles at the mill. Smoke rises in columns at intervals where villages and towns burn. Fire is a potent weapon against the plague, but it is indiscriminate. Its hunger rivals that of the plaguers.

"Do you see them?" Matheus asks. "In that village, do you see them moving?"

I look closely. Plaguers in a settlement less than a mile away. I can just make out their lurching steps.

"Demons," Matheus says. "There are scores of them out there. The village is called Boxford, and it was home to one of the largest foundling homes in Suffolk. Dozens of children lived happily there, cared for by monks. But look at it now. Look at it. The demons killed all the children and feed on their bodies still."

We stare in silence.

"I understand all of England is like that," Matheus says. "The dead walk and eat human flesh. Towns burn. The populations of entire villages live cramped inside churches and castles. Everyone lives in fear."

He motions to one side and the soldier holding the tapestry steps forward. Another soldier holds one end and they unroll the fabric. The two men pull the tapestry tight. Belisencia gasps, which is precisely what I feel like doing. I study the tapestry, then look out across the landscape of Suffolk, then back to the tapestry once more.

"You see it?" Matheus says. "Do you see it?"

I see it.

The tapestry looks like the view from this tower. The most striking things in the woven artwork are the plaguers. Perhaps they are not plaguers in the tapestry, but they certainly look like them: staggering, angry creatures that once were human. Lurching bloody monsters that claw and snarl. Towns burn behind them. Humans weep and hold their dead and dying close or shelter inside castle walls. The skies are dark and, in what I can only ascribe to divine coincidence, clouds above us roll over the sun and darken the landscape as we watch.

Matheus smiles, but it is a sad smile. "Do you want to know what God said to Hugh the Baptist?" He pauses dramatically. A scream shreds the pause as another pilgrim meets Hugh. "He said that we are already dead. All of us. That we are in purgatory, unable to find our way to heaven."

Not even Tristan responds to this.

Matheus points to the tapestry. "This was woven more than a hundred years ago. It was made at the request of Joseph the Devout, who in his lifetime had more than two hundred holy visions. Even Pope Nicholas III consulted with Joseph." He touches the weaving with his fingers. "And this, this is Joseph's vision of purgatory."

Belisencia kneels and crosses herself. "Oh Holy Father," she says, tears welling. "Oh Jesus, our Lord and Savior."

Tristan studies the tapestry, one hand on his chin. "The people's heads are too large," he says. "I'm not impressed with the artistry." He pauses. "Or does that come later? Will our heads swell?" He makes a show of touching his head at various spots. "Edward, does my head look bigger to you?"

"Shut your mouth, Tristan," I say. He believes in nothing, Tristan. As I stand and stare at this tapestry, I wish I, too, could believe in nothing. But the sight of this artwork sends chills crawling like demon fingers along the skin of my back. I am so hot and unsteady that I feel like shedding my armor. If I am in purgatory, then where is Elizabeth?

Tristan points to a soldier with a bulbous forehead. "Dear God!" he shouts. "It's started! That poor man!"

Matheus stares at Tristan with a look of infinite patience, then speaks.

"You wanted to see hell, Tristan?" He points toward Boxford and the smoke columns in the distance. "That is hell. Hell surrounds us. There is no plague. There are only the saved and the unsaved. Those whom you call 'afflicted' have ascended to the Kingdom of Heaven. And the rest? They are lost in the darkness. You are up to your necks in hell, my friends, and the fiery waters continue to rise. There is only one way out. You must take it before your souls drown and the devil claims you for eternity."

"In these times of madness," Tristan says, smirking, "only the plague will save us. So why have you not been saved, Matheus?"

"I will be, Sir Tristan," he replies. "I cannot wait for the day. But God and Hugh need a king here to help guide the lost back to their home."

Belisencia's fingers coil in her hair. Her green eyes are wide and shine with tears. "We...we are dead?"

"Yes, Sister," Matheus says. "And God waits for you."

"But...if the afflicted have gone to heaven, why do they still walk?" she asks. "Why do they not die?"

"Because this is hell, Sister. And when the spirit departs the body in hell, demons take its place. The bodies lurch and stagger because demons fight amongst themselves for control. Like snails fighting for a shell."

Belisencia's hair flutters in the wind. I stare out into the village. Is Elizabeth in heaven? Am I searching for something that she does not need? Am I searching hell without purpose? If I must afflict myself to reunite with my angel, then I will let the demons tear my body apart. And I will smile as they do it.

But what if he is wrong?

"I always..." Tristan scratches at his neck. "I always imagined hell with a bit more...well...fire. What was all that bollocks about fiery lakes and brimstone?"

"The fire is inside us, Sir Tristan. We burn with fear and shame. Do you not feel a smoldering within you?"

"Yes," Tristan says. "I thought it was the dried venison from the bandit camp."

"Listen to him!" Belisencia weeps and falls to her knees. Her hands claw at Tristan. "Look at the tapestry! Look out there!"

"You try to deflect the truth with your humor, Sir Tristan," Matheus says. "Do not harden your heart. Who do you know that has been afflicted? Are they not the devout? The innocent? The meek? The best of us?"

This last remark brings sweat to my brow. Elizabeth. Morgan. Matilda. I think of the priests and bishops. Of the monks and the holy devout. These are the people this plague has taken. Dear Lord, could Matheus be right? Is my Elizabeth waiting for me? I stare up into the sky, as if I might see her beckoning.

"You are right, Matheus," Belisencia says. "It is the most devout who are taken. I have sinned, so I remain here in purgatory. I have sinned." Belisencia tightens her lips and stops talking. I see the struggle on her face.

Matheus strokes her chin.

"Must you touch her so much?" Tristan asks.

"We are all sinners, Sister," Matheus says. "It was only by Christ's sacrifice that our sins were forgiven. We must make our own sacrifice. We must show God that we have faith. This plague is a test, my child. A trial of faith for those whom Saint Michael found unworthy of either heaven or hell."

"Hallelujah," Tristan says.

"God is merciful." Matheus keeps his eyes on Belisencia. "He has given us another chance. We must repent of our sins and show Him that we trust Him completely. Only then will He raise us to heaven."

I am uncertain what to think. This plague has seemed like a nightmare. Something unreal. A feverish hallucination. Are we dead already? Is this purgatory? I stare out at Boxford and watch a group of plaguers fighting over something that was once alive. Does hell truly rise around us? It is not a difficult thing to believe.

"You said earlier that you would burn us as heathens if we rejected the word of God," Tristan says. "Seems a bit excessive to kill us when we are already dead, doesn't it?"

Matheus nods. "A clever insight, Sir Tristan." He looks out toward the village again. "If we burn your bodies in purgatory, your soul will remain in purgatory until it is swallowed by hell. If you reject the word of God, then you sentence yourselves to eternal torment. It is not something I wish to do, but Hugh has decreed it should be so."

"Where is this Hugh?" Tristan asks. "I have a suggestion concerning his name."

"I will take you to see Hugh now," Matheus says. "He will free you from the darkness."

"We don't wish to see Hugh," I say. "We don't believe you." Although, in all honesty, I am not sure if that is true. If what he says is correct, it would answer many questions. But then it is the job of religion to find answers. Tristan once said that religion was created because humans cannot bear an unanswered question, that superstition grows in the unknown like mold in the dark. "We will not let you afflict us."

Matheus looks at each of us and sighs. "None of you wishes salvation? None of you seeks the Kingdom of Heaven?"

Tristan shrugs. "Not if it's full of monks and priests."

Belisencia says something quietly, but I cannot make it out clearly.

"You can't manipulate us into doing your bidding," I say.

Belisencia clears her throat and speaks more clearly. "I will do it."

Tristan and I stare at her, then at one another.

"Take me to Hugh the Baptist," Belisencia says. "I wish to leave purgatory."

Chapter 16

"ARE YOU MAD, WOMAN?" TRISTAN points to the plaguers in the distant village. "You will become like them. A drooling fool." He considers this, then adds, "More than you already are, at any rate."

"I forgot," she replies, her words hard and biting. "Tristan of Rye is always right. He knows the truth when so many others do not."

"That's not entirely correct," Tristan replies. "I was wrong once, about six years ago. Do you remember that, Edward? In Rouen? *That* was a long night."

"Belisencia," I say. "Whether he is right or not, you should not leap into this without thinking it through."

"We have leaped already," she says. "We leaped into purgatory. Look around, Edward. The dead walk. Madness spreads like fire upon dry reeds. Look at the tapestry. Fire. Hunger. Fear. Sorrow. Matheus is right. Hugh the Baptist is right. Their words are the only things that make sense."

Tristan takes her arm gently. "Belisencia…"

"No, Tristan," she says. "I told Edward that I do not want to live in a world where I cannot trust anyone. And I truly do not want to live here. We cannot trust, because no one is trustworthy in purgatory."

She shakes Tristan off and nods toward Matheus. He smiles and leads us back down the spiral stairs of the Norman tower. "Perhaps when you witness Belisencia's ascension, the two of you will change your minds," he says.

"Belisencia's ascension," Tristan says. "Sounds like one of those bawdy stories the minstrels tell when everyone is in their cups." He is joking but I hear the anger in his voice.

We leave the church and are guided back to the manor house. Four of the white-robed pilgrims sit carving their masks now. As I watch, the nine-year-old girl joins them. She sniffles and touches the wound on her shoulder, cries when her fingers brush the bloody, broken skin. I look at the afflicted girl and feel despair so deep that it makes me weary. I feel like sleeping. Like lying down and never rising again. But Elizabeth needs me. The slow kindle of fury burns away the weariness. A molten forge of injustice. I want to direct the anger at Matheus, but I am not yet convinced he is wrong. Has he killed the girl or given her eternal joy?

Belisencia takes Matheus's arm and walks toward the font. The soldiers shove us back with their spear shafts to keep us from following.

"Belisencia!" Tristan shouts. "Don't!"

Matheus speaks the same words that the bald priest spoke for the others, then tips the ladle onto Belisencia's head. The blood washes down her face, follows the long strands of dark hair to her shoulders and along her back. She flinches at the touch of blood on her skin. There is a suggestion of a smile on her face, but her gaze darts to the outbuilding and her fingers worry the sleeves of her robe.

"You won't go to heaven!" Tristan says. "He just needs more oxen!"

Matheus guides Belisencia toward the temple of Hugh the Baptist. Tristan's shoulders relax. He sighs deeply. Then he springs forward, surprising the guards. He manages five steps before they knock him down. I do not know what he would have done with his hands bound as they are.

"Belisencia! You will die!" he shouts. He strains against the soldiers, but there are too many holding him down. "You will die! Don't do it! *Don't do it!*"

I do not know if Belisencia is right in doing what she does, but Robert Knolles, my commander in France, once told me never to buy anything in a market until you have spoken to other merchants.

"I want to see it," I shout.

Matheus pauses and glances my way. "Pardon?"

"You said you would take us to Hugh the Baptist. I want to see him. I want to watch as she is saved. Perhaps it will sway me."

Matheus stares at me silently for a time. He glances toward the bald priest, who shrugs.

"You may watch," Matheus says. "Cut him loose." He raises a forefinger. "But you will have a knife at your throat. If you try to stop Hugh the Baptist, your life will spill out in the temple, and Satan will claim your soul."

I nod. The mercenary with the swollen cheek draws a seax from his belt, the metal blade ringing as it leaves the sheath. He cuts the ropes binding my hands and crowds next to me, brandishing the knife, grinning malevolently. Italian, I decide. Probably Genoese.

And together the four of us—Matheus, Belisencia, the mercenary, and I—go to see Hugh the Baptist.

The door creaks open. A small window high on one wall lets in a shaft of light. Dust motes rise and swirl in the sunbeam. The chamber is smaller than it looked from outside. No more than four paces in any direction. A thick candle burns on a shelf that runs the length of one wall. I expected to see plaguers, in a cage perhaps. But all I see is a man sitting in a chair. Presumably Hugh the Baptist. He wears a bishop's hat and robes, but I cannot make out any more details in the gloom. There is a small door behind Hugh, and I imagine that is where the plaguer, or plaguers, are kept.

The Italian mercenary closes the front door, then steps behind me and I feel the steel edge of the seax against my neck. "Perhaps I slit you even if you no make trouble." His whisper is fierce, his accent thick. "When he turns he back, I can say you try to fight me, no?"

Matheus turns his back. I stand perfectly still.

Belisencia crosses herself and mumbles a prayer as Matheus picks up the candle and places it on a trestle table beside the sitting man. The candlelight reveals Hugh the Baptist, and the sight of him shocks me. So much so that I jerk backward and crash against the mercenary. Belisencia lets out a short cry when she sees him. The Italian shouts in his language, spittle from his lips spattering my neck.

He grasps a shock of my hair and pulls my head backward with one hand as the knife returns to my throat.

I stare at the man sitting in the chair.

Hugh the Baptist is a plaguer.

The man's skin is pale and wrinkled and sagging. Blood stains his mouth and neck. He lost his nose at some point: a red splotch and shards of cartilage mar his features where it once sat. He looks like a drooping, black-eyed skull in a bishop's hat. A rope around his waist binds him to the chair.

"After Hugh heard the word of God, he was called to the Kingdom of Heaven," Matheus explains. "But the Lord sent him back to us. The Lord sent him back to spread the word. To offer a chance at salvation, even now, even to those who were found unworthy. Hugh shares his body with demons now, but he continues to do the work of the Lord."

Hugh opens his mouth and makes a creaking sound that rises in volume until it is a shriek. Belisencia takes a step away from him and steadies herself on the shelf from which Matheus took the candle. Hugh's scream ends abruptly. He sniffs at Belisencia, although without a nose I am not sure what he smells. He opens his mouth cavernously, wider than any human mouth ought to open, and hisses. Then Hugh the Baptist shocks me once more.

He speaks. A tumbling susurration of words, like many voices whispering, with no breaks. "Whodoesnotbelievewillbecondemned."

I have taken part in sieges on two cities and five castles. And on several of these sieges, we employed sappers to tunnel beneath walls or towers. Sappers set roaring fires beneath fortifications. They use dead pigs and timber to create flames so potent that the heat collapses the structure above. I have always been on the side that employs the sappers, so I do not know how defenders must feel when their most reliable fortifications crumble without warning. But after hearing a plaguer speak, I can imagine. Walls and towers within my mind crumble in the face of this incomprehensible demonstration.

A plaguer has spoken. I have no defense for this.

And neither, it seems, does Belisencia. She swoons and Matheus catches her. He brushes back her hair and blows softly across her forehead. His movements have a practiced feel to them, as if he has done this many times. Her eyes flutter open and she leans against him as she tries to find her feet again. Matheus nods to her, runs a finger along his shoulder to show her where she should accept the bite.

The nun's eyes are wide in the candlelight. She still looks unsteady, but she returns his nod, stares upward, and crosses herself.

"We are dead?" she asks.

"This is purgatory," Matheus replies.

Belisencia's chin rises. She leans toward Hugh the Baptist, her lips trembling. The plaguer's mouth opens again, a dark chasm rimmed by yellowed teeth. Lines of spittle span the lips, like cobwebs across the mouth of a barrel.

I try to rush forward but the knife cuts into my flesh and the mercenary's hands jerk at my hair as he chuckles. "You going next, knight man."

This is her choice, I tell myself. *This is her choice. And perhaps she is right.*

I have watched a plaguer speak. I have seen the tapestry of Joseph the Devout.

Perhaps she is right.

But it does not seem right, and I feel a coward for doing nothing.

Hugh the Baptist's noseless face becomes a mask of seams and creases as he opens his mouth even wider. As he prepares to send Belisencia to heaven or to hell or to a shambling existence of mindless hunger. He leans toward Belisencia, and I pray that Matheus is right.

Chapter 17

BELISENCIA WHIMPERS AND JUST AS I decide that I cannot allow this to happen, the sappers in my mind send another wall crumbling to dust.

Hugh the Baptist shrieks.

It is not like the previous cry. There is terror in the sound. The plaguer thrashes in his chair, shakes his head back and forth wildly, shrieks again and again. The old chair rocks backward and forward as the plaguer tries to flee from the nun.

Belisencia puts her hands to her ears and screams. She catches her breath and turns to Matheus, her eyes swollen with horror. "Wh-what is happening? *What is happening?*"

Matheus looks as horrified as she does. He pants a few breaths and looks from Hugh to Belisencia. "He..." But no other words come. Not even Matheus's eloquence can counter the horror.

Hugh's screams change to words. The same words over and over again. Wild cries, growing louder and louder.

"Who does not believe will be condemned.
Who does not believe will be condemned!
Who does not believe will be condemned!
Whodoesnotbelievewillbecondemned!"

His head jerks from side to side so powerfully that the flesh at his neck rips open and bleeds. The bishop's hat sails from his head and lands in a corner. Wet slaps resound in the room as his cheeks strike the back of the chair again and again. His body spasms and lurches against the ropes. The chair rattles and pounds the wooden floor in a ragged rhythm.

" *Who does not believe will be condemned!*
Who does not believe will be condemned!
Whodoesnotbelievewillbecondemned!"

The cries are so loud in the tiny room that they seem to pierce my brain. Belisencia screams and screams. Matheus clutches at his hair and stares at Hugh with widemouthed panic. The Italian mercenary lowers his knife. I glance over my shoulder and see him backing toward the entrance, his eyes on Hugh, his head shaking from side to side slowly.

The door flies open and three guards stare inside, their eyes wide beneath the rims of their kettle helms. One shouts into the room, "Matheus?"

"Out!" Matheus screams. "Everyone out! Everyone out!" He shoves Belisencia toward the door. The Italian pushes his way through the soldiers. I deliberate for a moment and think about taking Matheus or Hugh or both of them hostage, but I decide against it. I do not know what is going on here. I do not know who is friend and who is foe. And I do not want to make an enemy of anyone that could banish me from my Elizabeth for eternity.

I am the last to leave the temple. I look back at Hugh the Baptist and all at once his screams end. His convulsions cease and he sits still and quiet. I gaze into his tar-pit eyes and he hisses softly.

"Whodoesnotbelievewillbecondemned."

A silent crowd of soldiers and white-robed pilgrims stare at us as we step out into the sun. Matheus coughs. He licks at his lips, glances at Belisencia, then raises his hands in the air. The smile returns, but I note the tremble of his fingers.

"Hugh the Baptist has spoken," he says. "This nun is... she...she cannot yet return to God. There is work for her here in purgatory." He takes Belisencia's hand and kisses it. "Go forth from the Holy Lands, Belisencia, and spread the word of Hugh the Baptist. Bring the wayward sheep back to the fold. Be the voice of God in the darkness of this drowning land."

"I think there are many wayward sheep in the Hedingham area," Tristan shouts.

"Go forth," Matheus says. "Wherever God directs you."

"I will," Belisencia says, her chest still rising and falling quickly from the terror of Hugh's outburst. Her eyes dart to the outbuilding. She does not seem fully convinced by Matheus's words. "I will, Matheus. When should I return?"

Matheus's smile fades for an instant. "There is much work to do," he says. "Much work. Do not return overly soon. Jesus preached for three years, did he not?"

Our horses are returned to us. Matheus even gives us a basket of strawberries for the trip.

"Thank you, Matheus," Belisencia says. "Thank you for entrusting me with this important task."

"It is Hugh you should thank," Matheus replies. Belisencia looks toward the outbuilding and Matheus adds hastily, "I will thank him for you."

He takes her hand and kisses it, holds it as he stares into her eyes. "You are a beautiful woman, Belisencia."

She turns her head demurely. Tristan pulls their hands apart and places a strawberry in Matheus's open palm. "There is much work to be done, Matheus," Tristan says. "Much work. We should be on our way."

Matheus nods and eats the strawberry. "I hope enlightenment finds you, Sir Tristan," he says.

"I hope the burning crotch disease finds you, King Matheus," Tristan says.

Matheus's brows furrow and I wonder if Tristan has pushed him too far. The two men study each other in silence, then Matheus shrugs. "In hell crotches burn for eternity, Sir Tristan. And quicksilver has no effect. I hope God frees you from the darkness."

He nods to me, then turns and walks back toward the font, where the last of the white-robed pilgrims await baptism by blood. The Italian mercenary snarls at me from the doorway of the manor house.

We ride out of the Holy Lands in silence, a silence that lasts for several miles. I feel worse with every step of my horse. Something is wrong with me. I am burning with fever. Fear creeps through my soul like a muddy-pawed black cat. I push away the thoughts of affliction. The wound is festering. That is all. I will need to have the cut looked at and cleaned, but the plague has not found me. The nuns at Hedingham can take care of the wound. I steal a glance at Belisencia.

A plaguer refused to bite her. The more I think about Matheus, the more I doubt his motives. But there is nothing disingenuous about the woman riding beside me. I wonder who she is that God would protect her so.

She sees me looking. "Edward," she says, "do you think Matheus was right? Do you think Hugh the Baptist wanted me to spread God's word? Is that what happened in there?"

"Hugh the Baptist is a plaguer in a bishop's hat," Tristan says. "The only thing he wants spread is your blood on a husk of manchet bread."

Belisencia does not acknowledge his response but looks to me for an answer. I think about her question for a time as we ride.

Elizabeth reads often, so I brought her many books from France when I returned. Among them was a set of old volumes named *Roman de Renard*. Elizabeth took a fancy to these books and, after finishing them, tried for several days to make me read them.

"I am a soldier," I told her. "Books are as useful to me as swords are to monks."

"If more soldiers read books," she replied, "then we would not need so many swords."

"But a soldier I am," I said. "And you can't use a book to stop a sword."

"No," she replied. "A book cannot stop a sword, but it can stop a war."

I gave up and read the bloody books. It is no use arguing with her. She always outmaneuvers me. Probably because of all the damnable reading she does.

I thought the stories childish. They were about animals. A fox, a chicken, a wolf, a lion. But I recall one of the stories where the fox steals a chicken, then sees his reflection in a well on his way back home. He mistakes the reflection for his wife and leaps into the bucket. When he is at the bottom of the well he realizes his mistake but has no way to get out.

After a time the wolf looks down into the well and he sees the fox. But he also sees his own reflection, which he, too, mistakes for his wife. Fox calls up from the bottom of the well.

"We are dead, wolf, and this is heaven. Confess your sins and come down in the other bucket and you will achieve the realm of heaven, with fields full of cows and sheep and goats to eat whenever you please."

The wolf leaps into the second bucket, and while he descends, the first bucket ascends and the fox escapes.

I think of Matheus's smile and cannot help but feel like a wolf.

"I don't know if Matheus was right about any of it," I say to Belisencia. My horse seems to tilt from one side to the other. The sun feels too hot.

"Any of it?" she replies. "You mean about purgatory and all of us being dead already?"

"I don't feel dead," I say. "And my wife is not in the well. She is in St. Edmund's Bury. Where I must return with the cure."

Belisencia frowns and looks at Tristan. He shrugs and speaks to her with mock solemnity. "His wife is not in the well, Belisencia."

She looks to me again. "But you looked at the tapestry. You heard Hugh the Baptist speak. We saw the same things, Edward."

"And yet I think you saw more than I did." I feel wise and educated; I should read more books.

My smugness fades as I reflect upon what occurred in the Holy Lands. I cannot be certain that Matheus was wrong. I cannot be certain that we are not already in purgatory. There is only one thing I can be certain of, and that is my love for Elizabeth. I will not rest until I have found this alchemist. And if the plague sends the afflicted to heaven, then I will use the cure to bring Elizabeth back to me, if only for an instant. I will kiss her lips, stroke her long fingers, and promise that I will be with her soon. And if God keeps me from my angel, then I will storm the very gates of Paradise. I will lay siege to Kingdom Come. I will muster an army of sappers to topple the walls and towers of heaven itself.

I draw Elizabeth's glove from the pouch on my hip with as much subtlety as I can muster. I hide it in my hand and pretend to rub at my face so I can smell her scent. The lavender oil is fading.

"If you have doubts, we can return to Matheus," Belisencia says. "He can explain it again."

Tristan chuckles. "I don't think Matheus will be explaining much anymore."

"What does that mean?" she asks.

"King Matheus," he says, "has been saved."

"Saved?" I ask.

"Yes, Edward," Tristan says. "That's when your soul is redeemed by the Lord."

"I know what it means," I say. "But why do you say that?"

He reaches into his saddlebag and tosses me a ceramic phial. I study it. The seal has been broken. I look back at Tristan. He is eating a strawberry.

"No!" The world stops tilting. I yank my horse to a halt. "Tristan, no!"

"Yes," he says. "Most assuredly yes. God has freed Matheus from his darkness."

"What have you done!" Belisencia shrieks. "You fool! You terrible fool! He is a godly man! You have committed a great evil!"

"Tristan," I shout. "You can't go around afflicting people! It's…you…you just can't!"

His horse pivots in a full circle. When he has control again, Tristan looks at us with a raised brow. "I'm sorry," he says. "What exactly are the two of you so angry about? Is it because I sent a good man to heaven, or because I sent an evil man to hell?"

Belisencia opens her mouth but no words come out. She looks to me for help. But she will find none. Tristan reads far more than I do.

"It was not your choice to make, Tristan," I say.

He shrugs. "*Mea maxima culpa.*"

I sigh. "We can reach Hedingham before nightfall if we hurry," I say. "There's work to be done. Much work."

Chapter 18

It takes us several hours to find a place where we can ford the River Box. Boxford is the closest village, but it is not in my interest to visit a village that resembles a prophet's image of hell. We find a low point in the stream and our horses splash through. Belisencia dismounts and washes the blood from her hair in the river. Tristan talks to me as we wait, but I see his eyes drifting toward the nun kneeling by the water. I wish I could throw myself into that river. My skin feels as if it is on fire. My head pulses to a drumbeat of agony. My wrist is paralyzed with pain from the wound. It sends bolts of torment down my entire forearm. It smells bad and leaks a yellow pus. Tristan sees me sniffing under my gauntlet and chuckles.

"I don't know where they kept our gauntlets, but they smell terrible," I lie.

"Mine are fine." He gives me a wry grin. "I don't want to make you feel bad, but I don't think it's the gauntlets."

I feel a chill in the air and draw my cape tight around me. "You smell...as bad as I do, Tristan."

"I haven't been seducing cattle, Edward." He laughs, then stops laughing abruptly. "You don't look well."

"No," Belisencia says. She mounts her horse again. "He doesn't look well at all."

"I'm fine," I reply. "Just...just a bit chilly."

"Then why are you sweating?" Tristan asks.

"I'm fine, Tristan." The world tilts sharply to the right. The strawberries in my stomach threaten to escape.

"Show me your wrist," he says. There is something fragile in his voice. A jagged edge of glass. "Show me your wrist."

I take the gauntlet off and show him my wrist. He lets out a sharp huff of breath and runs a hand through his hair. "How?" he asks. "How did you get that?"

I shake my head. "I don't know. It happened when I was leaving the monastery."

"How long ago?"

"Two days," I say. "Too long for it to plague."

Tristan nods repeatedly. "Two days," he says. "Two days; that's good. It couldn't be plague after two days. It couldn't."

"It couldn't," I say.

"Are you certain of that?" Belisencia studies the wound warily.

"Of course he is," Tristan replies. "The wound is simply corrupted. He just needs a good leeching, is all. We need to get him to a barber or a surgeon."

"The nuns at Hedingham might mend it." I remember a novice at the nunnery binding my ankle when we first passed through. Has it truly been less than a week since we were there last? I try to count the days but my mind does not cooperate.

"You need a surgeon," Belisencia says. "Not a nun."

I try to argue with her, but I know she is right. I do not know if I will make it to Hedingham.

She kicks her horse forward. "Follow me. I believe I know where we can find one."

Tristan goads his horse forward, makes sure I am following, and rides after her. "Are you sure you don't want to simply pray the problem away, Sister?"

"If prayer was that effective at removing problems, Tristan, you would not be here." She sends her horse into a canter.

Tristan looks back at me and shakes his head. "I hate that woman."

"I'm not sure that you do," I say.

We kick our horses after her.

Belisencia leads us for two or three miles, to the *praeceptoria* of Maplestead. The compound is surprisingly clear of plaguers, which leads me to believe that the Knights Hospitallers might still man this outpost. The Hospitaller order, originally founded to protect pilgrims in Jerusalem, has properties and hospitals all over England. I have passed this particular property and the hospital within on many occasions during my trips from Bodiam to St. Edmund's Bury and back. But I have never had a call to use it. And now, when I have call to use it, I did not think of it. I find it difficult to think clearly at all.

"Are you from this area?" I ask Belisencia. "You don't have a Suffolk accent."

"This is Essex," she replies. "And no, I am not from this area. But I have passed through here before. I recognized the area when we forded the Box."

We ride slowly toward a rising church spire. I feel cold. The wound sends pulses of pain through my body.

"Where are you from, then?" Tristan asks. "What is your family name?"

"We're here," Belisencia announces cheerfully.

A cluster of limestone buildings sits among oaks and grassy fields. Meticulously groomed gardens of roses and lavender line the worn paths leading to each of the buildings. The church is the tallest, its tower capped by a domed and shuttered bell cot. Beside it is another large stone structure that I imagine must be the hospital or dorter. Other smaller stone homes sit among hedges and daffodils. An ivied trellis on one side of the church leads through a hedgerow into what looks to be an orchard.

A group of children play among the buildings. They are the first children I have seen playing outside since this ordeal began, and to hear them laughing brings sunlight into my soul. A child being scolded by a woman spots me. The woman scolding him looks to see what he is staring at. She starts and sends the children off toward one of the smaller homes.

"We should run," Tristan says. "We should run very fast and get very far from this place."

"What?" Belisencia scowls at him. "This place is beautiful. And peaceful."

"Precisely," Tristan says. "We should run."

But I cannot run. I can barely stay on my horse.

"Walter!" the woman shouts. "Walter!"

A man kneeling by the central path to the hospital stands and brushes loose soil from his trousers and hands. "I see them, Emma." The man wears what appear to be silk rabbit ears on top of his head. He stoops and picks up the largest crossbow I have ever seen, then points it at us. "If you seek strife, seek it somewhere else," he says. "We are a peaceful people."

"I can see that," Tristan says, laughing. He draws his hand bombard. "Aim the crossbow somewhere else or your warren will lose its bunny chief."

Another man runs from behind a building and takes position beside Walter. The new man has a smaller crossbow and wears a mouse nose made from felt. He aims the weapon at us and glances at Walter. "What's all this?"

"Some folk who apparently want to die, Roger," Walter says. "Some folk who want to die."

"We're already dead," Tristan says. "Haven't you heard?"

"Tristan, put your cannon away," I say. "Or this will get out of hand."

"Out of hand?" Tristan replies. "We're being threatened by a man wearing rabbit ears and another wearing a mouse nose. It can't get much more out of hand, Edward."

The sound of singing rises from behind the church. I glance over and spot a group of men and women holding hands and dancing wildly toward us. Their song is boisterous and their movements carefree, but there is no joy on their faces. In fact they look miserable. The line of them emerges from the orchard. They pass beneath the trellis and caper toward us. All five of us watch their approach.

They dance directly between the two men and our horses, between the crossbows and hand cannon, singing loudly, some of them weeping as they sing. Some throw their legs upward and toss their heads; others dip their shoulders below their waists and rise again. A young woman spins as far as she can while maintaining her hold on her neighbors' hands, then spins the other way. Her bracelets rattle and chime. Tears stream down her face. Spittle and foam fly from one man's lips as he skips and hops into the air. A woman rolls her head from side to side so swiftly that I cannot see her face behind the whip of golden hair. Another woman can scarcely sing through her sobs. The line jangles past us, then arcs toward one of the smaller buildings, until all the dancers disappear behind it. The faint sounds of their song echo in the distance.

Tristan clears his throat and shrugs. "I stand corrected."

Episode 4

1 mile

Sudbury

R. Stour

Bures

Suffolk

N

AD AMENTIA TALIS

Maplestead

Essex

Hedingham

Roman Road

Chapter 19

THE TWO COSTUMED MEN KEEP their crossbows leveled at us as the echoes of the dancers' song fade. My wound must have festered too long. I think, perhaps, I am in the throes of a fevered dream. And yet Tristan looks as stunned as I do.

The man who spoke to us, Walter, shakes his head but keeps his eyes locked on Tristan. "Who let the dancers out of the barn?" he says.

"Must you ask?" Roger replies. The felt mouse-nose wobbles when he talks.

Walter sighs. "If Paul let them out, he can go gather them up again."

"Something has to be done about him, Walter," Roger says. "He has no sense in his head. The children were out. Everyone was out. How many times is he going to leave that bloody door open?"

Tristan clears his throat. "Pardon me," he says. "Can we return to killing each other?"

Walter narrows his eyes. "We weren't killing each other," he says. "Roger and I were killing you." He spits to one side.

"Unless you want to take yourselves somewhere else. That's the last time I'm going to ask." He takes a step forward and his hands flex on the crossbow. Tristan edges his cannon closer to him.

"We need a surgeon," Belisencia blurts. "Is there a hospital here still?"

"Don't be rude, Bel," Tristan says. "We've only just met these men. We're still at the pointing-weapons stage of our association."

Walter and Roger glance at each other. Walter's gaze comes to rest on me, his eyes inventorying my condition. His hands shift and tighten on the crossbow, then he swings the weapon in my direction. "There's nothing a surgeon can do for the afflicted. Get him out of here before he changes."

I want to speak in my defense but I am tired. So tired. I lean forward and lie against my horse's mane. How could the wound have done this to me in so short a span? I think of all the men I know who have died in battle. The vast majority of them did not die on the battlefield. They died days later, sweating and vomiting, crying out from the agony, their wounds foaming with pus and reeking so badly that surgeons had to cover their faces with scarves. I would not like to die in that fashion.

"He's not afflicted," Tristan says. "Just a smelly wound. If you leech him and get rid of his stench, we'll let you see our horses' bums."

"If he's afflicted, we'll kill him," Walter says.

"You wouldn't be the first to try," Tristan responds.

I want to tell Tristan to stop being so aggressive, but I am tired. I rub at my eyes.

"Edward is very weak." Belisencia looks at me nervously. "Perhaps we should move him to a bed now." She glances back toward Tristan and Walter, who still point weapons at one another. "If the two of you are done with your barbaric rituals."

"Walter, I don't advise this." Roger takes the mouse nose off and tosses it to the ground. "They are knights. They have armor and cannons."

"Which is why we should let Paul treat the man's wound and get them out of here as fast as we can." Walter nods to Tristan. "Put your weapons away and we'll have a look at your friend."

"My apologies, did you say *Paul* would treat his wound?" Belisencia asks.

"Paul's our leech," Roger replies.

Belisencia glances at Tristan, then looks back at Roger. "But…you just said that Paul has no sense in his head."

Roger shrugs. "I didn't say he was a *good* leech."

Walter and Roger are Knights Hospitallers. They are the only remaining knights at the *praeceptoria* and they have turned it into a refuge of sorts. Each day they ride out with ten other men to look for survivors and to kill any plaguers they find.

"A majority of the survivors are children," Walter says. He and Roger lead us toward one of the cottages at the far end of the compound. "The poor souls. They have night-mares, all of them. They jump at every sound. Most of them will cry if you raise your voice. So Roger and I try to distract them at all times." He points to the rabbit ears on his head.

"Is that what those dancers were?" Tristan asks. "A distraction?"

"The wrong sort of distraction," Walter replies. "It began with two women. They started dancing, and they wouldn't stop. We thought they were just being silly. After an entire day of dancing, we grew a bit concerned. But how long can two women dance? We knew they would tire eventually. A few days later, a man joined them, and another woman. And after two weeks, we had a whole line of them. I don't know how to help them. They just dance and sing until they fall down with exhaustion. We've had one of them die from it. His heart just burst."

Tristan opens his mouth, then shuts it. I think he is trying to decide if Walter is serious.

"It's happened before," Roger says. "On the Continent. Hundreds of people dancing uncontrollably. They call it Saint John's Dance. It moves from person to person, like plague, so we keep them locked in a barn." He glances at Walter. "Or we try to anyway."

"Have you not heard the virtues of rope?" Tristan asks.

Walter shakes his head. "They get worse if you bind them. A woman named Mary battered herself to death. Cracked her pretty skull wide open trying to get free. We had to bind the wounds of a half dozen of them before we decided it was best to just let them dance."

A child peers out at us from behind the wall of a cottage. He is clean and his dark hair is trimmed, but I have trouble focusing on his features. My eyes water with this sickness and I want to close them and sleep.

"Is it a new sort of plague, then?" Belisencia asks. "Another one?"

Yes. It is part of the third plague. The relentless spread of madness.

"Perhaps this is God's new scourge." Tristan smiles. "It has a bit more flair than that tedious flood business from the Old Testament."

"There is nothing funny about this, Tristan," Belisencia says.

"No," he replies, rolling his eyes. "There is nothing funny about God cleansing the earth through dance." He laughs. "Perhaps we should gather pairs of animals into a boat and do needlepoint and other dull things."

"Stop it, Tristan," she says.

People do not understand Tristan. They call him an arse and say he has no consideration for anything. But I know Tristan. He is a man with a love for life. A man who sees the humor in everything. A man who rarely gets flustered or melancholy. I wish, sometimes, that I could be more like him. My mind drifts to the past, to our campaigns in France. I think I am feverish.

"It's too late!" Tristan shouts. "Dear Lord, it's too late!" He takes Belisencia's hands and dances, spinning her in a circle. "We are doomed!"

She scowls, but I can see the smile struggling to break free.

"Dance with me, Belisencia! Dance with me to heaven!"

They look into each other's eyes for a long moment, then she pulls her hands away, a smile shining on her face. Tristan would do well at this hospital. He is good at distraction.

The smile fades quickly. Belisencia smooths her skirts and shakes her head. "Those people are sick, Tristan," she says. "You have no respect for anything."

"On the contrary," he says, staring at her. "I have a deep respect for beauty."

She blushes, fights another smile, and runs a hand through her dark hair.

"And some day I will find it." He laughs.

Belisencia's mouth drops open; she looks to me and I shake my head.

Tristan is an arse.

Chapter 20

DOCTORS.

That is the new name for men who are somewhere between barber and surgeon. I despise doctors. We used to call them "leeches," because their primary course of treatment was to apply small bloodsucking worms to their patients. I do not know the reason for the name change, but I suspect the old title was too close to the mark. Doctors are a greedy lot. In my experience, they are always more concerned with payment than treatment. "Take while the patient is in pain." That is the philosophy of their profession. And I despise them for it.

But I need a doctor right now. My wound must be tended to so my journey can continue. I think of the black marks on Elizabeth's wrists and feel a wave of frustration. I need the wound tended to quickly.

Walter and Roger escort us into a cottage at the far end of the *praeceptoria*. It is not a hospital, just a small stone cottage with a tile roof, but Paul has set up his tools here. He is a plump man, with a matted auburn beard and the wild hair of a shipwreck survivor.

"We have a patient for you, Paul," Walter says. He and Tristan help me into the room.

"A patient?" Paul holds the lid to a ceramic jar in his hand. He replaces the lid and looks our way, but it is not me whom his eyes rest upon. It is Belisencia. The doctor rakes at his hair with thick fingers and smiles at her while Tristan and Walter help me out of my armor. Paul's mouth looks like an ancient ruin; the teeth that remain are twisted and soiled by years of decay.

"Are you a nun?" he asks Belisencia, his gaze roaming her body.

She nods quickly and puts her hands together. "Married to God."

Paul frowns and scratches at his beard, leans toward her. "Happily married?" He stares at her like a beggar looking through a window on a feast day. Belisencia flinches from him and touches the tips of her fingers to her nose. It appears the doctor's breath is as rotten as his teeth.

"Your patient is over here, Paul," Tristan says.

"Ah, the patient. Lay him over there."

Tristan and Walter help me into a bed in the one-room cottage. It is a sparse chamber: a chest, two chairs, and a table with the sundry instruments of a doctor. Paul studies my wound, sniffs at it, and recoils.

"Roger, please open the door," he says. "Or this smell will kill us all." I catch the briefest hint of his breath and consider the irony of his statement.

Paul asks me questions about the wound. When the fever started. What caused the injury. Where I received the wound. How long the wound has festered.

I answer his questions as best I can, then listen to him as he drones on about black bile and phlegm, about my humors being out of balance, and how the liver is an oven that, in my case, has overheated. He looks back at Belisencia often, as if explaining all of this to her.

"Incidentally," he says to her, "might I ask if your humors are in balance, my lady? I could have a look at y—"

"She has no humor," Tristan says. "Speak with me and Edward, not her."

"Yes, speak with Tristan." I see a glint of mischief in Belisencia's eyes. "But he's half-deaf, so you will have to lean in close."

Paul stands up and edges close to Tristan, who turns away from the man's mouth and darts a glance at Belisencia. Tristan's smile is a vow for revenge.

"On what day was the patient born?" Paul asks loudly.

"The seventh of June," I say.

Paul shakes his head and looks at me as if I have failed some test. "You were born to the House of Gemini."

I nod.

"That is not good, Sir Edward. Are you sure you were born on that day?"

"Listen to me," I say, my voice croaking, "I have answered all of your questions. Drain the wound and apply what you must to my wrist. I need to leave as soon as possible."

Paul, like many doctors, uses astrology to guide him. I know nothing of star signs, but looking to the heavens for answers is just prayer, no matter what form it takes. And prayer does little for me these days.

The doctor sighs. "I will treat your wound, but I do not take responsibility for what comes of it," he says. "Venus is transitive today, and the moon is three-quarters full. That does not bode well for any patient today. And it certainly does not bode well for someone who was born under Gemini."

"Edward was born under a goat," Tristan says. "So don't worry overmuch."

I would kick him if he were in reach.

Paul rises from the bed and walks to the trestle table that holds the tools of his profession. He picks a thin saw from among the tools.

"What are you doing with that?" Tristan asks.

Paul looks at the saw, then at Tristan. "I'm going to heal your friend."

"With a saw?"

"Yes. We will have to cut the hand off. It's the only way."

"Satan's hairy cock!" Tristan says. "You're not cutting anything off."

"Your friend's wound is like a month-old plum. It is rotted through. If he is to live, we must prune the rotted parts away."

"Your brain is rotted," Tristan says. "And I'll prune it from your skull if you get near him with that saw. I've seen surgeons treat festering wounds without any sort of *pruning*."

"Any other form of treatment will fail. If you could read the stars, you would understand that. I am the doctor here. You asked me to try to save him, and that is what I am going to do."

"There will be no pruning." There is steel in Tristan's voice.

Paul tries to push his way to me, but Tristan blocks his path.

"Put down the saw," Tristan snarls. "Or I'll prune your face, you charlatan!"

Paul sighs and looks to Walter. "Can you please take everyone away except for the patient? I must be allowed to work."

"You wanted us to tend his wound," Walter says to Tristan. "Step out of the way and let him tend."

"I wanted you to tend his wound, not remove it." Tristan points to the table that holds Paul's tools. "There are a host of things on that table, things that are not saws. Go pick one out and use it."

Walter aims his crossbow at Tristan. "If you prefer a different course of treatment, you're free to find a different leech."

"We're called doctors now," Paul says.

"Perhaps you could recommend another leech," Tristan replies. "One who doesn't mind that Edward was born on a summer day in June." I hear the frustration in his voice. Tristan does not get flustered or upset easily, but when he does, it can be a terrible thing.

"There are no other leeches within ten miles of here," Walter says. "So you might want to step aside and let Paul do what he's good at."

"What he's good at?" Tristan snaps. "Maiming people? Is that his specialty? I won't allow it!"

Walter studies Tristan over the top of his crossbow. "Then leave."

Tristan's lips draw into a snarl. "He will die if we leave."

"He will probably die whether you leave or not," Paul says. "The stars aren't in his favor."

I am dying already. I think I can hear the angels singing in heaven.

"I'm finished with this," Walter says. He motions toward the door with his crossbow. "Get out. All of you. And take Sir Edward with you. Ride away somewhere and don't return."

Tristan speaks with a calmness that terrifies me. "I will not leave until Sir Edward's wound has been treated."

"I told you not to let them in." Roger aims his crossbow at Tristan. "Didn't I tell you not to let them in?"

"I am finished with this too." Paul sets the saw down on the bed and walks toward the open doorway.

"You're not going anywhere," Tristan shouts, and this time the steel is not in his voice, but in his hands. He pulls Paul back to the bed by the hair and places a dagger blade under his throat. The doctor stops moving, his eyes wide as eggs.

Belisencia gasps. "Tristan, no!"

Walter's face reddens, his neck pulses. "Take your hands off our leech." He steps forward and jabs the crossbow toward Tristan. "Let him go!"

"God's bones, Walter!" Roger shouts. "You had to allow them in, didn't you? You couldn't listen to me, could you?"

Paul gropes backward with his hand until he finds the saw and tries to strike at Tristan with it. Tristan grabs the doctor's arm and twists it behind the man's back. Paul shrieks and drops the saw, but Tristan does not let go. "What do the stars say about broken arms, Paul? I hope you weren't born under Gemini."

"Let him go!" Walter aims the crossbow at Tristan's forehead. "Let him go or I swear I will make you a unicorn!"

Roger slips forward, his crossbow inches from Tristan. "Let go of him and get out!"

It is crowded at my bedside.

The voices of the angels grow louder in my head. I wonder if Elizabeth's voice is among them.

"I'll let this gong farmer go when he heals Edward!" Tristan shouts.

The song of the angels swells to fill the room. But they are not angels, they are dancers. Dancing men and women shuffle into the cottage. They hold hands and sing and weep and look at us with tortured eyes. The line is led by a woman with a blue silk veil wrapped around her head. She sobs and weaves between Belisencia and Roger, then knocks Walter backward and leads the line between him and Tristan.

Walter does his best to ignore them. *"Let him go!"*

Belisencia covers her ears and shrieks. "Stop it! Stop it all of you!"

"Everyone...everyone stop..." I feel faint from sitting up.

The dancers wind though the room like a living serpent. A man wearing a green muffin cap kicks Paul's trestle table over. Metal tools fall jangling to the floorboards. Ceramic jugs shatter, splashing fluids across the room. Linen bandages and leeches, silk thread and metal knives, needles and spoons—they fall in a rattling shower onto the wooden floor.

"This will accomplish nothing!" Roger shouts. "*Release him!*"

"I'm going to shoot!" Walter shouts. "I'm going to send you to hell!"

"Please, Tristan!" Belisencia cries. "*Please!*"

I can't make sense of what is happening. Everyone is shouting at the same time. Belisencia is crying and pulling at Walter's arm. Roger is trying to aim over her shoulder with his crossbow. The dancers are making a mess of the room. Tristan is screaming about astrology and gardening. And Paul shrieks as the dagger blade touches his skin.

A woman with fair hair meets my gaze, her blue eyes blurred with tears. She twines her long fingers in front of her face. A small silver cross dangling from her neck bounces and twists against her dress as she leaps and twirls.

I look at the fallen trestle table and spot a loaf of green bread on the floor.

God helps those who help themselves.

"Kill him, Walter!" Paul screams. "*Kill him!*"

It takes all of my strength to slip out of the bed on the side farthest from the cacophonous dispute. The fever has leeched me of my energy. I pick up the loaf.

Bolts of pain shoot through my head when I bend down to pick up a steel knife. The metal blade feels like ice in my warm fingers.

"Let him go, Tristan!" Belisencia shrieks. "This isn't helping!"

"All he has to do is say he will treat Edward," Tristan replies. "That's your way out, Paul."

Walter fires his crossbow.

I glance up but the bolt has buried itself in the wall.

"The next one goes in your head!" Walter shouts to Tristan.

"The next one will make me jump," Tristan says, "and Paul will have another mouth. Tell him to treat Edward. Properly!"

I toss the bread and knife onto the mattress and climb back into bed. I think of all the men I know who have died of battle wounds. For every two who died from rotting wounds, there was one who lived. One whose sickness healed. Battlefield surgeons had no time for astrology. They learned long ago that stars are fickle. That the gods of astrology do not care about the dying and the dead. It did not matter if the patients had been wounded when Venus was transitive or the moon full. The surgeons treated them in the same way. With moldy bread and cobwebs. With wine and leeches. And sometimes, the patients lived.

The woman in the blue veil dances out of the room. The other dancers follow her path, like colorful echoes, and snake back outside. I watch the blonde woman spin and prance out the door. Listen to their song fade away.

I will not die. Elizabeth's life depends on me. I will cut off my own arm if I must, but I hope it will not come to that.

"Walter, kill him!" Paul shouts. "Roger, for God's sake, help me!"

"I'll slit his throat, I will!" Tristan holds his head at an angle, his eyes wide like a madman's. "I'll paint the floor red! *By God, I'll make this room taste like Paul!*"

I pat the bed until I feel the cold steel of the knife. I take it in my left hand and cut into my wound. It hurts like the devil's pitchfork but I open the gash and let the pus run.

I squeeze until I cannot take the pain anymore, allow myself a few breaths, then squeeze again.

The shouting ceases slowly.

Walter and Belisencia stop first, then Roger, and finally, it is only Tristan bellowing threats. I look up. They are staring at me. Tristan follows their gazes and falls silent. Paul still has a dagger blade at his throat. The crossbows are still aimed at Tristan. Belisencia's hands are still in her hair. But they watch me.

Paul shakes his head. "You shouldn't be doing that," he says. "You haven't been trained."

"I need...wine," I mutter. The room seems too bright. Voices seem to echo. Fire surges from my wrist to my shoulder.

"Do you know what you are doing?" Paul asks.

"No," I say. "But...I'm a...clever chicken. I'll do what I can."

"Please, Paul," Belisencia says. "Can't you treat him? We can pay you for any supplies, and for your time. Just...please don't take his hand."

Paul scoffs. "Coin is worthless."

"We have food," she says, "and the knights have swords."

"Yes," Paul says, "and daggers. I don't need weapons. I'm a doctor."

"Surely there is something we can trade?" she asks.

Paul sweeps his eyes along her body again. "Now that you speak of it, there is something."

Belisencia takes a back step. "Wh-what?"

"You are a handsome woman, Belisencia."

"Paul..." She shakes her head.

"The next words you speak may be your last, Paul," Tristan snarls.

"A kiss," Paul says.

"No!" Belisencia shouts.

"A kiss?" Tristan cocks his head to one side. "All you want is a kiss?"

Paul holds one hand out toward Belisencia. "One kiss from you, my lady, and I will do what I can for Sir Edward."

"Paul, I'm a nun," she says.

Tristan looks at the ruins of the doctor's mouth and smiles. "I think one kiss is entirely reasonable."

"No," Belisencia says. "Tristan, stop it."

Tristan taps his ear. "My apologies, Bel, I am half-deaf and I can't hear you."

Paul leans toward Tristan and shouts, "On the lips!"

"Absolutely not!" Belisencia says.

Tristan nods and takes the dagger from Paul's throat. "Fine, but there will be no *pruning* in Edward's treatment."

Paul nods, leans in close to Tristan and shouts, "A long kiss!"

"Fine," Tristan says, covering his nose. "But we need medicine and bandages to keep the wound clean on our travels."

Paul nods again, his gaze locked on Belisencia. "A long kiss on the lips and it is agreed!"

"You think she'll kiss Paul and everything will be right between us?" Walter snarls.

"We could go back to pointing weapons," Tristan replies.

"I am not an ox to be bartered!" Belisencia shouts.

"She kisses him, Paul heals your friend, and we never see you again," Walter says.

Tristan nods. Walter lowers his crossbow.

"I don't understand why everyone is talking to Tristan," Belisencia says. "If anyone decides whom I will kiss, it is God, and God says nuns do not kiss men."

"I don't remember anything in the Bible about nuns not kissing doctors," Paul replies.

"That's because there is nothing in the Bible about nuns not kissing doctors," Tristan says. "She should give you several kisses, really."

Belisencia gives him a look that could wither plants. She looks at Paul, her gaze settling on his twisted teeth. Paul smiles. His gums are rotted and so dark they are almost brown. She sighs and shakes her head softly, the black waves of her hair rocking.

"If I kiss you," she says, "you will heal Edward?"

"With a kiss from you, I think I could heal the plague, my lady," Paul says.

She nods. "Heal him then. And I will kiss you."

Paul shakes his head. "I'm sorry my lady, kiss first."

Take while the patient is in pain.

Belisencia sighs. "You won't cut off his hand?"

"I will not," Paul says. He turns to me and smiles. "I'll do all I can for you, Sir Edward."

I turn my head away. His breath smells like a bedpan that has not been changed in days. He turns back to Belisencia and she makes a face. She is more hesitant to kiss this fool than she was to accept Hugh the Baptist's bite. But then, Hugh's lips promised heaven. And Paul's will be hell.

Belisencia sits and takes a deep breath. Paul drifts toward her and turns his head; he makes faint sucking sounds as his tongue moistens his lips. I watch his profile as he forms the faintest of puckers with his lips. Belisencia wrinkles her nose and leans closer, touches her lips to Paul's with a whimper.

The leech puts one hand on the back of her head. He runs his tongue across her mouth. Belisencia wails from her throat and tries to break away, but Paul holds her to him. His tongue explores her lips, drives between them. She cries out again and breaks free.

Tristan slaps the doctor in the side of the head. The blow sounds like a book falling on dirt.

Paul rocks to one side and wraps both arms around his head. "Why did you hit me?"

"Because something was wrong with your tongue," Tristan replies. "Thank the stars my blow put it back in its place."

Belisencia wipes at her lips with her robe. She scowls at Paul. "You got what you wanted. Now heal him."

Paul shrugs. "I'll do what I can. But he will most likely die anyway." He looks at my wound, pinches the skin around it hard enough to bring tears to my eyes.

I despise doctors.

Chapter 21

PAUL CLEANS MY WOUND WITH water and wine, then applies three leeches. I am not fond of the worms, but I feel nothing as they are attached. My surgeon at Bodiam told me the leeches have something in their saliva that keeps their bite from causing pain. Elizabeth was with me during the explanation, and she suggested that all knights should put leech saliva on their swords.

She is a gentle soul, my Elizabeth. When she wakes, I must never tell her of the multitudes I have killed in my quest to find and save her. She would never sleep again.

When the leeches are placed, Paul proclaims that I need rest, and everyone leaves the room. I lay in the bed, alone, for a long time. I think about the last bad wound I took, in Caen. The skirt of my armor had been torn off and a spear pierced the mail just below my backplate. Tristan says I was stabbed in the arse, but it was six inches too high for that. When I came limping home, Elizabeth told me I was never going back to France. But a year later, I was off again. I looked at her in our bed before I left, with her adoring terrier at her side, and told her I loved her in French. I thought it clever.

"*Je t'aime*," I said.

She smiled, but it was the impish smile. "No," she replied. "You are not tame. But someday, you will be. Someday you will tire of being away from me, and you will come home forever." She stroked her little terrier and spoke to it. "We will tame him, won't we, Monty?"

That was six years ago, and since then I have made three more trips to France with Tristan and Robert Knolles. It is how I have made my fortune, and how we can afford our castle. But I am done now. When Elizabeth comes back to me, I will stay home forever.

I fall asleep thinking about our castle. Elizabeth and I will make the strongest and most beautiful fortress in all of England. And we shall never leave its sheltering embrace. My dreams show me my castle as I will build it, rising from a moat in crenellated splendor. Four round towers and two square ones. No keep, for we shall live within the very walls. But in my dream those walls bleed. Bloody waterfalls that turn the moat crimson, spill over, and wash all of Bodiam with the stain of my sins.

When I wake the bed sheets are soaked with my sweat and I am shivering. Paul hovers over me, examining the wound.

"How long...have I been asleep?"

"Two hours or so," Paul says.

Two hours? I was hoping to be at Hedingham by now. Two more hours of my angel's life have passed.

Walter stands by the door, holding his crossbow. Tristan stands next to Paul and looks at me with concern, but he smiles. Perhaps I look better.

"How do you get thirty dancing men and women into a barn?" Tristan asks.

I shake my head. "I don't know."

"With great difficulty," Tristan says, laughing. "They really are an interesting mob. Walter tells me that they hate pointy shoes. Can you imagine that? Whatever makes them dance also makes them hate pointy shoes. And the color red." He smiles distantly. "I didn't believe him, so I took one of Belisencia's pointy boots and showed it to the dancers. God's teeth, Edward, you should have seen it! They *do not* like pointy shoes." He grows sober and shakes his head wistfully. "Not one bit."

"Where...where is Belisencia?" I ask.

Tristan shrugs. "She's in the barn with Roger, trying to get the remains of her boot back."

"Shush," Paul says. "I need to concentrate." I turn away from the blast of foul air. Paul slides a metal file beneath the edges of a leech until the suction breaks and the worm releases its hold. He does this with each of the leeches. When the swollen leeches are back in their jar, he sets strips of wet, mold-ridden bread over the wound using linen bandages to hold the bread in place. I have seen surgeons do this before. Something in the mold eats the infection, although I do not know how or why. And I do not think the surgeons do, either.

Paul turns to Tristan. "That is all I can do for him!" he shouts. He still thinks Tristan is hard of hearing. "As I said, the stars are against your friend! He will probably die in horrible pain!"

"Are...are you supposed to say that in front of me?" I croak.

Paul pats my arm. "False hope is no hope at all."

I despise doctors.

Paul tells me that I must remain in bed for at least two days, if I live that long. But if I am to die, I will die riding toward Elizabeth's cure. I stagger upright. The floorboards feel cold against my bare feet. "Tristan, my clothes."

"Edward, it pains me to say this, but perhaps Paul is right."

I nod to appease him, but he knows I won't change my mind.

I pick up my boots and perch on the bed to pull them on. Tristan sighs and helps me dress. Everything except my armor. He gathers my breastplate and cuisses and walks toward the door with them. "You can put your harness on when you feel better," he says. "Its weight will only make you weaker now."

I know he is right, but I mutter a protest to stave off one of his smirks and deny him satisfaction.

Belisencia waits for us outside, already on her horse, and wearing mismatched boots. Walter and Roger hold crossbows on their shoulders.

"No offense intended," Walter says, "but don't come back. Ever."

Tristan has to boost me into my saddle. Children peer out from behind buildings to look at us. Belisencia waves to them and a few wave back.

"The Bible says that children are a gift from God," she says as we ride away from the *praeceptoria.*

"That can't be in the New Testament," Tristan says. "Children are noisy, rude little people that act like drunkards and piss their pants. They are always getting into trouble and never listen to anything they are told. A gift worthy of the Old Testament God."

Belisencia looks thoughtful. "Noisy. Rude. Always in trouble. Never listen. Act like drunkards. Why does this sound so familiar to me?" She looks at Tristan and raises a brow.

"Sister Belisencia," Tristan replies, "how dare you suggest that Sir Edward is childish."

"Did Tristan tell you that he wet himself once on the battlefield?" I say.

"Edward!" Tristan shouts. "That was perspiration!"

"He had to...pardon me, my lady...piss before the battle started but the horns sounded and he had no time. A French bastard hit him low on the breastplate with a mace and suddenly Tristan had a groin full of *perspiration*." The jostling of the horse hurts my head, but I feel better. Perhaps the sleep helped.

Belisencia laughs. "I had no idea groins perspired so much."

"Sweat accumulates there," Tristan says. "Did Edward tell you that someone threw up in his great helm once?"

"Tristan..." I do not like this story.

"Edward didn't know until he put the helmet on, but he was already running toward the city walls, so he couldn't clean himself off. Fought the rest of the battle with chunks of rabbit stew dripping onto his neck."

"That is a total fabrication." I say.

We ride a hundred paces before I speak again.

"It was chicken stew."

Hedingham is only five miles from Maplestead, which is a good thing because I do not think I can ride very far. Fire still courses through my arm, and my strength has not returned.

A sprinkling of rain falls on us from the cloud-swept skies as we ride a muddy track heading westward. I call a halt a mile from the *praeceptoria* and slide down from my horse.

Tristan dismounts and joins me.

A dead fox lies among a patch of buttercups on the side of the old track. I kneel beside the corpse and unwrap the dressing that Paul made.

Tristan kneels next to me. "Oh Lord," he says, "we commend the soul of our friend, fox, into your arms. Forgive him his chicken-killing ways and accept him into your kingdom."

"Shut your mouth and help me collect maggots," I say.

"I didn't realize you had a maggot collection, Ed," he replies. "Not to cast judgment, but have you ever thought about wood carvings instead? Or maybe little ceramic statues?"

I pick maggots from the fox's flesh, feeling them flail in my fingers, and drop them into my helmet. The first time I saw a surgeon fill a man's wound with maggots, it nearly made me sick. But I have seen such treatment many times now, and I know how useful these little creatures can be. Leeches and maggots. I thought my own personal path to salvation depended on chickens. But it is worms that will deliver me.

Tristan shakes his head. "I'm sorry Ed, I can't. Have I ever told you of my deep disgust for maggots?"

"What are you two doing?" Belisencia walks toward us holding the reins of all three horses.

"Edward is hungry," Tristan says.

Belisencia looks at the rotting fox and shudders. "Have you both gone mad?"

Tristan grins. "In these times of madness, only *maggots* will save us."

When I have harvested two dozen of the maggots, I give Tristan the helmet and tell him to tilt it over my wound slowly, so that the maggots fall onto it a few at a time. He nods. I clench my teeth and open the cut with my fingers. Four maggots fall onto my wrist. One of them slips into the wound, another falls half in and half out but wriggles inside. The other two fall to the ground. Tristan tilts the helmet several times, until ten of the maggots have made a home of my wound. I smear the wet bread over the gash so that some of the mold settles inside.

"That is the second most repulsive thing I have ever seen," Belisencia says.

"It is vile," Tristan says. "But seeing you kiss that doctor was worse."

I wrap the moldy bread in the linen bandages and tuck them into my saddlebag. "What's the first most repulsive?" I ask Belisencia.

She sets her gaze on Tristan and crosses her arms.

I chuckle and kick my horse forward. My fever does not seem as bad. Perhaps Paul's treatment is working. I look skyward and pray to Saint Giles and Saint Luke for healing. I say a prayer to House Gemini, too, just in case.

We ride again through the worsening rain, leaning low in our saddles. Our horses send up crowns of water with each plodding step. A few hours before sundown, I see something that makes me yank the reins hard enough to make my gelding nicker. We stop on the muddy track, the rain nattering off Tristan's spaulders.

"Edward," Tristan says. "Where is Hedingham from here?"

I point to the southwest with a trembling finger. "There," I say.

We stare silently. A column of black smoke rises from the direction in which I point.

Chapter 22

WE RIDE SWIFTLY TOWARD THE column of smoke. The lively pace makes my head throb and keeps me gasping for breath, but I note these things absently. My only thoughts are of my friends, Morgan and Zhuri, and of the nuns of Hedingham.

We crest a small hill crowned with oaks and spot the nunnery. The walled convent used to lie among green fields and hickory rows, but today there is nothing but charred earth in a wide circle around it. We storm down the hill toward the convent. Countless skeletons lie blackened and smoldering upon the scorched ground, curled in on themselves in the agony of death. The nunnery itself does not seem affected by the fire. The limestone walls stand untouched. No smoke rises from the arched, tile-roofed buildings of the convent.

"It would seem they had plaguer problems," I say.

"Demons," Belisencia says. "They had demons at their gates."

We ride through the circle of death, our horses picking paths through the charcoal husks that once were humans.

Perhaps they were not plaguers. Perhaps the nunnery was attacked.

Two soldiers gaze at us from the wall. One calls down and the wooden gates creak open slowly. Our horses amble inside and two soldiers with spears approach as the gates close again behind us.

"Dismount and remove your clothing," the first man says.

"We're not plagued," I say as we dismount. "Tell Sister Margaret that Sir Edward of Bodiam has returned with what he promised."

The soldiers look to one another and back to me. One of them runs off toward the chapter house.

"What do you think of your new home?" Tristan says to Belisencia.

Belisencia looks around and shrugs. "It is a nunnery. They all look the same."

"Will you stay here then?" Tristan asks.

"I do not know," she says. "I miss my home. I may return to Hampshire."

"Hampshire?" Tristan says. "What is your family name? I know Hampshire well."

"Hampshire is lovely," she says. "I wonder how badly the plague has affected it."

"What is your family name?" Tristan says it firmly this time.

Someone shouts my name. I look toward the dormitories and see a familiar face. It is my friend, Zhuri, the Moor. He sprints the last ten paces and nearly knocks me over with his embrace.

"Edward! Tristan! It is wonderful to see you!" Zhuri still keeps a short and meticulously groomed beard, but he wears a leather gambeson from the garrison and tall brown boots. He almost looks like an Englishman.

We met Zhuri in Danbury, at a manor house that became overrun with plaguers. Zhuri escaped with us and we traveled to Hedingham, where he has remained to watch over our afflicted friend, Morgan.

"We thought the monastery had been fired," Tristan says as Zhuri embraces him.

"We are fine," Zhuri replies. "A mob of plaguers found us. The walls at the nunnery are not completely sound, so we decided to strike them before they discovered a way in." Zhuri glances toward the gate, his lips clenched tightly. "May Allah forgive us."

"He will," Tristan says. "You look well, Zhuri. I trust living in a fortress that houses three-dozen women and only a handful of men has been satisfying?"

Zhuri smiles. "It has Tristan. It has."

"You were right to strike first," I say. "I don't like the way the stones lean on the eastern wall. They'll tumble if enough pressure is put on them."

"Thank you, Edward. I will let the nuns know." Zhuri claps me on the shoulder. "Tell me, Edward, did you find her? Did you find your Elizabeth?"

I say nothing. We found Elizabeth. Locked in a hall with dozens of plaguers. Three men in that hall had shown signs of plague, so the monks at St. Edmund's Bury sealed the doors, locking everyone inside. Dooming the lords and ladies of Suffolk—and one angel from Bodiam—to either death or plague. I found my Elizabeth. And I suppose I should be happy that it was plague and not death.

166

Zhuri sees my expression and bows his head. "I am so terribly sorry," he says. "Is she alive, Edward?"

"She is alive"—I take a breath to steady myself—"but she is not herself."

"My sorrow has no words, dear friend," he replies. "Perhaps I can provide a small amount of cheer."

I look into his eyes. "Cheer?"

He smiles. "I have acquired some information that may bring you a gleam of hope. But first..." He turns to Belisencia with a dashing smile and a deep bow. He takes her hand and kisses it several times. "Who do I have the pleasure of setting my eyes upon?"

Tristan takes Belisencia's hand from Zhuri's. "That's Belisencia. And she is promised to a doctor in Maplestead."

"Do not listen to him," she says, smiling at Zhuri. "He is full of lies."

"My lady," Zhuri says, "I learned long ago to ignore the words of Sir Tristan. I am Zhuri of Granada."

"Belisencia," she replies, "of...Hampshire."

"Tell me the information." My voice is gruffer than I intended. It chases away their smiles. Zhuri nods and glances back as the doors to the rectory open and Sister Margaret emerges. "Do you remember the witch Isabella?" he whispers.

I cannot possibly forget Isabella. A woman we rescued in Chelmsford. After saving her, we discovered that she was spreading the plague, selling poisonous phials like the ones Tristan still carries. It was her afflicted dogs who put Morgan in the wine cellar of this nunnery. And it was

Isabella who spoke to us about the alchemist and a possible cure for the plague. The witch was killed in a gun explosion not long after setting her dogs on us, and pieces of her body may still litter the northern reaches of Waltham Forest.

"What of her?" I ask.

"Do you remember she said that an alchemist had the cure for the plague?" he whispers.

"Yes," I say. "We're trying to find the simpleton that Isabella spoke of. The man who works for the alchemist."

Zhuri beams. "I know where he is," he says. "I know where the simpleton lives."

Sister Margaret arrives with another nun and two soldiers. We greet her and I hand over Saint Luke's thighbone. Margaret speaks to me; her tone is a grateful one, but I do not hear her words.

Zhuri has found the simpleton.

We are one step away from the alchemist. One step from a cure. I imagine myself pouring drops of elixir into Elizabeth's delicate mouth. I see her waking. Her long fingers reaching up to touch my face. A smile playing across her lips. I know what I will say to her when she wakes. I will gaze into her blue eyes and say, *"Je suis apprivoisé."* I am tame. She will call me a wonderful fool, wrap one arm behind my neck, and kiss me. I can feel her warm body against mine, feel the tears of joy stinging my eyes.

"Are you not well, Edward?" Sister Margaret asks.

I take a breath and wipe at my eyes. "I had a wound that festered," I say.

"Father in heaven!" Margaret says. "Let me see it."

I show her my wrist. The tail of a maggot pokes out from the cut. Or perhaps it is the head. "It is healing," I say.

"Yes," Tristan says. "He received the kiss of life, didn't he, Belisencia?"

"Maggots?" Sister Margaret shakes her head. "You should put moldy bread on it. And spider webs. I will have someone tend to you."

We follow her toward the dormitories.

Tristan grows sober. He puts a hand on Zhuri's shoulder as we walk. "How is Morgan?"

Zhuri does not speak at first, and when he finally does, he looks furtively at Sister Margaret's back, then whispers, "You should go find the simpleton first thing in the morning. I was preparing to go before the plaguers found us. We must find that cure."

I do not like Zhuri's evasiveness. I stop walking. "Zhuri, tell us about Morgan."

Zhuri takes a deep breath, rubs at his face. He will not meet my gaze. "He is not well, Edward." Zhuri glances toward the hall that houses the nunnery's wine cellar. "He is dying."

Chapter 23

WE WALK DOWN THE STONE steps leading to the wine cellar. The smell of old wood, earth, and lye brings back memories of that terrible day when we locked Morgan in a chamber of this cellar. My heart pounds as I descend the stairs. Morgan has a young daughter, Sara, in Hastings. And I am responsible for what happened to her father.

Mea maxima culpa.

Screams ring out in the darkness. Savage screams with no humanity left in them. I hold a candle in front of me and breathe heavily from the exertion of descending the tall steps. The door to Morgan's chamber is closed, but the casks that we barricaded it with are gone.

Zhuri brushes past me when we reach the bottom, holding his own candle. He opens the door and peers inside, then steps into the room. Light flares as he fires a lantern and I get my first look at Morgan since we left him. And what I see makes me fall to my knees.

Morgan is rotting.

They have tied him down onto a wooden platform lain over two rows of casks. Large swaths of his skin are black. Black like the rotted peels of Spanish bananas. Black like the scorched skeletons huddled outside the monastery. Broad patches of his beard have fallen out. The skin on his hands has been torn to bloody shreds, and a wound along the side of his chin reveals the white bones of his jaw among mangled red meat.

"Morgan..." I walk to his side. He growls and strains against the ropes. His eyes are so black and smooth that I see myself reflected in them. His chest rises and falls erratically. He tries to scream again but his strength fades halfway through and the cry ends with a groan.

"Why is he so bad?" I ask. "Why did this happen so quickly?"

"He was battering himself to pieces on the door," Zhuri says, "so we tied him down. I do not know what is wrong. But I know he is dying. He gets weaker every day."

I stare at Morgan, and I see Elizabeth, tied with padded silk to a mattress in St. Edmund's Bury. Is her skin black like Morgan's? Does she struggle for breath too? The room seems to sway. I feel sick.

The lantern gutters. Zhuri taps it and the flame grows stronger, but it gutters again. "It's almost out of oil."

"You said..." I am short of breath. Speaking is a struggle. "You said you know where the simpleton lives."

"Yes," Zhuri says. "Some pilgrims stopped here two days ago and spoke of an alchemist living in a fortress. They did not speak favorably of him."

"They wouldn't." I recall the alchemist I saw burned at the stake when I was a child. *Prayer is the only true and righteous weapon against illness.* "I don't want details, Zhuri. Just tell me where the simpleton is."

"I would have spoken with him already, but the plaguers found us first. They surrounded the convent. We finally set fire to them this morning." He shakes his head. "It was a horrible sight, Edward. It is the worst thing I have ever done."

"Zhuri," I look into his eyes, "where is the simpleton?"

"The pilgrims said he lived in a place called Bewer," Zhuri says. "That's what the simpleton told them. I searched the maps in the library for hours before I realized that he probably meant—"

"Bure," I say and run for the stairs. I imagine Elizabeth's long fingers shredded to the bone. Her slender chest rising and falling erratically. I take one last look at Morgan, tied to the casks. He, Tristan, Zhuri, and Belisencia are lit by the guttering orange glow of the lantern. The oil will run out soon.

"Where are you going?" Zhuri shouts. Tristan and Belisencia chase after me.

"To find the cure!" I call back. The steps are difficult to climb at a run. I grow fatigued as I reach the top and lean against the wall to catch my breath.

"Edward," Tristan says, "you need to rest. It makes no sense to leave now. The sun will set in less than two hours and Bure is ten miles away."

"I can travel ten miles in less than two hours," I say.

"You won't make five miles in your condition, Ed," he replies.

"I'll be fine." I have to be. Morgan is dying. Elizabeth may be, too. The oil is running out.

"Edward." Tristan shakes his head. "We can ride in the morning."

I think of Morgan dying in the wine cellar. It is my fault. I was selfish. I should never have brought others with me on my errand. I look at Tristan; he would do anything I ask of him...except stay behind. "Very well," I say. "We'll leave in the morning." I try to sound sincere.

We eat a simple meal of bread and leek stew in the great hall. Sister Margaret and three other nuns join us. I speak to Zhuri, recounting our adventures since leaving him. Tristan and Belisencia sit next to each other. Belisencia had a bath in the dormitory and two of the sisters combed out her hair. She wears new robes, too, and looks quite lovely. Tristan's eyebrows disappeared beneath his hair when he saw her. The two of them laugh throughout the dinner, poke fun at one another, and their hands touch accidentally every so often. I do not know how they truly feel about each other, but seeing them laugh together makes me think of my Elizabeth. She always makes me laugh, my angel. I hope I will hear the chime of her laughter again, soon. When she wakes, I will never leave her side again.

Je suis apprivoisé.

After the meal, Sister Margaret has a nun tend to my wound. The portly woman plucks the maggots from my wrist and tells me the creatures have done a good job. "The wound has been cleansed of dead flesh."

She douses the injury with more wine and applies a salve that she says is made from bread mold and cobwebs. A proper remedy, just like the battlefield surgeons make. She wraps the wound with bandages and gives me a small bottle of the salve to take with me. "Clean the wound with wine and apply the salve every day," she says before leaving. "With God's help, you will defeat the festering illness."

Sister Margaret loans Belisencia a novice's room and has beds made up for Tristan and me in the dormitory. There are already three-dozen men from the village sleeping in the dormitory, most on the floor, so Tristan and I give up our beds and lay on blankets upon the rushes.

"How's the wound?" Tristan asks.

"Better," I reply. "I found a good doctor."

"She didn't mind that you were born under House Gemini?" Tristan chuckles.

"And her breath was better, too." I try to sound cheerful, but Elizabeth haunts me tonight.

"Belisencia is coming with us," Tristan says.

"Is she?" I ask. "She still wants to spread the word of Hugh the Baptist?"

"No," he replies. "I don't think she truly believes that anymore. I don't think she knows what to believe."

"Tristan, that plaguer, Hugh, he didn't bite her."

"I know," he replies. "I've thought about it for a long time, Edward. And I can't come up with any answers."

I, too, have thought long and hard about the events in Hugh's temple: the talking plaguer; his refusal to bite Belisencia; Matheus's confusion. I, too, have no answers. Perhaps Matheus was right. Perhaps we are in purgatory.

Tristan's breathing becomes deep and regular. I count to two hundred, holding Elizabeth's glove to my nose as I do, then rise as quietly as I can. My head still hurts and I have trouble finding my balance in the darkness, but I make my way out of the dormitories. I creep quietly to the stables. A soldier sits on a stool and challenges me when I approach.

"I am Sir Edward of Bodiam," I reply. "I need my armor."

The soldier leads me to the last stall, where my armor and that of Tristan has been scoured of rust and hung on pegs. I grow winded as I strap on the various plates and have to ask the guard for help. It takes a long time to get the harness on. When I am done, I ask him for a lantern. He hesitates, then pulls one down from a peg on the next stall and gives it to me. I thank him and walk to the stall that holds my horse.

"Do you need help saddling him?"

It is not the guard speaking. I sigh.

Tristan and Belisencia sit on a bench just inside the door. They are in their bedclothes.

"No, Tristan," I say. "I need the two of you to go back to sleep."

"I think I *am* sleeping," Tristan says. "This must be a bad dream. My friend Edward Dallingridge would never abandon me in a nunnery." He thinks about what he said. "Although, I suppose there are worse places to be abandoned."

"You cannot do this alone," Belisencia says. "The Bible says, 'Three are better than one. For if they fall, they fall together. But woe if one should fall alone.'"

I try to make sense of the quote. Tristan looks equally mystified.

"That's not quite right, my lady," the soldier says. "'Two are better than one, for if one falls, the other will lift up his fellow. But woe to him who is alone when he falls and has not another to lift him up.'"

"Yes, that is what I meant," she says.

"What kind of a nun are you?" the soldier asks.

"One who will lift up her friend when he falls," she says.

"Morgan fell," I say, "and I can't lift him up. I don't want the same fate for the two of you."

"God has blessed Morgan with a trial," Tristan says. "If He chooses to bless me, too, then that is His choice, not yours."

"Hallelujah," Belisencia says.

Tristan and I look at her, but she is serious. Tristan laughs and we say it together: "Hallelujah."

I know it is selfish, but I am glad for their company. If I fall, Elizabeth and Morgan will need someone to lift me up again. I know now that Tristan and Belisencia will be there to do it. "Don't try to leave us again, Ed," Tristan says, "or I will tell everyone that you buggered a cow."

I shrug. "Least it wasn't a horse."

We laugh. It feels good to laugh, even though the black mist of Elizabeth's sickness coils in my stomach.

The soldier looks at me with horror. I shrug again. "She was a beauty, that cow. You'd have done the same."

Tristan laughs loud and long. Even Belisencia chuckles.

"Off to bed with us," I say.

"You won't try to leave us again?" Belisencia asks. "That wasn't a nice thing to do."

"No, I won't try to leave you again." I nod and look into her eyes so she can see the gratitude that I cannot express. "*Mea maxima culpa.*"

We rise at first light and I go to Zhuri's chamber to ask if he wants to come. He shakes his head. "I swore I would guard Morgan," he says, "and that promise will keep me here until he is healed. I will continue to take care of him and check his health every day. I am glad you arrived when you did, or I would have had to leave him."

Something moves next to him and I catch a glimpse of long brown hair. Zhuri clears his throat. "Besides, I like it here."

"Until next time, Zhuri," I say.

"Until next time, Sir Edward."

I walk to the stables, where I meet Tristan and Belisencia.

"How is the wound?" Belisencia asks.

"Much improved," I say, and it is. My head feels clearer. Walking no longer tires me, although I still feel weak. Tristan helps me into my armor and I help him into his. We tighten our sword belts, nod to one another, then mount. Or try to mount. After my third attempt, Tristan gives me a boost into the saddle.

"You could use a day or two of rest," Tristan says.

"You could do with a day or two of shutting your mouth," I reply.

"Hallelujah," Belisencia says.

As we ride out of Hedingham, the panic returns to my soul. I must find the cure. It feels as if someone has punched a hole in Elizabeth's sandglass. It feels as if her life is seeping away faster than ever.

Chapter 24

WE RIDE EASTWARD AGAIN, PASSING south of Maplestead. Tristan asks Belisencia if she wants to visit her husband, Paul, but she ignores him. Thick black clouds drift and swirl overhead, turning day to twilight. We keep a good pace, stopping only to water the horses.

Just past Pebmarsh we spot a pilgrim walking on his knees southward, probably toward Canterbury. I have seen this before. Pilgrims walk on their knees to atone for their sins. But I cannot imagine doing such a thing amidst this plague that has swept England. I have no doubt that he is afflicted by the other sickness: the third plague. Only a madman would walk on his knees through this England. He does not look at us and we leave him to his pilgrimage.

"Someone should give that man a horse," Tristan says. We slow our pace to give our steeds some rest.

"I admire him," Belisencia replies. "He is a devout, God-fearing man looking for a way to atone for his sins."

"I'd prefer a God that I don't have to fear," Tristan says.

"Only sinners need to fear him," she says. "And yes, that means you."

"But aren't we all sinners?" Tristan replies. "The Bible has us sinning before we are even born, doesn't it?"

"It does," she replies. "Because of Adam and Eve."

I spot movement up ahead on the side of the road. A plaguer is eating a horse.

"Some mad strumpet eats a crab apple and the rest of us have to suffer forever? What sort of God does that?"

"Do not blame God for our faults, Tristan," Belisencia says. "It was Adam who caused this. Not God."

"God, Adam, Eve, does it matter?" Tristan says. "I don't even *like* apples. Why should I be born a sinner? Why must newborn babies carry a stain?"

"Newborn babies acquire Original Sin from their parents," she says. "Parents transmit the sin through their procreation."

"Through procreation?" Tristan shakes his head. "So Original Sin is like syphilis and the burning crotch. It's all starting to makes sense."

"That's not what I am saying at all," she replies.

Thunder rumbles distantly. We approach the plaguer and I realize I was wrong. It is not a plaguer at all. It is a man buggering a hobbled horse. The man does not even look at us as we pass. He continues pumping at the prone horse, his eyes closed, his face strained. The mare grunts resignedly. Belisencia gasps and looks away. Tristan and I exchange glances. We ride silently for a few paces. Tristan clears his throat, looks back at the man and horse. We ride a few more paces.

"So," Tristan says, "maybe a little mercury ointment, applied liberally, would clear up this Original Sin affliction."

"Think of it in this way," Belisencia replies. "Humanity is like a pail of white paint. Adam dropped a spot of lampblack into it. It does not matter how much more white you add to the pail. It will never again be pure."

"Interesting," he says. "So, if the pail will never be white again, why not just add more lampblack and make a nice gray? It would be a lot more fun than spending your entire life trying to make it white again."

"Because gray is dark and unpleasant," Belisencia says. "White is bright and virtuous."

"I like gray," Tristan responds.

Thunder rumbles again, loudly this time, and the three of us look up at the dark clouds.

"Gray." Belisencia points toward the skies. A few thick drops spatter down onto us, and after another dozen paces the dark clouds unleash a torrent of rain. I give Belisencia a saddle blanket to cover her head and we ride hunched against the deluge.

The storm eases after a mile or so. We ride the remaining miles in a spitting rain that comes and goes, but I barely even notice. Bure is not far. The simpleton is near.

Bure is a quiet place upon the River Stour, with ivy-wrapped tree trunks and mild, rolling hills. A humble stone church and a mill sit by the river, surrounded by shaggy willows, marsh grasses, and water lilies. A forest crowds the village on the east side, just a kicked stone's distance from the church, and two-dozen thatched homes spread out from both banks of the river. The Stour winds lethargically through the village and disappears into the forest.

It is a normal English settlement. But there is something quite abnormal occurring on the far riverbank. The entire population of the village seems to have gathered at the Stour, near the forest. Tristan and I look at one another. If we did not need the simpleton, we would stay well clear of such a sight. But we ride past the church, which is devoted to the Virgin Mary of course, and head toward an arched wooden bridge that spans the river.

One of the tallest men I have ever seen clutches a long staff that bears a crucifix at the top. He has close-cropped black hair and wears red and black robes that hang off his thin frame like sails. Two men in front of him hold a bound and gagged woman in their arms. The rest of the villagers form a half circle around them.

Tristan and I break into a gallop. Only bad things can happen to a bound woman when priests are around. But we are too late. The tall man makes the sign of the cross and the two men throw her into the river. We cross the bridge and lose sight of the woman, but the villagers see our horses rumbling toward them and pull back. I see the bound maiden again. It is not deep where she has fallen, so she lies, kicking, on her side, the water covering only half her body. Her head is still clear of the river.

Tristan and I dismount and push our way through the crowd. I point at the tall man with the staff. "Are you mad?" It is a question I should not ask anymore. The third plague is easy enough to spot.

"Mad?" the tall man asks. "Would that it were madness and all our pain just a tormented dream. Would that I could wake in the morning in my cottage and say to myself, 'Good Lord, what a foul dream I had.' Nay, 'tis not madness, my good sir. 'Tis survival."

Tristan nods. "Yes," he says. "I've lost count of the number of bound women I have thrown into rivers so that I might survive."

"Mock our pain," the tall man says. "Mock our suffering. Go on."

Tristan looks puzzled. "I've never had this sort of invitation before." He clears his throat. "All of you are fools! I laugh at you! You deserve—"

"Tristan." I put an edge in my voice.

Belisencia arrives and shuffles through the crowd. She stares into the river. "Why is that woman in the water?"

"Survival," Tristan says. "Do you know nothing?"

"You, priest," I say. "What is your name?"

"My parents christened me after my grandsire, a fine man who made a living from tanning hides," he says. "And he was christened Ralf."

Tristan snickers at the name.

"Why have you thrown that woman into the river, Father Ralf?" I ask. I feel like sitting on the bank. It tires me to stand.

"Because a great evil has descended upon us," the priest says. "Sent from hell, or perhaps from some other wicked place, but it has descended upon us all the same. A terrible menace that has terrified the people of Bure. Something so wicked that—"

"*What is it, man?*" I am anxious to find the simpleton and this priest will not stop talking.

Ralf flinches at my raised voice. "A dragon," he says. "We are plagued by a dragon."

Tristan laughs. "Truly? A dragon?"

Ralf nods his head. "Yes. A dragon."

Tristan looks at the bound woman in the river and raises his hands. He turns toward the crowd. "When will you people stop acting like sheep? You deserve to be mocked! Your priest tells you there is a dragon in the area, so you allow him to tie up your women and throw them into the river? Is that what Christians do these days?" He points to the woman in the Stour. "This river is probably tidal. You will go home and, during the night, the river will rise and she will drown. Her body will be carried out to sea. You will come back in the morning and she will not be here, and this priest will tell you a dragon took her. And you will believe him, won't you? And you will allow him to murder more of your women! If you have any women left, that is. Do you people have no minds? Do you *truly* think a dragon simply swoops down and—*Satan's hairy cock! Holy Christ almighty! House of fucking Gemini!*"

Tristan staggers backward as a dragon bursts from the forest and roars. I am too stunned to react, and so is everyone else. The dragon leaps into the river, hisses, then snatches up the woman in its toothy maw.

Episode 5

Chapter 25

FATHER RALF IS CORRECT. IT is a thing of hell, this dragon.

Every scabrous fold and ripple of its body is a testament to the evil in its soul. It crawls upon its belly like the Snake of Eden, long as three men lying head to foot and thick as two armored knights standing shoulder to shoulder. Its crusted skin is dark and stony, as if chiseled from the jagged walls of hell itself. Thick scales of deep, mottled golds and blacks ripple along the creature's knotted body, glimmering in the daylight with the promise of invulnerability.

I shake my head and gather my senses, feeling the calling of honor upon me. A maiden's life is in danger. And it is a dragon that threatens her.

Every priest dreams of sainthood. Every merchant dreams of riches. And every knight, no matter how much he may deny it, dreams of slaying a dragon. It is in our blood. Tristan and I nearly knock each other to the ground in our haste to reach the creature.

I vault into the water and sink up to my calves in the soft mud of the river bottom. The Stour is only knee-high near the shore but gets swiftly deeper. I slog toward the wyrm, my sword flashing in the cloud-baked sunlight. The water-line licks at my stomach. Cold water seeps through mail and numbs my thighs and groin. Tristan takes long sloshing leaps at my side.

The dragon's jaws are clamped around the woman's legs. It pulls her deep into the river and rolls like a twirling log, taunting us, the water splashing and churning violently. The woman is a whirl of white skirts and blue corset, of black hair and pale skin: an explosion of fabric and flesh that disappears into the Stour. The monster completes a roll and she becomes visible, her gurgling shrieks muffled by the gag, then she disappears once again below the surface.

The cruel beast is having sport with her.

Tristan reaches the wyrm first. He shouts and hacks at the creature with his sword, sending up an eruption of water. I sheathe my weapon and clutch at the bound woman, my mailed fingers brushing against the hard, warted skin of the dragon. The water makes her clothing slick and I have trouble taking hold of her. Something long and spiked lashes across the water, so fast that it is just a blur. It strikes Tristan's back with a metallic crack that echoes across the river. The dragon's tail. Tristan's shout is cut short as he falls forward and under the water.

Tristan!

I stare into the river where he went under and hold the woman's torso with both arms. I hug her close as the dragon rolls again. It drags me forward so powerfully that I almost roll with her. I dig my heels in and groan against the creature's pull. The woman's shrieks turn from horror to agony, so I release her. She plunges under the surface again. If I had kept my grip, the monster's teeth would have torn off her legs.

I lunge at the twirling monster. A spurt of water splashes into my mouth as I inhale, making me cough. The wyrm thrashes, making deep grunts, then curls its body through the water, heading downstream and into the forest. I claw at it, clutch at its knobbed body, and take hold of the tail, feeling the double row of spikes flexing under my hand. The creature flails, frothing the river, and its terrible strength nearly knocks me underwater. The dragon makes a sound: something between a hiss and a deep, throbbing grunt. It coils backward, releases the woman, and lunges at me. The mouth is as big as a treasure chest. Big enough to accommodate my head and torso. I fall backward, raise an arm as the flashing rows of bone-white teeth clash against my bracer and glance off. The impact knocks me back, the water roaring around me. People on shore cry out in terror. The Stour swallows me. Feathery milfoil brushes my face. There is silence. A cloudy brown darkness. I am in purgatory.

I kick my feet and surface, taking in a deep breath and shaking the Stour from my hair. Sound returns to the world. Water splatters. Villagers scream from the shore.

The dragon has vanished.

The undulating river washes against me, makes me lightheaded and unsure of my balance. I pant from my exertions, feeling weak and more tired than I should be. I draw my sword again and spin in the water, my eyes darting wildly. Tristan stands in the river, holding the bound woman in his arms. He nods to me, water dripping from his armor, and sloshes toward the rush-hemmed shore. A lily has settled onto his right shoulder. I spin again, sword held high in one hand, and search the Stour as I back toward shore. Something moves to my right. I whirl and threaten a sprout of waving spearwort on the riverbank. I search downstream, but there is no sign of the dragon.

Perhaps it has returned to hell. Or maybe we have angered it into bringing hell to Bure.

The woman is alive, but her legs are torn and bleeding badly. She sobs through her gag.

"Is there a leech in this village?" Tristan asks, but no one will meet his gaze. "For God's sake, she'll die! Do you have a barber?"

I climb from the river. "We seek a simpleton who is said to live in Bure."

Father Ralf slams the butt end of his staff against my breastplate. "We had a pact with that dragon!" He strikes me with the staff again. "You have enraged it! We had a pact!"

"A pact?" I shove the priest backward. "You made a pact with the devil?"

"Our survival is at stake!"

"What kind of pact?" I ask. "You feed it villagers so it will leave you alone? Is that your pact?"

The priest raises the staff to strike me again, then appears to think better of it. He shakes his head and walks away, toward the village. I take hold of his cape and pull him backward with a little more force than I intended. He stumbles and falls to the wet grass.

"Is that it?" I say. "Are you feeding your flock to the dragon so it will leave you alone?"

The crowd becomes more active. I note a ripple of discontent at the edge of my vision. I should not have pulled on the cape so hard.

Father Ralf crosses his arms and says nothing. The priest would not stop talking when we saw him first, and now he will not speak at all.

"*What kind of pact?*" I shout.

He flinches and holds up a trembling finger. "The dragon demands one virgin each month," he says. "And in return it protects our village."

"This woman will die if she is not tended to," Tristan calls. He still holds her in his arms. "Who among you can bind her wounds?"

Belisencia speaks soothingly to the woman, who is still bound and gagged.

Father Ralf shakes his head. "She is our sacrifice," he says. "She must be returned to the river."

Tristan scowls at the priest. "I'm certain that she doesn't see it that way."

A bearded man at the front of the crowd speaks up. "She does," he says. "She agreed to it."

Tristan opens his mouth to speak, shuts it again. He looks at the woman, who nods tearfully.

Chapter 26

THE WOMAN'S NAME IS SARA, and her family is to receive an allotment of three shillings every month for five years. In return, Sara is to be sacrificed to the dragon and her name etched into the floor of St. Mary's Church as a martyr for God, England, and the village of Bure.

"They might even make me a saint," she says tearfully.

It is an unsettling thing. Maidens are supposed to cheer their heroes, to weep with joy at being pulled from the jaws of the beast. But Sara looks at us with tearful indignation.

I sit on the damp grass and rub at my face. "Tend to her wounds," I say to the priest. "Tend to her wounds while we talk. You can always throw her back after she has been bandaged."

The priest purses his lips and stares at the woman. A damp circle at the back of his robe marks the spot where he fell onto the grass. He nods at a thick-armed man in the crowd. The man takes Sara from Tristan and trudges off toward the village. A pox-faced older man—the leech or barber no doubt—follows him.

"Now, where is your lord?" I ask.

"Sir Richard perished," the priest replies. "He died fighting the dragon."

"Sir Richard?" I say. "Sir Richard Waldegrave?"

The priest nods. I knew Sir Richard. He was a good man. He would never have allowed the atrocity of human sacrifice in his village.

"Very well," I say. "Then I will ask you for your help. We seek a simpleton who lives in Bure. Is he among you? Can you point him out to us, Father?"

Father Ralf turns away from me halfway through my request and looks to the crowd. "We will throw Sara the Martyr to the dragon tomorrow. Gather here at noon once again, and we will perform the ceremony."

"Tell me, priest," Tristan says. "How does this dragon protect your village?"

The priest sweeps the crucifix in a broad arc. "Look around you," he says. "Simply look around. Do you see any demons? Is there even one afflicted soul in sight? The dragon devours them. It keeps our lands free of plague. And all it asks is for one virgin a month." He sneers at Tristan. "Although I think perhaps its demands may change now that you fools attacked it."

I scan the crowd for anyone who might look simple. "The dragon eats the afflicted?"

Ralf nods. "It protects us."

"How do you know the dragon requires virgins?" Tristan smirks. "Did it speak with you?"

"There are other ways to communicate," Father Ralf replies.

"You're insane," Tristan says.

"The dragon," Belisencia says. "Does it...does it breathe fire?"

Ralf nods. "It burned down Wormingford a month ago. Seeking revenge for wrongs committed long ago, you see? Avenging its kin. Everyone in the village was killed. Not even the animals escaped."

Wormingford is a village south of Bure. I have heard people say that Saint George slew a dragon there, when the place was known as Withermundsford. Those same people say that a mound of earth and grass has covered the dragon's body, but that the creature's bones still lie where it fell. That is why they changed the name to Wormingford: to honor England's patron saint. Why they did not change the name to St. George's Ford is beyond my understanding.

"And you are happy with this pact you have made?" I ask. "This is an acceptable way to live? Feeding your daughters to this beast of hell?"

"Bure does not burn," the priest replies. "Our children are safe. The village is protected."

"And what happens when you run out of virgins?" I say. "Will you make a new pact?"

Father Ralf takes a long, deep breath. "What choice do we have?"

"You can kill it," I say. "You can send it back to hell."

The priest shakes his head solemnly. "We cannot kill it. No one can."

"And why not?" I ask.

Father Ralf closes his eyes. "I had a vision," he says. "A dark and terrible vision. Long before this foul beast arrived. A most prophetic vision. An image sent to me from God himself. A terrifying message that foretold of the coming anguish. A waking dream that made me cry out with horror. 'No!' I shouted to the heavens. 'Lord, tell me this is not the future I see. Tell me that such terrible things will not—'"

"The vision," Tristan snaps. "Get to the vision."

Father Ralf clears his throat. "My vision was that a serpent would come to Bure. And that no man alive could slay it. In the vision, I was made aware that only the blood of virgins would appease the dragon."

"I have a solution," Tristan replies. "What's say we rid the town of virgins? I'd be happy to offer my assistance."

Belisencia crosses her arms and quotes scriptures with a sour look on her face. "'Put to death the earthly things in you: sexual immorality, impurity, passion, evil desire, and covetousness, which is idolatry.'"

"A rather complete list," Tristan replies. "You might as well add happiness. What a sad place this world must seem to the truly devout. Does God allow for any enjoyment of the beauty He has created?"

Father Ralf clears his throat and recites another verse. "'Let your fountain be blessed, and rejoice in the wife of your youth, a lovely deer, a graceful doe. Let her breasts fill you at all times with delight; be intoxicated always in her love.'"

Tristan laughs. "Father Ralf!"

The priest shrugs. "I like that verse." He repeats a portion of it in a sing-song voice: "'Let her breasts fill you at all times with delight.'"

"If my priest had read verses like that, I would have been in the front pew at every mass," Tristan says. "Tell me, Father, what other wonderful things does the Bible say about breasts?"

The priest scratches at his cheek. "There is not much else. Mostly the Bible talks about breasts withering."

"That's not appealing, Father," Tristan replies. "What does it say about virgins?"

"They're not virgins," the bearded man shouts from the crowd.

"Sorry?" Tristan says.

"We only had four virgins in the village," the man replies. "So we had to start feeding the dragon ordinary—"

"I have no time for this," I snap. "Father, I seek a simpleton who lives in your village. Do you know him? Is he there in the crowd?"

Father Ralf stares at me, then looks downward and rolls the staff between his fingers absently. He does not meet my gaze. "Why do you seek him?"

"I need to talk with him," I say.

"His master is an alchemist," Belisencia says. "And some say this alchemist has a cure for the plague."

The priest's eyes grow wide. He crosses himself and backs away from me. "Alchemy is a mortal sin!"

I give Belisencia a scathing look, then address the priest. "We must seek any help we can find in these terrible times, Father."

The priest backs away farther, holding the staffed crucifix to the sky, like Moses. "'There shall not be found among you any one that useth an enchanter, or a witch. Or a charmer, or a consulter with familiar spirits, or a wizard, or a necromancer. For all that do these things are an abomination unto the Lord.'"

Tristan shakes his head. "I liked the verse about the breasts better."

Chapter 27

"I propose a new rule," I say as we knock on another door. "Belisencia is not to speak to anyone we meet on our quest."

"Hallelujah," Tristan replies.

"I was trying to help," she snaps.

I knock again at the door as a light drizzle washes down on us. It is a thatched cottage a dozen paces south of the Stour, with a small window beside the entrance. This is the third such cottage we have approached. Father Ralf sent the crowd back to their homes after Belisencia's revelation and told the villagers not to speak with us or they would be guilty of abomination. So we search for the simpleton without their help.

"Can you believe that priest?" Tristan says. "He has no qualms feeding virgins to a dragon so plague will not find his village, but he draws the line at alchemy."

"They're not virgins, Tristan," Belisencia replies. "They ran out."

Tristan laughs and she smiles, but it is a guilty smile. "I should not laugh. It is cruel."

"No, it is human," Tristan says. "In these times of madness, only human sacrifice will save us."

It grates on me that they are joking when we have no way of finding the simpleton, but there is no sense imposing my anguish on them.

"Tell me, Belisencia," Tristan says. "What happens to a soul when it is eaten by a dragon in purgatory? Does it spend eternity in a steaming pile of wyrm dung?"

Belisencia's smile fades. "That's not funny, Tristan."

I bang on the door as loudly as I can. Someone moves inside the cottage. A gaunt face peers out from the window.

"Don't tell me you still think we are in purgatory," Tristan says.

"I do not know where we are," she says. "But there was a dragon in the middle of this village. How many dragons have you seen on earth, Tristan?"

Someone shouts from behind the door. "Go away! Alchemy is a sin!"

"So is human sacrifice," Tristan calls.

"Please," I say. "My wife is dying. Please."

"Alchemy is an abomination!"

Red rage rises in me, burns in my cheeks. I grip the latch on the door with the strength of my fury and twist slowly until the wood creaks. I could tear down this door and search the cottage for the simpleton. It would be easy. But I take three deep breaths and walk away instead. Cold rainwater seeps under the collar of my breastplate and trickles down my back. The rain beads on our armor and glistens like jewels in Belisencia's wool cloak.

"Someone will talk to us," Tristan says.

"Of course they will," Belisencia adds. "We just need to find the right person."

I do not respond. The simpleton may be within a few hundred paces of me but I am powerless to find him. Perhaps we are in purgatory. Perhaps this is my punishment, to seek this simpleton for an eternity.

There must be twenty-five or thirty homes in the village, as well as a tavern and twin rows of flint-faced buildings that house vendors and workshops. It would take a full day or more to speak with everyone. And we still might not find the answer.

"We need help," I say.

It is a new church, and it seems as if the tower is not yet completed. An ornate porch frames the central doorway. A thing of cusped and foiled arches made from great beams of ship wood and smaller curving planks. We walk through the door and I sweep my gaze over the interior.

Angel carvings decorate the corbeled arches. Thick, fluted columns rise skyward and latticed stained-glass windows turn sunlight into colored patterns on the walls. We sit in the frontmost pew in the nave of St. Mary's Church, only a few paces from the altar. I pray at times and speak with Tristan and Belisencia at others. I do not know what to expect. All I know is that the Virgin helped me once. And, if nothing else, I want to thank her properly for what she did for me at the Lutons' Manor.

The doors to the church open again and I look back to see Father Ralf enter with a short, stocky man. The priest flinches when he sees us and whispers to the man at his side. Only one hissing, echoing word makes it to my ears: "heretics." The two men stride down the nave, past us, their footsteps ringing out across the church. They vanish through a small, iron-studded door at the east transept.

"Want to hear something humorous?" Tristan asks.

"No," Belisencia and I say together.

"When I was a child," Tristan continues, "my parents took me to London to watch as a dozen sinners were hanged."

"Quite humorous," Belisencia says.

"We gathered in a square, where soldiers raised thick wooden poles from which they would hang the sinners," Tristan says. "The poor condemned souls were paraded in front of us. People in the crowd threw vegetables at them. Some spit at the sinners. But what I thought cruelest of all were the horrible insults that were shouted. One insult in particular. Men and women in the crowd called these poor people 'hairy ticks.'"

"You are a fool," Belisencia says. "Heretics?"

"I was seven years old," he replies. "That's what it sounded like to me. It was the vilest insult I had ever heard. A hairy tick. Ticks are repulsive, but hairy ones? The thought of them made me shiver. It was worse than maggots."

"Then the priests addressed the crowd, and they spoke of a hairy sea, which was where I assumed hairy ticks went when they died."

Belisencia laughs. "To the hairy sea?"

"Can you imagine how horrible such a place would be? Feeling those hairs creeping over you as you drowned, over and over for eternity—because I imagined that's what you would do in the hairy sea: drown. I told my older brother about all of it when I returned home and he tormented me for years. Whenever I was caught in mischief, he would call me a hairy tick and tell me I would be sent to the hairy sea. It gave me nightmares." He shakes his head. "It still gives me nightmares."

Belisencia and Tristan laugh, their voices echoing in the church. But the laughter stops when the great wooden doors of the church rattle open again.

An old woman approaches, hunched and holding a woolen shawl over her head against the drizzle outside. "You are the knighth," she says, her lisping voice like wind through dead reeds.

"We are," I say. "Do you know where the simpleton lives?"

Faded green eyes peer out at me from a face cracked like the desert floor, creased and weathered, the lips sunken in a toothless mouth. She looks like my grandmother, may God protect her departed soul. And, as I think on it, a bit like Tristan's grandmother, too. It is odd how age turns all women into the same person.

"I know where he ith," she says.

"Tell me, old woman." I stand and nod to her.

Someone laughs from the east transept, behind the small door that Father Ralf and his guest disappeared through. The old woman looks to the door. Her milky eyes grow wide and she turns to leave.

"Wait!" I grab her thin arm gently. It is like holding a staff wrapped in wool. I glance back toward the door and speak quietly. "I will pay you."

She shakes her head and whispers, "I have no need for coin."

"Surely there is something you want," I say. "Tell us where the simpleton lives and we will repay you however we can."

The cracked desert floor splits as she smiles. I was wrong; she has one tooth left in her mouth, a yellowed pebble that juts above her sunken bottom lip. She points a finger at me. "I will tell you where the thimpleton ith, but you will pay me firtht."

Take while the patient is in pain. I live in a world of doctors now.

"We will pay you if you can repeat the sacred words," Tristan says. "Simon sows seeds sinfully in the summer sun."

"Stop it, Tristan," I say. "What is the price we must pay, woman?"

She leans forward and glances toward the door before speaking.

"Thlay the dragon, mighty knigth. Thlay the Dragon of Bure."

Chapter 28

"Father Ralf says the dragon cannot be killed," I say.

"Then you will never find the thimpleton," she replies.

I study the old woman. She smiles, but there is no humor in her eyes. There is only desperation.

"Why do you want the dragon killed?" I ask. "I thought it protected Bure."

She shakes her head. "The dragon protecth Father Ralf and the men of the village. It doeth nothing for the women."

"So you represent the women of the village?" I say.

"I reprethent Sara," she replies. "Thee is my granddaughter."

"I see. And Sara is to be sacrificed tomorrow."

"No," she says. "Thee will not be. Becauthe you will kill the dragon today."

The rain will render our cannons unreliable, so we leave them with Belisencia and run whetstones over the burrs in our blades. We secure the worn leather straps of our armor, don our helmets, and we stride out of the church into a gray world. It is late afternoon but the thick clouds overhead and the ceaseless, hazy drizzle turn day into evening. The cooling temperatures have wreathed the Stour in a thick, coiling mist that cloaks the water.

How many times have Tristan and I marched out to battle like this? The sounds are as familiar to me as the song of the thrush or the feel of the wind on the downs: plates clanking, weighted footsteps on soft earth, breath echoing in helms. I look to Tristan and put my hand on the hilt of my sword. He nods and we draw our blades together.

We have killed Frenchmen, Tristan and I. We have defeated Italians, Spaniards, and Scots. Fought bears and witches, man-eating dogs and angry bulls. We have vanquished whatever enemies this world has sent at us and enjoyed the earthly prizes that came with the victories. But today is different. Today's foe is not of this world. Today we fight hell's champion, and Elizabeth is the prize.

A blond-haired boy of eight or nine plays in the rain, throwing rocks at a small wooden boat in a large puddle. His wide eyes study us, from our mailed boots to our steel helms. I nod to him. He stands and reaches a hand out to touch our armor as we pass. I take off my gauntlet, dig into a purse, and toss him a handful of pennies. The boy picks them up and hurls them toward the ship and into the puddle. Not even children will take coins anymore.

We follow the smoldering Stour into the forest. Push through reed and sedge, our mailed boots sinking deep in the waterlogged soil. I hear a second rush of the river in my helmet, like the ocean in a shell. I glance into the misty Stour but see only white nothingness. It is like staring into oblivion. As if the world simply ceases in that channel.

"If the dragon is in there," Tristan says, "I don't think we will find it."

"Let's hope it finds us, then." I did not consider the possibility of not finding the beast. I wonder if Saint George had to search for his wyrm.

"Edward," Tristan says. "I don't want the dragon to find us first. If it finds us before we find it, we will spend eternity in steaming wyrm dung."

"Then stop talking and search." I pick up a branch from the forest floor and push my way through oak leaves to the river's edge. The branch is taller than I am, and when I dip it into the river I cannot touch the bottom. "It's deep here," I say. "Don't fall in."

I push through a scatter of purple harrow, the thorns clawing at my mail like skeletal fingers. It is even darker in the forest. Rain trickling through the leaves mimics footsteps in every direction. At least I hope it is the rain making those sounds. The mist makes it impossible to be sure. Something dark moves by the riverbank. I jump backward, my armor clattering against Tristan's.

"What?" Tristan shouts, breath coming in ragged blasts through his helm, like some great guttering furnace.

The darkness coils and slips past me into the river, which lies a few paces to our right. A water snake.

"Wrong sort of wyrm," I say.

"I propose a new rule," Tristan says. "No jumping unless you are certain you see the dragon."

"You can go first if you want," I say.

"Proceed, Sir Edward."

I proceed.

Dragons have lurked in England for centuries, although I cannot recall hearing of one that lived in my lifetime. The tales of knights slaying these monsters are always ancient ones. Saint George is the most famous of these knights. It is said he slew several dragons in England, including the one at Withermundsford. Lancelot, a knight who lived in the time of a king named Arthur, slew one too. And there are others. Each territory of England has half-forgotten stories of local knights fighting local dragons. But all lived long ago.

"Who was the last knight to kill a dragon?" I ask Tristan.

He chops at a bramble with his sword and shrugs. "Saint Gilbert, I think."

"He was a Scotsman, wasn't he?"

"Aye, Sirrr," Tristan says in a brogue. "Kilt the dragon Dubh Giuthais, he did. Said the words, 'Pity of you, dragon,' and fired an arrow into its heart."

"But Gilbert killed his beast a hundred years ago at least, didn't he?"

Tristan nods. "We could be the only dragon slayers of our time."

"We have to kill the dragon to become dragon slayers, Tristan."

We push through ever-thickening brush. Water trickles into my helmet through the eye slits and air holes, spatters my face. I stumble over fallen, half-buried branches and push through thick patches of bur reed and saxifrage. I worry that we will not find the creature. What happens then? Will we waste days searching for the simpleton? What if he is not in the village? How long will it take to find him? I wonder how Elizabeth is doing and pray her body is holding up better than Morgan's.

"Edward," Tristan says. "Did you see the dragon's eyes when we fought it in the river?"

"No, Tristan," I say. "I was distracted by the massive teeth that nearly took my arm off."

"I saw them," he says. "They were yellow."

"Very good," I say. "Maybe you can paint a picture when we get home."

"Edward," he says. "They were yellow."

"I heard you, Tris…" I stop walking and look back at him. He nods. "Yellow."

"The priest said the dragon eats plaguers."

"And yet its eyes are yellow."

"Maybe the priest lied," I say. "Maybe it doesn't eat plaguers."

Tristan shrugs. "Then where are the afflicted? We haven't seen any in the village. Not one."

I stare back toward Bure and wonder. "That's quite a mystery, Tristan."

"It quite is, isn't it?"

We continue walking. I am tired already. The festering wound still drains me of strength. When we are about fifty paces into the forest, something moves in the mist. I crouch and hear Tristan doing the same behind me. My helm makes it difficult to see, but I do not want to remove it. If the dragon breathes fire, it is the only thing that might save me. I look into the mist. It is no snake this time.

I put a finger to my helm at the place where my lips would be and turn toward Tristan, point to the dark shape. Tristan's helmet bobs up and down. He sees it. I tap him with my hand, then motion with my finger that he should loop around in front of it. Then I tap my chest and motion that I will circle behind it. His helmet shakes side to side. He taps me and motions that I should go in front of it and he behind. I sigh.

The shape moves closer. Slowly, so slowly. I do not think it has spotted us. Despite the danger, I allow myself a smile.

We found the dragon before it found us.

I stay crouched and creep toward the front of the monster. I wish I had a shield. I do not know how many times I have wished that on this quest. Knights do not use shields anymore. They are unwieldy on horseback and our armor is so strong these days that we do not need the extra protection. Not using shields also allows us the use of two-handed weapons. Tristan would laugh if he saw me with a shield, but if dragons are returning to the world, then I think shields should, too.

Tristan creeps forward and loops toward the dragon's flank. We are only a few paces from the Stour, which worries me. It would not be wise to pin ourselves between a dragon and the deep river if things go badly. But if things go badly, then Elizabeth will die. I shake my head. There will be no retreat.

The shape makes a sharp movement, then freezes. Has it heard us? I sit unmoving, breath held. We need to take the beast by surprise. It does not move. I think it knows we are near. We should strike before it finds us. I take a long breath, count to three, and charge.

My war cry is "Elizabeth." I shout it with all my strength and storm toward the dark shape, knowing, as I approach, that it is far too tall to be the dragon. Far too lanky and frail. My war cry echoes flatly in the forest.

The deer plants on its front legs, then leaps to one side and bounds away from me. But Tristan charges from its flank, his war cry of "Hallelujah!" echoing as well. The doe shifts to one side, crouches, then leaps effortlessly over Tristan's hunched form. She lands behind him and vanishes into the mist.

Tristan laughs and turns to me. "Did you see that? Did you see it Edward? She jumped right over me!"

More deer silhouettes appear behind Tristan. I open my mouth to tell him that more deer may jump over him, but they are not deer.

"Tristan!" I slog through lady fern and old leaves, raising my sword high. "Tristan!"

He turns and nearly falls backward from the surprise. Plaguers. At least a dozen of them. And the mist gives birth to more and more of them as I watch.

"To me!" I shout. "To me!"

But Tristan is already backing toward the river. Fool. He will be pinned between river and plague. I run to his side.

"The other way! Back toward the village!"

But I realize why he backed toward the river. There are plaguers behind me too. The afflicted approach in a half circle of snarling death. The mist leeches them of details. They are rotting silhouettes that claw at us, their footsteps like an exhausted army on the march.

Tristan and I stand shoulder to shoulder. One of the plaguers trips in the brush and falls at our feet. I drive Saint Giles's blade through his back, pinning him to the earth. Tristan thrusts over and over again into the back of the man's neck until the head is severed.

Two more approach. I hack through the leg of another man, nearly severing the limb. He topples to the ground. Tristan frees a woman's entrails. When she doubles over in pain, he shatters her skull with a two-handed rising cut. My plaguer crawls toward me and I smash his skull with my boot, knowing I will remember the slow crackling sound for the rest of my days.

Three bodies. A good start.

But many more approach. I think back to a night on the banks of the Thames. Sir Morgan and I shoulder to shoulder, rotting, clawing death closing in on us from all sides. But this is different. There aren't so many against us today. And, unlike the Thames, the Stour does not appear to be tidal. The river is deep, so the dead cannot flank us.

I would be more confident if I did not feel so tired already. My breaths echo in the great helm at the same speed as my thundering heartbeat.

Tristan savages the throat of a thickset man. Three more of the afflicted approach. Then a fourth and fifth. There are too many to count. We give as much ground as we can. Until the river strokes our heels. Our swords carve room for us, but the space we make is taken back instantly as more of the afflicted crowd forward. Some of the plaguers we cut down continue to attack. I feel their hands clutching at my legs, their teeth searching for weakness in my mailed boots. There are too many. Too close. They are inside my fighting distance and I cannot retreat. My sword is now a liability.

I drive the blade down through the back of a crawling man, plunge it deep as I can, hearing the man's high-pitched shrieks as I pin him to the earth. I draw my dagger. And I begin a more personal fight.

My head hurts. There is a whine in my ears, a high-pitched tone that grows louder. I slash the dagger two-handed at a young woman's face and almost lose my balance with the follow-through. I stagger backward and one of my boots slips into the river. I fall to my knees and feel hands grasping at me. Bodies overwhelm me.

I stab and stab at the bodies that hang from me. I do not know where I am striking, only that I am rending flesh, releasing blood, tearing screams of agony from the plaguers. I grab hair, gouge eyes, use my helmet to break skulls, and slash, always I slash. Still on my knees. I must stand or they will smother me.

Tristan holds one gauntleted hand at the center of his sword and swings the weapon like a staff, hacking with the blade and piercing with the tip. He rips open the face of a man who wears a blue silk shirt. The flesh splits like a sliced gourd, revealing the bright red pulp inside.

He turns to me and extends a hand. I take it and he pulls.

For if one falls, the other will lift up his fellow…

I thank God, Mary, and Saint Giles that Tristan is beside me.

The world spins as I stand. Exhaustion. I have reached the point of exhaustion. My limbs feel like limestone blocks. I am still not well. But the dead do not stop. They smother me with their heavy flesh. Get between me and Tristan. I lose sight of him among their bodies. More and more plaguers press against me. I have to push back to keep them from driving me into the river. I plunge my dagger blade into the eye socket of a fat man who has boils over his entire face.

I must find the simpleton.

They hurl themselves onto me, one after another, dangling from my arms and shoulders, holding my waist and legs. Their teeth scrape loudly against my armor, like tiny saws working at tree trunks. They push at me from three sides. We sway dangerously, back and forth. I pry my arm free and raise the dagger over my head. Aim at the nape of a woman wearing a wimple. I have no strength to put behind the blow; I simply let my hand fall. The blade sinks two inches into her neck. She shrieks and throws her head back, which yanks the dagger out of my hand and sends it into the darkness.

I must find the cure.

I raise my gauntlet and drop it on her face. The lobstered plates rattle against her forehead. A man lunges at my neck, his teeth scraping at my bevor. I gather all my strength and strike the woman's face again. Her bones crunch and grind beneath the metal plates of my gauntlet. She screams, her voice nasal behind a shattered nose and cheek.

I must cure Elizabeth.

I put one hand behind her neck. The man pushes at my helmet. I can feel the strap straining against my chin. I draw back once more and use the strength of blooming hysteria to drive my gauntlet through the woman's head. Her face becomes soft and curved. I smell something briny and rich, feel the back of her skull against my fingers.

I will never leave her side again.

Tears come to my eyes as I let the woman drop and turn to the man pulling at my helmet. I grab his face in my hands, feeling a dozen other hands pulling at my armor. Plates rise, straps strain. The man opens his mouth and I slam my great helm into him, shattering his teeth.

Je suis apprivoisé. I am tame.

The tears flow freely, my screams of rage muffled and echoing in the helmet. I cannot stop screaming. I draw back my head and deliver another blow, then another and another. My throat hurts. I slam my helmet into the man's forehead again and again. I do not stop even when the man's hands fall limply to his sides. My helm slips against the wet mess of his skull but I do not stop.

I'm sorry, Elizabeth. Mea maxima culpa.

There is not enough of the man's head left to strike, so I look for the next plaguer. I spin in a half circle and see one wearing armor. I grab his shoulders and realize that it is Tristan and that he has been shouting at me. I do not know for how long. He places both hands on my helm and looks into my eyes. His mouth moves; he is saying something, but I cannot hear it. All I hear is my breathing and the echoes of my gauntlets striking the woman's face. Caving in her skull. The Stour is like a thunderous waterfall in my great helm. Each breath I take is like the roar of a bear. I cannot focus. My knees tremble.

"Gone!" Tristan shouts. "All of them! They are gone! Speak to me, Ed! *Speak to me!*"

I blink my eyes and stoop, then collapse to the ground. My wrist hurts. Why does my wrist hurt? I hurt it. The doctor…the nun…

I claw at my helmet. I cannot breathe.

Tristan kneels beside me and helps me with the straps. I throw the great helm off and take deep gasps of air. Steam rises from beneath my bevor. I pull off my gauntlets and look at my wrist. It is red and swollen and I feel the familiar fire in my arm.

Plaguer bodies form two half-moon ramparts around us. They lie in twisted, bloody, mangled stacks. Some of them writhe. I estimate fifteen or twenty bodies. Not enough.

"What...what happened to the rest?" I say.

Tristan takes his gauntlets off and scoops water from the Stour in his cupped hands. He pours it over my head. "I don't know. They just left."

"What do you mean they left?" It is lighter by the river. The setting sun is burning its way through the clouds, turning the skies into a blazing forge. "Plaguers...don't just leave."

Tristan looks up the Stour, then down it, then collapses to his knees by the river, his breathing labored. "I'm...very wary of it. I felt a chill when they left, but I'm glad they did." He scoops more water from the river. "I don't think we would have made it. Maybe the—"

The Stour explodes in a roaring eruption of white water, foam, and the most terrifying jaws I have ever seen. Craggy, sculpted jaws lined with jagged white teeth the shape of thorns and as long as my forefinger. The creature's head is nothing but mouth, and it is a mouth like nothing on earth. It is Lucifer's man-trap. A cave with knife-blade teeth. Plateaus of gnarled rock splitting and swallowing the world. It is the very gateway to hell.

And it shuts on Tristan with the sound of a cell door slamming forever closed.

Chapter 29

THE DRAGON'S JAWS CLAMP SHUT around Tristan's waist and
the beast tosses its head to one side, scaled muscles rippling,
whipping him effortlessly off the riverbank and into the
Stour. Knight and beast vanish underwater. It happens so
quickly that a moment after the attack it seems like Tristan
was never there.

"*Tristan!*" The mist roils and water churns but I cannot
see them. There is nothingness again, an oblivion that has
swallowed them both. "*Tristan!*"

I scramble to my feet and crouch, ready to leap into the
river after him, but I hesitate. I cannot help Tristan if I am
trapped at the river bottom. The weight of my armor will
sink me, and we will both drown. If we are not eaten first.
But what choice do I have? Tristan dies while I debate. I lean
toward the river, bend my knees and—

A gauntleted hand rises among the mist. It waves violently, slaps the surface. I reach toward it. "Tristan! *Tristan!*"
My fingers brush against his fingers. I grab the thin tendril
of an oak branch and lean forward, my entire torso now

over the water. My fingertip touches his gauntlet. My fingers close on his fingers. And then he is torn from me.

The hand travels upstream swiftly, appearing and disappearing in the mist for ten or fifteen feet. It becomes an arm, then shoulders and a great helm. Tristan sucks in a deep, wheezing breath. He screams my name, his voice cracking and high pitched. The mist parts and closes behind him as the dragon propels him through the water. He strikes at the dragon with his fist. The monster rolls. Tristan flips sideways and vanishes into the Stour once more.

I run along the bank, pushing through branches and shrubs and unbuckling my sword belt. I glimpse the white belly of the dragon as it rolls and then the mist hides even that from view. But they are less than ten feet from the bank.

I wrap the leather belt tightly in both hands, feel the bite of the cold metal buckle. Then I leap into the Stour.

In these times of madness, only madness will save us.

I spread my body to its full length as I leap. I stretch my arms out forward, the belt forming a two-foot link between my hands. It seems like I hang in the air forever, suspended over coiling white clouds. The water will never come. I am in purgatory again. I am a hairy tick and I dangle over the hairy sea.

When I finally hit the water, I find it surprisingly warm. It surges over me. Floods in through every crevice of my armor. I can see nothing but frothing river. My arms hook around an object that I pray is Tristan. One of my hands touches rough warts and scales. My chest falls on something that does not like being fallen upon. It thrashes and whips its body. Tosses me like a hound's toy. But I am hooked to Tristan.

The water froths. I think it has released Tristan, because he and I drift downward. The monstrously spiked tail sweeps past my eyes. Dirt and debris cloud the water. And then I see something gleaming and white. The jaws of the beast. Breath leaves me in a thousand bubbles. The dragon flashes past and I get a closer look at its lunatic grin. Meet the gaze of one jutting, serpent-slit eye. The tail thumps me and sends me reeling in the water as the wyrm sweeps past.

Tristan and I sink. My lungs feel like lead. My head throbs. My boot touches soft mud and sinks to my shin. I shove toward the shore, drag Tristan with me. My other boot sinks into the mud a few feet closer to the riverbank. I feel like sleeping. The lap of the river is soothing. The milfoil caresses my cheek. Sleep. My arms relax. Darkness eats at the edges of my vision. I struggle against it, bubbles rising from my lips. But the last breath escapes my mouth and I ascend to heaven.

I open my eyes and cough. If I am in heaven, then I am terribly disappointed. I cough again, on my hands and knees, water leaving my mouth like vomit. Heaven is a leafy riverbank in a dark forest and apparently it is full of coughing men. I cough and look sideways. Tristan is on his hands and knees, and he too coughs water. It trickles from the breathing holes of his helm. I recall, somewhere in the shadowy depths of my mind, him pulling me from the river. He throws off his helmet, vomits more water, then sits up on his knees, and tosses me my sword belt. His eyes scan the river carefully.

"I propose a new rule," he says. "If plaguers run away, then we should too."

I cough. Did the plaguers really run from the dragon? I have never seen plaguers run from anything. "Are you injured?"

"Yes," he says. "That monster tore off a large chunk of my pride."

"A mortal wound for you," I reply.

"No. I'm not injured." He runs his hands over his face. "Why, exactly...are we hunting this thing again?"

I shrug. "The only dragon slayers of our time. Something of that nature."

"We've done quite a bit in our time," he says. "We're quite selfish really. Young knights need accomplishments, too."

"And old knights need to find a cure for the plague."

"Yes, yes, but did you see its teeth, Edward? Those claws?" He shakes his head, then smirks at me. "Besides, alchemy is a sin."

There is less than an hour of sunlight left, but I resolve not to leave until we have slain the dragon. I recover my sword from where I left it in the ground. The plaguer I pinned to the forest floor with it grasps and hisses, tries to stand. I jam the blade into the back of his skull and he stops moving.

We scour the shore, using leaf-strewn branches to sweep at the fading mist. I feel lightheaded and my wrist throbs with pain. Perhaps that idiot doctor was right. Maybe the stars are not in my favor. I have fought nearly everything there is to fight in Europe and have never been defeated. But a one-inch gash on my flesh threatens to put me in the ground.

"Perhaps we should wait until tomorrow," Tristan says. "They will throw Sara into the river again. The beast will wander to the village to be pampered and fed. Then we can leap out from the forest and give it a little of *God's Love.* See how *it* enjoys being ambushed."

I continue walking, waving my branch at the river and holding my sword out toward the water. Tristan lost his sword in the Stour. I think that is the third sword he has lost on our travels.

"We don't know if the dragon will come for Sara," I say. "And if it does, it might not come for hours."

"Of course it will come for her, Edward. No monster can resist a free meal." He frowns. "I can't resist a free meal either. Does that make me a monster?"

"No," I reply. "The things you do and say make you a monster."

The mist is not so thick now. I spot something in the water. Eyes staring from beneath the river? I reach forward and shake the branch at it. The leaves chatter but the object in the water does not move. I pick up a flint and throw it. The stone glugs and sends a tiny crest of water into the air directly in front of the eyes. But it is no dragon. Just a submerged branch.

"Ed, let's go back to the village and get a fair night's rest so we will be ready for the dragon tomorrow. It doesn't matter if we spend the next two hours walking up and down this river. We won't see it—it's too dark. The dragon is going to find us first again. Remember how we fared the last time that happened?"

"It won't find us first," I say.

"How can you be so sure of that?"

I point to a row of white teeth that seem to glow in the dark, thirty paces farther up the riverbank. The branches of a shaggy chestnut dip down to the ground by the Stour and the dragon has pulled its upper body onto them.

"We found it first." Tristan sounds surprised.

I study the creature. It is the first time I have seen it at rest. Its back is studded with rows of squat, stony spikes, like sharpened warts. The size of the monster's head staggers me. It is nearly as long as my arm, the jaws so wide that I could place my breastplate inside them without touching the creature's flesh. The eyes sit atop the head like burled knots in petrified bark. Its legs, flopped on either side of the thick body, look ridiculously small: bent things, armored in scales, and clawed. I wonder how they can support the weight of the mighty creature they are attached to.

"How do we get to it," Tristan says, "without it either slipping into the river or burning us to cinders?"

"I'm not convinced that it breathes fire," I say.

"It burned down Wormingford."

"And who told you that, Tristan?" I ask.

"Father Ralf," he replies. He sees my look and shrugs. "The man who sacrifices women to keep himself safe."

"So tell me, how would Father Ralf know it burned Wormingford?" I ask. "And if the dragon could breathe fire, don't you think the priest would have seen it by now? He would have mentioned that when Belisencia asked him if the monster breathed fire."

"Very strong points," Tristan says. "But the dragon can refute all of them with one breath."

"Then why didn't it?" I ask. "It had us both sitting on the riverbank within a foot of each other. It could have roasted us together. But it didn't."

Tristan shrugged. "Maybe it wasn't that hungry. You know how quickly roasts go bad. And it doesn't look like it has much patience for salting and drying."

"I'm not saying we shouldn't be careful. But I think if it were going to burn us, it would have done so earlier."

"Very well, Sir George," Tristan says. "So how do we slay it?"

"The same way it tried to slay us."

"Sounds like a good plan," Tristan says. "But I'm not going to be the one that bites it."

Chapter 30

WE CREEP THROUGH THE FOREST slowly, as silently as we are capable, inching forward with infinite patience. Knights are not good at moving silently through forests. Tristan and I break branches and shatter leaves no matter how slowly we walk. But fortunately dragons do not seem to have good hearing. We reach the chestnut upon whose branches the dragon rests and I glimpse the white blades of the creature's teeth in the dying light. I can only just see Tristan at my left. The waxing moon turns the river to quicksilver, but in the forest there is only pitch. There will be no other chances tonight. I must kill it now, or Elizabeth loses another day. And I do not think she has many days left.

I skulk forward, my sword wrapped in a cloak I tore from a dead plaguer. The dragon is less than three paces from me. The creature looks more evil now that the night has leeched the color from it. It is a black demon on the riverbank, and I have come for its blood.

I take one more crunching step and stop when the dragon's head swings to one side. It has heard us. Or perhaps it has known of our presence all along but will not tolerate us to come any closer. A gap in the branches allows me an unobstructed view of the beast. I hope I am right about the flames. The creature lies motionless again, its massive head tilted away from us. Perhaps it sees from the side, like falcons.

I nod to Tristan.

"How did I end up as the bait?" he whispers.

"Because we know that it likes the taste of you." My whisper sounds metallic in the great helm.

Tristan rises and creeps away slowly. If the dragon hears him, it does not react. Tristan slinks farther to my left, a choir of snapping branches, mashed leaves, and clinking metal. The dragon does not move.

When Tristan is ten paces from me, he turns toward the river and trudges forward. He looks my way and crosses himself. He is joking but I know there is terror in his heart. The dragon nearly killed him last time.

He reaches the riverbank and rises to his full height ten paces from the monster. I wonder how fast the beast is on land.

"What say we try this again, you ugly serpent?" he says. The dragon does not react. "I was named after a dragon slayer, Sir Tristan, who slew a dragon much larger than you to win a princess."

The dragon remains motionless.

"You're nothing like Tristan's dragon." He jumps up and down, making his armor clatter. "I'll be lucky to get a one-legged whore for the night when I kill you."

The dragon turns its head toward me and I imagine that it is looking at Tristan now.

"Didn't like that, did you?" Tristan laughs. "Maybe I'll tie a rope around your mouth and lead you into the village, like Saint George did before killing your kin."

The beast pivots toward Tristan and hisses, its mouth opening like a trapdoor to hell. I rise to my feet slowly.

Tristan hunches down and stares into the caverns of the creature's mouth. I can hear his breathing from here. Nothing stands between him and the dragon. One burst of flame can turn Tristan to charcoal. But I know I am right about the fire. Nothing in this forest has been burned.

I pray I am right about the fire.

I creep forward and draw my sword from the cloak, place the fabric on the ground silently. The dragon's mouth is still open and it still faces Tristan. I have one chance. I may never get another opportunity like this. I take a long, slow, quiet breath. I think of Elizabeth and crouch.

"Pity of you, dragon," I whisper.

And I leap.

Dragons are faster than they look. Those flimsy legs at their sides are capable of quick, powerful movements. The monster lurches to one side and then back toward the water as I crash down with an overhead thrust of my sword. The shift to the side was a bit of tactical brilliance by the beast, because the thrust of my blade does not end in the creature's spine as I had hoped. The sword buries itself halfway into the soft clay of the riverbank. But the dragon does not escape cleanly.

One of the floppy, clawed legs gets between the blade and the ground.

Saint Giles's sword pierces the scales, cuts through flesh, splinters bone and severs the foot. The dragon's mouth springs open and a rattling, guttural roar—so powerful that I feel the wind of it through my visor—shreds the quiet night. If it were ever going to breathe fire, this would be the time. I cover my helmet with one arm and raise the sword for a second strike.

The dragon slips backward, roaring once more. My sword cuts a gash into its snout before the beast slips into the Stour. I dive forward and slash again, but the blade cuts only water as the dragon pulls its legs flush to its body and the massive tail catapults it downstream.

"I see it!" Tristan shouts. He runs downstream, stepping over branches and pushing through shrubs. "Hurry!"

The dragon shows up well: a deep black shape among the bright shine of the moonlit river. Much of the mist has lifted and we track it downstream.

It moves swiftly, curling its body from side to side and thrashing its tail. We follow it, crashing through the underbrush until we come to a jumble of massive stones that lie against the river. We try to clamber over them, but clambering and armor are things that do not go well together. I peer over the first boulder and watch as the dragon slips to the side of the river and disappears in a watery hole beneath one of the massive stones.

"It's under the rocks," I say. "It's trapped itself."

"I believe what you mean to say," Tristan replies, "is that it has entered its lair to await our arrival so it may eat us."

He shoves me up onto the boulder and I pull him up after me. His breastplate scrapes against the stone as he struggles to his knees and stands beside me. I can just see the dragon hole from where I stand. A small, waterlogged cavern at the base of the rocks. We would have to wade the river to enter. I am not certain I can fit comfortably inside the cave with my armor. And I am not certain I want to try.

"It'll die now," I say. "Won't it? It will bleed to death."

"I'm not certain," Tristan replies. "It doesn't seem like a creature that would die from losing a foot."

I dwell on the likelihood of such a wound killing the dragon, watching the underwater cave for any sign of the monster. "Course it will die," I say. "Remember that Danish king who killed the dragon? Tore its arm off and the beast scurried away to die?"

"That was Beowulf," Tristan replies, "and he tore the arm off a different sort of creature. The dragon killed Beowulf."

"Oh." I stare at the cave again. I do not want to fight this creature anymore.

The river brushes the boulders, but there is a tiny jut of soggy land just downstream of us with a scattering of smaller boulders upon it. An idea comes to me.

I navigate along the ridge until I am directly above the jut of land. It is six feet down.

"Lower me," I say.

Tristan takes my hand and lowers me slowly. This would be a terrible time for the dragon to emerge from the cave. I watch the opening in the rocks carefully as I descend. When I land, my boots squish onto the grassy earth.

"Come down," I say.

Tristan lays flat against the rock, belly down, and clambers toward me. I glance into the cave. Something white glimmers. Is that a tooth? I grab Tristan's legs, my eyes on the cave, and guide him downward. "Hurry up!"

Tristan slides down to the soggy earth and draws his dagger. I point to the rocks on the ground. "Help me with these boulders."

We lift one of the larger ones. It is about the size and shape of an anvil. We lug it toward the cave, swing it back and forth a few times and hurl it toward the opening. It lands with a splash that soaks us both, but the stone blocks part of the entrance.

"We could have been the only dragon slayers of our time," Tristan says as we heave another boulder from off the ground.

"No, you were right," I reply. "We should leave some accomplishments for the younger knights." We hurl the boulder toward the cave and it lands crookedly but blocks more of the cavern entrance. "Besides," I say, "it will die in there. So we are just slaying it slowly."

"One more boulder ought to do it," Tristan says.

We pick one with a shape similar to the opening that is left in the cavern, but it is half-buried. We dig with our fingers.

"Dig faster, Edward," Tristan says.

I glance at the cavern and can just make out a row of white teeth. I dig faster.

We rock the stone back and forth until it is free from the earth, then roll it to the water's edge. The white teeth move and the moonlight shines off a bleeding snout.

"Hurry!" I say. We groan and lift the boulder, stagger into the knee-deep water.

"It's coming out!" Tristan shouts.

The head of the dragon peers out from the cave. It opens the great mouth again, and I imagine a gout of flame spraying out. I imagine my armor growing red hot, my skin searing to the metal, flames flooding through my eye slits and breathing holes, melting the flesh of my face.

"Throw it!" I shout.

We swing the boulder back once, then hurl it as the dragon crouches and readies itself to spring. I fall to my hands and knees in the water with the effort.

Perhaps the creature's missing foot keeps it from springing. Or maybe it simply feels safe in the cavern. I do not know how dragons think, but the beast doesn't leave its cave. It lowers itself onto its belly, floating in the water, and backs into the cavern as the boulder falls and seals the monster into its tomb.

Chapter 31

THE LITTLE BOY STILL PLAYS with his boat outside the church. His eyes are even wider when he looks at us. We are caked in mud. Our armor is gouged and scraped from the rocks. Tristan bears monstrous teeth marks on his right cuisse and across the tasset and fauld that sit upon his waist.

"I suppose Saint George was spotless after his dragon?" Tristan says without looking at the child. We wade through the puddle, overturning his boat, and enter the church.

Belisencia and the old woman still sit in the frontmost pew. Belisencia runs to us and hugs Tristan tightly, then she backs away, clears her throat, and embraces me. Not as tightly.

She looks us up and down and covers her mouth with her hand. "You look awful. Are you hurt?"

We remove our helmets, and I shake my head. "Nothing that a pint of beer won't cure."

"Ith it done?" the old woman says.

Tristan nods. "We have thlain the therpent that thtalkth the River Thtour," he says.

The woman squints and cocks her head. "What?"

"Yes, it is done." I throw the dragon's foot onto the floor in front of her. "The beast will never bother this village again."

The woman cackles. "You did it! By God and Mary, you did it!"

"We have fulfilled our part of the bargain, old woman," I say. "Now take us to the simpleton."

The woman stops laughing. She studies me for a long moment, then nods. "I will take you to him."

She pulls the woolen shawl over her head again and we leave the church. The boy picks up the boat when he sees us and follows.

We walk around the church, past a small cemetery, and toward a field crowded with wet sheep in their thick summer coats. The woman takes us to a stone wall bordering the field and points to a rotted wooden hut in the distance. "There," she says. "The thimpleton lieth there."

"He lives in that rotting husk?" I study the building. It looks abandoned. A sheep bleats in the distance.

"No," she replies. "There." And I see what she is actually pointing at: a crudely cut tombstone jutting from the earth like the old woman's single tooth.

"The thimpleton was the dragonth firtht victim."

Episode 6

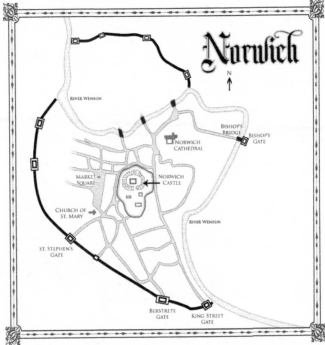

Chapter 32

I AM PLAGUED.

I have no direction. No thoughts. No *reason*. Only a hunger for something that I will never have. A driving, mindless hunger for the smile of a woman who will never smile again. The rain lashes down, drenching me, the drops striking distant leaves like muffled laughter. The world laughs at me. I am a lost soul, and I will wander purgatory for eternity. My mind has nothing to bind it to this world.

The third plague has found me.

It is difficult to see tears in a driving rain, but I slip the great helm over my head anyway, sealing my grief within its metal walls. I fasten the strap without taking my eyes from the crooked gravestone that lies only a caber toss away.

"Go," I say, but no one notices. "Go! Leave me!"

"Edward." Tristan places a hand on my shoulder, his mailed gauntlet grating against my pauldron.

I shrug the hand off and push him backward, roughly. "Leave me! Go away! Go!"

"There is still ho—"

"*Get away from me!*" I do not want to hear the word that Tristan was about to speak. Not when the only link to the alchemist is a crudely carved, half-buried granite slab. Tristan's jaw tightens. He stares at me, a bead of water dangling from the tip of his nose. He nods, dislodging the droplet. "I'll be in the tavern." He trudges back toward the village. Belisencia embraces me and follows, the old woman not far behind.

I fall to my knees, bring my hands to the great helm and cry. Violent sobs shake my body. I pound the wet earth with my gauntlets, the rattle of plates like the jangling keys of a jailer—a jailer standing just out of reach, laughing, laughing, laughing. I reach into the pouch at my belt and draw out Elizabeth's glove. It is soaked from the river and stained with silt and mud. I can no longer recognize it as Elizabeth's. I hold it in both hands and let the grief ravage me.

"Was he your son?"

I stifle the sobs and straighten my back, tuck the glove back into my pouch, and look behind me. Rainwater blots my visor slits. I have to shake my head to get a clear view. It is the blond boy who followed us from the church.

"Get home, child," I say, my voice gravelly.

"He were always kindly to me, your son," he says.

"*Was* always." I think of Zhuri when I correct the child. The Moor and Tristan used to correct everyone's English. "And he wasn't my son."

Elizabeth and I never had children. The Wardieu women were not known for their fertility and I was in France too often to give it a proper effort.

The boy looks at me with narrowed eyes. "A carpenter we had in the village tried to bugger a boy named Thomas, once."

It takes me a moment to realize his implication. "I wasn't buggering the simpleton. Does your mother know you talk like that?"

"I ain't got no mother," he replies. "So I think she don't know. If he weren't your son and you weren't...wasn't buggering him, then why are you so sad?"

"*Weren't* buggering him," I say. "You were right the first time."

He squints at me. "Right about him being your son, or about you buggering him?"

"Neither," I say. "You said *wasn't* bugg...Oh, never mind. Go home."

"He was nice to me. I cried when he died, too." He walks back toward the village.

I watch him for a few heartbeats, then call out, "Did he ever talk about the island?"

He stops and looks over his shoulder at me. "Island?"

"Yes. I understand he worked for an alch...a man who lives on an island fortress." The boy stares at me and I wave him away. "Never mind. Go home. Get dry and warm."

"He couldn't go there no more," the boy says. "He couldn't work for that man no more."

My heart quickens. I take three cautious steps toward the child. "Did he ever tell you where it was? Did he talk to you about the island? About the man who lived in the fortress?"

The boy studies me for a long time, the rain flattening his blond hair into spikes that fall past his eyes. "He didn't like to talk about that."

"What did he like to talk about?" I ask.

The boy shrugs again. "Mostly he just talked about some stupid cure for the plague."

Chapter 33

THE BOY TELLS ME HIS name is Theodore. I walk with him into the village and join the others at a table inside the The Six Bells, a tavern on the Essex side of the Stour. It is a low-ceilinged, smoky, great-hearthed place with dozens of old horse bridles dangling from the thick beams. Men sit at tables and stare at us with unveiled enmity. They do not approach us; perhaps the two hand cannons at our side have something to do with that.

Conversations are whispered, punctuated by the sound of wooden mugs against wooden tables. I recognize the bearded man who revealed that the village had run out of virgins. He sees me staring and looks down into his mug.

I trade the silver cross around my neck for four bowls of a pottage stew, three mugs of warm cider, a tankard of murrey for the boy, and four plates of smoked herring.

Theodore tells us that the simpleton's name was Stephen. Pilgrims brought the man to the village after finding him wandering near the Norfolk border. For some reason that Theodore is unaware of, the simpleton told the monks that he lived in Bure. But no one in the village had ever seen Stephen before. The simpleton took to living in the forest, until a man named Humfrey took pity on him and gave him employment as a shepherd. Humfrey fed Stephen and allowed him to sleep in his barn.

"And Stephen spoke of a cure?" The spoon trembles in my hand. I cannot tell if it is from the thrill of hope or from the fever that rises once more inside me. "Did he say it existed?"

"Yes, m'lord," Theodore replies. "He had some of it with him. In his wagon. But I don't think it were a proper cure. He said he were going to sell it and get horses for his wagon and go back to Bure. That's funny, ain't it? Because he *was* in Bure. But he kept telling me he wanted to *go* to Bure. I always tried to explain it to him, but he got confused and sometimes he got cross."

Tristan draws a phial from his shoulder sack. "Did the cure look like this?"

The boy smiles, his eyes wide. "Yes! That's it. You have it too?"

"Don't mind that," I say. The simpleton gave Isabella, the witch, racks and racks full of plague, claiming it was the cure. But Isabella was certain that he had mistakenly brought the wrong phials to her. "Could there be another Bure somewhere?"

Theodore shrugs and slurps at his stew.

"We need a map," I say. "I'll wager there is an island called Bure somewhere, and that's where the simpleton came from." I feel a smile creep across my face and can do nothing to stop it. "We have a name. We can find the fortress now. We can find the alchemist."

"Alchemy is a sin," Theodore says absently, tipping the bowl to drink the broth.

"Everything's a sin," Tristan replies. "Haven't you heard? Except, apparently, breasts. Hallelujah."

"Don't you poison him with your wicked ideas," Belisencia says.

"He's already poisoned," Tristan says. "He was born a sinner. Weren't you, Theodore?"

"You mean that Adam and Eve stuff?" Theodore asks.

"Don't listen to him," Belisencia replies. "Be righteous and faithful and you will be saved."

Tristan turns back to me. "Perhaps we should talk to a ship's captain. A captain would know where this island is for certain."

"We could go back to Hedingham," Belisencia offers. "The de Vere family has a library in their castle. We might find maps that show where this island is."

"How do you know so much about Suffolk?" Tristan asks.

"I think there's a library in the Lutons' Manor at Long Melford," I say. "It's closer than Hedingham Castle." I think of Abigail and sigh. "Although we'd have to fight through plaguers to get at it."

Theodore wipes at his mouth. "Sounds like heaps of work," he says. "I could just show you how to get to the fortress if you like."

Theodore leads us through the rain to the west side of the village, where a whitewashed barn stands on a hill. A thatched farmhouse sits a dozen paces away from it. The blond child tugs at the barn doors, then puts his shoulders to each one and shoves until they are wide open. He gestures inside. An old wagon sits in the dark barn.

"Not much of a fortress," Tristan says.

"It's not a fortress," Theodore replies. "It's a wagon."

"I always mix those two up." Tristan points to the cart and repeats the word "wagon" over and over again to himself. He draws something from his shoulder sack. "Get down off there and I'll give you a slice of anvil."

Theodore laughs. "That's bread."

"Bread?" Tristan looks at the raveled loaf and shakes his head. "It all makes sense now. Edward, remind me to apologize to the blacksmith when we return to Sussex."

Theodore laughs again and Tristan laughs with him. Belisencia smiles. She looks at Tristan with an expression I am certain she does not realize she wears.

"Why are you showing us a wagon, Theodore?" The food has given me strength. Perhaps I will conquer this wound after all.

"Because it were Stephen's," he replies. "And you can't find the fortress without it." He climbs onto the wagon and pats two enormous sacks that lie in the bed. "These are walnuts," he calls, giggling. "That's how he found his way back to the fortress whenever he left. But he couldn't go there no more."

"Walnuts?" Belisencia asks.

The boy jumps down with a thump and runs to the back of the cart. He bounces his thumbnail against a piece of metal jutting from the frame of the wagon just above the wheel. It rings like a tiny bell. "He used to have to get food and things for his master. So he traveled. But he was a baboon. Couldn't find his way back to the fortress.

He weren't…wasn't good with remembering stuff. But he could count." He points to another piece of metal protruding from the rim of the wheel itself. "Every time the wheel spins, the metals hit and they ding. And every ten dings, he tosses a walnut out of the bag. When the bag is empty, he knows he has to turn, and he's only three miles from the fortress."

I think about this, but there is a lot of information the boy has left out. I force myself to remain calm. "That makes no sense, Theodore. How would he know how many walnuts to put in the bag?"

Theodore raises his hands and twists them in childlike bafflement. "I don't know. He said he always went to the gate on the east side of Norwich and started pulling the nuts out of the bag from there. He only needed one bag, but he said he always brought a spare." The boy holds up a flat piece of wood with two curved lines painted into it. "This told him how far to turn the cart when the walnuts ran out. His wagon tracks had to look like this in the grass so that he didn't turn too much, or not enough. He was the cleverest baboon I've ever seen."

"Theodore," Belisencia says. "You shouldn't call people that."

Theodore looks at her, his lip drawn up. "It's a sin to call people clever?"

"I did warn you," Tristan says. "*Everything* is a sin."

"Stop it, Tristan," Belisencia snaps.

"So no matter where the baboon went," I say, "he would return through Norwich?"

"That's what he said."

"A genius among baboons," Tristan says.

Belisencia shakes her head. "Baboon? You two shouldn't be allowed near children."

"Hallelujah," Tristan replies.

I look at the cart in the barn. It will slow us down, make us easy prey. But I do not see a better solution.

Tristan pokes at one of the large sacks and grins.

"In these times of madness, only nuts will save us."

Chapter 34

It is twenty-five miles to Norwich, and another ten to reach the coast. If we could ride swiftly, with little rest, the trip would take a long day. But two of our horses are hitched to the wagon and Tristan rides the third. Barring any delays, it will take us nearly two days to reach Norwich. Two more days for Elizabeth and Morgan. Do they have two days left? The despair saps my strength, rakes my soul like dragon claws.

Our trip would be swifter if I knew the destination. But Stephen the Simpleton did not know how to return to the island. Stephen the Simpleton had to travel to Norwich every time he wanted to find the fortress. Stephen the Simpleton needed a bell, a bag, and a piece of wood to make his way home. I sigh and glance back at the two sacks in the bed of the wagon. My eternal salvation now depends on walnuts.

God is testing me. This is simply a trial I must endure.

"Norwich should be lovely at this time," Tristan says. "With the dogwoods in bloom and the fires of hell bathing the buildings in that warm tangerine glow."

The wagon wheel chimes every time it makes a full spin. We have gone scarcely a mile and already it is driving me mad.

"It is a wonderful city," Belisencia says. "Norwich has the most beautiful cathedral I have ever seen."

"Perhaps the demons inside will sing us a tortured hymn," Tristan replies. "Have we thought this through, Edward? Are we going to ride our singing wagon into the largest city in East Anglia? You saw how much plague there was at St. Edmund's Bury. What do you think Norwich will be like?"

"If you have a better plan, I am anxious to hear it," I reply.

"I think *a* plan would be a good start," he says. "We're just going to roll up to the gates and ride eastward?"

"That's exactly what we're going to do," I say. "We're going to ride eastward until the walnuts run out." I pick up the painted panel of wood. "And then we're going to turn south so that our wagon wheel tracks look like…" I glance at the panel. The curving lines point to the left now. I flip the panel and they point to the right.

"Oh my," Tristan says.

I run a hand over my eyes. The wood clatters as I toss it into the wagon bed.

Hallelujah.

We follow the Stour northward, the relentless chime of metal strips on the wagon wheel attesting to our brisk pace. I know the sound cannot be as loud as it seems, but I cannot help imagining that every plaguer and mad king in England will hear the chime echoing across the heathland.

That our approach is announced for miles by the simpleton's singing wagon.

"I do not mind the sound," Belisencia says. "It makes me feel safe."

Tristan scoffs. "Safe? That sound will kill us all."

Belisencia shrugs. "In the North, when someone dies, they hire a bell ringer to walk at the front of the funeral procession. They say the bell frightens away evil spirits."

Tristan stares at the wagon wheel. "This isn't the North, we're not dead, and this bell won't frighten off evil spirits, it will attract them, silly woman."

"Why must you always be so unpleasant in your blathering?" Belisencia says. "Why must you always disagree with what I say? You can be a vile, arrogant, cruel, and disagreeable man."

"You go too far, woman," Tristan replies. "I don't blather." He leans low in the saddle and squints at the wheel. "Maybe we can take one of the strips off and replace it near Norwich."

"There is no way of replacing the metal strip if we take it off," I say.

Tristan shrugs. "I'm going to scout ahead." He sends a dark gaze toward Belisencia and whips his reins. "Maybe I'll spot the evil spirits as they flee from us." His horse gallops from us swiftly. We watch him for a time without speaking.

"How about that?" Belisencia finally says, her arms crossed. "The bell works."

When we are a few miles outside of Sudbury, we veer off to the northeast. I learned, early in my travels through this plague-swept England, to avoid cities and large towns. The afflicted haunt these places, either because it is easier to find food here than in the fields and forest, or because of some dim, half-remembered attachment to their homes. I do not know why they stay. All I know is that in this plague-swept kingdom, cities and towns are death.

We spot plaguers wandering through dying furloughs of beets and barley. Only a scattered few swivel their heads in our direction and lumber after us as fast as they can, but the cart is too swift for most of them.

A plagued man wearing rusted mail walks into our path a dozen paces away. The skin of his face is cracked and marked by scores of blood-ringed yellow boils. He hisses at us, his teeth black and shattered into sharp edges. Tristan hunches low in his saddle and canters at the man, sword flashing to one side of the horse. Blood spits from the man's throat as Tristan rides past. The plaguer's black eyes stare at me as he falls to his knees. I think he tries to hiss again, but all he manages to do is spray another gout of blood from his wounded neck. He thumps forward like a bag of barley dropped on the road. The wagon wheels chime as I veer the cart around him.

The skies darken as we ride. We have little sunlight left, but I do not plan to stop until we are well on our way to Norwich. We find the Roman road a few miles farther and follow it eastward. Boxford and the Holy Lands lie some-where to the south. I lash the horses with the reins and stare into the distance as if I might see Hugh the Baptist lurching toward me with his cracked lips and bishop's hat. We pass south of Edwardstone, and I listen for the sound of bowstrings, but all I hear is the rattle of the wheels and the ceaseless chime of the simpleton's cart.

Tristan rides at our side and stares southward. "Do you remember Gilbert?" he asks. "All that talk about *reason*."

"I remember," I say.

"And yet, he's nothing but charred bones now." Tristan shakes his head. "This plague doesn't care what you believe in. It eats priests and philosophers alike."

"It is not death that matters," Belisencia says. "It's what happens after death that is important."

"Yes, it's better to rot in a coffin than on a wet field," he replies. "Tidier."

"Someday you will die, Tristan. And you will come face-to-face with God. You will bear witness to the Divine Being that you have denied for so long. And what will you say then?"

Tristan shrugs. "I will thank him for not making breasts a sin."

She shakes her head. "You will regret your constant blasphemy. Sometimes you are worse than the barbaric pagans."

"Barbaric?" Tristan asks. "And why are they any more barbaric than Christians?"

Belisencia scoffs and looks away. "There's no sense talking to you about it."

Tristan laughs. "Go on, tell me. I would like to know what's more barbaric than drinking the blood of our savior every week. Or eating his flesh." He laughs again and sweeps his hand to encompass the countryside. "Maybe all of these plaguers are just good Christians that got carried away. They're drinking *everyone's* blood. Maybe they are more devout than any of us."

"Stop it, Tristan," I say.

"Jesus should have been more precise in his instructions. I'm certain he knows how easily confused we mortals are."

I turn to Tristan and scowl, but he pretends not to see me. He is having too much fun to acknowledge me.

"What was it Jesus said? 'Whoever eats My flesh and drinks My blood has eternal life.'" He waggles his finger and frowns as if lecturing us. "But please, good people, this only works with *My* flesh and blood. Not each other's. Are we clear on that? Do not force me to make another commandment. I am trusting that all of you will remember the distinction. I will be most annoyed if I return from heaven and find all of you shambling around eating one anoth—"

"*Stop it!*" Belisencia's scream is like a thunderclap. "Stop your blasphemy! You may have no respect for God and Jesus and Christianity, but I do. Did no one ever teach you to be silent when speech might offend?"

"Yes," Tristan replies. "The same priest who taught me that I should pluck out my eye if I look with lust upon a woman. And I didn't take that very seriously either."

The day dies slowly as we follow the Roman road for four milestones. We turn at the fourth stone and leave the road, traveling northward upon the flat heaths of northern Suffolk. It was my first time on that particular Roman road, but I have been told it ends after five or six miles at a place called Coddenham. It is a large town, no doubt drowning in plague, and I want no part of it. Cities and towns are death.

A soft rain falls once more. After another mile or so, we turn eastward again until we find yet another Roman road that leads north, to Norwich. I have been on this one.

My wrist is red and throbs with pain. I feel the stirrings of another fever and it makes me irritable.

"Are we still rolling straight into the city with our musical wagon?" Tristan asks.

"We won't go to the very gates," I say. "Two hundred paces away is fine. We can drop a few walnuts before we start."

"Such a shame," Belisencia says. "I would love to see the beauty of Norwich once more. Have you ever been there, Edward?"

"Once," I say. "But I couldn't appreciate the beauty."

"Why not?" Belisencia asks.

"Because I was there with John of Gaunt." The name twists venomously in my mouth. John of Gaunt is uncle to my king, Richard II. I spent three nights in a dungeon because of John and have challenged him to a duel three times.

"You do not like John of Gaunt?" Belisencia asks.

"He is the worst of men," I reply. "Scheming and avaricious. A man who cares only for himself. A man who bullies the weak and cowers before the strong."

"Edward and John are old friends," Tristan says.

The metals chime as I spit. "The worst thing about him is that he is always at King Richard's ear, weakening the boy."

"Is it he that weakens the boy," Belisencia replies, "or is Richard simply a weak boy?"

I open my mouth to speak, then close it and look at her for a long moment before responding. "Richard is my king. And yours too, my lady."

"If he is my king," she replies. "Then where is he?"

"Not knowing where he is doesn't strip him of his crown."

"But I have heard you ask it yourself," she says. "Where is Richard? Where are England's armies? I would like to know this also. Where is Richard? Where were England's armies when the nuns of my convent were being eaten alive?"

"He is our king," I say. "I'm sure that whatever delays him is no fault of his."

"Of course not. According to you, it's never Richard's fault. All of this must be John of Gaunt's fault."

I yank the reins hard and stop the wagon, turn to face her. "Listen to me, woman. Perhaps you have listened to too many stories. There are schemers everywhere in the kingdom. Men who would pull a kingdom from the hands of a boy simply because he is a boy. Richard is inexperienced, but he is brave. He rode out among ten thousand angry peasants when he was fourteen years old and had them cheering for him by the time he was done. It is not lack of courage that keeps him away. It is death, injury, or the pig-licking John of Gaunt that keeps him from acting. Richard is still king, and you would do well to remember that. Do not meddle in affairs that have nothing to do with you, silly girl."

Belisencia's face is flushed red, her lips drawn tight. One of her brows twitches, but she says nothing. She looks away from me and stares at the horses. I feel Tristan's hand on my shoulder.

"Let's talk about something less offensive, eh?" he says. "Do you remember the man buggering that mare on the roadside? That was something, wasn't it?"

I take a long, deep breath and flick the reins. The animals hesitate, so I shout to get them going. They are not wagon horses, and so are not used to the trace and collar. I shout again and they dig into the Suffolk clay and drag us forward once more. Belisencia's gaze never wavers from the two geldings.

We travel for another half mile before darkness consumes the world. I take the wagon far off the road, to the edge of a sparse forest, and unharness the horses. We rub them down and tie them to a grizzled oak. Tristan and I stack rocks and logs on either side of the horses and the cart; with luck, the obstacles will slow plaguers if we are found.

Belisencia sleeps in the bed of the wagon. The space is not long enough for her, so she has to sleep with her knees curled. Tristan volunteers for the first watch, and I am grateful. I strip off my armor and crawl beneath the cart. The last thing I see before sleep claims me is the bottom of the wagon bed, wooden planks that make me feel like I am inside a coffin.

Chapter 35

THE NIGHT IS BLESSEDLY UNEVENTFUL. We hitch the horses to the wagon again and set off at first light. The day has dawned bright and clear, but this is England and I know the clouds will gather soon. I apply more of the salve that the nun gave me at Hedingham. My wrist looks even worse today. The pain has returned to my head. I remember the words that Paul the Doctor spoke to Tristan: *The stars are against your friend. He will probably die in horrible pain.*

Doctors.

Belisencia does not speak to me, nor even look in my direction as we ride. It is probably for the best. I do not want another discussion about the king. Richard lives under the shadow of his father, the Black Prince—may God bless his soul—and his grandfather, Edward III. Both were great men. And though Richard has stumbled at times, I always remind myself that he was only ten years old when the crown was placed on his head. King Richard has his father's blood in him, and with the right guidance I know he can be a mighty king like his grandfather. But he does not have the right guidance. He has John of Gaunt.

Thick, black smoke columns rise in the distance, to the east and north. More of England returning to dust. We pass an abandoned field of barley, the ridges and furrows arching gently in S-curves. I remember my ploughman at Bodiam making those same curves when working the manorial fields. He would drive the oxen onto the fields at an angle, let them drift back to true by midfield, then slowly angle them again for the next furrow. His passes would trace gentle, perfect curves upon the land. I miss Elizabeth, and I miss Bodiam. We had the perfect life and I was completely unaware of it.

Our cart chimes past deserted villages. Millhouses still run but grind nothing. The fields are riddled with skeletons that have been picked clean. There are so many bones that I stop noting the differences between animal and human: they become another part of the landscape. Like hedges and flints.

Our pace is good and sometime in the afternoon we pass out of Suffolk and into the windswept chalklands of Norfolk. We ride ever northward, the winds snapping Belisencia's robe and fluttering the tops of the walnut sacks. A relentless wind that brings earaches and tears.

We make Caistor St. Edmund a few hours before sunset. Caistor is an old Roman village, and I have heard stories that it was a stronghold of the British tribes who were here even before the Romans. I passed through it when I came to Norwich with John of Gaunt. It is large enough that I fear the plaguers that might wander its streets, so I turn the wagon off the road before we enter the village.

I gaze toward Caistor as we pass it, squinting, searching for any life. I spot something near a thatched cottage on the outskirts of the village. A shape moving toward us. The figure stops and watches us pass.

"Is that a plaguer?" Tristan asks.

I shrug.

Another shape limps toward the first. Both are dressed in white and blend in with the pale daub of the cottage. We watch them and they watch us, until the cottage fades from view.

After another mile, we reach a river, the Yare I believe, and I stop the wagon at its bank.

"Norwich isn't far," I say. "We should settle our plan."

"A plan?" says Tristan. "We have a plan?"

"We're going to come at the city from the east. I'm going to bring the wagon as close to the gate as I can. But there will be plaguers. Tristan, you keep them off the cart. When there are too many of them to fight, I'll turn the cart around and we can ride toward the fortress. Belisencia, for every ten chimes you hear, take a walnut out of the bag."

"A fine plan," Tristan says. "Nothing could possibly go awry."

"Do you have a better plan?"

"Yes. We start our journey to the island a mile away from the city. How many walnuts can there be in a mile? Twenty? Thirty? We throw twenty or thirty walnuts out and avoid the city completely."

"And what if it's fifty?" I say. "What if it's eighty? We could miss the island completely."

"What's the difference?" Tristan replies. "We'll hit the coast and be within fifty or eighty walnuts of the island."

"No we won't," I say. "If we turn our cart at the wrong point and go two miles, we could end up a long way from the island. And we don't even bloody know if we have to turn north or south. How many miles would we have to cover then, Tristan? Five miles of coastline? Ten? And Norfolk is full of swamps and rivers. What if we come to something impassable? We could end up on the wrong side of a river and have to travel back for miles before we found a ford." I shake my head. "This mad ritual with the walnuts was created for a reason. It probably navigates past all the obstacles. We are going to do this as accurately as possible." My breath is coming too fast. My chin touches the bevor at my neck and the metal feels icy against my fevered skin. "We are going to get as close to the gate as we can. And we are going to do this properly."

We travel eastward. I spot the first of the plaguers to the north. Small groups of them wandering without aim. They turn to face us and there is a moment of hesitation before they lurch toward us. I have seen many plaguers do this. As if they are startled to see us. As if, for one heartbeat, they have forgotten that we are food. But they remember quickly.

I lash the horses with a branch and the wagon outpaces the afflicted. Tristan rides close to us. "That chiming probably sounds like a dinner bell to them."

When I think we have gone a mile, I turn the wagon northward again, toward Norwich, and I find the first problem with my plan.

Chapter 36

THERE IS A RIVER IN our path.

The Yare again, or perhaps the Wensun. I should have thought this through. I stare into the dark water and watch small clusters of bodies drift peacefully downstream. The bodies do not move, but I know better than to think them dead. Morgan, Tristan, and I found out in a catastrophic way that dead bodies in rivers are rarely dead these days. There were more bodies than this in the Thames when we crossed it. Many more. So many that when they started moving and climbing onto our boat, we capsized. We tumbled into hell itself, plaguers above and below the surface of the water. It was the hairy sea and we were nearly devoured in it.

I stand on the driver's box and squint. I can see the walls of Norwich from the bank of the river. They sweep around the city, a city punctuated by squat, round towers every hundred paces or so. There is no wall on the east side of Norwich, because the river is barrier enough. The east gate is flanked by tall drum towers. We are too far to see if there are plaguers at the eastern bridge. It does not matter. We do not need entrance into the city. We just need to get closer. I sit back down. It is not even possible to start our journey from here, because we are on the wrong side of the river.

I think of the child in Bure. Theodore. What was it he said about the simpleton and the fortress? *He couldn't go there no more.* I begin to understand.

Tristan and Belisencia are silent. I rub at my eyes. The fever is growing worse.

"There is only one choice," I say.

"I truly hope it's not the choice I think it is," Tristan replies.

"Does the choice you are thinking of involve us riding eastward for miles until we find a ford or bridge?"

Tristan cocks his head and squints. "Actually, no."

"Good," I reply. "Because that's not the choice."

"Wait…I like that choice."

I turn the horses to the west and goad them toward the south gate of Norwich.

He couldn't go there no more. Of course he couldn't; he always had to go *through* the city. And sometime in the last few months, the city had succumbed to plague. The afflicted occupy Norwich now, an invading army with soldiers recruited from nightmares.

"Edward," Tristan says. "Let's talk about that eastward choice, shall we? I just want to discuss it a bit. Please? Edward?"

Nothing he says will deter me, and he knows it. This is the only way. We must enter Norwich and cross the entire city to reach the east gate.

Belisencia brings her hands together, closes her eyes, and prays.

We pass an abandoned priory on the banks of the river; high grasses and wildflowers slowly devour the stone buildings. Just past the priory is the first gate. A sign over the entrance declares it to be King Street Gate. It lies just west of the river but it is not the main gate of the city. I do not want to travel through winding streets trying to find our way to the east gate. So we ride past.

Berstrete Gate is a few hundred paces to the west. It is an imposing stone gatehouse with a tall round tower on the left and shorter one on the right, but it is not the one I want, either. I have never been through Berstrete Gate and I do not know where it leads. We rumble past it, and a quarter mile to the west I spot an old leper hospital that I passed the last time I arrived in Norwich. It, too, looks abandoned, and just beyond its overgrown garden lies St. Stephen's Gate. That is the entrance John of Gaunt took me through. It rises like a castle keep from the flint walls of Norwich. Thick, crenelated towers flank the gatehouse. Angels and saints decorate the stonework, and statues of dead priests and bishops fill niches along the walls.

Saint Stephen was a deacon who was stoned to death for disagreeing with church doctrine. I think about the church view of alchemy and grit my teeth as I guide the wagon toward his gate.

"Edward, we will be trapped in that city." There is no humor in Tristan's voice as he calls to me from his horse.

I slow the cart so we can talk. "We won't be trapped, because there won't be enough time. We will storm through the city so quickly that the plaguers won't be able to gather."

Tristan shakes his head and pulls his helmet on. "We'd have a chance if we were all riding horses, but with a cart?" His helmet shakes from side to side.

I put my own helmet on and lash the horses to a canter. "Lie as flat as you can in the cart," I call back to Belisencia. Her lips quiver as she curls up in the bed. I wish I had a dagger to give her, but I lost mine in the forest outside of Bure.

St. Stephen's Gate is open. The spikes of the portcullis poke from the top of the gatehouse like Lucifer's teeth. I take a long, slow breath. In this plague-swept kingdom, cities and towns are death.

I pray to Mary, Giles, and God.

Let us make it through the city. Keep us alive.

I cross myself, kiss the pommel of Saint Giles's sword, and take the wagon through the devil's open mouth.

And I find nothing.

It is a city, nothing more. No armies of plaguers. No dead bodies. Just an abandoned city. Rows of tile-roofed, narrow houses line the northwest side of the cobbled street. Derelict fields lie to the southeast, the ridges and furrows sprouting the first stubble of grass. Our wagon wheels sound like thunder on the silent lane, the chime of the metal strips like a church bell. I squeeze the velvety reins tightly and turn my head to one side, then the other, searching through twin rectangles for the first of the plaguers.

"Where are they?" Tristan shouts. He holds his sword in one hand, swinging the blade toward our own echoes.

I understand how he feels; the anticipation is dreadful. It is like a crossbow pointed at my face. I would prefer them to come all at once than to suffer the torture of waiting.

I spot Norwich Castle up ahead, soaring above us on a motte nearly a hundred feet high. I can make out the great white keep and the walls of the inner bailey. We pass the fields and the houses and reach a baffling junction of streets. Roads split off to the south, the east, the northeast, and the northwest. I stop the wagon and think. The helmet makes my head hurt. It is too hot inside my armor. I do not know which way to go.

"Ed?" Tristan's horse tosses its head. It looks as nervous as Tristan does.

"Give me a moment," I say.

"Why are we stopped?" Belisencia's voice is shrill behind me.

"A moment!" I shout. The Bishop's Gate. The name comes to me from nowhere. Perhaps Mary or Giles felt pity on me. The Bishop's Gate is the eastern gate. It lies near the cathedral, which I remember is northeast of the castle. I study the northeastern road. A trickle of filthy water runs down the central gutter, smelling of sewage and old waste. The road appears to lead directly to the castle. Not where we need to be.

I slap the reins and turn the cart to the northwest. The crisp clatter of our horses' hooves spills out across the city again. A stone church with a Norman tower rises in front of us. The sign by the gravestones declares it to be St. Mary's, and I know I have taken the correct road.

The thoroughfare widens abruptly into a long market square, but there are no stands or marquees. It is empty and eerie. A gust blows a child's filthy hat across the cobble-stones as we rumble through. Homes of wood and halls of pink carstone stand shoulder to shoulder along the square, but no one moves in them.

When I was young, I was often taken to Rye, where French stone shipments arrived with some frequency. My father loved Caen stone, despite its French origins, and used nothing else on the buildings of his manor. Father would lead me to the docks before the sun rose so we could be the first to see the consignments. He taught me to read the stones, to find weaknesses in the great slabs, and to only buy stones that would outlast civilizations. I was often in Rye before the sun rose, before the world woke. It was quiet on those mornings, but you could still hear the town's pulse. The rattle of handcarts. The waking cries of gulls. The boom of sailor's voices. The creak of ropes upon pulleys and the rumble of wooden crates dragged onto ramps. The heartbeat of a city at rest.

But here in Norwich there is utter silence. There is no pulse, no heartbeat. The city does not rest; it is dead. And not even the plaguers want its corpse.

Fear rises in my throat like bile. Why would the afflicted avoid a city? I think of the dragon in Bure. The last time plaguers ran from something, Tristan nearly died. But something else pulses just beneath my fear: a wild hope. Could we cross the city without encountering even a single plaguer? Will our journey through Norwich be bloodless?

We pass a thatched, wooden tollhouse and the market square ends at another crossroad: East or west? I stop the cart. We are still not completely past the castle. It is too early to go east. But the western thoroughfare takes us in the opposite direction to where we want to go.

"East." I call to Tristan, but he looks at something on our left. I follow his gaze across the square to a narrow alley between a row of three-story homes and workshops. A figure walks toward us. A normal gait. No lurching. No shambling.

My breath quickens and for an instant I mourn humanity; I mourn because I have learned to fear my kinsmen even more than I fear the plaguers ravaging our kingdom.

The figure walks toward us more quickly. There is something odd about its head. Tristan and I draw our swords at the same time.

"Stop!" I shout. "I am Edward of Bodiam. What do you want?"

The figure does not stop. It walks toward us at an even faster pace.

"Halt!" I shout. But the figure trots, then runs slowly, then sprints toward us, its arms pumping wildly. The thing shrieks, its cry like the trumpet of Judgment Day in the noiseless city. I get a good look as the figure clears the shadows. The world spins.

Matheus was right. Hugh the Baptist was right. We are in purgatory.

The creature running toward me is a demon.

Chapter 37

THERE IS NO TIME TO escape. I leap from the wagon, feeling unsteady from fever, feeling the faint protest of my ankle, which still throbs occasionally under weight.

I have no doubt that the creature is a demon. The left side of the fiend's face oozes and bubbles as if the flesh were made from melted wax or boiling pitch. The forehead bulges monstrously on the left side, like ten loaves' worth of yeast rising, a deformation so large that I wonder how it keeps its head from lolling to one side. It wears a torn and filthy white robe.

The demon howls again as it nears us. Tristan canters toward it, his sword raised high in the air, but his horse rears. It is not a warhorse, but I imagine even warhorses would rear at such a creature. The fiend hurls itself at Tristan. Its hands reach forward, its misshapen mouth open. The demon crashes into the rearing horse, battering it with its grotesque flesh, knocks the animal to one side so that it almost topples. The fiend's oversized teeth rip into the animal's neck. The horse cries out and tries to rear once more, but the demon's weight holds it down. Tristan leans low and hacks again and again with his sword, sending spatters of blood and strips of dirty cloth into the air.

Belisencia screams just as I reach Tristan. I whirl and see another demon sprinting toward the wagon from the opposite side of the square. One of its arms is far too big. I run back toward the cart and see another figure emerge from a workshop door. And yet another leaps from a second-story window. This last one falls to the cobblestones, then scrabbles to its feet and runs at the wagon, screaming the gibberish of madmen.

I take position between the cart and the approaching monsters. The first has a nose so misshapen and swollen that it simply looks like a thick cut of meat thrown across the face. The left eye is a black, glistening slit that lies slanted halfway down the cheek. One arm is swollen to an impossible size, as if pigs had burrowed beneath the skin and died there.

It leaps at me from three paces away. I slash and spin, and the demon's body strikes my shoulder and tumbles to the cobblestones. I stagger to one side and fall to a knee. The creature rises. Blood from my slash seeps into the chest of the white woolen robe. Its good eye is dark as Satan's arsehole and ringed in red.

"Tristan, they're plag—" Something strikes me in the back with enough force to knock me prone. I roll onto my back and kick at the grotesque form above me. One eye protrudes from the side of the face like that of an enormous frog; a great bubble of an eye that looks as if it was nailed haphazardly against the melted flesh of its temple. I thrust my sword through that bubble and a rancid brown fluid erupts from it, trickles into my air holes and spatters warm upon my cheek. It smells like rotting milk. The creature does not even hesitate. It continues to claw at me, its shapeless teeth snapping. Do these demons not feel pain?

Belisencia calls for Tristan. The other fiends. I grab the creature's bloated shoulder with one hand and shudder as my fingers sink deep into the soft flesh. I push the demon backward and try to drive my sword into its mouth. It is too close to me. The tip enters its mouth, but at an angle, and I have to slowly carve my way into its skull, straightening the sword little by little. Blood runs down the length of the blade. The demon makes choking sounds but does not stop clawing at my helm. I withdraw the blade and slash its neck. Then angle the blade deep into its other eye. The creature gurgles and flails like a herring in the net, but still it claws at me. I drive the blade all the way to the hilt. Twist it. Saw at the head until the monster stops moving. Then I kick the body away and scramble to my feet. I sway and look for my next foe.

Tristan's horse is dying on the cold stones of the market square. Its legs kick and its eyes roll. Tristan staggers in front of the wagon. The demon I slashed at the start of the melee is wrapped around one of his legs. Another fiend lies motionless in front of him. Belisencia stands in the cart holding Tristan's knife. The body of the very first demon lies on the other side of the cart.

I run to Tristan's side and together we plunge our swords into the last demon until it stops moving. It takes a long time. These demons do not die as easily as Frenchmen or plaguers.

We scarcely get two breaths before we hear more footsteps. These are on the far side of the square, near the crossroads we passed.

"Get in the cart!" I shout. Tristan lunges half into the wagon bed and kicks at the air. Belisencia pulls at the bottom edge of his backplate until he tumbles inside.

I climb onto the driver's box and whip the reins. I lost my branch but the horses do not need it anymore. They hear the demons behind us, same as we do. Their shoes slip and strike sparks from the cobbles as they flee to the east.

My eyes flash across a sign that names the road we are on—St. Giles Street. I do not know if it is a good thing or bad thing to be on a road named after the patron saint of insanity. The horses gallop at a pace faster than I have ever seen from them. The wagon rattles and jolts on the stones. Chimes ring out like a servant bell rung by a furiously impatient lord. The castle rises above us.

St. Giles Street circles the great castle motte to the northeast. And as we loop to the rear of the castle, I hear the mad slaps of leather shoes and bare feet behind us on the cobblestones. I glance back. Six or seven of the demons chase us.

"I'll deal with them!" Tristan shouts. "Just get us out!"

A lane splits northward and I take it. The horses turn so quickly that the wheels on the right side rise off the cobblestones. I let go of the reins and claw at the seat to keep from sliding off. A crash sounds from behind me as Tristan and Belisencia tumble against the wooden wall of the cart.

The wagon drops back to the ground and I grab the reins. The demons are a dozen paces back, but more appear from alleys and doorways.

Tristan lifts one of the bags and dumps the walnuts out of it. The nuts fall in a noisy shower and clatter behind us as we go.

"Are you mad?" I shout. We have lost our spare bag.

"Watch," he replies.

I glance back again. The demons reach the walnuts. They run over and past them without slowing. Tristan brings both hands to his great helm. "How did that not work?"

"You are a *baboon!*" Belisencia shouts.

The road ends in a junction that branches to the east and west. I have to bring the wagon almost to a halt to make the sharp turn. We turn eastward.

And the demons are upon us.

The cart lurches as fiends hurl themselves at it.

I glance back and see one demon halfway into the cart. Its lips are swollen to horrifying proportions, thick as sword blades, bulging and glistening across half of the monster's enormous face. It hisses. Massive jaws open to reveal over-sized yellowed teeth, each tooth thicker than my thumb.

Boil-covered hands claw for purchase at the back edge of the wagon, where another demon looks to be dragging behind us. More demons reach for the cart. I glance forward and notice, for the first time, the great cathedral of Norwich. The spire stabs the sky like a sword, white in the sunlight. The Bishop's Gate lies past that great church.

I peer over my shoulder. Tristan grunts as he kicks at the boulder-jawed demon. Belisencia cowers at the opposite wall and makes hesitant jabs at the hands holding the back edge. Another demon leaps at the cart and scrambles into the wagon near Belisencia. A thick globule of skin, as big around as a shield, dangles from its chin and sways with the jostle of the cart. Belisencia screams and kicks at the creature. One of her feet catches the dangling skin and sets it rocking like a cauldron in a gale. She grunts and kicks at the creature's legs.

The cathedral ward opens up ahead of me. I follow the curving road around the ecclesiastic buildings. We are close. So close.

Tristan gives a cry of victory. I glance back and see both the demons that were in the cart now rolling on the cobblestones. Several of the pursuing fiends stumble over the fallen bodies.

The elaborate arches of the Bishop's Bridge lie directly ahead. I slap the reins, shouting at the horses, but they need no encouragement. Froth spatters back from their mouths, lather blossoms on their necks, but they run. God bless the poor creatures, they run.

I look back once more as Tristan hacks at the hands of the dragging demon. Our wagon outpaces the other monsters, and many of them do not run so swiftly anymore. Perhaps they have given up. I feel a stab of apprehension. I have learned to fear those moments when our enemies grow quiet.

Tristan slashes at the pair of grotesque hands that clutch the back of the wagon, taking two fingers. He positions himself for a better angle and hacks down toward the monster's wrists with a swift precision. But the demon gives a roar and lunges forward at the same instant, pulling its bloated chest into the wagon. The sword blade buries itself into the fiend's back instead of severing a hand.

Thick folds of pinched skin obscure most of this monster's features. The eyes are barely visible, black raisins in mangled dough. Tristan draws the sword free, then uses his hands to shove the monstrous, sagging face backward. It is a struggle. The two fight a silent battle of will and leverage. Tristan gains ground with each heartbeat. The demon pounds at Tristan's helm as its neck arches backward farther and farther. Tristan wedges a booted foot under its chest and shoves. The demon screeches and tumbles to the cold stones.

But it takes the last sack of walnuts with it.

Chapter 38

I HEAR THE WALNUTS CRASHING and rattling to the stones behind us. The demon lies on the road, still clutching the sack, staring at us with misaligned black eyes. Two more demons run toward us; they pick up their pace as if regaining lost motivation. I do not look at them. All I can do is watch the flood of walnuts washing violently along the road, skittering in all directions like a routing army seen from far away.

Tristan and Belisencia look at one another, then slowly turn their heads to look at me. I am already yanking on the reins, even as I watch the walnuts tumble and roll. Each of those nuts is a day of Elizabeth's life. A day I get to spend with my angel. And I will not be cheated of a single one.

"Leave them!" Belisencia shouts.

Tristan vaults from the wagon, his sword in the long guard—pointed forward in two hands, one leg thrust forward. He and I have faced death together too many times to not understand each other. He knew even before I pulled the reins that I would stop the cart. He understands that my salvation depends on those walnuts.

"Are you mad?" Belisencia shouts. "*Leave them!*"

I leap from the driver's box before the horses come to a stop. I am not as fancy as Tristan. I take position beside him, holding my sword at my side and in one hand, ready to cleave in whatever fashion I can.

"Belisencia, the walnuts," I call. "Use the extra sack!"

I do not look back to see if she responds, because the first of the demons catapults through the air at us. Tristan is clever. The long guard, apparently, is perfect for impaling leaping demons. His lanky, bubbling-faced monster throws itself onto the blade. My sword master did not talk nearly enough about the best methods of fighting demons and dragons.

The other two leap. I spin away from one and manage to bury my blade in the other's neck as it crashes into me. We fall with a clatter to the stones. Small, dark circles flash in front of my eyes. The armor is too hot. Sweat washes in rivulets down my face. The demon rises, my sword still buried in its neck. Its arms are enormous and grotesque. Like flesh growing unchecked and without direction. Bubbling like boiling water. There is no shape to the arms. Only knotted, twisted flesh, like God's half-mashed and discarded clay.

It takes the blade in one hand—the perfect fingers in that roil of flesh make the creature even more repulsive— and pulls the sword from its neck. I rise to my feet as the sword clatters to the stones and the demon leaps again. I put my hands between it and me, grab the monsters pulpy

271

neck, and squeeze. The creature snaps its jaws at me. My hands sink through the gash in its flesh. I rip at the neck. Sinews pop, sounding like saplings torn and twisted. Muscle shreds. Blood spurts toward my visor and I close my eyes. The creature's head is nearly off and still it pounds at me with its blubbery arms. It is like being struck by swinging pigs. I gather the last of my strength, give a long cry, and snap the demon's spine with a crack. The swine arms stop swinging.

I open my eyes. Tristan stands over the last demon and twists his sword in the monster's neck. Blood covers his armor in streaks and beads. Footsteps echo in the distance. Howls echo through the city, growing louder.

I look back at Belisencia. She is picking up walnuts and tossing them in the sack, one at a time.

"Are you a *baboon*?" Tristan shouts. He takes off his helmet and runs the edge along the cobblestones, scooping walnuts into it. He dumps the nuts into the sack and scoops up more of them.

"I don't *have* a helmet," she replies. "Maybe we shouldn't have stopped!"

I take my helmet off as well and use my hand to sweep walnuts into it. Sweat trickles from my hair onto the cobblestones. The footsteps grow closer. I feel ill.

Between the three of us we manage to gather most of the remaining walnuts. I crawl along the road, reaching for solitary nuts in distant crevices.

Tristan stands and straps his helmet back on. "More of those things, Edward."

I stand slowly, stoop, and catch my breath.

"What's wrong, old man?" he says.

"Nothing," I reply. "That creature hit my breastplate hard. Just need to catch my breath."

He stares at me, the great helm hiding his expression. "There are only three," he says. "I'll take them. You get the rest of the walnuts."

I shake my head and stand straight. "You want all the glory." I hold my sword in the long guard and take a deep breath.

The demons hurl themselves at us.

I hit the cobbled road again.

The impact blackens my world and fills the back of my nose with the taste of fire. I struggle against the creature, but I have so little strength. My sword is in its stomach, but it does not seem to care. One of the demon's eyes is as large as a bracelet. The monster gouges at my visor. Its twisted teeth clack against the bevor at my neck. It gibbers as it searches for openings in my armor, making desperate groans and growls. Its hands batter my helmet, make my ears ring. I push at its chest. A thin black tongue thrusts out from its neck in a bloody spray. Not a tongue. The tip of Tristan's sword. I shove the demon's head to one side hard. Tristan pulls the blade back and hacks two-handed at the neck. Once, twice, and the third stroke cleaves the head from the body. Blood spurts as the misshapen head tumbles to the cobblestones. The arms continue to rake at me for a three or four heartbeats before the demon realizes it is dead.

"Excellent strategy," Tristan says. "Letting it get on top of you so that I could kill it easily."

"Shut your mouth, you baboon," I say. He helps me up.

"I'm glad we shared the glory, Edward."

I wave him off and we pick at the last of the fallen walnuts.

"Ed," says Tristan.

"I hear them." More footsteps. Many more. They come in far greater numbers than we can fight. These are not just plaguers. They are stronger, faster, and more intelligent. I reach down to pick a walnut from a groove between two stones and nearly topple over.

"Get in the back, Ed," Tristan says. "I'll handle the horses."

I nod and climb the driver's box, then crawl to the back of the wagon. Tristan throws the sack into the cart as Belisencia joins me. She studies me with furrowed brows.

"Did you get hurt, Edward?" she asks.

I pull the great helm off and shake my head. "Just a bit winded."

Tristan shouts at the horses and the wagon rattles toward the Bishop's Bridge. We pass the sprawling Hospital of St. Giles on our left and I know we will make it out of the city; I remember now that the hospital is that last building before the bridge. I lean to one side and look back. White-robed demons sprint toward us. Dozens of them. A white-capped flood of hunchbacked death hurtling down the thoroughfare.

The wagon wheels tremble on the smaller stones of the Bishop's Bridge. The Wensun winds beneath us. The east gate looms ahead. Freedom.

"Edward!" There is hysteria in Tristan's voice.

I squint at the gate, then let my head fall back against the wagon. *Of course.*

The gate is closed.

Episode 7

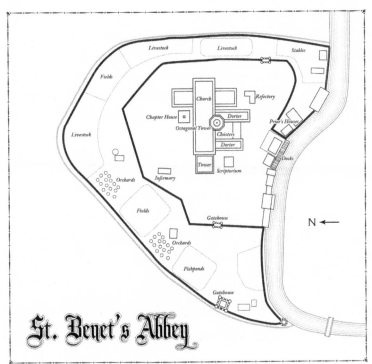

St. Benet's Abbey

Chapter 38

THE HORSES SLOW UPON THE bridge and toss their heads as they approach the iron portcullis. One of the geldings nickers. They appear as unhappy as I am to find the gates closed. The nickering animal glances back at us and I am certain I see accusation in its eye.

"Satan's barbed cock!" Tristan leaps from the driver's box in a clamor of steel plates and vaults the four steps leading to the arched gatehouse entryway.

Belisencia stands beside me in the wagon bed. "Tristan suggested finding a ford to the east!" she shouts. "But you wouldn't even consider it, would you?"

Dozens of the creatures rumble toward us, their gaits wild and unsteady. One clips its enormous left leg against its normal-sized right one and sprawls to the stones. The other demons stampede over their fallen comrade, smashing its nodding head into the cobblestones with their grotesque feet.

"Every other gate we passed was open," I say. "Every other gate! And you blame me for this?"

"No, of course not, Edward," she replies. "It must be John of Gaunt's fault!"

I can hear the hysteria in her voice, so I forgive her the sarcasm. A winding rattle cuts through the demon howls. Tristan is cranking the windlass in the gatehouse. I glance back. The portcullis is rising too slowly. We do not have enough time.

"They're coming!" Belisencia stands in the wagon and points to the lunging horde of disfigured creatures, as if I cannot see them. *"Edward, they're coming!"*

I step over the back edge of the wagon with one leg and lower myself gingerly onto the bridge. My skin burns with fever. I do not know if my legs will hold my weight for long. I draw Saint Giles's sword, staggering as I do.

Perhaps she is right. Perhaps we could have found a ford or another bridge and come back to the city, as Tristan suggested. In my haste I have put her life in danger, and that of Tristan's.

Mea maxima culpa.

Saint Giles's sword feels heavy in my hand—a steel anchor, made ponderous by the lives it has taken. I have sinned more times than I could ever account for. Sins that span six countries. Sins that have left broken lives and broken families in my wake. Sins that have shattered hearts and driven Christians from God. It would be far easier to count the commandments I have not broken than the ones I have.

If each sin leaves a dark stain, then my soul must be black as a hanged man's tongue. Can it get darker? I do not know if I can bear the weight of Tristan's and Belisencia's deaths.

Woe to him who is alone when he falls and has not another to lift him up.

And woe to him who is pulled down while trying to lift his friend up.

The first of the demons is twenty paces away. They have reached the bridge and stampede toward us in lopsided fury. The chains continue to rattle as Tristan winds the windlass. A foot of space is visible beneath the teeth of the portcullis.

I glance at Belisencia. I can see the tremble in her shoulders, but the fear does not stop her from hopping down from the cart.

"Get back in the wagon!" I shout.

She shakes her head. "If those are demons, then we are in purgatory," she says. "And if we are in purgatory, then Hugh the Baptist was right." She takes the cross from her neck. "And if Hugh the Baptist was right, then God has a special purpose for me."

"Get back in the wagon, you stubborn cow." I hold my trembling sword in both hands and straighten my arms. The first demon has a copper bell around its neck, and bloody bandages around its hands. I aim the tip of my blade at the monster's right eye, which is as large as the mouth of a tankard. And Belisencia steps in front of me.

"*No!*" I drop Saint Giles's sword to the stones and grab her shoulders, but even as I pull at her the demon lunges.

And it recoils from her.

I stop moving and gape. Belisencia holds the cross out toward the advancing horde, but the first row of creatures shriek and fall back, like summer wheat rippling from a gale. They howl and collide against the next row of clomping monsters. The bloated creatures in the first two ranks stumble and fall over one another, creating a dam of writh-ing, white-cloaked flesh.

I pick up my sword and hack at them as they try to stand, glancing back at Belisencia. She gives me a look of unbri-dled self-righteousness an instant before a keg-faced demon slips past me and knocks her to the cold stones. I leap to her side, stumbling as I do.

The demon roars and opens a mouth so cavernous that you could thrust a dagger into it sideways. The brown teeth are broken and jagged. The creature lunges at Belisencia's face but I jam my sword into the demon's mouth before it can reach her. The fiend gurgles as the tip of the blade breaks through the back of its skull. But it does not die.

The fiends on the bridge are disentangling themselves. One throws its body at me. My sword is trapped in the skull of another, so I raise an arm against the hurtling flesh. The weight of the swollen demon knocks me backward. I leave Saint Giles's sword in the mouth of the other demon.

Belisencia screams. "Shut the gates!"

Shut the gates? Is she mad?

I gather a dram of strength and throw the monster off me, glance back toward the gate.

Belisencia is back on the wagon. She faces the gate-house and is bent almost double with her screams. "*Tristan! Shut the gates!*"

I look past her, toward the rising gates, and my dram of strength fades. Exhaustion returns like a black tide.

Woe to Tristan and Belisencia. Woe to Elizabeth.

I see more white cloaks outside the gate. How many, I cannot tell. What I can tell is that we are surrounded. Demons on either side.

Chapter 39

I LOOK AWAY FROM THE portcullis and kick at the fiends advancing on this side of the gate. They fall upon me with their ungainly weight. Pin me to the stones and pull at the plates of my armor. They are clever chickens, these demons. They know they cannot hurt me until my armor is off.

Two of them pull at my helm with both hands. The strap at my chin bites into my flesh. My sword is still trapped in the head of a demon. I cannot find the weapon. I flail with my hand, striking a swollen arm. It is like punching dough. The strap tightens against my chin and creaks. Either the rivet holding it to my helm will break or my jaw will. I strike at the demons with my hands, pull at them, scratch at their flesh with my gauntlets.

More and more of them tug at my armor. I kick a gourd-nosed monster in the face three times, crushing cartilage and tearing flesh, but it continues to pry at the greave on my left shin. The greave snaps off and the creature falls backward holding it in two misshapen hands. I swing wildly at another demon with my fist. It is a good blow. An astounding blow.

So powerful that it causes the monster's head to explode in a cloud of blood and bone and flesh.

I made a demon's head explode.

I look at my gauntlet. There is no blood on it. I look back up at the creature as it falls sideways. A man in rusted chain mail stands beside me. I did not make a demon's head explode. He did.

The man swings something heavy and black and another demon head erupts. The pressure on my helm ceases. I glance back at the portcullis. It is up at about waist height. The demons outside make no attempt to enter.

"Get up!" The man in the rusted mail holds a flail. His entire body lurches as he swings the spiked ball in a slow, wooshing circle. I roll onto my side and struggle to rise. *"Get up!"*

I get up and steady myself against the wagon. The creatures on the outside of the city gate still do not approach. There are only a few of them and they stand motionless, watching. But these look different from the ones inside the city. Thinner. Their bodies proportioned correctly.

I glance back at the man in the chain mail. He is even taller than I am, his shoulders like curtain walls. He stands less than a pace away from me. The flail carves a deadly arc. One of the demons launches itself at him but the spiked ball catches it in midair. The fiend drops to the ground in a cloud of blood as the warrior spins away. But more approach.

Belisencia leans over the back edge of the cart and reaches past me with her cross. *"In nomine Dei Patris omnipotentis!"* she shouts. The demons back away, hissing, but approach again warily. Whatever power she has over them seems to be fading.

"In nomine Dei Patris omnipotentis!" Belisencia shouts. *"In nomine Dei Patris omnipotentis! In nomine Dei Patris omnipotentis!"*

"Isn't there more to that?" the man in the chain mail calls.

"It's all I know!" she shouts back.

He swings the flail, grazing one of the monsters on its log-sized chin. "What kind of nun are you?"

Tristan bounds out of the gatehouse and leaps toward the driver's box. He does not lift his foot high enough and it catches on the edge of the platform, sending him clattering off the cart and onto the bridge. "Gate's up!" he shouts from his knees.

A demon crawls away from Belisencia. I see a flash of steel in its mouth. My sword.

"There you are," I mutter.

I step forward and take the hilt as the others advance. The man in the chain mail puts a foot on the creature's back and I pull the sword free.

Tristan calls from the driver's box. "I'd like to leave Norwich now, please."

"Into the cart!" I shout. The world seems to sway, as if I am on the deck of a lurching ship. I scramble for purchase but cannot lift myself. Belisencia yanks at the back of my bevor.

"Help him!" she shouts.

Strong arms shove me into the wagon bed. The man in the chain mail swings the flail in a vicious arc, cracking the skull of an advancing demon, then he leaps into the wagon. He curses as a three-fingered hand grabs his leg and pulls him backward. I break all three of the fingers with my hands and punch at another creature trying to board the cart. The man drags his leg into the wagon bed and spins back to face the horde. The horses pull and the cart lurches forward with a happy chime.

Belisencia looks at the warrior beside us and gasps. "You've been bitten!"

He lashes the spiked ball with a grunt, skimming the top of a demon's tuberous head and sending a shower of blood into the Wensum. I see torn flesh on the man's bare hand. He has indeed been bitten.

The cart passes under the portcullis. Demons clutch at us, then stop abruptly. They do not pursue us past the gate.

The white-robed figures outside do not appear to be demons. Not hostile ones anyway. There are only three of them, and they follow behind the cart, a dozen paces back.

My eyes sting with the hot tears of fever. I close them. "That bite," I say to the man at my side. "You'll plague."

He shakes his head. "Any of you would plague with this bite," he says. "But not me."

"And why is that?" Belisencia asks.

The man slumps beside me as we leave the city. I look through the Bishop's Gate, back into Norwich. The demons roar from inside the city. They leap and raise their clawed, nightmare hands into the air, but they do not follow.

"I won't plague," the man says, "because I'm already dead. I died five years ago."

Chapter 40

THE HORSES SNORT AND FIGHT the bridle. They want to
run. They want to flee Norwich as quickly as they can.
I understand. I, too, want to put the city behind me. But
I know I will not. Not ever. The things I saw in that place
will haunt my dreams. The stub-fingered hands will lash
at my face. The bloated, misshapen faces—detritus from
a butcher's block—will appear from darkness and shriek.
I will run from them forever, but in my dreams they will
always be faster.

I look at Belisencia. She held off the demons. They
recoiled from her as if she were the Archangel. She sees
me looking and stares down at the cross on her neck, then
glances at me. She fidgets with the hem of her robe and
looks back at Norwich.

Tristan shortens the reins, makes the horses walk. The
metals chime once more and one of the white-robed, bandaged creatures limping beside the cart rings a handbell in
response. They are not demons, these poor souls that walk
beside us. They are lepers.

The man in the chain mail stares into the city. His face could be carved from granite for all the emotion he displays. He is a powerful man. The chain links of his armor strain when his muscles tense. His arms are like sea serpents that have swallowed a quarry of stones; they bulge with muscles that I did not know men had. He is the healthiest dead man I have ever seen. Belisencia notices too.

"You were magnificent in there," she says.

Tristan's helmeted head turns back to look at us.

"Who are you?" I ask. "Where did you come from? And why are lepers following us?"

The man looks away from the city, studies me. "You plagued?"

"No." I take my gauntlet off and wipe the sweat from my forehead. "I can't get the plague, either."

The man's eyes narrow. "Why not?"

"Because God needs me to heal one of his angels."

His hand brushes the pommel of a thick dagger at his belt and he asks again. "Are you plagued?"

Tristan stops the horses and stands on the driver's box, fingers touching his own dagger. "He's dead too," he says. "We are all dead and this is purgatory. Didn't you see those men in the city? Swollen heads are one of the signs of Judgment Day. I saw it in a tapestry, so it must be true."

The man stands, his eyes nearly even with Tristan's despite the eight-inch drop from driver's box to wagon bed. "You'd've been dead, that's clear," he replies. "If we hadn't followed you up here to Norwich and saved you. I see you're too full with emotion to thank me proper."

"I'm not plagued," I say.

"Then why the fever?"

"He's afflicted by the House of Gemini," Tristan says. "And judging by the symptoms, you've got a serious inflammation of your self-worth. We were almost out of there when you appeared."

Belisencia taps the man on his mailed shoulder and curtsies when he glances back. "Thank you for saving our lives."

"Saving our lives?" Tristan laughs. "We had the gate up already. He's one of those men who runs forward after the battle and puts his foot on the carcass."

The man turns back to Tristan. "It would have been your carcass." His thumb brushes the dagger's grip. "Still might."

"I can see why you're dead. I'd have killed you too." Tristan unstraps his great helm and tosses it into the wagon bed, at the man's feet. "Still might."

I stand with a groan. "Yes, why don't the two of you kill each other and save the demons the trouble? Don't you think we have enough enemies without picking fights with each other?" I spit over the side of the cart and fix both of them with a stare. "Is this what we've become?"

Tristan shrugs. "I was like this already."

"All I need to know is why you're sick," the man says. "You're sweating too heavy for just that fight, and you can barely hold your feet. If you ain't plagued, then why the fever?"

I show him my wrist. "Because doctors are useless."

He studies the wound. "That weren't a bite?"

"No." I point to him with my chin. "Now, tell me about your death."

Chapter 41

HE TELLS US THAT HIS name is Praeteritus. My Latin was never good, but I think it means "forgotten," and I am certain it is not his real name. I am also certain that someone gave him the name, because he is not the sort of man who would know Latin. His accent and phrasing mark him as Suffolk peasantry, so deeply rooted in farms that I can almost smell the loam on his breath.

"What sort of ridiculous name is Praeteritus?" Tristan says. "Sounds like a monk sneezing. You look more like a Ralf."

"What was it that killed you?" I ask.

"The plague," Praeteritus says, then he shakes his head when I try to speak. "Not this plague. The other one. The Black Death. There are still pockets of it left around, you know."

"If that one was black," Tristan says, "then what color is this one, Ralf?"

"Red," I reply.

I was a child during the Black Death. The disease spared me and most of my family, but it withered England.

It crept through every corner of my kingdom, spreading rot and boils, and killing so many that entire villages ceased to exist. Bodies were rolled into great pits and buried in lye, or set aflame like some Old Testament offering. My father told me it was the worst thing that ever happened to England.

But this sickness is far worse. Entire villages still disappear, but neither lye nor flame will give proper rest to the victims of the Red Plague. This plague does not wither England; it rips the kingdom into a thousand bloody pieces and swallows them all.

"I got sick from the Black Death five years ago," Praeteritus says. "And it killed me."

The old plague still creeps through the land, still claims victims, but not very often.

"I realize you serf stock aren't given much in the way of learning, Ralf," Tristan says, "but I think you missed an important lesson about the results of death."

Praeteritus darts a lethal glance at Tristan. "You mean the idea that dead people oughta stay dead?"

Tristan opens his mouth, then closes it. "Probably not the most important lesson these days."

Praeteritus is a smart chicken.

"How are you alive?" I ask.

"God sent me back."

Figures in the distance lurch toward us. I am almost relieved to see ordinary plaguers.

"God?" Belisencia touches the cross at her neck. "Why would He send you back?"

"I used to think I was His arrow. That He sent me back to punish bad people. To give them the 'wages of sin.'"

I give Tristan a glance. If this man has the third plague, he will be a danger to all of us. Tristan's shoulders tense.

"Wages of sin?" Belisencia says. "You mean…kill them?" She takes the smallest of steps backward.

Praeteritus nods. "I used to kill men for the Bishop of Ely, before this new plague got started."

"The Bishop of Ely?" Belisencia says. "You killed for a man of God?"

Praeteritus smiles. "All men are men of God. Bishops just profit from the relationship."

"Do you still think you are God's arrowhead?" I tap the pommel of my sword with a thumb as subtly as I can so I can draw it in an instant if needed.

He looks at the lepers that have huddled about twenty paces away. "I ain't certain of anything anymore."

I study the lepers as well and remember the white-robed figures that watched us in Caistor St. Edmund.

"Well, you are clearly not dead anymore," Belisencia says. "You should not say that you are."

"You're wrong, m'lady," he says. "I will always be dead. The priest gave me the rites. Put the oil on my body."

"But you were alive," I say.

"I ain't certain if I died or not. All I know is that the Church said I was dead. The odd thing about the Church is they have a ceremony for when you die, but they ain't got one for when you come back. And priests are too stubborn to admit they're wrong. So they just pretend you don't exist. Once you're dead to the Church, you don't never come back."

I have heard of such things. Men and women declared dead, anointed and given last rites, then rising from their beds. They are shunned as abominations. The lucky ones are merely driven from their homes and villages.

"You poor man," Belisencia says.

The plaguers continue toward us. Some of them wear mail. It is time to move on. The island fortress is two miles and a bag of walnuts away.

"We should continue this conversation somewhere else." I nod toward the lepers. "Are they with you?"

"They are," Praeteritus replies. "They live in Caistor St. Edmund for now, with three hundred other lepers. And I am their king."

"Ralf the Leper King." Tristan sits on the driver's box and takes the reins.

I open my mouth to invite the lepers into the cart but hesitate. These men followed us from Caistor St. Edmund to save us from the demons, but they are lepers. Blighted men and women. They are the unclean. Unloved by God. Damned and confined to the shadows by the magnitude of their sins. So reviled that the church declares them dead and strips them of their possessions. I understand why Praeteritus has found kinship among them: they, too, are the living dead.

"Where are your horses?" I ask. "Are they nearby?"

"Our wagon is two miles east, on the south side of the river," Praeteritus replies. "There are rafts there, on the Wensum, to allow crossings."

Tristan and Belisencia look back at me without expression and I do not acknowledge them.

"Tell them to climb in," I say. "We'll take you to the rafts."

Belisencia stares at me with wide eyes. I know she will not enjoy traveling two miles while squeezed into a cart with lepers, but it will be good for her. A trial to teach her humility and tolerance.

"Edward," she whispers. "They're lepers!"

I nod. "Hallelujah."

I think about my own sins and wonder that I am not a leper already. Perhaps bringing them onto the cart will afflict me with their disease. Three months spent avoiding this new plague only to contract leprosy. But if humanity is to live, then we must show ourselves to be human.

Praeteritus calls the lepers over. The three men approach slowly. One rings a bell, another rattles a clapper.

"Unclean!" they shout as they approach.

"Stop that," Praeteritus shouts. "I told you, you don't have to do that no more."

Two of them have only stumps for hands. I reach out and take one of the stumps, fighting revulsion, and help the man up.

"Don't pull too hard," Tristan says.

"That's not funny, Tristan," Belisencia says.

"My apologies," he says. "Are they all on board?" He glances back, brows furrowed. "Maybe I should rephrase that."

"You are a horrible man," Belisencia says, but she edges away from a second leper that Praeteritus helps up. Blood has soaked though his filthy white robe in blotches.

I reach a hand out to the third, but Praeteritus shakes his head. "Not him. He stays here."

The leper makes no attempt to board the wagon.

"You cannot leave him to be…to be…" Belisencia glances at the approaching plaguers.

"He won't be eaten," Praeteritus replies. "Plaguers don't eat lepers."

"And what about you?" I ask. "You were bitten."

"Plaguers don't eat lepers, and survivors of the Black Death aren't affected by this plague."

"You've been bitten before?" I ask.

"More than I care to remember," he replies.

The only way all five of us can fit in the cart is if we stand. The arrangement is not ideal. I do not think I can stay on my feet for very long. The fever is not as bad as the one I had when we visited Paul the Doctor, but it is worsening.

We take hold of whatever section of the cart is nearest us as Tristan snaps the reins. The horses strain against the added weight, but once the wagon creaks forward they have no trouble trotting away from the city of Norwich. The metal strips chime and the leper with the blood spots rings a bell in response.

"Unclean!" he shouts.

"You don't have to do that no more," Praeteritus says.

Belisencia swallows with effort and smiles at the leper. "Yes," she says. "Your past failures do not put you beyond redemption. Pray to Christ and he may forgive your sins and make you worthy once more."

"That man's disease is no more his fault than this Red Plague," Tristan says. "People get sick. It doesn't mean they have failed or that God is punishing them."

"How do you know?" Belisencia asks. "Leprosy spreads through wanton, impure sexual habits and through immoral character. That is known. Why is it that you think you know more than everyone else? Why must you deny all common knowledge? Don't be such a baboon."

"If God gave him leprosy," Tristan says, "then God also gave the plague to the nuns of your convent."

"And how do you know that it was not Lucifer who gave them the plague?"

"Because it wasn't," I say. "John of Gaunt gave them the plague. Let's stop talking and watch for plaguers."

The metals chime on the wagon. I have lost count of how many chimes there have been. I draw a walnut from the sack and toss it onto the cart floor. Praeteritus looks at me curiously but says nothing.

The leper we leave behind pulls one of the bandages from his face, and even from fifty paces away I see that his chin is badly swollen on one side. Things begin to make sense to me. The keystone falls into place.

I point to the leper in the distance. "Is he plagued?"

Praeteritus rubs one of his hands slowly against the other. "The plague affects lepers different," he says. "Some of them can't get the affliction. But the ones that can...well, it affects them different. They become..." He shrugs and points toward the city. "They become those."

The leper turns away from us and walks slowly toward Norwich. "There were five leper hospitals round Norwich before the plague came on. And more than four hundred lepers outside the city. When the townsfolk ran off or got ate, the lepers took the city as their own."

"What about the plaguers?" Belisencia asks.

"Like I said. Plaguers don't eat them. Norwich became a leper city. A place where everyone was the same. Where no one was cursed, and no one was spit on."

"Sounds lovely," Tristan says. "A leper Eden."

"But the serpent found them, didn't it?" I say.

"Just because the plaguers don't eat lepers don't mean they can't hurt them," Praeteritus says. "Most of the afflicted left the city. I guess not even plaguers want to be near lepers. But a few plaguers stayed. And if backed into a corner, the afflicted will even bite lepers. I don't know what happened. But plague spread in Norwich again. The city got overrun."

"I thought you said not all lepers can become afflicted," Belisencia says.

"They can't. But if only half of them could get the plague, that's still more than two hundred afflicted lepers running through the streets. The unafflicted lepers fled. And they have been looking for a home ever since." He stares at the white-robed men standing in the cart. "A band of soldiers found the wandering lot of them and got to killing them. They said the plague was caused by lepers. I been told it was a bloodbath. Fifty dead. Lots more wounded. The survivors made it to Caistor, where I found them. But there's not much there. Just a ruined Roman city. They want a home. Something safe. I promised I would find them one."

"The bloated ones in the city," Belisencia says. "Why don't they leave? They wouldn't follow us past the gates."

Praeteritus looks back toward the city, then gazes at one of the three lepers in the cart. "I don't know. I think they remember a little. They know it's home. The world was hell for them. But in Norwich, they weren't damned no more. It was their Promised Land. God forgave them." He shrugs but there is something painful in the gesture. I do not think the lepers are the only ones seeking God's forgiveness. Perhaps these poor broken men are Praeteritus's penance. He turns back to Belisencia. "Why would you leave Eden?"

The cart rattles over a rabbit hole as I think on his words.

"So the things in Norwich are plagued lepers," Belisencia whispers.

Praeteritus nods.

"And they're not demons," I say.

Praeteritus watches the man walk through the gates and into Norwich. "Depends on who you ask."

The wagon chimes and the leper rings his bell once more. "Unclean!" he shouts.

"You don't have to do that no more," Praeteritus says.

"Unclean!" the leper cries. "Unclean!"

We leave Praeteritus and his subjects at the bank of the Wensum, where two rafts of reed have been drawn up on the mud. I call to him as he drags one of the rafts into the river.

"Praeteritus, did you come here to save us, or to bring that afflicted leper to Norwich?"

He picks at grass wedged into the raft reeds. "There always got to be one answer to everything?" He tugs the raft into the river current and helps one of his lepers onto it, hands the man a long wooden pole.

"Good-bye, Leper King," Tristan shouts.

"Good-bye, baboon," Praeteritus replies.

We continue our eastward journey, through golden fields of cowslips and flat expanses of wild grasses and forgotten furlongs. I lie on my back while Belisencia and Tristan fret about my condition.

"How bad is it?" Tristan's jaw is tight as he glances back at me.

"Perhaps there will be another doctor at the island fortress," Belisencia says. "We should pray for that."

"Yes," I say. "That's precisely what I want to pray for. Another doctor."

The nun draws a walnut from the bag every ten chimes. The constant rattle of the wagon makes me restless, so I sit up and watch the flat landscape.

The walnuts run out about five miles from Norwich and I feel a welling of disappointment from deep within my marrow. We are still far from the coast. If we turn to the northeast or southwest, as the painted wagon tracks show, and travel two miles like the boy at Bure said, we will still be far from the coast. I know from my last visit to Norwich that the shore is nearly ten miles from the city.

"I knew this wouldn't work," I mutter. "A bag of walnuts? What in God's teeth was I thinking?"

"Settle down," Belisencia says. "The boy said that we had two more miles after the walnuts ran out. We have to turn the cart and keep going."

Fever and failure form a noxious cloud in my mind. I turn on Belisencia. "Until what?" I shout. "Two miles will put us more than three miles from the coast. Or didn't they teach you nuns to count? We'll still be in the middle of nothing after two miles! There are no islands in the middle of Norfolk, Belisencia! There are only fields. Endless fields and hedges and flowers and great heaps of bloody nothing! Look around you! What do you see? Fields! Tell me if you see an island. Tell me if you get the scent of the ocean. Tell me if you catch sight of a single bloody gull! We have failed! We are landlocked, don't you understand that?" It feels good to shout, and I want to continue shouting, but Belisencia is not looking at me anymore. She is staring over my shoulder, eyes wide.

I whip my head around, but there is only a half-ploughed field and endless stretches of flatlands. The woman must be going mad.

And then I see it.

Cutting through the middle of the farmer's plot is a square sail. It drifts westward across the field and into a meadow that brims with tall stalks of red valerian. I point to the sail, feeling like an idiot for pointing when the others have clearly already seen it. But I cannot stop pointing. A sail is cutting through a meadow. Does this ceaseless Norfolk wind allow sailors to tack through farmland? Could the specter of a dead sailor's ship haunt these plains?

I follow the square sail with my finger as it turns southward. A midge buzzes into my open mouth. I spit it out and watch with my mouth closed. A second sail comes into view in the farmer's plot.

I look back to my companions. Belisencia looks at me with no expression at all.

I scowl at her. "Stop being so bloody smug."

Chapter 42

TRISTAN GIVES A SHOUT AND flails the horses with the reins. He sends us toward the sails and I do not stop him. I want to know how ships can cross meadows.

I get my answer when we are a fifty paces away: a narrow channel of water has been carved into the land. The channel is steep-sided and invisible from a distance, and the two clinker-built cogs sail westward through it.

Both ships are on fire.

"This is like some bizarre dream," Belisencia says. "Are we going insane?"

"Allow me a moment to consider this," Tristan says. "You have been witness to a plaguer that talks, a dragon that eats virgins, and a chain of crying men and women who dance themselves to death. And this is where you begin to question your sanity?"

Belisencia sighs. "They weren't virgins, Tristan."

He barks a laugh.

"The ships aren't burning," I say.

Something has been attached to the boats. Rails of some sort that extend from the hulls. The rails encircle the cogs completely, and it is these rails that are on fire.

"I wouldn't be amused by those if I were a plaguer trying to board," Tristan says.

"Exactly," I reply. "Those captains are used to sailing through plaguer-infested waters."

We could overtake the ships if we tried, but I do not want to try. There is no way to tell how many men are on board and what their motivations are. I have a suspicion that the ships are coming from the fortress. I do not know why; I simply have a feeling. Perhaps we are not as far from the coast as I had thought. Hope blossoms. Even the fever seems to have weakened.

We ride back to the place where we first spotted the sails. I find the plank of wood and hold it in front of Tristan with the painted tracks curving left. The horses turn to the northeast and, with a glance back at our tracks, we begin our two-mile journey to the island fortress. In two miles, I pray I will learn that my Elizabeth can be cured.

It is roughly a mile and a half before my hopes dwindle again. The landscape has not changed. There is no island. No smell of the sea. Not even a single bloody gull. We are still miles from the coast. It has been a colossal waste of time. The walnuts. Norwich. Everything. I have squandered two days of Elizabeth's life. I understand now that I am not worthy of her. Another knight would have found the cure by now. Another knight would not have wasted two days riding in a chiming cart and tossing walnuts from a sack. We ride the remaining half mile in a tense silence. Tristan does not stop. He keeps the horses moving long after we have traveled the two miles. Our heads swivel from one side to the other as we search out anything that might lead us to an island.

"Stop the wagon," I say.

Tristan does not stop the wagon.

"Tristan…"

"Maybe it hasn't been two miles yet, Edward."

"Let's go back to where the walnuts ran out," I say. "We can try turning the wagon to the southeast." I am not hopeful. Northeast was where the ships came from. It was our best chance.

"Just a little longer," Tristan replies.

Black smoke rises a few miles to the east of us. Another village consumed by hellfire. I spot an old monastery far to the north. Just walls and a glittering spire from this distance.

"There!" Belisencia says. "A monastery. We can talk to the people there. They might know something useful."

"Yes, good thinking," Tristan replies. "Pardon me, but have you seen an island in your fields? Or perhaps your vineyards?"

"And *your* plan consists of riding aimlessly through Norfolk," she replies.

"I'm not aimless at all." Tristan points forward. "I'm going that way."

"Go to the monastery," I say. "Maybe they'll have a surgeon."

Tristan turns the horses northward. Something in my memory nags at me. I once heard something about an abbey east of Norwich. Yes. Richard FitzAlan, earl of Arundel, spoke about this abbey. His family gave vast amounts of money for its construction. I try to remember the name of the place. Was it St. Benedict? St. Bernard? Lord Richard told me he visits the monastery once a year, when the abbot holds a feast for its patrons. Perhaps my family's ties to the earl will be helpful in procuring a surgeon at this abbey.

More of the narrow channels crop up in the fields, and those fields become more and more sodden. The land becomes a swamp. Our horses have to work hard to keep us moving. I fear for their safety in the treacherous muck.

A vast, muddy pit becomes visible to the west, and one of the narrow channels of water passes to one side of it. I remember Lord Richard telling me about the peat mines in the area and imagine a hundred mud-caked diggers cutting peat sods from that massive hole and loading them onto barges in the channel.

The spire of the monastery church glints in the late-afternoon sun. I see thick curtain walls and a gatehouse to the northwest, where the main entrance lies. A river flows between us and the monastery, but a triple-arched stone bridge just west of the abbey crosses the waterway. The wagon wheels spin and hiss in the wet soil as we ride toward the river. Our horses snort and take careful steps in the slick mud. The cowslips and daisies give way to fen orchids and fleabane. For the first time, I am thankful for the strong Norfolk winds; without them the midges would feast on us.

It is an elegant stone bridge. The three arches are reflected in the water below, completing the circles and looking like an elaborate pillory. Tristan glances back at me and I nod. The horses lower their heads and heave the wagon onto the bridge. The wheels rumble and grind along the thick sandstone blocks. When we have crossed, we turn toward the monastery.

A portion of the river has been diverted toward the abbey so that the water forms a moat around the curtain walls. The gatehouse is opulent as only buildings owned by the Church can be. Statues of dead men who were famous long ago fill the niches on either side of a massive arched window at the top of the gatehouse. Tracery of limestone and knapped flint covers the spaces above the niches and at the crest of the structure.

Tristan stops the wagon at the moat, directly in front of the entrance. The thick, oaken drawbridge is raised. I wonder that there are no plaguers out here. Surely a place this large must be full of villagers and townsfolk.

I peer upward at the central window. Is there movement there? I stand and cup my hands to my mouth. "We seek entry to the abbey!" The shouting makes me cough, and I have to sit again. The fever has returned, like a hot tide coming in.

Tristan gives me a worried look, then calls up to the gatehouse. "Open the gates! We'd like to buy indulgences! And tithe! And donate ale!"

"That won't help," I say.

But perhaps it does, because a woman pushes open one side of the hinged windowpane and leans out. I can only see her head, neck, and one shoulder, but she appears to be naked.

"Good day!" She laughs as the other pane opens and a stout man, also seemingly unclothed, leans out and kisses her on the mouth. They appear to be drunk as well as naked.

"What sort of abbey is this?" Belisencia asks. She cups her hands to her mouth and calls up, "Stop your lewdness at once!"

"Yes!" Tristan shouts. "You'll catch a terrible bout of Original Sin!" Belisencia glares at him. He shrugs. "And leprosy!"

The man looks down at us and calls back. "We ain't allowing carts in through the main gate no more. Everything gets loaded by ships now, on the River Bure."

All three of us fall silent. We gaze at each other and I know the same thought has come to us all.

"What did you say the river is called?" Tristan shouts.

"You have to unload on the river," he calls back. "We'll send a ship."

"I understand that!" I shout. "What is the *name* of the river?" More coughing.

The man says something to the woman beside him. She laughs and he addresses us again. "The Bure," he says. "Just go back over the bridge and wait at the riverbank."

My breath catches. Tristan gazes at the moat, then turns to me. "Do you think that moat goes all the way around the abbey?"

I understand what he is implying. My heart rumbles, thunder in my chest. "It would be useless if it didn't."

I stare at the crenelated curtain walls. At the hulking gatehouse and the thick-planked drawbridge. It is fortified, this abbey. And it is completely surrounded by water. Tears sting my eyes.

We have found the island fortress.

Chapter 43

"In the name of King Richard and the earl of Arundel, I order you to lower the drawbridge," I say.

The smile leaves the man's face. He looks at me, brows drawn downward. "King who?" He laughs loudly, and the woman at his side joins him. Is it a sin to despise people you have never met?

"Open the gates, or you will hang for treas…" I cough and do not stop coughing for a long while. Belisencia helps me sit down in the cart and wipes at my forehead with the hem of her robe.

"He is sick," she shouts. "He needs a surgeon."

The man shakes his head. "We don't need plague here."

"It's not plague!" Belisencia shouts. "He has a festering wound."

The man looks down at us silently.

"We can pay," Tristan says.

"Did you say the earl of Arundel?" The man replies.

"Yes, he did," Tristan says. "He is good friends with the earl."

"You aren't here to cause trouble? Because we will hang you and flay your skin and torture you if you are."

"No trouble," I call, my voice gravelly.

"I'm sorry," Tristan says. "Did you say hang, flay, and *then* torture?"

"We'll make you very unhappy if you try to hurt anyone here."

"Please don't take this badly," Tristan says, "but this *conversation* is making me very unhappy. Can you open the gate, please?"

The man frowns and says something to the woman at his side, then calls down, "You said the earl of Arundel is your friend?"

"Like brothers," Tristan says. "Brothers who really like each other."

"Wait there."

He disappears, and the woman entertains us by singing an out-of-tune Norfolk tavern song of some sort.

It takes a long time for anything to happen. I doze in the cart and dream of clawing hands and eyes black as a sinner's soul. I wake with a start when Belisencia touches my shoulder.

A deep rattle of chains and the clanking of a massive windlass resound across the countryside. The drawbridge tilts downward. Thick chains guide the oaken platform until it rests on the damp soil. Four men wearing hardened leather vests and holding halberds stand in the gateway. The thickset man from the window stands between them in linen breeches and a loose tunic of wool.

"Is the alchemist here?" I ask as we roll into the gatehouse. Despite my fever, I tremble at the thought of being this close to Elizabeth's salvation. No one replies to my question. Instead, they inspect us. They do not seem surprised at the walnuts in the cart, but they are impressed with the two hand cannons. Tristan draws his dagger when one of the halberdiers walks away with both guns. The window man holds up a hand. "You'll get them back. No weapons allowed in the monastery. I'll have your swords and daggers, too." His breath smells of wine.

"You'll give us back our cannons now," Tristan says. "And maybe we won't kill all of you."

"I knew they were trouble, John," one of the halberdiers says. "They're like the others."

"No trouble." I unstrap Saint Giles's sword from my waist and hand it to the portly drunk man, John. "We're no trouble at all."

Tristan looks at me, sighs, then hands the dagger over.

"Where's your sword?" John asks Tristan.

"At the bottom of a river," Tristan says.

"How'd it get to the bottom of a river?"

"Is the alchemist here?" I ask.

"I thought you needed a surgeon," John says.

"I do. But I also need an alchemist. Is he here?" I try to keep the desperation from my voice.

John studies me for a long time. "Let's have a look at your wound."

I show him my wrist. He inspects it, then nods. "We don't have a surgeon, but we might be able to help. You said you're friends with Lord Richard? What's your name?"

"Edward Dallingridge, of Bodiam."

Knights do not live long unless they have a finely honed sense of danger. The glance that passes between two of the halberdiers is a fleeting one, but even in my fevered state I recognize something dangerous in it.

"Tristan, why don't you and Belisencia wait outside," I say.

"Nonsense," Belisencia replies. "We will stay with you, Edward."

Tristan does not reply but I see his posture change. I do not think he saw the glance between the halberdiers, but he knows something is wrong now.

"Wait here in the gatehouse," John says. "I'll see what can be done for you."

He walks off, slightly unsteady, toward a smaller gatehouse and another curtain wall of napped flint. It is a hundred paces easily to the gate, so we watch him walk for a long time.

There are no makeshift tents or mattresses in the monastery grounds. There are fishponds and buildings along the river, vineyards and plowed fields, stables and orchards, but there seem to be few people in the abbey grounds. I wonder why the place is not flooded with villagers. I wonder how many soldiers guard this place. I wonder if I will die here, perhaps a hundred paces from my goal.

John stumbles back after a time and climbs into the wagon with us. "Go to the church. Past that small gatehouse." The wheels chime and John glances at the strips of metal on the wagon wheel. He kicks at the walnuts in the wagon bed. "Where'd you get this cart?"

"It belonged to a simpleton," I say.

John nods. "Where is the simpleton?"

"He's with my sword," Tristan replies.

The church is not impressive for a monastery of this size. It is larger than most village churches but lacks the grandeur of abbey structures. The only interesting feature is an octagonal tower, plated in lead, which rises high above the church. The turret is crowned with a tall spire that juts into the sky, far higher than the smaller Norman tower on the west end. This spire was the one I saw from the marshes.

We leave the cart near the great, iron-hinged doors and John leads us into the church. I feel unsteady on my feet. Belisencia and Tristan try to take my arms but I shrug them off.

"Are you taking us to the alchemist?" I ask.

John does not reply. I have a terrible foreboding. He could be leading us anywhere. We have no weapons, and even if I had my sword, I do not think I could swing it more than once or twice.

The church is narrow. It has no aisles and the choir just past the crossing is a cramped one. The ceiling is vaulted and ribbed, with the faces of monks staring down wherever two ribs intersect.

John walks quickly through the nave to a small arched doorway just before the south transept, and then up a long set of spiral stairs. The stairs wind anticlockwise, of course, and they prove too much for me. I have to stop and sit down several times, my coughs echoing in the stairwell.

John sighs and shuffles his feet each time he has to wait for me. Eventually I get to the top. Small spheres, like tiny beads of glass, appear in my vision and pop like bubbles. I have to lean against the tower wall to stay on my feet. My breath rasps. Tristan looks at me and I nod reassuringly.

John raps on a thick door at the very top of the tower and, after a moment's wait and the clank of a thick metal latch, the door opens.

Belisencia gasps. Even Tristan backs up a step at the sight. I look past them and see a thin man in the doorway. But he is like no man I have ever seen; this man has the head of a bird.

"Are you ready to die?" the bird man says.

Chapter 44

THE BIRD-HEADED MAN TURNS HIS beaked face slightly and peers at us. "Oh, these are the knights." He backs into the octagonal chamber and motions for us to enter. "My apologies. I thought you were someone else."

John enters the chamber but the three of us remain outside the door. I think Tristan and Belisencia would have fled already if I was in good health. I have seen a bird man like this before. I have had nightmares about such a creature. Long, long ago. But I cannot place the time. I study him closely and realize that he does not have a bird head at all. He merely wears a long-beaked mask.

"You can go in," I whisper to Tristan. "It's a mask."

"I know it's a mask," Tristan whispers back. "But knowing doesn't make me any more inclined to go in."

I brush past him and understand his hesitation. There are three long trestle tables in the room and all three have bodies chained onto them. The closest is of a powerful-looking naked man. He turns his head toward me. His eyes are like a plaguers' eyes, only a deep blood red instead of black. He opens his mouth and a monstrous tongue lolls from it as he hisses.

"He is bound by chains," the thin man says. "He cannot hurt you."

I step inside. Tristan and Belisencia follow, taking short shuffling steps. Two men in leather jerkins stand just inside the door, short swords at their waists. They watch us carefully, hands on hilts.

The room is like a scholar's library—the ones where bookshelves have been stacked to dizzying heights and affixed to every wall. Except the shelves do not contain books. They contain phials and flasks, ceramic jars, leather pouches, pestles and mortars, funnels, and round-bottomed flasks, and all manner of what I can only assume are alchemical tools.

"You..." The words will not come out. "You..."

"Yes, his case is quite severe," the thin man says. "He seems terribly disoriented."

"You are the alchemist," I say finally.

The thin man takes off the wide-brimmed hat and slips the mask off his head.

I remember where I saw such masks. When I was a child, during the Black Death. I think doctors used to wear them to keep from contracting the Plague.

The alchemist walks to a peg and carefully hangs the hat, then places the mask on a shelf beside the peg. He studies the mask, uses both hands to adjust its position, studies it again, and nods.

"I am a scholar," he says. "Alchemists search for what *might be*. I study what *is*."

"So, is there a cure?" I say.

The alchemist studies me for a long moment, then shrugs. "Might be."

He threads his way through the tables toward the back wall of the tower.

"You cannot imagine the things we have gone through to get here," I say. "Tell me, please, is there a cure for this plague? I must know."

"Patience is bitter," the alchemist says, "but its fruit is sweet. Come to my workspace first so that I might look at your wound."

I follow the alchemist past the first table, the one with the powerfully built naked man. The man hisses again; his red eyes follow me.

The second table holds another naked man, but this one's eyes are normal. His bound hand stretches toward me as I pass and a single tear streaks down his cheek. He opens his mouth and I see no tongue. His throat is blistered and yellow and raw, but he manages a sorrowful croak.

I cannot look closely at the last table. It is like a butcher's block. A man has been cut open from throat to groin, and his ribs have been pulled apart. I have seen men cut wide open on the battlefield, but there is something ghastly about seeing one cut up in such a methodical fashion and displayed in this way. As I pass, the head turns toward me and I jump back so sharply that I clatter against the second table.

"He's alive!" I shout. Mother Mary, the man is still alive. His eyes are completely black. Belisencia squeals and covers her mouth, buries her face in Tristan's chest.

The alchemist has taken position at a wide wooden shelf that is set into one wall and supported by chains that rise to the ceiling. He glances back. "Yes, he is alive. Do not disturb him."

"Lucifer's bollocks!" Tristan says. "He's disturbing me!"

"What are you doing to him?" I ask.

The alchemist sighs deeply. "You are fighting men," he replies. "It is beyond your understanding." He sees my expression and holds up a hand. "I mean no offense. Such things are simply beyond the scope of men like you."

"How could that possibly be offensive?" Tristan says.

"Who are these people?" I ask.

The alchemist crosses his arms. "I had been led to believe one of you had a wound that needed tending."

I hold out my arm and the alchemist studies my wound, smells it, then holds my wrist up to one of the arched windows. I glance out and see a lone horseman riding south. The alchemist shakes his head. "English medicine can do nothing for this wound."

Tristan takes a step toward him. "What kind of—"

"And so," The alchemist says sharply, "it is a good thing that you came to me, for I do not rely solely upon English medicine." He walks a few paces along the perimeter of the tower and gestures to one of the guards at the doorway. "Daniel, the ladder, if you please." The guard, blond and sharp-eyed, fetches a ladder leaning near the doorway and brings it to the alchemist. When the guard nears me, I notice strange mottled scars across his forehead and one side of his jaw. "Fifth shelf," the alchemist says. "In a jar with a green circle painted on it."

Daniel climbs the ladder, takes the thick jar in two hands, and carefully steps down. The alchemist brings the jar to the workbench and removes the thick cork from the top. A vile odor fills the air. It is like the smell of a dead fish left out in the sun for days, then dropped into a bowl of rotted eggs. Inside the jar is a brown paste.

"What is that filth?" I ask.

"That *filth*," the alchemist says, "is Malta fungus. It is a medicine found on a rock off the coast of an island called Gozo. The Knights Hospitaller discovered the rock upon which it grew and they guard the site as if it were the king's bedchamber. To take fungus from the rock without permission is punishable by death." He holds up the jar and waves it under his nose. "This *filth* is so rare in Europe that only royalty can afford it. The Muslims call it 'The Great Treasure' because of its almost magical curative powers." He wedges the cork back onto the jar. "I have fifty-four drams of it left. Perhaps I should save it for someone who appreciates it."

I look at the jar. In my travels throughout Europe I have discovered a curious thing. The farther something travels, the more power it is perceived to have. A fruit that not even children will eat in Jerusalem will become an expensive cure for shingles in England. And a gourd grown in England will take on magical powers in Italy. But I have exhausted my country's best cures. And something about this alchemist gives me confidence.

"How does it work?" I ask.

He tsks and shakes his head. "As I mentioned before, you are fighting men. You would not understand even if I explained it to you. And as before, I mean no offense. Such things are simply beyond the scope of men like you."

I look into the jar and nod. "Cure me. Do what you have to do."

What he has to do, apparently, is bring me incomparable amounts of pain. He cleanses the wound with a fluid that makes me feel as if burning coals are being thrust under my skin. Then he cuts at the wound—his knife making sounds like footsteps in a distant swamp—to open it wide. The workbench trembles under my grip. I look away until I hear the sound of a cork being pulled free and smell the putrid odor of the Malta fungus.

"Interestingly, it is not really a fungus," he says. "It is a tuber."

"That is truly fascinating," Tristan says. "Don't you find that fascinating, Edward?"

I stare into Tristan's eyes and let him see my displeasure. I do not want to anger this alchemist. He is the last man on earth I want to anger.

The alchemist glances up at me. "You said you were a friend of Richard FitzAlan?"

I nod. "I am Sir Edward Dallingridge. My family and his have been very close for many generations."

The alchemist nods. "Perhaps, then, before I finish the treatment, I could ask something of you."

Take while the patient is in pain.

I let out a long breath. "I'm not in a position to refuse, am I?"

"Do you know the earl of Warwick?" he asks. "Thomas de Beauchamp?"

"I have met him several times," I say. "But I don't know him well."

"He is my patron," the alchemist says. "And I need to get a message to him. I understand Lord Richard and he are good friends. Perhaps you could deliver a message for me?"

"I haven't seen Lord Richard in six months," I say. "And I haven't seen Warwick in longer than that. I can't even tell you if they are alive."

The alchemist sighs. "Do you have any men?" he asks. "Any soldiers you could lend me?"

I shrug. "Back in Sussex I have men. But I haven't been to my home in nearly three weeks. Heaven knows if anyone is left back there. But if you have a cure for the plague, I will give you everything I have."

The alchemist shakes his head and uses a cylindrical brush to apply the salve to my wound. It stings but is also quite cool.

"Why do you need the men?" I ask.

"Because people are learning that I am here," he says. "They are discovering what it is I am doing. And they do not like it."

"And what exactly are you doing here?" I ask. "Have you found a cure? An alchemical cure? Is that what people don't like?"

He covers the wound with a linen pad soaked in a clear fluid, then bandages it neatly with linen strips.

"There," he says. "In two days you will be cured."

I thank him as he cleans up the clutter of his tools, but I can't help wondering what the House of Gemini has to say about his cure.

Tristan pulls a ceramic phial from a rack on the workbench. He takes a phial from his belt and compares them. The two look identical.

"Where did you get that?" The alchemist straightens the rack of phials so that they are perfectly flush with the edge of the bench again.

"From you, apparently," Tristan replies.

"Give it to me," the alchemist says. "That is dangerous. You should not have it."

"Dangerous?" Tristan puts his phial away and unstoppers the other. "I bet it's a cure for the plague." He lifts it toward his mouth. The alchemist crosses his arms and watches. "You aren't going to stop me?" Tristan asks.

"I warned you already," he replies. "The world is better off without fools who drink things they have been warned not to. Besides, I am running out of murderers and rapists. I could use another test subject."

"You are a pitiless bastard." Tristan stoppers the phial.

"Pity is a luxury," he responds. "And, at times of calamity, luxury is the first thing to die."

"Murderers and rapists?" Belisencia asks.

"Yes. Lord Warwick gave me thirty prisoners from his dungeons to help test my work." He nods to the phials. "Those contain the blood of plaguers. It is how I afflict the prisoners."

The mystery is solved. The simpleton gave Isabella phials of plaguer blood. I say a prayer for the souls of Danbury. Souls that we afflicted with our good intentions. A thought comes to me.

"You have a cure," I say. "That's why you didn't stop Tristan when he pretended to drink from the phial. You have a cure."

The alchemist looks at me curiously. "A peculiar conclusion. How did you reach it?"

I glance at Tristan, then look back to the alchemist and shrug. "Reason?"

"A warrior playing with reason is like a child playing with a loaded crossbow."

"So there is no cure?" Fear stabs at me.

"I didn't say that."

My chest rises and falls with each breath. I force myself to unclench my fists. "Stop playing games, man!" I say. "Is there a cure?"

The alchemist glances toward his guards, then at the men strapped to the tables. He looks back at me and sighs. "There is—"

A multitude of distant shouts rise up from outside. Even from the top of this tower I can hear the hatred in the voices. The violence.

The alchemist rushes to the arched window and looks out. He appears calm, but his fingers turn white on the sandstone ledge.

"They're back." He says it quietly, then turns toward the blond guard. "There are too many this time, Daniel." He looks at us with drooping eyes. "I am so very sorry. You will die with us now."

Episode 8

Suffolk

Norfolk

Yarmouth

Lowestoft

St. Benet's Abbey

Norwich

Caistor St. Edmund

Ipswich

Coddenham

Bures

St. Edmund's Bury

Roman Road

Sudbury

Hedingham

2 miles

Chapter 46

I PUSH PAST THE ALCHEMIST and gaze out from the tower window. A priest is the first thing I see, and it makes me sigh. Men have become savage as dogs in these dark times, and priests are the huntsmen who set those dogs loose upon the world.

The priest is a longbow shot away, on the opposite side of the River Bure, but I can see his robes clearly. Two younger clergymen trudge at his side, their heads cowled and bent forward. Behind these three men march scores of peasants wearing wool, linen, and scowls. Some of the men drag small rowboats along the marsh. It is the peasants who shout. I cannot make out their words, but the sharp, angry cries and the weapons in their hands deliver the message clearly: they are hounds, and the hunt is afoot.

"Between ninety and a hundred of them," I say. "And six boats. Looks like they're out for blood. Are you the fox?"

The alchemist collapses onto a stool beside the workbench and shakes his head. "There are only seven guards here at the abbey," he says. "Remember when I asked if you could bring soldiers?"

Tristan looks through the window. "It's just priests and farmers," he says. "What do you need soldiers for?"

"This is a monastery, not a castle," the alchemist replies. "They have spent weeks searching for a way in. And they have found it. They know the docks are our weakest point, and today they have brought boats to get them there."

"What do they want?" Belisencia asks.

The alchemist picks a thread from his robe. "They want to apply flame to my body. Alchemy, apparently, is a sin."

"So is murder," Tristan replies.

"There's still time," I say. "They haven't reached the Bure yet. You were about to tell us if there is a cure."

"What does it matter?" the alchemist replies. "It's not the plague that will kill us today. There is no cure for fire or steel."

"We will rid you of those peasants," I say. "Tell us about the cure."

The alchemist looks toward the window as the shouts grow ever louder. "You cannot defeat a hundred men."

"We will," I say.

"We will?" Tristan asks.

The shouts are dangerously close now. Other voices rise against them. Probably the halberdiers from the abbey warning then off. The alchemist gazes toward the window and straightens a cross that hangs from his neck. He looks back at me. "How can you possibly fight them all?"

"You said it yourself," I reply. "I am a fighting man."

A unified cry rises from the mob. The huntsmen are working the dogs into a blood-frenzy.

"Is there a cure?" My heart batters my chest. If I knew there was a cure, I could fight ten thousand peasants and whistle as I did. *"Is there a cure?"*

The alchemist glances toward the window again, runs his hands through his hair, then nods. "Yes," he says. "There is a cure."

Chapter 47

It is as if every voice in heaven erupts into song. As if the skies rain gold and silver. It is as if all of God's angels explode in my heart and shower my soul with the blood of Christ. I am not certain that is a good thing, but if it is, that is what I feel. I am drunk with exultation.

Hallelujah!

It is the most spiritual moment I have experienced. I feel the touch of God, and it is an alchemist's sin that is responsible.

There is a cure!

A beam from the setting sun splashes through the arched window like God's smile. Tears flood my eyes. I fall to my knees and cover my face with my hands. There can be no words more beautiful, more powerful, more heavenly.

There is a cure!

I will start a new religion, and its bible will hold only four words.

There is a cure!

I will climb the mountains of Asia and shout madly from their peaks.

There is a cure!

I will dance with the King of France, laugh wildly, and sing the words.

Existe un remède!

And Elizabeth will be at my side through it all. My Elizabeth. I will see her crooked half smile again. I will kiss those long, pale fingers. I will trace figure eights around the freckles of her legs and bury my nose in her flaxen hair.

There is a cure!

The alchemist clears his throat. "There is a cure," he says. "But I do not have any left. And I cannot make any more."

Chapter 48

I DREAM THAT I AM under a red ocean. Perhaps it is the hairy sea. And in that dream I am killing a man.

My hands hold his neck. My fingers squeeze, but as in all dreams, something stops me from achieving my goal. Something keeps my fingers from closing around the man's throat.

Tristan is in that dream. And so is Belisencia. Their faces are wild. Their mouths move as if they are screaming, but I cannot hear them. Probably because I am under the red waves of the hairy sea.

Some unseen force latches onto me from behind. Perhaps it is a hairy tick. More of them latch onto me and pull. The red water slowly turns clear.

A murky droning sound drifts to my ears. An urgent song of the sea that becomes more and more persistent. It sounds like Tristan.

"Let him go!" Tristan shouts. He holds one of my hands.

"You'll kill him!" Belisencia shrieks. She holds my other hand.

A guard behind me has his arms around my waist. Another has his hand on my face and is pulling my head backward. The man I am killing is the alchemist, of course.

I should not be killing the alchemist, so I release him.

The guards wrestle me to the ground, shouting for me to cease. One of the guards clouts me on the back of the head. Tristan kneels and shelters me from the guards.

"It's all right, Ed," he says. "It'll be all right."

"He is desperate," Belisencia pleads with the alchemist. "His wife is plagued."

The alchemist looks at me and something in his expression softens. All of the shouts from outside have quieted except for one. A single voice screaming in the singsong of prayer.

I look up at the alchemist, my breath coming in gasps. He has fallen back against the workbench and instead of looking at me, he studies the mess behind him. He holds one hand to his throat and with the other he absently picks up toppled jars and phials. He does not look at me until all the objects are righted.

"What...what do you mean?" I say. "If you have the cure, you must make more."

The alchemist straightens himself and tugs at his tunic. "I cannot make more. It is impossible."

The guards loosen their hold on me. I push myself upward with one hand, and my arm trembles under my weight.

"Why?" I ask. "Why is it impossible? I don't understand."

The alchemist returns his attention to the workbench, his hands shifting each of the objects by the barest of degrees. His eyes are calculating, comparing, judging their positions. But his hands shake, and a flush stains his cheeks. "Because sometimes there are no bridges across rivers," he says. "Sometimes you have no boats and the currents are too strong. I cannot make more of the cure."

"You are the only one capable of saving this kingdom," I say. "You must make more! It is injustice to sit by idly while the kingdom dies!"

The alchemist whirls around, his elbow brushing a round-bottomed flask and knocking it off the bench. The glass shatters with a crisp finality.

"What do you know about injustice?" His eyes are slits beneath his brows. "I haven't left this monastery in nearly three months, and I have spent most of that time here, in this tower. I work all day every day long into the night, sleeping only after the sun has risen again. But not even sleep allows me escape from my labors, because my dreams are of waters and waxes and tinctures and inductions. But I continue. I continue despite the priests and villagers at my gate. They call me a demon and a miscreant and Satan's dog. I suffer dead animals hurled over the walls. I have been burned in effigy a dozen times. The very people I am trying to save want to murder me. But I continue. Always I continue. And do you know what the true injustice is?"

"That we are subjected to your boring rant?" Tristan asks.

"That I cannot make a cure!" The alchemist closes his eyes and the rage melts away. His shoulders shake and tears squeeze past the clench of his lids. "I have failed. And I continue to fail. All of the suffering has been for naught. I am incapable of making a cure. *That* is the true injustice." He collapses back into the stool.

I swallow a flood of bile and will myself not to vomit. "But you said…" I cannot speak.

"You told us there was a cure," Belisencia says gently.

The alchemist nods without opening his eyes. "There is a cure," he replies. "But it is not mine. That is the second great injustice of my existence."

Tristan helps me rise to my feet. "Whose cure is it?" I ask, my voice shaking.

The alchemist opens his eyes and looks skyward. "It belongs to an old man," he says. "A traveling peddler named Gregory the Wanderer."

Chapter 49

I AM GLAD TRISTAN IS holding my arm because I think the alchemist's words would have toppled me otherwise. Gregory the Wanderer. The peddler who traded us the phials of plague, calling them a cure. We gave one of those phials to the villagers of Danbury and afflicted the lot of them. Why would Gregory have traded with Isabella the Witch for phials he thought contained a cure if he already had a cure? Phials that he obtained from this very alchemist.

Someone pounds on the tower door and tells us what we already know. "A mob approaches! And they have boats!" It sounds like John, the drunk from the gatehouse.

"I answered your question," the alchemist says. "I believe you have a hundred peasants to drive off." His tone implies that he has little faith that we will be true to our word. The pounding on the door grows more violent.

"Daniel! Wilfred! We need you at the docks!" shouts John.

"I have more questions," I say.

"Shall I answer them on the pyre?"

"We are not finished with this conversation," I say.

The peasants cheer loudly outside. The priest is no doubt giving them a rousing speech. I stride to the window and look out. The crowd is assembled at the far riverbank, the boats poised on the shore. In a few moments, the Bure will be swarming with angry men. If they reach the docks, there are only wooden doors to stop them. I have seen what happens when frustrated armies finally breach a city wall. It is a hell that makes the scenes in Matheus's tapestry look like children at play. I have never been on the wrong side of that hell, and I do not wish to be today.

"Give us our weapons back," I say. "We'll send those dogs home."

John the drunk gives us back our cannons, my sword, and Tristan's dagger. I take a lit prayer candle from the chancel and we run from the church to the cluster of abbey buildings along the river.

The priest and his mob are still on the opposite bank. Three of the four halberdiers from the monastery face them from the docks, crossbows in hand. A square-sailed cog, similar to the ones we saw in the narrow channel east of Norwich, is moored to one side of the docks. The Norfolk winds tug at the furled canvas of the sail.

Tristan and I take positions on the dock with the rest of the guards. Belisencia and the alchemist stand just behind us.

I call to the priest: "Is this one of those open-air masses?"

"Yield!" shouts the priest. "I am Father Simon, and I say yield, heathens! Yield the abbey to us and pray to the Holy Father for forgiveness! You must open the gates of St. Benet's and allow God's Justice to enter!"

"We let God's Justice in a few hours ago," Tristan calls. "He says to tell you He is having a lovely time and that all of you idiots should return home."

The alchemist clears his throat at my side. "Perhaps we shouldn't antagonize them."

"Alchemy is a sin!" the priest shouts. "Alchemy and witchcraft are the cause of this plague!" He gestures to the crowd behind him. "And we shall be the cure."

"I thought prayer was the only true and righteous cure," I shout.

"Yes," says the priest. "We will pray for you as you burn."

"But..." Tristan squints and shakes his head. "We're not plagued. And if we were, we wouldn't need to be cured, since you were going to burn us alive anyway. This metaphor is confusing, Father."

"*Open the bloody gates!*" the priest shouts. His shoulders rise with a deep breath, then he calls in a calmer voice. "Open the gates and I promise we will let everyone live, except for the alchemist. All servants and soldiers will be spared. But the alchemist defiles holy ground! Saint Benet would weep if he knew that a sorcerer had turned his abbey into a cesspit of foul magic and sin."

Saint Benet is the patron of scholars and students, so I believe this abbey to be a fitting place for an alchemist. The poetry of this observation would likely be lost on Father Simon, though. The priest has a look in his eyes that I have seen too often in the eyes of men with power. In the ancient times, an old soldier and king named Caesar crossed a river called the Rubicon on his way to attack Rome. A monk told me that when the army crossed this river, there was no turning back. He was committed to the attack. The priest before me has not crossed the Bure, but I believe he crossed the Rubicon long ago. There is no turning back for him, and so there is no point talking to him any further.

"I'm tired of this conversation, Father," I say. "This man is doing nothing wrong. He is searching for answers. Nothing more."

"God is the answer! And death is the wage of sin!"

"Did you hear that, Tristan?" I ask. "He says God is the answer."

Tristan draws his ten-shot hand bombard from the sack at his shoulder. "Truly," he replies, "is there any question that cannot be answered with God's Love?"

I hand Daniel the prayer candle I took from the church and draw my own cannon. Tristan lights two firing cords and gives one to me as the priest continues to blather.

"It is God, not the works of a sorcerer that will save us!" he shouts. "'For by grace you have been saved through faith. And this is not your own doing; it is the gift of God, not a result of works!' That is written in Ephisians!" He gestures toward the mob behind him. "These men gathered with me are God's warriors! God shall be our sword. God shall be our armor! We will not leave until God's Justice has been done! We are unshakable in our faith! Do you hear me? We are unshakable in our faith!"

Tristan and I raise the cannons.

"What are you doing?" the alchemist asks.

"Shaking their faith," I reply.

"This plague is a test!" Father Simon shouts. "And by turning to sorcery, you have failed! 'Count it all joy, my brothers, when you meet trials of various kinds, for you know that the testing of your faith produces steadfastness.'"

"Hallelujah." Tristan and I say it together as we light the guns. The thunderous blast of the explosions and the thick belch of smoke startle me, as they always do. But if the guns make my heart stutter, I can only imagine the terror the peasants on the far bank must feel.

They fly like startled pigeons.

Our guns were aimed into the river. We were not looking to put holes in flesh, merely to send flesh running. And run it does. The peasants do not stop.

The three priests flinched at the explosions—the two younger men dropped to their knees at the sound—but none of them took even one step away from the riverbank.

"God's Warriors are going the wrong way, Father Simon." Tristan shouts. "Do the Ephisians speak about cowardly flight? Or abandoning faith in the face of overwhelming noise?"

"You will not laugh when the flames melt your flesh," Father Simon says. "You will weep when you feel the fiery lakes and the sting of brimstone. You will pray that God forgives you when you see the hell that awaits."

"I've seen it," Tristan says. "And the fiery-lakes-and-brimstone thing is bollocks. It's just people with large heads."

Chapter 50

THE SOLDIERS AND SERVANTS OF the abbey laugh and whistle as they board the cog and row it to the far shore. They attach ropes to the six rowboats and tie the ropes to the cog. Off in the distance I spot a group of peasants stumbling back toward us. I watch them for a time, then realize that they are not peasants at all but plaguers.

"They've been coming more regularly," says the alchemist. "And in greater numbers. We are remote here and surrounded by rivers and marshes. But the afflicted can smell our animals. I fear more and more of them will come, until we are overrun."

"More mindless enemies," I say.

The alchemist walks a dozen paces away and kneels. He offers a prayer to Saint Benet and the Virgin. Our alchemist is a religious man. I try to wade through the many ironies of this fact, but Belisencia interrupts.

"It is God's Will that we came here when we did." She looks toward the alchemist. "Or they would have killed him."

I shake my head. "I doubt it. It's almost impossible to break into an enemy fortress."

"It can't be that hard," she replies. "Our armies have taken many fortresses in France, have they not?"

I study her for a moment. "Do you know how most enemies get inside fortifications?"

She thinks on this. "Climbing the walls?"

I shake my head. "Someone on the inside opens the gates."

She looks at me as if trying to gauge my sincerity, then glances at Tristan.

"It's true," he says. "Either a traitor opens the gate or the governor surrenders and opens them. I've been trying to convince Edward not to put any gates or doors in his castle wall at Bodiam."

"Castles with no gates or doors are called tombs, Tristan," I say.

"Yes," he replies. "And have you ever heard of an army getting into a tomb? It never happens."

The alchemist tells us that he will dine in two hours at the refectory and invites us to join him. He will answer no questions before supper and suggests we bathe and let his servants wash our clothing.

John the drunk, who seems more sober after the peasant confrontation, leads us to the bath, below the dormer. A wooden tub sits at the center of the ribbed undercroft. Servants scurry past us with buckets of hot water, pour them into the tub, then rush off to fetch more. Other servants dump boiled chamomile and brown fennel into the rising water. Tristan does not wait for them to finish. He walks toward the tub.

"Thanks be to House Gemini," he says. "Even the filth on me has filth on it." He strips off his armor, letting each piece fall to the stone floor with a clatter, then pulls off his mail shirt and gambeson in one motion. "Unclean!" he moans, mimicking the lepers from Norwich.

Belisencia blushes at his shirtless body, but she does not leave the room. Her gaze drifts across Tristan's muscled back.

"Pardon me, but can you..." Tristan calls back to a servant girl, then trails off when he notes Belisencia's gaze.

She starts and averts her eyes. "You...I didn't know you were going to..."

Tristan shakes his head. "'But I say to you that every woman who looks at a man with lust has already committed adultery with him in her heart.'"

"I wasn't looking...I simply...you removed everything so quickly..."

He walks toward her. "And since it is in your heart already..."

She backs away from him. "Tristan..."

"Modesty is what separates us from animals," he says, circling her slowly. "Why don't you join me in the bath? We can be animals for a time."

"Tristan..." Belisencia follows him with her eyes, turning her head to keep him in sight. Her gaze brushes across his bare chest.

"We can pretend we're baboons. Pick the filth from one another."

"If only...if only I could pick the filth from your brain." Her words are almost a whisper.

I have seen Tristan besiege women like this before. It has always amused me, watching him break through their defenses. Today is different. Today I feel like a defender. As if I should protect Belisencia. But she is like one of those French cities in Normandy where half the population supports the attackers. It makes for a difficult defense.

"Why do you hesitate?" he says. "It's Paul, isn't it? That bastard. I'll challenge him to a duel, I will."

"Stop playing games, Tristan." A flush darkens her face from neck to cheeks.

The smile fades from Tristan's face. "I'm not playing games."

She lifts a hand to brush at her hair but he grabs the hand and kisses it, stares into her eyes. They remain frozen in that position until Belisencia slowly pulls free. Tristan steps closer to her so their bodies are almost touching. She returns his gaze for a long moment, then blinks and shakes her head.

"I...I will wait upstairs until the two of you are done. I can have my bath later." She whirls around, tripping over the hem of her dress, and stumbles toward the stairs. With a final glance toward Tristan, she gathers her skirts and flees the undercroft.

The refectory is sparse. A tall wooden crucifix hangs on one wall and a statuette of the Virgin Mary holding the babe, Jesus, sits on a shelf on the opposite wall. There are no other ornaments in the building. All of the guards and three women join us for the meal. The two halberdiers who exchanged dangerous looks earlier sit across from me and do their best not to look my way. I stare at them for a long time.

Belisencia looks radiant again. She wears a new dress—green and simple, but pretty—over her kirtle. Her hair has been brushed and plaited into spirals on either side of her head, with a netted caul holding the plaits in place. Tristan's gaze never strays from her as he pulls a chair out beside his.

The alchemist leads us in a short prayer, then the servants bring supper from the kitchens. It is a feast. A pig and five not-so-clever chickens have been slaughtered in our honor. It is the finest meal I have seen since leaving St. Edmund's Bury.

"How is it that Gregory the Wanderer has a cure?" I ask.

The alchemist chews slowly without looking at me. He drinks wine and wipes at his lips carefully with the tablecloth before answering. "He traded with a ship captain from Damascus."

Damascus. Syria. Ships from the Arab lands often visit England. They trade silk and spices and perfumes for English wool, which they covet. If a Syrian captain had a cure, then this plague must have struck Arabia as well. Is the entire world crawling with the hungry dead? Or have they completely cured the plague in Syria? Must I travel to Damascus to heal my Elizabeth?

"Arabian and Persian medicine is far better than ours," the alchemist says. "They do not see science as sin." He touches the cross at his neck.

"So if I want the cure, I must go to Syria?" I ask. My heart aches at the thought. It would take weeks to get to Syria. Perhaps months. Elizabeth does not have months.

"I do not think you will find it there, either," the alchemist replies. "I spoke with a shipmaster who had arrived from Alexandria. The plague runs unchecked through the Arab lands. He said there are no ports left to dock upon, and fires rage in all the major cities. Whoever created this cure did not create it in time. I do not expect any more to be made."

"And Gregory gave it to you?" I do not trust the wandering peddler, and after his last cure, I certainly do not trust this one.

"He was starving. So he traded seven ampoules of the cure for ten pigs."

"And you have tested the cure?" I ask.

"Of course I have." He and Daniel exchange glances. "I tried it on two subjects. One ampoule each."

"And it cured them?" I try to keep my voice from trembling.

"It cured one of them, yes."

"And the other?"

A silence falls over the table. Guards exchange glances. The alchemist cuts into the pork and chews slowly, then wipes his mouth again. "The other was not successful."

Tristan and I look to one another.

"Not successful in what way?" I ask.

Another silence settles in the hall. One of the guards clears his throat. A wooden plate clatters to the floor in the kitchens.

"Did the person remain plagued?" I ask.

"Yes," says the alchemist. "Let us leave it at that, shall we?"

I do not want to leave it at that, but the alchemist cuts at his roast and does not meet my gaze.

"So the cure only works for some people," Belisencia says.

"I believe so," the alchemist replies. "It is common in such things. Everyone's humors are in a different state of balance." His gaze grows distant, his voice almost a whisper.

"It is possible that the second ampoule was mixed incorrectly. I doubt we will ever know for sure."

"So you still have five ampoules left," says Tristan.

The alchemist drinks his wine for a long time. He sets the cup down gently and moves it an inch to one side, then half an inch to the other. "I...used the other ampoules in my studies." He stares at the tabletop. "I have none left."

"And you can't make more of it?" I ask. "You can't determine what was in them?"

"Oh I know what was in them. Each ampoule has a strip of parchment attached with the ingredients written in Arabic."

It takes me a moment to respond to this. "You...you have the ingredients?"

He nods.

"So why can't you make more?"

"Because it isn't like making stew," he snaps. "You do not simply pour ingredients into a bowl and stir. It is complicated work. And I do not expect men who fight for a living to understand it." His chair grates across the floor as he rises. "I have work to do. I hope you will pardon me." He stands, sets his knife down carefully on the table, and leaves the room.

I look to Tristan, but he and Belisencia are engrossed in conversation. My eyes fall upon the tapestry of the Virgin Mary.

"He is torn apart by guilt." It is the blond guard, Daniel, sitting at my side. I note once again the deep, mottled scars along his jaw and above his eye. And realization nearly knocks me to the floor.

"You...you were his subject."

He takes a long breath and nods. "He cured me."

My breath quickens. I study him closely. There is no trace of black in his eyes. The only evidence of his affliction is the scarring on his face. "Dear God." I look closely at his skin, at his hair and fingers. I know it is unseemly to stare at him in this way, but I cannot look away. He had the plague and he is cured. "The alchemist must have caught your affliction early," I say. "I can scarcely tell you were afflicted."

He shakes his head. "I was far gone. They tell me that my skin was splitting and turning black. Boils all over me." He strips his sleeve back and I see scars along his forearm. "The cure removed my affliction. And my body did the rest. It just healed."

I close my eyes. Think of the black bands on the skin of Elizabeth's wrists. I think of Morgan's peeling, blackened skin. I can save them both.

"Has...has he come close?" I run a hand along the skin of Daniel's forearm, feeling the scars. "Is he close to copying the Syrian cure?"

Daniel shrugs. "He's trying. But whoever made the Syrian cure wrote the names of the ingredients in a mysterious way. Made them into riddles. One of the elements was called 'the juice of hadeed.' Dominic...the alchemist... he told me that hadeed means metal or iron, and he had to work out that 'the juice of metal' was quicksilver. They were all like that. Each of the elements. He's very clever, Dominic. But there's one element that he can't work out."

I'm terrible with riddles, but if Elizabeth's life depends on the answer, I will read an entire library to find it. "What riddle is giving him trouble?"

"One of the element calls for blood from the ah-teen," Daniel replies. "Ah-teen means..."

I stand, gasping. Daniel trails off, his eyes wide. "Are you not well? I can call the—"

"I'm fine," I say. But I am not. The room is spinning. I can hear the wash of blood through my ears. I think of Sir Ethelbert, the old knight whose grandfather used to tell stories about the crusades.

They didn't call them dragons. They called them aw-teen.

"I know what ah-teen is," I say. "It's not a riddle. I need to speak with the alchemist at once."

Chapter 51

"Ludicrous." The alchemist shakes his head again and again. We are in his tower once more. "I have no doubt that the cure requires blood, but it is preposterous to think that he meant the blood of an actual dragon."

"Why?" I reply. "Why couldn't it be the blood of a dragon?"

"First and foremost, because dragons *do not exist*!" he snaps. "Alchemy is not sorcery. We do not use pieces of mythical beasts to make medicine. We use books and learning and experiments. The person who made that cure was cryptic about each of the ingredients. Why would he then be straightforward about the last one? I appreciate that you want to help, but you are knights. These things are beyond your comprehension. No offense meant. Such things are simply not in the realm of your understanding."

"But what if I could bring you dragon blood," I say. "Would you try using it?"

"Why not bring me fairy dust?" the alchemist replies. "Or a feather from the tail of the phoenix?"

"Because I don't know where to find those things," I say. "But I can bring you dragon blood. How much do you need?"

"We might as well bring him the entire dragon," Tristan says.

"Too right, Tristan. We'll bring you the entire dragon."

The alchemist shakes his head, his lip drawn into a snarl. "You are fools. Where do you intend to find a dragon?"

I smile at him and cross my arms. "You are a simple scholar. It is beyond your comprehension."

"No offense meant," Tristan adds. "Such things are simply not in your realm of understanding."

We sleep that night in one of the dorters on straw-filled mattresses meant for monks. There are twenty-six beds arranged in two rows in the long chamber. I wonder what happened to the monks.

I think for a time about the dragon blood. It sounds foolish now that I consider it carefully. The alchemist, Dominic, is right of course. He is not making a witch's spell. He is making a medical tincture. And medical tinctures do not rely upon dragon blood or bat wings or bear bollocks. But I have to believe it can work. If it does not, my only hope lies in tracking down Gregory the Wanderer and obtaining the cure from him. And Gregory the Wanderer is not an easy man to find.

Tristan creeps out of bed sometime in the night. I know where he is going. I feel an urge to stop him, to protect Belisencia's honor, but I do not think she wants her honor protected. And in this time of darkness and misery, how can I disapprove of two people seeking happiness in one another?

I think of Elizabeth again and feel the wash of hot tears in my eyes.

I wake from a nightmare of grasping hands and hissing mouths into the far worse nightmare of my life without Elizabeth. I check that my weapons and armor are beneath my bed. Tristan is back in bed, facedown and snoring. I let him sleep and walk down the day stairs into the cloisters, where I hear voices. Belisencia sits on the grass with three servant girls and one of the two halberdiers who earned my suspicions yesterday. The five of them eat bread and strawberries and walnuts. Belisencia's smile is a spring that has bubbled up from the depths of her soul.

"Good morning to you, Sir Edward." She practically sings it.

I grunt a good morning and take a seat.

"Are we leaving today?" Belisencia asks.

"Looks that way." I stare at the halberdier—a thin, auburn-haired man with eyes that bulge—and take a husk of bread from a basket on the grass.

Footsteps sound in the arcade. The second of the two suspect halberdiers steps into the garth and freezes in place when he sees me. He is even thinner than the first and has a nose so long you could churn butter with it. He looks like he wants to flee, but he simply exchanges a look with the other halberdier and joins us.

Gooseflesh rises on my arms. There was true fear in the man's eyes. I want to get our horses and leave the abbey right now, but I know I am overreacting. These men would not be the first commoners to fear me. Perhaps they heard about my outburst in the alchemist's tower.

"I've done nothing but travel since I met Tristan and you," she replies. "It's madness."

One of the halberdiers shrugs and speaks through a mouth full of bread. "Im dese dimes of madness, ondy madness will dave us."

I stop chewing and stare at him. My breath quickens. I try to convince myself that I am being foolish. "What did you say?"

He holds up a forefinger, swallows, then says, "In these times of madness, only madness will save us."

I rise slowly. "Where did you hear that?"

He shrugs, his smile drying up. "I...I just...I don't know. I've just...heard it somewhere."

I throw the loaf of bread at him. "*Where did you hear it?*"

He bats the bread away, flinches at the tone of my voice. "I...don't remember," he holds up a hand toward me. "Calm yourself. It's just a saying."

It is indeed just a saying. Sir Gerald's saying.

I recall the lone horseman I saw riding south yesterday when I looked out the tower window.

"Belisencia, get Tristan!" I run through the arches of the arcade.

"What?" She remains seated, her face twisted with confusion.

"We're leaving. Now!" I yank the door to the church open and run through the nave, feeling like a fool for reacting like this. Perhaps the expression came from a poem that many people have seen. Perhaps I should read more books. I throw open the front doors of the church.

Yes, I am a fool. But only because it took me so long to react.

A long column of horsemen file through the inner gate-house. I run south, toward the river, but a dozen men in brigandine and kettle helmets race toward me from the docks. I break toward the north wall. I can loop around. If I reach the stables I can...I can...I'm not sure what I can do, but I must try something. Belisencia peers out through the church doors.

"Get Tristan!" I shout. "Head for the stables!"

I curve around the north side of the church and run as fast as I can. Fatigue sets in swiftly. My wound is better, but I am not fully healed yet. My pace slows as fire sweeps through my lungs. I hear the deep thud of hoof-beats behind me. A fit of coughing forces me to slow even further. Two horsemen holding spears rumble past and wheel to face me. I fall to my knees, coughing. Spearheads gleam before me.

"This one might die before we can kill him," one of the horsemen says.

The horsemen lead me back to the church doors. Belisencia and the two halberdiers are in the company of the soldiers that I saw arriving from the docks. At least twenty horse-men have assembled halfway between us and the inner gate-house. Two standards flutter above them. The first is a lion and staff, which I do not recognize. But I know the second very well: the three roosters. Sir Gerald of Thunresleam.

The doors to the church swing open and a group of soldiers in chain-mail tunics walk outside. Two of them hold Tristan. I close my eyes. We are surrounded, they have Tristan, and I am a fool for leaving my weapons in the dorter. At least I could have died fighting.

"Tristan!" Belisencia tries to run to him but a guard holds her back. "Who are they?" Her voice trembles. "Why do they have Tristan?"

"They are Sir Gerald's men," I say. "We might have mentioned Sir Gerald on our travels. Insane. Cruel. Wants us dead."

"No!" The thick tears leap from her eyes. "How did he get into the monastery?"

I watch the horsemen make their way toward us. "How do most enemies breach enemy walls?" I pound one of the halberdiers in the face as hard as I can, shattering his broomstick nose. He drops to the earth like pigeon shit as Sir Gerald's men take hold of me. "Someone on the inside opens the gates."

Chapter 52

Most of the horsemen stop a dozen paces from the church, but two of them amble closer until they are directly in front of us. Both are fully armored. The first rides a dappled charger and wears one of those hideous new hounskull helmets with the muzzle-shaped visors. The other rides a monstrous black destrier and wears a bascinet helm. The visor of this man's helmet has been replaced with a steel mask made to look like an animal face—a roaring ape of some sort. I have not seen the helm before, but I have seen the black destrier.

Sir Gerald has been on the wrong end of cannon blasts the last two times we met. The most recent was the gun explosion that killed Isabella the Witch and ravaged part of Gerald's face. His new helmet hides the scars of that meeting. There will be torture in store for us. I do not know what kind of torture, but I imagine it will make Alexander the Cruel seem saintly.

"Sir Edward." Gerald's voice trembles, although I cannot tell if it is with excitement or hatred. "Sir Tristan. How wonderful to see old friends." His voice sounds tinny from behind the mask.

"What's that on your face?" Tristan says. "A baboon?"

The steel mask turns toward Tristan. "It is the great gorilla of the Africas. The most powerful creature of the jungle."

"Is that how you see yourself?" Tristan laughs and points to the three roosters of Gerald's crest. "You Thunresleam knights and your little cocks. Always getting above yourselves."

Sir Gerald turns to the man at his side. "I shall wear his tongue as a pendant before the day is done."

"Release him," I say. "Tristan had nothing to do with Sir John's death." Sir John, Gerald's hero, died at the Battle of Lighe, fighting a French army. The same French army whose survivors Alexander the Cruel strapped to wagon wheels. But the French did not kill Sir John. He was torn apart by plaguers that I led to the battlefield.

Mea maxima culpa.

The ape mask turns toward me. "There is more than enough guilt for both of you." He gestures to the man at his side. "This is my new ally, King Brian."

The man raises his dog-face visor and frowns. "Am I allowed to call myself a king?" Sweat glistens on his trimmed, black beard.

"Of course you are," Gerald replies. "King Brian of Yarmouth. Those with land and castles are the new kings. We must each carve out our kingdoms."

The man nods. "As you say." He leans forward in the saddle and addresses us. "I am Brian Hastings, King of Yarmouth. And any enemy of King Gerald is an enemy of mine."

Belisencia sucks in a sharp breath and slips behind Tristan.

Gerald points to the halberdier behind me. "You there. I need to take these two men somewhere. A place where I can peel their skin off and urinate on the pulp." He cackles and looks at King Brian. "You can piss on them, too. We can piss on them together!"

King Brian's smile is a strained one. "Very kind, really, but—"

"No, no, I insist. It will seal our alliance. A symbolic gesture. Pissing on our enemies together."

King Brian shrugs meekly. "I suppose."

"You can take them to the undercroft of the dorter," says the halberdier. "There's a tub there."

Someone shouts "No!" from inside the church. The alchemist steps outside and blinks against the sun. "No. Take them to the cellar of my tower. There is only one door and no windows. No chance for them to escape."

"You filthy bastard!" I lunge toward him but soldiers pull me back and drag me away from the church doors.

"Who are you?" Sir Gerald asks.

"I am Dominic of Norwich, granted this monastery by the earl of Warwick."

"And why do you wish these men harm?"

"Because you do, your highness. And in these dark times we must bow to the new order of things. I wish to keep the monastery and to be allowed a continuation of my studies. In return, I will serve you however I can."

"We should have let you burn!" Tristan shouts.

"The monastery belongs to King Brian now," Gerald says. "You may appeal to him. But in the meantime." He claps his hands together. "Guards, bind Sir Edward and Sir Tristan and take them into the cellar of the tower."

We are pushed toward the church. Belisencia tries to follow but two soldiers bar her path. "Tristan!" she shrieks. "*Tristan!*"

King Brian stands in his stirrups and points to Belisencia. "Wait!" The guards stop. "I know that woman."

All eyes fall upon Belisencia, who wipes at her tears roughly and spits toward King Brian. "You know who I am, but you do not know me. You never have."

"She's comely," says Gerald. "Who is she?"

"She's—"

"Elizabeth of Lancaster," Belisencia spits. "Countess of Pembroke. Cousin to King Richard, and sister to Henry of Bolingbroke."

"Elizabeth of Lancaster?" The thoughts jumble in my head too quickly to make sense of things. "You're…you're…"

She looks at me, and more tears fall from her eyes. "Daughter to John of Gaunt. Though I hold little love for him."

"You're John of Gaunt's daughter?" Tristan asks.

"And wife to my cousin, John Hastings," King Brian adds. "She escaped from his household and has been missing for months. We shall be rewarded for her return."

"Wife?" Tristan's voice is sharp as a razor. "You have a husband?"

Belisencia, or Elizabeth, or whoever she is, reaches past the guards and runs a hand along Tristan's face. "I can explain it. I can explain all of it."

Sir Gerald laughs. A loud, uninterrupted stream of madness. "This is…this is the best day of my life. I could not have planned it any better. Take them away."

We are shoved through the church doors. Belisencia shouts after us. "It's not as it seems! Tristan! *Tristan!*" The boom of the closing church doors cut off her scream. The guards bind our wrists with iron manacles and we are dragged through the dark nave toward the octagonal tower. The alchemist walks ahead of us, holding a set of keys, the jingle of them echoing in the church.

"The peasants were right!" Tristan shouts. "You *are* Satan's dog! Burning is too good for you!"

"Why?" I shout. "Why betray us?"

The alchemist stops at the beveled archway leading to the tower stairs and looks back at me. "You are fighting men," he says sadly. "It is beyond your understanding." He takes a candle from a sconce on the wall and walks down the stairs.

The cellar is a low-ceilinged room. So low-ceilinged that I have to duck as they shove me inside. Tristan does the same. It smells of feces and urine in the room. The alchemist reaches in and lights a torch on the wall beside the doorway. It is a large room despite the low ceiling. The torchlight does not illuminate much of it, so the alchemist steps inside and extends his arm. The candlelight shines on something cylindrical to our left. The smell seems to emanate from there.

"Do you see it?" The alchemist whispers. He slips a dagger into my hands. "Do what you must. Then get to the top."

An instant later the two guards enter the room. I fumble to hide the dagger beneath my wrists.

One of the guards, a fat man with a tangled beard, covers his nose. "Oi, but that's a horrid smell!"

"A hermit lived here," the alchemist replies. "I'm afraid we never cleaned this chamber when we took over the monastery."

The two guards flip a penny to see which one will stay in the room. The portly one loses and groans; the other laughs and takes position outside the door. As the alchemist departs, he glances to my left one last time. The door creaks shut and the lock clanks true. The portly guard pounds on the door. "It ain't right leaving me here with this smell!"

The lock clanks again and the door groans open. "What are you thumping about?" the other guard asks.

"It ain't right, this smell!"

"You lost square. Shut your mouth and do your job." The door slams shut again and the lock slides into place.

The fat guard waves us away from the door. "You two stand over there, right? Don't come near me." He puts the back of his hand to his nose and grimaces. "God's Thumb, this smell is awful. This is the worst post I've ever had."

It's about to get worse for him. I flip the dagger so the blade is out and find the man's throat with my eyes. I have to be quick and cut deep or he will cry out.

An instant before I raise the dagger, something in the room growls deeply. A long, winding, animal growl that echoes in the circular chamber.

Chapter 53

I HIDE THE DAGGER AGAIN and stare into the darkness.

"What the bloody hell was that?" the portly guard asks.

Whatever made the noise is on the opposite end of the room. The three of us huddle against the door and stare into the darkness. Something laughs. A woman's laugh. Musical. It continues for a long time, growing higher and higher pitched until it becomes a shriek. And when the shriek ends, the echoes throb in the low chamber. Something pants in the darkness.

"Oh Jesus," the guard says. He bangs on the door behind him. "Oh bloody Christ."

A woman's whisper slips from the darkness: "I love you."

I hear Elizabeth in that voice. It is a knife thrust through my heart. The woman giggles, and there is malevolence in the sound. Evil.

"Who's there?" the guard calls out. He continues to pound on the door as he speaks.

Another long growl rolls out from the other end of the room. "I will care for you always," says the woman. More laughter.

The words batter at my conscience. I think of Elizabeth waiting for me in the monastery. Wondering if I would come to save her. And I never did.

I'm sorry, Elizabeth. I'm so sorry. Mea maxima culpa.

"Eat my fingers. Please. Won't you eat my fingers?" A thunderous roar nearly knocks us over. The voices and sounds blend into one another. It seems impossible, but the same creature is making all of those sounds. More laughter echoes across the chamber. Scraping footsteps approach us.

"Christ in heaven, it's coming for us!" shouts the guard.

I have known abject terror many times in my life. But never has the sweat risen on my body so swiftly. Never has the fire of terror burned through my limbs quite so fiercely. I want to pound at the door and scream. But all I do is suck in deep breaths of the damp, dusty air.

The portly guard pounds on the door. "William, open the door! Open the bloody door!"

William calls back from outside, but the door is so thick that I cannot understand what he says; I can only hear his laughter.

"The torch," Tristan whispers. "Take the torch, you baboon."

The guard pulls the torch from the sconce and aims it toward the sounds. Something scuttles on all fours through the light and disappears in shadows. Something pale and filthy and skeletal. The three of us jump back at the sight.

The guard swings the torch to one side then the other, creating long, swirling shadows. The light flashes from withered and bleeding eye sockets. No eyes. Just black, scabrous holes like open graves. A face that has lost much of its skin.

Wisps of hair like windblown scraps of hay. A shriveled mouth opens and hisses, then the creature is gone.

"It's a demon," the guard says. "They got a demon locked up in here."

But it is not a demon. The torchlight glitters off a chain on the floor. Someone has bound the creature to the wall, and I suddenly understand who this poor soul was.

The guard sconces the torch and draws his dagger. He aims the pommel of the dagger at the door and lifts his fist to pound on the oak. "I ain't gonna be killed by no demon."

"No," I say. I raise the dagger in my bound hands, fight through a twinge of guilt, and plunge it through the back of his neck. "You ain't."

He tries to turn but I hold the dagger tightly as he gurgles and spasms.

The woman's voice rings out from the dark. "I will care for you always."

More mad laughter.

I lower the dead guard to the floor of the room. "I'm sorry," I say. "I'm so terribly sorry."

"What is that thing?" Tristan gestures toward the darkness with his bound hands.

"It's the alchemist's failure." I nod toward the darkness and borrow the alchemist's words. "The other was not successful."

I wipe the blade on the guard's trousers and tuck the dagger into my boot. "Gerald will want his horse seen to," I say. "Hopefully, he'll drink something. Maybe eat before he deals with us." It is wishful thinking. Gerald's hatred of us will keep us foremost in his mind. While we live, we are an itch in his mind. And I do not think he will wait long to scratch.

I aim the torch toward the left side of the room. The cylindrical object I saw before looks like a well. I step forward and realize with dread what it is.

"God's Boils," I say.

"What?" Tristan asks.

"What's the second most common way for an army to breach a fortification?"

He steps forward and looks. "No, no, no, no, no." He shakes his head. "I think I'll let Sir Gerald have me."

It is a cesspit. The place where all the garderobes in the tower empty into. We must wade through the cesspit and climb a shit-covered, piss-soaked shaft to freedom.

I lower myself down into the cesspit. It is like climbing into a giant intestine. The filth reaches my stomach. A deep swamp of human excrement. I take two steps and gag, then vomit.

"Lovely," Tristan says. "Shit, piss, and your vomit."

The creature behind us cackles.

I wipe at my mouth with a sleeve. "Someone finally finds you funny," I say.

Chains rattle and clink as they go taut again and again. The creature is struggling against its bonds.

I hear Tristan gagging behind me, but I do not have the will to look back and gloat. I reach the stone shaft that leads up to the various floors of the tower and pull myself into it. The shaft is wide enough for me to brace my knees against one wall and my back against the other. Square niches pierce the shaft at intervals, putlock holes used by the builders to support scaffolds. To climb, I simply have to shove with my knees so that my shoulders slide upward along the wall. I then place my bound hands in a putlock hole and pull my knees upward until they are bent again. I am a human inchworm. My shoulders push through the feces as I glide upward, like a plough through a muddy field.

I vomit again as I climb. My eyes water, but still I climb. I hear Tristan pull himself into the shaft.

"I'm...sorry about Belisencia," I say, trying to think of something other than what we are doing. "I had no idea."

He does not respond immediately. Only the sounds of our shuffling climb interrupt the silence, the moist scrape of bodies through feces-caked walls. I know now what a turd's journey through the body feels like. And smells like.

"I'm glad she's married," he says. "It'll be easier to get rid of her."

Something drips onto my cheek just below my eye. I am not certain if it is liquid or solid, and I do not want to know.

"You don't mean that," I say.

The shaft splits at an angle away from me. The alchemist said to get to the top. Of course he did. It is not him climbing through four stories of shit. I continue inching my way up through the main shaft.

"No," Tristan says. "I don't mean it." His sigh echoes in the tunnel. "How could I have gotten involved with her? She's been nothing but trouble since the start."

Down below the chain rings over and over, faster and faster, as the creature yanks against it. I brace a foot against the angled shaft and push as hard as I can, until my back begins to rise along the lubricated wall. A thought rises in my head and I chuckle.

"What?" Tristan calls.

"Belisencia," I say. "She's John of Gaunt's fault."

Tristan chuckles, then laughs, and I laugh with him. Our laughter rings loudly in the tunnel, so we stifle it as best we can. Tristan's snorts echo.

"I'm sure there's more to her marriage than we imagine," I say. I fought for John of Gaunt once, but he became my enemy years later, when his avarice and hunger for power turned him into a monster. He has many children. I have heard of Elizabeth of Lancaster but I know little about her. And even less about John Hastings, who apparently is her husband.

My foot slips in the branching shaft and I have to brace myself with my hands to keep from becoming wedged in the tunnel. "God's Teeth!"

"If you fall on me with your shit-stained bum and send me into that cesspit below, Edward, I swear our friendship will be over."

I take hold of a putlock hole and pull with all my strength. "Your loss," I say. "'Woe to him that is alone when he falls into the cesspit and has not another to lift him out of the shit.'"

We laugh again, quietly, and for the next two floors our giggles intersperse our groans.

A jingling crack sounds from far below. Then the sound of a dragging chain.

"Edward?"

"Just keep climbing."

My nose stings with the stench of this place. I wipe at it and manage only to smear feces across my face. Tristan vomits again.

"At least…at least if we are caught again," Tristan says, "I won't mind so much being pissed on by Sir Gerald and his new friend."

We pass a second branching. Two more floors to go. I lean forward and brush at my back, dislodging the mound of tepid shit that has accumulated across my shoulders.

"Oi!" Tristan calls. "*Oi!* What's wrong with you?"

"Sorry." I try not to laugh as I continue my climb.

I chuckle again as I push myself upward, then cough as the acrid fumes of the tunnel fill my lungs. Light shines faintly from above. I say a prayer to Saint Giles; when navigating a tunnel of shit, you can only really pray to the patron saint of the insane.

"The alchemist should really see a doctor," Tristan says. "Urgently."

Something hisses below us. Then the sound of nails on stone and faint grunts.

"Edward, I can't look down in this position!" Tristan's words come out fast and loud.

"I'm fairly certain you don't want to," I say. "Keep climbing. She'll never catch us."

A woman's voice calls up, resonant in the shaft. "I love you."

"I get that a lot," Tristan calls down. "I like you, I do. You're a lovely…thing. Someday you'll make some…other thing…a lovely wife. But I prefer my women to have a certain bit of…well…sanity, really. And eyes. And maybe a touch more hair. Does that make me shallow and tedious?" His words tumble from him swiftly and I know he is on the edge of hysteria.

The scraping nails grow closer. The grunts grow louder. How can she be gaining on us?

"Edward, move faster!" Tristan's hand shoves at my legs. "Why am I always on the bottom?"

The light above us grows closer. I squirm upward, rocking back and forth, hearing the wet sounds of my progress and Tristan's labored breathing down below. The glow becomes a circle of light. The top of the garderobe. I wedge my fingers in a putlock hole and drag my knees upward. The worst physical experience I have ever had is almost over.

"We're almost there, Tristan."

"So soon?" he replies, but his voice is tinged with fear.

Something growls from below us. Then a voice so sweet that I can't imagine it came from the same throat. "May I suck the juice from your eyes?"

A voice calls down from above. "Hello?" The word echoes in the garderobe shaft. Tristan and I stop moving. The voice sounds again, but much fainter. "Sounded... someone there..." I hear the murmur of another voice but cannot make out any of the words.

I continue to climb as quietly as I can, not certain whether the voices are friend or foe. The first voice rings out again, louder. "Hurry up. I want to watch King Gerald piss on those knights. I'm going to squat. You'd best be done when I am."

Foe, then. I use both hands to pull the dagger from my boot. The circle of light is blotted out and I know I must act. Immediately.

I wriggle upward, take a breath, and sheathe the dagger in the arse above me. It is not a plaguer scream that rings out, although it is similar in volume and passion. When a man sees a plaguer, he screams from the soul. But when a man has a dagger shoved into his arsehole, he screams from somewhere else entirely.

The dagger is pulled from my grasp. Light returns to the shaft. I jam my toe into a putlock hole and push with all the strength I have. A thick slab of wood with a hole cut from it is the only thing separating me from clean air. I brace my back against the wall and pound with my fists until I dislodge it, then hook my elbows over the stone ledge and pull myself upward. I brace myself for an attack, but none comes. The alchemist kneels with his back to me in the center of his workshop. The man I stabbed lies on his stomach and groans.

"I could use some assistance," I say.

"That is out of the question," he replies. "You are covered in filth. There is a tub and two buckets of water just outside the necessarium. Use them and stay there. Do not step into my workshop until I am done here."

I claw my way out of the shaft, groaning and straining with the effort. Clumps of wet shit splat onto the floor beside me as I bend low and hold out a hand to Tristan. He takes the hand and scrambles out, then peers into the hole. "I felt her hand on me, Edward! I kicked at her and I think she fell back to the bottom." He places the slab of wood back over the shaft opening and looks at the alchemist. "Did he just call this privy a necessarium? My grandmother calls it that." He brushes feces from his clothes. "What are you doing with that man? You're not buggering him, are you? A priest once told me that buggery is the cause of this plague."

"I'm not buggering him," the alchemist replies calmly. "Your friend stabbed him in the anus. A filthy canal. The wound must be treated at once."

"You don't have to talk to me about filthy canals," Tristan responds. He peers warily into the garderobe.

"You stabbed me in the...the anus!" the man whimpers. "You're a bastard and a knave! In my filthy canal!"

I strip my fouled clothes off and step into the small wooden tub just outside the garderobe.

"If I do not treat him, the wound will fester and rot," the alchemist says.

"You are treating one of Sir Gerald's men," I say.

"I am treating a human," he replies. "Are the plaguers not enemies enough? Must you fight each other, too?"

I squat down in the tub and pour one of the buckets of water over my head. The alchemist is right, of course. I spoke similar words to Tristan and Praeteritus not long ago. Humans should look after each other now. It is difficult to remember that when one particular human wants to strip your flesh and piss upon your pulp.

Chapter 54

WE WAIT, WRAPPED IN WOOL blankets and still smelling of shit, as the alchemist finishes salving the guard. "Wash the area thoroughly after each bowel movement and apply this ointment," says the alchemist as we tie the man's hands with cord.

"So what happens now?" I say.

"Sir Gerald is touring the wine cellars at the moment," the alchemist replies. "I told him there was something of great interest to him there. Something he had to see immediately."

"What is it?" I ask.

"There is nothing of great interest down there," he says. "My man will show him a vintage of wine made in Thunresleam. I doubt Sir Gerald will be very impressed by it, but it has given us time."

He motions us to his workbench and lifts the lid off a large glass bottle. "Pull your hands apart as far as you can."

I pull my hands until the chain between them is taut. The alchemist tilts the bottle over the links and a few drops of liquid fall from it. The drops sizzle and smoke when they touch the metal chain. He tilts the bottle again and a few more drops fall free. More smoke rises from the chain. One of the links falls, ringing across the floor, and then I am free.

"What is that?" I ask.

"A very powerful acid." He frees Tristan in the same way, then seals the bottle. He takes an even larger bottle from his desk and gives it to me. The bottle is empty. "You can collect the dragon blood in this."

"He'll know you did it," I say. "Gerald will know you set us free."

The alchemist hands us our cannons, my sword, and our shoulder sacks. "You will strike me once in the face to give evidence to the fact that I did no such thing," he says. "And this noble creature that you stabbed in the anus will vouch that you overpowered the two of us."

"Why will he do that?" Tristan asks.

"Because that wound you gave him will take a long time to heal. It is a tricky wound in a filthy place, so it might never heal. If he wants my best care and a chance at recovery, I think it only fair he assist me. I might even spare some Malta fungus if he is convincing."

"Malta fungus?" asks the guard.

"It's not really fungus," Tristan whispers to him.

The alchemist lifts two folded brown robes from a chair and hands one to me. "I apologize. I could not bring your armor without attracting suspicion. You must let God be your armor now."

I take a robe and look at the alchemist. "That woman in the cellar," I say. "She was the second test subject, wasn't she?"

He clears his throat and uses the hem of Tristan's robe to wipe a fallen chunk of feces from the floor. "Yes." He hands the robe to Tristan, his lips drawn tightly. "She was." He closes his eyes and makes the sign of the cross.

"You loved her?" I ask.

Tristan scowls as he takes the robe, examines the soiled hem.

"I, too, know what it is like to lose a wife, Sir Edward." He looks into my eyes and lets out a long, ragged breath. "I will help your Elizabeth. Whether the dragon blood works or not. I promise I will help." There is something in his eyes, a message for me that I do not understand. He quotes scripture: "'Faith is the assurance of things hoped for, the conviction of things not seen.' I will heal your wife, Sir Edward."

I stare at him for a long moment, and he back at me. He clears his throat and turns away. "Go to the docks one at a time, and board the cog. I have men waiting to take you wherever you wish to go."

I put a hand on the alchemist's shoulder. "You are the best man I have met on my travels, Dominic. I grieve for your wife."

He nods, his eyes growing glassy, and clears his throat again. "Where is it you will go?"

"South," I reply. "We have a dragon to slay."

Tristan thrusts his robe toward me. "Edward, would you mind terribly if we traded?"

We leave the tower and walk halfway down the stairs before I realize that I forgot to hit the alchemist. I return to his chamber and push open the door, only to find him on his hands and knees at the base of the wall that holds the window. The guard is still on his stomach, head toward the workbench, eyes closed.

I enter the chamber. The alchemist jerks upright at my footsteps and stands abruptly. His body is taut as a strung bow. "What...what is it?"

"Is everything well?" I scan the room for any danger.

The alchemist glances back at the floor just beneath the window, and the tension drains from his shoulders. "Just a little preservation. Rain sweeps in from the window sometimes and mold grows along the floor. I cannot tolerate filth in my workspace. I must scrub it away. All of it. Do you understand? I will abide no dirt or disorder."

I look at the floor. It is perfectly clean. I look back at the alchemist. There is something damaged about him. Some species of the third plague courses through his veins and affects his thoughts. But in these dark times I suppose all of us suffer some sort of madness.

"I'm afraid I have to bring a bit of disorder to your face," I say.

"Oh." He touches his cheek. "I had forgotten. Good of you to remember."

He walks toward me and I hit him before he expects the blow. He falls backward with a grunt and nods, touches his cheek again, and winces.

No one finds anything strange about two cowled monks in a monastery. We slip past armored men like two ghosts. Two of Sir Brian's guards linger by the docks, but they run past us as the first shouts go up from the church. Daniel, the man who was cured of plague, waits for us in the cog.

He looks in the direction of the shouts and shakes his head. "Someone's about to get very angry."

Tristan and I leap into the ship. A charcoal fire burns in a clay pot that has been lashed to the mast, probably to light the cloth-covered rails that surround the hull.

"Put your blade to my back," Daniel whispers. I draw Saint Giles's sword and touch the tip to Daniel's back.

"Head toward Norwich," I say.

"We can't leave Belisencia," Tristan says.

"We don't have a choice," I say. "We'll come back for her."

"Sir Gerald won't be happy," he replies. "He'll torture her."

"Not a chance," I say. "She's King Richard's cousin and she's married to Sir Brian's brother. Even if Gerald dares to cross Richard, he won't cross his new ally." I shrug. "The worst they'll do is piss on her symbolically."

Six servants at the oars paddle against the current, pulling the cog forward slowly. Daniel and another servant unfurl the square sail. Figures approach the abbey from the south. Maybe ten of them. Lurching slowly through the swamps. More and more plaguers are being drawn to St. Benet's.

We drift downstream along the river, following the winding waterway through Norfolk. After a time Daniel anchors the boat and tells us that we are two miles northeast of Norwich.

"How long will you be?" he asks.

"Four or five hours at most," I say.

"I'll wait until dusk," he replies. "I can't stay any longer than that. We can only light the ship's rails on fire once, and there are plaguers in these waters."

We drop down from the boat into waist-deep water and wade through reeds and cowbane and onto the shore. We strip and bathe in the river to wash away the remnants of our journey through the garderobe.

"So why are we here?" Tristan asks. "Why not go straight to Bure?"

I tug his robe. "God is our armor," I say. "But a suit of chain mail never hurts."

Chapter 55

Praeteritus and his lepers live within the crumbling flint walls of an old Roman fortress in Caistor St. Edmund. Soiled tents and crude wooden huts fill the spaces inside the walls. It looks more like a siege encampment than a home. Lepers sit around fires or walk the tent village in their white robes.

"There are better places to live," I say. "Abandoned homes everywhere."

Praeteritus shrugs. "Abandoned homes don't have curtain walls." He touches the flint wall as he walks. "Besides, this place was Roman once. I like the Romans."

A beautiful sound rises from behind us. Voices. Dozens of voices. A choir of lepers stands near one of the walls, singing a hymn. Another leper stands with his back to me, guiding their voices. I have heard many choirs in my days. Some of the finest choirs ever assembled. But I am ambushed by the song of these poor, cursed people in this desolate and filthy camp. An ache resonates somewhere deep inside me. A sorrow for our race. I hear the voice of God in their song.

Praeteritus takes us to one of the wooden huts and pushes through the linen curtain that serves as a door. "Sit," he says, motioning toward a trestle table that is little more than a board on stone blocks, and four chairs cut from logs. He rummages through a chest and returns with something in his hand. "Have a look at that." He places two metal disks on the table.

They are ancient coins. On the front of the first coin is the profile of a man wearing an ivy wreath on his head.

"That's a Roman on there," he says. "A real Roman."

I look carefully. There are faded words on the perimeter of the coin. I recognize one of the words. "Caesar."

Tristan reads one of the other words. "Nero." He glances up. "He was a king of Rome once."

"Was he the one who crossed the River Rubicon?" I ask.

"No, that was a different one. This one was a musician, I think."

"A musician-king?" Praeteritus asks.

"A fiddler, I think," Tristan says. "I'm not certain."

The second coin bears another Roman. This one wears a helmet with a great crest upon it. The words on this coin are unreadable. Praeteritus walks back to the chest and draws a helmet from it. It is a Roman helmet, and it bears a similar crest to the one on the coin, except it uses white feathers instead of horsehair. I have seen ancient helmets before, but none in such good condition.

"I found this buried. Right here, in Caistor, when we tried to dig ditches to make the fortress stronger. This helmet was in a tomb for a Roman solider. Maybe it belonged to the man on the coin." He holds it up and turns it in the light. "I've spent days polishing it. And I put pigeon feathers in the crest. Not sure what they used to use."

"They used horsehair," I say. "But it looks fine with feathers."

"Horsehair? How'd they get the hairs to stick up?"

I shrug. "Some Roman trick, I suppose."

"Interesting people, the Romans," Praeteritus says. "They built things—amazing things. They conquered everything. They could make hair stand straight. And their kings were musicians." He shakes his head. "Where'd they go? What happened to them? No one can tell me where they went to."

"They went home," Tristan replies. "They went home to fiddle and make helmets."

Praeteritus stands and draws the curtain aside. He looks out at his empire of lepers and sighs. "Home." He gazes out for a time, then returns and sets the helmet on the table. "You said you needed help."

"We hoped you might have some armor we could borrow," I say. "And perhaps a sword."

"Preferably ones made less than five hundred years ago," Tristan adds.

Praeteritus looks at our robes. "You lose your armor and weapons?"

"We know where they are," I reply. "So they're not truly lost."

"You only want to borrow some?" he asks.

I nod. "We'll return them tomorrow."

He leans back in the log chair and crosses his arms. "Lending armor is like lending a ship. You don't never know if you'll get it back, do you?"

"You'll get it back," I say. "We have a small task that would be easier to accomplish with armor."

"Sounds interesting. What kind of task?"

"I'm afraid I can't tell—"

"We're going to slay a dragon," Tristan blurts. "We're going to be famous, Edward and I."

Praeteritus finds us two coats of leather brigandine, an old bascinet helm, and a rusted sword. But he will only lend them to us if we allow him to accompany us.

"I ain't never seen a dragon before," he says.

"We'd be glad for your company," I say.

"But keep your distance," Tristan says. "We found the dragon. We will slay it. It belongs to us. You understand that, leper king?"

"I understand that you'll likely need me to save you again," he replies. "But I just want to see it. Dragons are like Romans, ain't they? They were here once. Strong and everywhere. And now they're gone. They're just ghosts."

"Yes," Tristan replies. "And like the Romans, this dragon will make your hair stand up straight. So stay back and let us deal with it."

Tristan and I walk back to the ship in our new armor. Praeteritus wears the Roman helmet with its pigeon-feather crest and his chain-mail hauberk. He carries a spear in his hand, a shield on his back, and a short sword at his side. In the fading light he looks strange and imposing.

Daniel takes us eastward, toward the coast, tacking along the maze of small waterways until we reach the North Sea. We sail along the Norfolk coast for a time, crossing into Suffolk sometime in the early evening. A bright moon hangs in the sky and paints a band of rippling white upon the sea.

Daniel moors the ship in a cove near a village that he names as Lowestoft and we sleep huddled on the deck.

We continue early the next morning, pushing slowly through a thick mist until the sun burns our way clear. A few hours into the day, Daniel points to what looks like a bay.

"Estuary of the River Stour," he says. He takes us into the gaping estuary and we wind through the narrowing river until it becomes too small for the boat to go any farther. "Won't be but three miles or so from here," Daniel says. "I'll moor out in the estuary and come back tomorrow morning, if that's enough time."

I borrow a coil of rope and thank him as we hop down into the river. The water is chest high, so we hold our weapons and armor over our heads and wade through reed and nettles and onto shore. I point toward the west. "Our dragon awaits."

The last time we came to Bure, it was from the west. This time we come from the east, which is for the best. We will not have to enter the village to get to the dragon's cave. We spot two or three outcroppings of stone that look similar before we finally reach the jut of massive boulders that Tristan and I scaled. The cave mouth remains sealed.

"That's it," I say.

Praeteritus squints toward the cave, then looks at me, the pigeon feathers quivering on his helm. "That? That's the dragon's lair? What sort of tiny dragon did you fight?"

"Tiny?" Tristan scoffs. "That thing will shake you about like a straw doll. It can swallow half of you with one bite."

Praeteritus shrugs. "I suppose it don't matter how big it is. Fire breath can kill, no matter the size of the dragon."

Tristan and I exchange glances. "It...we don't think it can breathe fire," I say.

Praeteritus laughs and stands straight. "What's wrong with you? You're knights. You can't kill a tiny dragon that don't breathe fire?"

Tristan leans in toward the tall warrior. "Just wait till you see it, leper king. You'll run screaming, you will."

"Course," Praeteritus replies with a smirk. "I'll run screaming from that little chameleon."

We pull the stones away one by one, pausing each time to look and listen. When only one large stone remains, I tell Praeteritus to wait upstream, towards the village.

"You'll be able to see the dragon from the shore there," I say. "And still be out of harm's way."

He wades the waist-deep water reluctantly and climbs the far bank of the river. "Shout if you need me," he calls.

"We won't," Tristan replies. "Just stay there, pigeon king."

Tristan and I take hold of the last stone and roll it away from the cave and into the river, then we scramble back as far as we can and draw our cannons. Tristan lights a firing cord while I watch for the beast.

"It doesn't seem fair," I say. "Killing it with a cannon."

"Course it's fair," he replies. He curses because the flint has gotten wet and is not sparking well. "Saint Gilbert killed his with a bow and arrow."

Tristan keeps striking at the flint. I throw small rocks into the cave until I see motion.

"Tristan."

He glances up, nods, then continues to work the flint.

The creature glides forward slowly. It has no expression. It might as well be a statue slipping through the river. The rows of shining white teeth glimmer in the afternoon light.

"Tristan."

"I know." He keeps striking the flint. A few sparks fly from it, but not enough to light the cord.

The creature finds a submerged stone and props itself on it, so that much of its body is exposed.

"Tristan!"

A shower of sparks fly from the stone. "There!" he cries.

The cord ignites and Tristan uses it to light a second cord, which he hands to me.

We aim the cannons, lift the firing cords, and shout, "Hallelujah!"

The blasts from the guns are especially loud here by the river. My ear rings with the sound. Thick, white smoke swallows the dragon, and when it clears, there is no sign of the creature.

"Cack!" Tristan raises his head to the skies. "House of Gemini! We blew it into nothingness!"

A shriek of terror sounds from the far shore. I turn in time to see the dragon leap from the water, mouth agape, and lunge at Praeteritus. The tall warrior holds his spear out and topples backward. Man and beast fall to the shore in a writhing mass of scales and metal links, teeth and pigeon feathers. Praeteritus screams as I wade through the river toward them.

When I reach the far bank, the dragon has stopped moving. And so has Praeteritus. I look at the beast. There is no sign that our cannons hit it. Praeteritus's spear is in the dragon's mouth. Only two feet of the shaft protrudes from the massive jaws. The rest of the weapon is inside the beast, except for the spearhead, which juts out from the creature's spine. The dragon impaled itself.

Praeteritus moans. I kick at the corpse, hoping to roll the body away, but the creature is too heavy. Tristan and I kneel and shove with all our strength until we get the top half of the beast off Praeteritus.

"Are you hurt?" I ask.

He peers up at me, blood on his face, his eyes wide. "Is… is it dead?"

"It's dead," I say.

"It leaped at me. It would've had me if you didn't kill it."

"I didn't kill it," I say. "You did."

It should not upset me so much that Tristan and I did not kill it. The dragon is dead. We have its blood. And yet there is a great sadness inside me. Every priest dreams of sainthood. Every merchant dreams of riches. And every knight, no matter how much he may deny it, dreams of slaying a dragon. It is in our blood.

"God's bollocks!" Tristan shouts at Praeteritus. "I told you to stay away from it, didn't I? *Didn't I?*"

"I killed it?" Praeteritus sits up and kicks the dragon's body off his leg.

I point my chin toward the spear. "You killed it."

"You didn't kill it," Tristan says. "It leaped onto your spear because we frightened it so much. So, in actuality, it was our kill."

"I killed it," Praeteritus says with a chuckle.

"You planned this all along!" Tristan says. "You wanted to kill it! I ought to stab you in the filthy canal!"

"Praeteritus, Slayer of the Bure Dragon," he says, smiling.

Tristan imitates the scream Praeteritus made before the dragon leaped, making it sound girlish, then he shakes his hands and mocks the man in a childlike voice. "Is…is it dead?"

Something rustles in the trees. I stand and draw my sword.

"A wonderful story for the ages that will be," Tristan says. "The peasant boy so ugly that a dragon killed itself rather than—"

"Quiet!" I whisper. I scan the forest. Figures approach slowly. I remember the last time figures approached us in this forest. We only survived because the dragon scared off the endless mass of plaguers. I glance at the dead carcass next to us. We will get no such reprieve this time.

A voice calls out from the forest. "Who's there?"

"Not a plaguer." Tristan waves off the voice and turns to me. "I propose a new rule. We do not bring vulturous spectators when we are hunting dragons."

A figure pushes through the branches of a hazel tree and peers at us from the north bank. It is Father Ralf, the priest of Bure. "What are you doing here?" he shouts.

I take hold of the spear shaft and lift it so the dragon's head rises. "Renegotiating your pact," I shout.

Other villagers appear at the river's edge. The priest stumbles back at the sight of the dragon. He shakes his head vigorously. "That…that cannot be! I had a vision. A prophecy. No man alive can kill that beast!"

"Then it's a good thing we brought him." I point to Praeteritus. "He's been dead for years."

Chapter 56

I DRAW OUT THE EMPTY bottle that the alchemist gave me and wash it in the river. Tristan and Praeteritus tilt the dragon's body sideways, and blood from its wound trickles down into the bottle. When I have as much blood as it will hold, I stopper the bottle and place it back into my shoulder sack.

We tie Daniel's rope to the creature's back legs and take turns dragging the massive corpse back toward Dedham. The blood in the creature will likely harden on our journey, but perhaps some will be left when we reach the abbey. The beast is heavy and is forever getting caught in among logs or stones or brambles. It is a long journey back.

It is night when we finally yank the dragon corpse into an abandoned fisherman's hut along the Stour estuary and fall asleep sitting against one of the walls.

We spot the square sail of Daniel's cog early the next morning and wave until he spots us from the prow. He waves back stiffly.

He leaps onto the dock and starts tying the mooring lines. "Your friends at the monastery have made things difficult for us."

"Difficult in what way?"

He clears his throat. "I spoke with the captain of a hulk coming south from Norfolk. He said he stopped at St. Benet's to trade last night. They're building a palisade along the riverbank where the docks are."

"Covering their weak spot," I say.

"He also said that they were slaughtering cows outside the monastery walls."

"What a waste," Tristan says.

But it is more than a waste. It is a strategy.

"Sir Gerald is summoning an army," I say. "He's a fool. Doesn't he learn?"

Daniel nods. "There's worse news." He licks at his lips and takes an interest in the mooring lines. "They let Father Simon in."

"Father Simon?" Tristan says. "The priest who led the mob?"

Daniel nods without looking at us. "Gerald wouldn't let the mob in. Just the three priests." He turns to face us, his nostrils flaring. "But how long will it take before the priests convince Sir Gerald to burn Dominic at the stake?"

"Not long, I would imagine." I say. "Sir Gerald sees himself as a devout man. I am certain he has no love for the alchemist, and I have no doubt he could be persuaded to dispose of him. Especially if he had any suspicions that the alchemist helped us escape.

"We're wasting time," Tristan says. "We should get back to the monastery as quickly as we can."

"And how will we get past the army of plaguers that will be waiting for us, Tristan?"

He rubs at his cheek. "We can...well..."

"How will we get into the monastery?" I ask.

"There must be..." he stares toward the estuary and thinks.

"How will we defeat forty armed-and-armored men?"

No one speaks for a long time. We would need at least fifty men to assault the monastery. Eighty would be better. And we would need armor and weapons for all of them. Cutting a path through plaguers is dangerous enough with a full harness. In brigandine, with exposed legs, arms, and hands, it would be suicide. And even if we did have our full kits, it would be pointless if we could not find a way into the abbey.

A wind gusts, and one of Praeteritus's pigeon feathers comes free from his crest and hits me in the face. I turn to him, irked at the interruption, and am struck by a thought so powerful that I know I cannot take credit for it. It is divine intervention. I hear the voice of God.

"I...I know how to do it," I say. "Dear God in heaven, I know how to do it."

Chapter 57

THE CLOUDS STRANGLE THE SUN slowly as our army marches toward the Abbey of St. Benet's. We are two hundred eighty-four strong, but our soldiers do not march properly. They stumble in the marshy fenland, and their ranks grow farther and farther apart as they slosh onward. Only a few of them have well-crafted weapons. They carry clubs and sickles, rusted axes and sharpened plough blades. There is not a single plate of armor among them, but we need none. Because God will be our armor.

We loop around a thick stand of alders and the walls of the abbey come into view. Everything around them comes into view as well. I draw up so short that one of my soldiers steps on the dragon carcass Tristan and I drag behind us.

"House of fucking Gemini." Tristan looks toward the monastery, both hands holding the rope that passes over his shoulder. We all gaze toward the monastery.

I have not seen so many plaguers since leaving St. Edmund's Bury. Hundreds of afflicted men and women crowd the landscape. Rank upon rank of them howl at the walls. They are like ocean waves, rippling and crashing against the abbey. The skies continue to darken and a spattering rain falls upon us, striking the exposed backs of my hands like dull pins.

"Every plaguer within twenty miles must be here," I say.

"It shouldn't matter," Praeteritus says. He holds a tall cross made from yew branches. Moses leading his people out of Egypt.

"*Shouldn't matter* isn't the most reassuring thing ever said to me," Tristan replies.

"Forward!" I shout to our soldiers. "Forward!" And our soldiers advance.

When the abbey walls are a quarter mile away, my army begins to sing. Their voices echo hauntingly across the marshland. No monks could ever hope to match the harmonic passion of my soldiers. It is the song of angels, risen from the bodies of demons.

"*Dies iræ!*" they sing. "*Dies illa Solvet sæclum in favilla: Teste David cum Sibylla!*"

I recognize their song. It is the "Dies Irae." Day of Wrath. A hymn about Judgment Day, often used in funeral masses, so it is appropriate on several levels.

Some of the plaguers turn to look at us when they hear the song. Many shamble in our direction. Tristan and I move deeper into the ranks of our army and pull the cowls tightly around our faces. My heart is like a maddened sparrow. This may be the worst idea that has ever come to me.

"*Quantus tremor est futurus, Quando iudex est venturus, Cuncta stricte discussurus!*"

The first group of plaguers reaches us. A dozen or so. Men and women with blackened skin, bleeding sores, and terrible wounds. Their hair is plastered to their scalps by the rain. They fall into step with the leper army and stare with inkwell eyes, turn their heads to one side, then the other. I imagine they can smell me and Tristan and Praeteritus. Or perhaps they smell the dead dragon. But they do nothing. They turn away a few at a time and slosh back toward the monastery.

God is our armor.

"It's working!" Tristan whispers. "It's working! This is the stupidest brilliant idea you've ever had, Edward, but it's working."

Two banners hang from the abbey gatehouse: Sir Gerald's three roosters, and Sir Brian's lion and staff. Both flutter in the Norfolk wind despite the rain. The song of the lepers falters and many point toward the banners. Praeteritus tells them to keep singing, and they do.

"What's wrong with them?" I ask.

Praeteritus gestures toward the banners with his chin. "Remember how I told you that soldiers massacred a lot of the lepers?"

I remember. When the lepers left Norwich, soldiers attacked them on the road, blaming them for the plague. The survivors settled in Caistor St. Edmund, where Praeteritus found them.

He spits to one side. "The men who attacked them wore the lion and staff."

"Sir Brian of Yarmouth," I reply. "He and his soldiers are inside."

Praeteritus's hands clench tightly around the cross. "Not for long."

"*Mors stupebit, et natura, Cum resurget creatura, ludicanti responsura.*"

None of the lepers objected when Praeteritus told them about St. Benet's. Not one of his subjects spoke out against the idea. He promised them a home, and today they will fight for one.

"*Quid sum miser tunc dicturus? Quem patronum rogaturus, Cum vix iustus sit securus?*"

The true test of my idea will come when we reach the moat. Plaguers quiver and snarl at the water, four or five ranks deep, their skins glistening from the rain. Occasionally, one of them topples into the water. I peer through breaks in their lines and see that the moat itself is full of floating plaguers. And beyond the moat, at the abbey walls, two dozen dripping plaguers stand wailing and clawing at the flint.

Our army is undaunted. They march directly at the moat. Their song grows louder as we near the howling mass of plaguers, as if the coming confrontation gives the lepers strength. And when the first rank of my army touches the last rank of plaguers, something astounding happens. The afflicted move away. They retreat from the lepers, shoving one another in their haste to get clear. A dozen more bodies fall into the moat as the ocean of plaguers parts before us. Praeteritus lifts his cross high for the full Red Sea effect and he leads his people into the gap. The wind whips our white cloaks and the rain falls more violently.

Two hundred eighty-four men dressed in white robes and singing hymns part a legion of plaguers without even lifting a sword. If I had not conceived the plan, I would be dumbstruck.

We stop at the edge of the moat, opposite the gatehouse, and the lepers stop singing all at once. Faces peer at us from the gatehouse window. Many faces. I am too far back to tell with certainty, but they certainly do look dumbstruck. The plaguers drift closer to our ranks. A few jostle with the lepers, and a chill sweeps through me. One incident could turn this field into a slaughterhouse. Tristan huddles closer to me. A flash of lightning burns the sky in the distance.

"Now!" I say, seeing the moment. "Quickly!"

Praeteritus clears his throat and shouts the words that we rehearsed. "We are the Sacred Brothers of Justice! We have come from Canterbury to reclaim St. Benet's Abbey in the name of God! I demand that you open the gate, or we shall drown you in a holy flood!"

A roll of thunder shakes the flint fields of St. Benet's.

Tristan grins next to me. "Ah, showmanship."

A plaguer at the left side of the formation hisses. He is bald, with thick shoulders and a face that was no doubt frightening even before the boils and sores. He sniffs at one of the lepers, his head moving with animal jerks. The leper trembles but does not look at the monstrosity that inspects him.

There is much activity among the people in the gatehouse. After a time, a thin man with a pointy beard thrusts his head out.

"The Sacred Brothers of what?" he shouts.

"Justice," Praeteritus calls back. "Open the gates. It's raining."

I give Praeteritus a glare, and he offers the faintest of shrugs without looking my way.

"King Brian of Yarmouth owns this monastery now," the man shouts. "He decides what will be done with it. Why aren't the plaguers attacking you?"

I whisper, "God owns the monastery," and Praeteritus nods.

"God owns the monastery!" he shouts, adding a tone of indignation consistent with priests. "And the plaguers don't attack us, because we got a sacred relic with us."

"Have," Tristan whispers. "*Have*."

"What relic is that?" calls the man at the window.

Praeteritus motions to a leper at his side, and the man holds up the pigeon-crested Roman helmet. "It is the helmet of Pontius Pilot!"

The bearded man turns to one side and speaks with someone next to him, then faces us again. "Why is Pontius Pilot's helmet a relic?"

"For Christ's sake!" Praeteritus shouts. "Open the gates and we can talk about it."

There is more discussion inside the gatehouse. An afflicted man paws at one of the lepers, who rings a hand-bell at him. Two plaguers snarl and hiss at one another as they study yet another leper in the ranks. I do not think God's Armor will protect us for much longer.

A new face peers out from the arched gatehouse window, and I recognize this one. Father Simon.

"Steady, Praeteritus," I whisper.

"Who are you?" shouts the priest. "I have never heard of the Brothers of Justice."

"We're very popular in Canterbury," Praeteritus replies.

"Consecrate the monastery," I whisper. "Man who defiled it. Keep to what we rehearsed."

"We are God's Justice," Praeteritus shouts. "We're here to consecrate the monastery and to give justice to the man who defiled it."

"And to smite the large headed among you," Tristan adds.

Praeteritus nods. "And to smite the—"

"No!" I hiss. "Tristan, you're going to get us killed!"

Praeteritus licks at his lips. "And to smite the...bad people...of the...of the world!"

The priest stares at us for a long time, then he disappears. A moment later, Sir Gerald appears at the window. "We welcome the Brothers of Justice," he says. "I know of your scared order and all the good works you have done."

I doubt very much that he does, since I invented the order a few hours ago.

"But unfortunately," he continues, "we can only allow one of you inside. I hope you understand."

I know that he is suspicious, but he cannot deny robed men who have warded off plaguers, men holding a cross and claiming to be God's Justice. I did not think he would allow three hundred men into the abbey. But I was certain he would not turn all of us away.

"You'd deny our sacred order?" Praeteritus says. "You'd keep God's People out in the rain while you feast in the Lord's house?"

"Yes," Gerald replies. "Terribly sorry."

Praeteritus shakes his head. "You ain't a good person. But if only one of us can go in, then I guess it'll be me. Open the gates, sinner!"

The winch cranks, and chains rattle as the drawbridge opens. Every one of the lepers rings a handbell or rattles a clapper at that moment. It is a clamor that I hope cuts through the rain and carries across the monastery. The plaguers directly beneath the drawbridge stumble away from the descending planks. Two of them are knocked into the moat. The others reach clawed hands over the top of the wooden platform as it descends.

Eight men come into view at the gate. Four hold crossbows and four carry halberds. All of them wear chain mail. The crossbowmen fire on the nearest plaguers. Two of the plaguers fall instantly, with bolts in their faces. Another two howl and claw at the quarrels that have pierced them. The halberdiers reach forward with their weapons and shove at the plaguers.

"Hurry!" Gerald shouts. "Run inside!"

The lepers ring their handbells all at once again. Then shouts rise up from the south side of the abbey, where the docks used to be. More shouts go up from inside the abbey itself. A horn blows from the tower on the curtain walls. Sir Gerald disappears into the gatehouse. For an instant, the open gate is unwatched.

And my army charges onto the drawbridge.

Chapter 58

WE REACH THE EIGHT SOLDIERS at the gate almost before they realize we are charging. Tristan and I pull with all our strength at the dragon carcass and do all we can to keep up with the lepers. Neither of us wants to be left outside the monastery without God's Armor. The planks of the drawbridge rumble under nearly six hundred feet. And in that instant the Brothers of Justice become the Brothers of Vengeance.

I am awed by the fury of the lepers. They spent years as the unclean. Years living in shame. Years suffering insults and scorn. They suffered it all silently, swallowing their words, accepting their roles. But tonight they will be heard. Tonight they have a new role. Tonight David has become Goliath, and there is no sling nor sword that can stop him.

The soldiers at the gate are hacked down by plough blades and clubs, sickles and axes. I watch two lepers pound a halberdier's head to jam, one holding a wooden mallet in his three-fingered hand, and the other using a staff. Another leper hooks a crossbowman's neck with a sickle and drags him along the ground, the blade cutting deeper and deeper into the man's neck. The lepers fly over the soldiers' bodies like a herd of deer over logs. They search out their enemies, enemies that hacked their friends and families to pieces on the road from Norwich, and they return the gesture.

Four of the lepers stop at the gatehouse, as I had asked them to, and make a human gate to keep out the plaguers, but there is too much food inside the monastery. The afflicted shove at my sentries, so I call more lepers and make a second rank.

The winch in the gatehouse sounds and the drawbridge rises slowly. Plaguers climb onto it, lie prone upon it or grasp the chains, and are lifted into the air, howling. If they get inside, someone else will have to worry about them. I have other immediate goals.

Tristan and I haul the dragon carcass to one side and run toward the monastery buildings, swords in hand. Small skirmishes are taking place all over the monastery grounds. Perhaps the word "skirmish" is a bit kind. The soldiers of Sir Gerald and Sir Brian are being butchered. Praeteritus leads his lepers across the monastery grounds. He wears the pigeon-crested roman helmet again and has cast off the white robe. The sticks forming the cross-staff have been discarded, revealing his spear. He screams to the white-robed soldiers around him and brutalizes men with his spear like an ancient Roman king.

Bodies lie scattered near the inner gatehouse, including one with a shield. I pause long enough to pick up the shield, and tell Tristan to bugger himself when he smirks. We run through the inner gatehouse and head toward the church. I glance toward the docks as we pass, but all I see are the freshly carved stakes of the new palisade. Daniel attacked the palisade from his cog when he heard the handbells. He was the distraction I knew we would need. Leftover wood from the palisade lies smoldering to one side.

We reach the church ahead of most of the lepers and three soldiers in chain mail charge in our direction. One runs off at the sight of us or perhaps the sight of the leper army behind us. I rush in on another swiftly, getting inside his swing and knocking him to the ground. I point my blade downward, raise it for the killing blow.

The soldier holds one arm up, his head turned away, his eyes closed. I kick his sword away from him. "Stand up," I say. "Run away. Hurry!"

He looks at me with disbelief, then scrambles to his feet and runs toward the postern gate. But he is not fast enough. Three lepers tackle him and bludgeon him with wooden sticks and a metal spike. I turn away, sickened.

"Belisencia," Tristan says. He pulls open the church doors and runs inside. I follow.

"Belisencia!" he shouts. *"Belisencia!"* His voice echoes through the nave. I run past him to the door of the alchemist's tower, feeling for the bottle of blood in my shoulder sack.

A woman shouts from the chancel. "Tristan!" Someone rushes toward us.

"Belisencia!" Tristan nearly knocks her over, then picks her up and twirls her, his forehead against hers.

"I was praying for you," she says. "I was kneeling there, praying to the Mother that you would come, and here you are!"

They laugh and embrace, then she pulls away from him. "He's thirteen years old, Tristan."

"What?"

"My husband. He's thirteen years old. They married me to him when he was eight. Our marriage was never consummated. I will have it annulled. I swear it."

"Married to an eight-year-old boy?" Tristan asks. "What kind of nun are you?"

"This kind," she says and kisses him on the lips.

He smiles when she pulls away. "I like those kind of nuns."

"Belisencia," I say. "Where is the alchemist?"

She sees me and her smile fades. "Edward..."

"I don't have time, Belisencia. Just tell me where he is."

"Edward..." She shakes her head. "I...I tried to stop them..."

A fear grips me. A terror so powerful that it paralyzes me.

Belisencia pulls away from Tristan, and tears tumble down her cheeks. "Oh Edward. I am so sorry. I cannot express how sorry I am."

The paralysis leaves me. I barrel through the church doors and out toward the docks.

He is alive. He is alive. He is alive. He has to be.

The pile of wood by the palisade continues to burn. I cannot look directly at it. I know what I will see. The scent of burning flesh drifts on the wind, but I still cannot accept what I must accept.

He is alive. He has to be.

I look directly at the burning woodpile. It is not leftover material from the palisade. It is a pyre. Three priests stand in front of it, shouting. One holds up a Bible. The lepers do not dare attack priests. Many of them have gathered to listen.

Mother Mary. Saint Giles. Heavenly Father. Holy Spirit. Jesus Lord…No.

"Whatever you ask in prayer," the priest shouts, "you will receive if you have faith!"

The burning husk of a man is tied to a stake at the center of the woodpile. I fall to my knees and pull at my hair.

"'For by the grace given to me I say to everyone among you not to think of himself more highly than he ought to think, but to think with sober judgment,'" the priest shouts. "This man we burn today thought he was greater than God. But no one is greater than God. And no one can seek to undo His works."

Sparks rise in a gust of wind, and blue smoke tumbles from the pyre. My hopes burn with the alchemist. He is dead because of me.

Mea maxima culpa. Mea maxima culpa.

I stare into the skies, feeling the sting of raindrops on my forehead. How could the Virgin be so cruel? How could she bring me through this journey, then take it all away at the last mile? I am in hell. The realization finally settles on me. I have died, and I am in hell.

"'Trust in the Lord with all your heart, and do not lean on your own understanding!'" The priest shouts. "'Faith is the assurance of things hoped for, the conviction of things not seen!'"

It is the same line the alchemist quoted to me before I left the tower. How can the same verse be used by two people with such different views?

"I will help your Elizabeth," the alchemist said. "Whether the dragon blood works or not. I promise I will help."

How could he have helped? If the dragon blood did not work, he would have been in the same situation as before. Stuck. Frustrated. Nearly defeated. His words had rung in my ears like an empty promise. A reassurance meant to show camaraderie or to motivate me in my journey. But as I think on them, I wonder. He was a clever man, and his gaze that day held a hidden meaning.

The conviction of things not seen.

I am running before I realize it. Lepers walk aimlessly through the monastery, staring in awe at their new home. Tristan and Belisencia are on their way to the docks. I dart past them and storm into the church, then run up the endless circle of spiral stairs until I reach the alchemist's workshop. It is in ruins. Shattered glass everywhere. Tables overturned. I hope he did not live to see this mess. Only his workbench seems unaffected.

I step over a table, my boots crunching on broken glass, and a voice calls out from the far side of the room.

"At least one good thing will come of this day." Sir Gerald sits against a wall to my left. He wears his armor, but no helmet. Twisted scars wind along his face like gnarled tree roots. I draw my sword as he stands, but he shakes his head. "You will not deny me this time, Sir Edward. I may die today, but I will die holding your cold, black heart."

I walk toward the workbench, avoiding a fallen jug and a broken mortar. "You can live, Gerald. I will tell them to let you go. I don't want to kill you."

He raises something toward me. A sculpted pipe so old that the iron has gone green. It is half again as long as his hand and looks as if its surface was once ornately carved.

He holds a tiny candle in his other hand. "King Brian gave this hand bombard to me," he says, gesturing toward the pipe. "It's smaller than yours, but it will do the task required of it."

I hear Tristan's voice in my head, a half dozen irreverent replies to Gerald's comment, but I remain silent.

"This one came from Asia. You light the back and death erupts from the front." He takes a step toward me. I notice a familiar glass bottle on the workbench. "We tortured the alchemist. He told me that he had a cure for the plague," Gerald says. "He said it was on the shelf closest to the door, but he lied. All I found were dried plants. And by the time I got back to him, the fools were already burning him." He takes another step. "But I knew that you would know. That's why you're here, isn't it? To find the cure. You and he were thick as mud, weren't you? Did you truly think I would believe that ridiculous story about how you escaped?"

"Put the cannon down, Gerald," I say. "I will walk out of the tower with you and tell them to let you go. I swear it."

Gerald raises the cannon and takes another step toward me. He is two strides away. "God will reward me for killing you, Edward. He will give me everlasting glory." He draws the candle toward the touchhole. "I will cut off your head and shit in your dead mouth, and God will smile."

"I don't want to kill you, Gerald," I say. "Put down the cannon and yield."

"You don't want to kill me?" He laughs. "You don't want to kill me? You are the one on the death side of this gun, Edward. And you ask me to yield? Are you mad?"

In these times of madness...

"I am truly sorry." The sword of Saint Giles hums as I swing it with all my strength. The blade strikes the glass bottle on the workbench, shattering it, sending glass and liquid toward Gerald. He flinches as the fluid spatters him. For an instant he looks at me with confusion and perhaps a touch of humor. But only for an instant. Then his screams tear through the workshop.

He howls as the liquid eats away at the flesh of his hands. The cannon falls, clattering, to the wood floor. I kick the weapon away as Gerald screams and works madly at the strap of his bevor. The acid eats slowly through his breast-plate. He yanks the bevor off his neck and hurls it away, then fumbles at the straps of his breastplate.

No man deserves to die like this. I sheathe my sword and run toward the garderobe. The water in the tub is full of feces and urine, but it is all I have. I use a bucket to scoop some out and return to Gerald.

"It's eating me!" he shouts. "It's eating me!"

I dump the feculent water over him and when I turn to gather more, he barrels into me, knocking me to the ground. I land on my knees, but before I can turn to face him I hear my sword slide from its sheath.

"That…that is…agony," he says, glancing at his burned hands. I spot the hand cannon beside one of the toppled tables. Too far away. "I'm done with you, Edward Dallingridge! Die, demon. *Right fucking now!*"

He raises Saint Giles's sword in both bleeding hands and jabs it down at me with a wild howl. I roll toward the hand cannon, knowing the brigandine won't stop Gerald's blow. Knowing that I must try to live, for Elizabeth. I feel pressure at my ribs. Soldiers often do not feel the sword blows that kill them. I feel only a slight pressure. My hand clenches the cannon.

"*No!*" Gerald's scream echoes across the room. "*No! No! No! No! No!*"

I tumble to one wall and snatch a candle from a sconce, but I needn't have bothered with the dramatics. Gerald hasn't moved. He stands with tears in his eyes.

"Why won't you ever die?" He looks at my sword in his burned hands. Only the hilt remains. Shards of steel litter the floor. I look at my sheath; holes have been burned through the leather.

Gerald tosses the hilt aside and slumps against the wall. "The sword shattered. It just shattered."

I touch the spot where he stabbed me and shrug. "God is my armor."

I let him leave the tower. Every instinct says I should kill him, but I let him go. If humanity is to survive, then we must show ourselves to be human. And perhaps by letting him live, I will buy Elizabeth's life.

I kneel by the window where I saw the alchemist before I left. I run my fingernails along the wooden planks. One of them is loose. I rock it from side to side, pulling upward with my nails, until the short plank rises. I toss it aside and draw a tiny brass coffer from the hole. My hands tremble as I work the latch. I take a long breath. Then I flip open the top.

Inside are three ampoules with Arabic writing on them.

Chapter 59

I walk toward the docks. Many of the lepers have gathered by the pyre and listen to the shouting priests. A dismembered heap that I believe was once Sir Brian has been staked to a spear a few paces away. The Brothers of Justice have obtained their vengeance. Tristan and Belisencia are there, too, as is Praeteritus.

"The monastery is yours now." Tristan sounds unusually sober. "Looks like your lepers found a home."

I take my place beside them and once again watch as a man burns for mixing tinctures to cure the plague. I do not know if he smiled as the flames licked his body. His body is beyond expression now. The fire has turned him into a shadow. A husk. An empty vessel from which no cures will ever flow again. My teeth grind with such force that a chip comes free from one of them.

The priests shout, spittle flying from their lips. They tell the gathered crowd that alchemy is a sin. That prayer is the only true and righteous weapon against plague.

But they are wrong.

I look down at the three phials in my hand. The baked clay glows orange in the light of the flames. Alchemy may be a sin, but prayer is not the only weapon we have. I hold a new weapon in my fist. And if I burn in hell for using it, then I, too, will smile as the flames lick my flesh. For I will have saved the woman I adore and earned eternal salvation in her eyes.

Episode 1:

Historical Note

THE EPISODE YOU HAVE JUST read is as historically accurate as I could make it. As I mentioned in the previous book, Sir Edward Dallingridge is a real knight. He was favored by King Richard II and the earl of Arundel and went on to become a knight of the shire and warden of London (for a time). But perhaps his most enduring accomplishment was the castle he and his wife, Elizabeth Wardieu, built at Bodiam, in Sussex. Visit it if you have a chance; I can't recommend it more highly. Of all the castles in England, Bodiam is my favorite. I believe it embodies the romance, the chivalry, and the adventure of the Middle Ages, even though the interior was gutted in the seventeenth century, during the Civil War.

In this episode I mention a manor house called Lutons' Place, in Long Melford. That manor house still exists, although it is now known by the name Kentwell Hall and is another place worth visiting. It does not look as it would have looked in Edward's time, but it is still a quirky old manor with centuries of history. The poet John Gower, a close friend of Geoffrey Chaucer, owned the manor for a time before the Clopton family moved in.

I make mention of the Flemish settling in Sudbury, but I couldn't find room to talk about Simon of Sudbury, one of the town's most famous sons. Here are Edward's thoughts on Simon, in a paragraph that was cut from the book:

> Sudbury also had a connection to the peasants' revolt a few years back. Simon of Sudbury, the inventor of the poll tax and archbishop of Canterbury, was beheaded by wild-eyed peasants in London during the riots. The peasants were not appreciative of his invention. Tristan likes to say that Simon's head was staked to a poll.

In the chapter where Edward is being taken to the bandit camp, he sees Frenchmen strapped to carriage wheels with their limbs hammered to rubbery pulp. This is nothing invented. This sort of torture device is called the Saint Catherine Wheel and it was, unfortunately, popular during the Middle Ages. An unknown writer from long ago described a victim of the wheel in far better terms than I do. He said the victim looked like "a sort of huge, screaming puppet writhing in rivulets of blood, a puppet with four tentacles, like a sea monster, of raw, slimy and shapeless flesh mixed up with splinters of smashed bones."

Something inside me shrivels when I read that. I can't imagine the excruciating pain these poor victims must have felt. I feel shame for being nervous at the dentist.

The other form of torture I mention is the Spanish Donkey, and this, too, was a real form of punishment. It was reportedly still used well into the eighteenth century.

It's sobering to think that human cruelty might actually be more terrifying than flesh-eating demons.

Episode 2:

Historical Note

MOST PEOPLE THINK OF THE Middle Ages as a time of ignorance. A time when knowledge and the pursuit of scientific truths were suppressed. And in many ways, this is true. But a great many theories and discoveries were made during those so-called Dark Ages.

The Venerable Bede was one of the greatest scholars of the medieval age, and he came from some of the darkest years of the Dark Ages—the seventh century. Bede, a monk, wrote more than sixty books on a wide variety of topics, including, as Edward stated, a treatise claiming the earth is spherical and not flat. Did I mention this was in the seventh century? He was versed in the classical philosophies as well as the religious and scientific ideology of his time. Not bad for an old man in the dark age of history.

Edward spends much of this episode in the village of Edwardstone, in Suffolk. The village, which is to the east of Sudbury, has existed for more than a thousand years. It was one of the many locales to be swept up in Suffolk's cloth trade, and it prospered in Edward's time. The church is lovely. Battlemented on one side, with a thick, handsome Norman tower. It was renovated in the nineteenth century but still maintains much of its medieval feel, and the church has a thirteenth-century font that would have been there long before Edward was born.

Okay, now for a confession. Some of you may know this already, but the Scottish sport of tossing the caber is generally thought to date from the early sixteenth century. I say generally, because no one knows for sure. There is much discussion about the origins of caber tossing. But like any sport, it probably predates the written historical records. I like to think that some form of caber tossing was around back in the fourteenth century, even if it had a different name. Not convinced? Then think about ice hockey. Variations of ice hockey were played in the early Middle Ages by the Danes. That's more than a thousand years before it became recognized as the sport we know today. But were Scots really throwing twenty-foot-long poles into the air in Edward's day?

I'd say there's a wee chance.

Episode 3:

Historical Note

IN THIS EPISODE, EDWARD REFLECTS upon the reason for spiral stairs going anticlockwise instead of clockwise. He would know a lot about such things because, as I have mentioned in the past, he designed and oversaw the construction of Bodiam Castle, which was—and is—in my opinion one of the finest castles in England. Edward was knowledgeable in the finer points of fortresses of all sorts. So knowledgeable, in fact, that he was appointed to survey the strengths and weaknesses of many English castles and settlements, including the towns of Winchelsea and Rye, and the castles in Calais and Picardy.

Edward's assertion that the church considered the left hand to be evil is correct. All knights were anointed in the eyes of God and had to be right-handed. So when invaders stormed up spiral staircases, you could be fairly certain that the attackers would be at a disadvantage because of the tower walls.

Edward is a master of military tactics and defenses, but his Elizabeth wants him to be more than that. She goads him into reading the French *Roman de Renard* books. As Edward recalls, the *Renard* books were mostly about animals. They were a sort of twelfth-century *Aesop's Fables*, except they rarely had a moral. They were simply snapshots that explored human emotions and motivations. The story Edward thought about is one of the most well known.

The order of the Knights Hospitaller is a real order, one that has been around as long as the order of the Knights Templar. Both were started during the Crusades for the purpose of protecting pilgrims making their way to the Holy Lands. The Knights Hospitallers held a wealth of lands in England, including the Little Maplestead Preceptory, which was founded in circa 1186. A preceptory is simply a community of Knights Hospitaller or Knights Templar. Not much is known about the preceptor at Maplestead except that it held a messuage (dwelling house and outbuildings) and a garden, a hospital, three hundred and eighty acres of land, sixteen acres of meadowland, thirty acres of pasture, and a dovecote.

I'm glad they documented the dovecote.

Episode 4:

Historical Note

THOSE DANCING PEOPLE?

Yes.

There really was a sickness in the Middle Ages that caused men and women to dance uncontrollably. It was, as the knight Roger noted, called Saint John's Dance, or, sometimes, the Dancing Plague. Although some cases of this peculiar illness were recorded as early as the eighth century, the first *major* outbreak was in Germany, in 1375. Thousands of people danced until they fell to the ground with exhaustion, and even after falling to the ground they would writhe and spasm. The theories as to why this occurred range from food poisoning to mass insanity, but nobody seems absolutely certain.

History often provides subjects that are stranger than anything writers can come up with. Case in point: Tristan said the dancers hated pointy shoes and the color red, which, according to historical records, is true. The dancers reacted violently to pointed shoes, the color red, and any attempts to stop them from dancing. Entire novels could be written about this odd illness.

Treatment for these people usually involved exorcism and isolation, and the success rate seems to have been about as low as you would expect. Which brings us to the treatment of wounds in general.

Barbers in Edward's time were no longer mere cutters of hair. They knew how to leech patients and performed routine, if crude, surgeries. Doctors had more learning, although the profession was riddled with superstition, astrology, and false knowledge. Humorism was a medieval belief that the body was controlled by four humors: blood, yellow bile, black bile, and phlegm. All illnesses were caused by an imbalance in these humors, and to recover one's health, one had to realign them. Often this involved drawing blood with leeches, or prescribing herbal medications. And while humorism seems a bit backward to us, it was a very complex system that sometimes arrived at the correct conclusion. Although usually for an incorrect reason.

Paul and the nun at Hedingham use mold to treat Edward's wound. Mold, which is used to make penicillin in modern times, has been used to treat infection from as far back as the days of ancient Greece. In the Middle Ages, the mold often took the form of wet bread and cobwebs. I'm not entirely sure what the cobwebs added to the formula, but webs were often used to stop bleeding.

Maggots were also used to treat infection, especially on battlefields, where surgeons observed that wounds with maggots in them were cleaner than wounds without.

Maggots only have the ability to eat dead flesh, and they leave healthy tissue alone. Clever maggots.

As with most areas of life in the Middle Ages, fraud was rampant in medicine. Some doctors or peddlers sold elixirs which they said would cure almost any illness. These elixirs were rarely useful in any way. Eventually a Latin term was applied to these sorts of worthless medicines that promised miracle cures.

Nostrum.

Episode 5:
Historical Note

DRAGONS HAVE BEEN A RICH part of the history of England and Europe. Looking back with modern sensibilities, it may seem as if the people of England were a bit silly to believe in such things. But the beliefs of a society change as education and discovery shine light into the dark areas of our knowledge. There are many people today who believe that lifeforms from alien planets come down and abduct humans. I can't be certain this is not true, because our society has not explored the planets and galaxies of our universe. Perhaps, someday in the future, we will have irrefutable proof one way or the other, and the people of that distant age may look back with humor at *our* archaic beliefs.

The creature that Edward and Tristan fight in this episode is not a dragon. Not in the strictest sense of the word. What they fight is a particularly large, particularly aggressive Nile crocodile. And though it seems a bit farfetched that a Nile crocodile would prowl the waterways of England, it has happened at least once, and probably more times than that.

King Richard I, while on crusade, was reportedly given a crocodile as a gift. He is said to have sent the creature back to England and kept it in a menagerie at the Tower of London. The caretakers of this "dragon" had no way of knowing how to properly pen this creature, and the croc escaped in the Thames and drifted along the east coast of England, terrorizing villagers of Essex and Kent.

Another crocodile seems to have escaped from the Tower in 1405. And, after leaving the Thames, this one found the River Stour and the village of Bures (called Bure back them). The croc horrified the people of the village, ate a few sheep, ate a few shepherds, and grew fat and lethal. The people of Bures called it a dragon and discussed sacrificing virgins to it, but Sir Richard Waldegrave prohibited any sacrifice and sent his archers after the beast. They shot the croc, and the animal, in one story, fled to Wormingford, where it was killed by a knight (another Sir George, oddly).

The village of Bures still recalls the glory of its brush with a dragon. If you visit Bures today, you can see the massive silhouette, outlined in white, of a dragon upon a hillside. There is, from what I understand, another dragon artwork in the village. It is in the St. Stephan's Chapel, a historic church where King Edmund was crowned in 855. There is, reportedly, a dragon etched or painted on the wall of the church.

But finding St. Stephan's in the maze of farmyards and bridle trails is a quest worthy of Sir Edward himself.

Episode 6:
Historical Note

NORWICH, IN THE MIDDLE AGES, was one of the largest cities in England. Its history fluctuates like a pendulum between the wonderful and horrible. In 1174, one of the most magnificent cathedrals in England was built there. Four years later, a boy was killed in the city and the large Jewish community was blamed for it. The result was a horrendous massacre of the Jews of Norwich. The Hospital of St. Giles (now known as the Great Hospital) was built in 1249 and became one of the finest hospitals in England. But in 1274 the entire city was excommunicated because of a riot against the monks of the cathedral. From sacks by the Flemings and the French to the flourishing of the wool trade, Norwich's history is a fascinating one. I have yet to find any reference to disfigured demons roaming the streets of the city, but if Sir Edward speaks of such things, it must be true.

King Richard II had a tumultuous twenty-year reign. His father, Edward the Black Prince, died a year before his own father, King Edward III. The Black Prince's death no doubt came as a shock to the people of England, who adored him and were expecting a long and successful reign from the prince. So when Edward III died a year later, the people were likely not impressed that instead of heralding the reign of the Black Prince, the crown was placed on the head of ten-year-old Richard. Not an auspicious start.

A council was created to advise the young king. The boy's uncle, John of Gaunt, lobbied to have himself appointed regent, to rule England until the boy came of age. But a council was appointed to advise the boy instead, and John of Gaunt was on that council.

Richard showed occasional flashes of brilliance, as in his handling of the Peasants' Revolt, but as he grew and took control of the kingdom, he became insular. He relied on very few advisers, close friends whom he rewarded and spent his time with. He did not interact well with the rest of his nobles and this brewed a resentment that spilled over in 1387, when a group of lords calling themselves the Lords Appellant wrested control of the kingdom for a short time.

Although Richard regained his throne from the Lords Appellant, his reign did not end peacefully. Years later, Henry of Bolingbroke, one of the three leaders of the Lords Appellant, raised an army and ousted the embattled king. Henry became King Henry IV, and Richard became a prisoner in the Tower of London and, it is said, died in captivity.

Another of the leaders of the Lords Appellant was none other than Richard FitzAlan, earl of Arundel and patron to Sir Edward Dallingridge. Edward must have been torn by loyalties when it came to King Richard. On one hand, FitzAlan, a personal friend of Edward's father, was leading a revolt against the king. On the other, Richard signed the order allowing Edward to build Bodiam Castle, which was Edward's crowning achievement.

Episode 7:

Historical Note

IT WAS NOT MY ORIGINAL intent to make the island fortress a monastery. I had in mind a windswept island off the coast, and a stormy boat journey in the driving rain for Sir Edward. But something happened to me on a day-trip to Norfolk that changed my mind. A man handed me a booklet on St. Benet's Abbey, a place that had fallen into ruin in the area now known as the Norfolk Broads.

For those not familiar with the Broads, they are a series of interconnecting waterways and lakes that are believed by many to be mostly man-made. Why were these huge lakes and channels created? There is a lot of speculation, but in this episode, Edward tells us one of the most widely held views. Peat. In the Middle Ages, peat was one of the most common forms of fuel. It was used for ceramics, baking, glassmaking, brickmaking, brewing, and just about any process that involved running a hot fire for long periods of time.

What is peat? It's basically a type of dead vegetation and soil, common in bogs and marshes. The northeast corner of Norfolk had vast amounts of peat, so men were hired to dig it from the earth. And dig they did. The massive pits they dug eventually flooded and created the many lakes of the Broads. And the channels? Some speculate that the channels were dug to allow the peat to be stacked onto ships and sent off to wherever the peat was stored and dried.

On that day in Norfolk, the day I was sold the booklet, I saw for the first time exactly what Edward, Tristan, and Belisencia saw: a ship sailing through a meadow. If you get a chance to visit the Norfolk Broads, I recommend visiting St. Benet's Abbey, if only to see the miracle of sails cutting through pastures and fields, which they still do.

St. Benet's never had the religious importance of St. Edmund's Abbey, but it had a storied history. It was built in AD 1020 as a monastery for Benedictine monks, but even before that it was a place of religious importance. Hermits formed a community there in the ninth century, and churches were built and destroyed on the site several times before King Canute granted the land for the Benedictine monks.

Historians have pieced together what the abbey might have looked like in its prime and, sadly, we must rely on their vision. The monastery survived Henry VIII's reformation only to fall into a slow spiral of decay and ruin. Fortunately, there are old illustrations and documents detailing what the church looked like and, in this story, I have tried to keep the descriptions as faithful to history as I can. The only embellishment I added was the bridge across the River Bure, outside the abbey. Edward always seems to need bridges where there were none.

There is not much left of the abbey now. A gatehouse that was turned into a mill in the eighteenth century, a few battered flint walls, and impressions on the ground of old fishponds. But the site is still consecrated, and an open-air mass is held on the grounds once a year by the bishop of Norwich.

When I toured the remains of the abbey and read the history of the place, I realized that I had found my island. Not only would it be unexpected for the fortress to be inland, but it was a real fortress on a real island; I wouldn't have to invent one. Edward's story is one that has always been grounded in history, and when writing it, I always prefer the resonance of true history to places I conjure.

Edward is healed (he hopes for the final time) by the alchemist using something known as Malta fungus. The fungus, scientific name *Cynomorium coccineum*, is real. It grows in the Mediterranean and in the Middle East. Crusaders brought some back to Europe and, as the alchemist points out, the Knights Hospitaller found a large store of it growing on a rock near the island of Gozo (one of the Maltese islands). The fungus was highly sought after by everyone, from the Europeans to the Chinese, as a curative for a long list of ailments, including infection. And modern-day science seems to cautiously agree with history: there is some evidence that Malta fungus can help with everything from HIV to impotence. Thanks to my copy editor, Marcus Trower, for pointing out this wonderful tidbit of history.

Episode 8:

Historical Note

SOMETIME IN THE MIDDLE OF the fourteenth century, a disease crept into England. Historians to this day still disagree as to the cause of the affliction, but whether it piggybacked into the country on fleas or hurtled in on nasal discharges, one thing is certain: the Black Death changed England more profoundly than any other event in history. There was no cure for this disease, but not from lack of effort. History records hundreds of attempted remedies. These ranged from eating crushed gems to drinking vinegar and water, from washing in urine to covering the victims with feces, and, perhaps one of the oddest attempts, rubbing a live chicken over the patient's body. Chickens may be clever, but they weren't smart enough to cure the plague.

The so-called Red Death in my story, Edward's plague, would have been similar in many ways to the Black Death of the mid-fourteenth century. It is unlikely that the citizens of England could have developed a cure for Edward's Red Death. Prayer was still seen as the primary weapon against such illnesses. And even in the Middle East, where science and medicine flourished among Muslim and Jewish scholars, it is doubtful that a cure would have developed, especially in such a short amount of time. But the concept of using dragon blood, though it might sound a bit fanciful, is not as farfetched as it may seem.

The dragon that Praeteritus kills in this episode was, as I mentioned earlier, a Nile crocodile that escaped from a menagerie into the waters of southeastern England (something that happened a few times in the Middle Ages). Crocodiles are very special creatures. They are fiercely territorial, leading to vicious fights among them. These fights result in terrible wounds, but the wounds almost never become infected. Odd, considering that crocodiles marinate in warm rivers seething with bacteria. Their ability to resist infections is so extraordinary that scientists have been studying crocodile blood for years. And their studies have yielded some amazing results. Apparently the crocodile's immune system can kill HIV and a host of other infections. It is entirely possible that, in the future, new medicines for old diseases will be developed on the basis of these studies.

The power of dragon's blood.

In this final episode, Belisencia revealed herself to be Elizabeth of Lancaster, daughter to John of Gaunt and cousin to Richard II. Elizabeth, in reality, was the feisty third child of Gaunt and eventually became the Duchess of Exeter. As mentioned in this episode, she was married to John Hastings, the earl of Pembroke, when she was seventeen and he only eight. But perhaps Elizabeth's greatest claim to fame is as the sister of Henry Bolingbroke, a man whom Edward Dallingridge might encounter in a future Scourge novel. Elizabeth of Lancaster's marriage to John Hastings was annulled in 1386, and she married twice more, finally finding happiness with Sir John Cornwall.

History has no record of her love affair with a knight named Sir Tristan of Rye.

As for Edward, his quest for the cure may be at an end, but he has yet to see Elizabeth's smile. It is a long journey from St. Benet's Abbey to St. Edmund's Bury, and in these times of madness anything can happen on the English trails.

Acknowledgments

I WOULD LIKE TO THANK the countless employees of English Heritage and the National Trust for their tireless assistance. In particular, I would like to single out Mike Williams for answering my questions about Bodiam Castle and for providing crucial information about Sir Edward Dallingridge.

Thanks should go out once again to the Fairfield Scribes, the best group of writers and friends in the world. And to David Pomerico, my editor, for continuing to believe in *The Scourge*. Alex Kahler was the content editor for *Nostrum*, and I am forever in his debt for his unerring judgment and for motivating me to do my very best. I would also like to thank Marcus Trower, my copy editor, for his wonderful work with the manuscript and for his plot inspirations.

Most importantly, I want to thank my fiancée, Annabelle Page, for driving me anywhere I want to go in her country, for reading and critiquing each and every word I write (usually more than once), and for doing anything and everything I ask of her (without a single complaint).

About the Author

Eunice Musvasva, 2013

ROBERTO CALAS HAS WORKED AS a graphic designer, newspaper reporter, magazine editor, and once owned a company that sold swords and armor. The second-generation Cuban American is the author of *The Scourge* and *The Beast of Maug Maurai,* and is an aficionado of fencing, ice hockey, and history. He lives in Sandy Hook, Connecticut.

Kindle Serials

This book was originally released in Episodes as a Kindle Serial. Kindle Serials launched in 2012 as a new way to experience serialized books. Kindle Serials allow readers to enjoy the story as the author creates it, purchasing once and receiving all existing Episodes immediately, followed by future Episodes as they are published. To find out more about Kindle Serials and to see the current selection of Serials titles, visit www.amazon.com/kindleserials.